FROST

F R O S T

Thomas Bernhard

Translated from the German by Michael Hofmann

ALFRED A. KNOPF
New York 2006

THIS IS A BORZOI BOOK
PUBLISHED BY ALFRED A. KNOPF

Translation copyright © 2006 by Alfred A. Knopf,
a division of Random House, Inc.

All rights reserved. Published in the United States
by Alfred A. Knopf, a division of Random House, Inc.,
New York, and in Canada by Random House
of Canada Limited, Toronto.

www.aaknopf.com

Originally published in Germany as *Frost* by Suhrkamp
Verlag, Frankfurt, Germany, 1963. Copyright © Insel Verlag
Frankfurt am Main, 1963.

Knopf, Borzoi Books, and the colophon are registered
trademarks of Random House, Inc.

Library of Congress Cataloging-in Publication Data

Bernhard, Thomas.
[Frost. English]
Frost / Thomas Bernhard ; translated from the German by
Michael Hofmann.
p. cm.
ISBN 1-4000-4066-3
I. Hofmann, Michael, 1957 Aug. 25.   II. Title.

PT2662.E7F713 2006
833'.914—dc22   2006040886

Manufactured in the United States of America
First American Edition

FROST

First Day

A medical internship consists of more than spectating at complicated bowel operations, cutting open stomach linings, bracketing off lungs, and sawing off feet; and it doesn't just consist of thumbing closed the eyes of the dead, and hauling babies out into the world either. An internship is not just tossing limbs and parts of limbs over your shoulder into an enamel bucket. Nor does it just consist of trotting along behind the registrar and the assistant and the assistant's assistant, a sort of tail-end Charlie. Nor can an internship be only the putting out of false information; it isn't just saying: "The pus will dissolve in your bloodstream, and you'll soon be restored to perfect health." Or a hundred other such lies. Not just: "It'll get better"—when nothing will. An internship isn't just an academy of scissors and thread, of tying off and pulling through. An internship extends to circumstances and possibilities that have nothing to do with the flesh. My mission to observe the painter Strauch compels me to think about precisely such non-flesh-related circumstances and issues. The exploration of something unfathomably mysterious. The making of sometimes very far-reaching discoveries. The way you might investigate a conspiracy, say. And it is perfectly possible that the non-flesh-related, by which I don't mean the soul—that what is non-flesh-related, without being the soul, of which I can't say for certain whether it exists, though I must say I assume it does, that this thousand-year-old working assumption is a thousand-year-old truth—but it is perfectly possible that the non-flesh-related, which is to say, the non-cell-based, is the thing from which everything takes its being, and not the other way round, nor yet some sort of interdependence.

Second Day

I took the earliest train at four thirty. Passed through sheer rock. When I boarded the train, I was shivering. Gradually I warmed up. Further, the voices of the workers coming home off the night shift. I felt for them right away. Men and women, old and young, but all with the same voices of utter exhaustion, from their heads and their breasts and their balls down to their boot soles. The men in gray caps, the women in red headscarves. They wrapped their legs in scraps of loden cloth; that's the only way they know of keeping the cold at bay. I knew at once that they were a group of snow-shovelers who had got on at Sulzau. It felt as warm as in a cow's belly: the air felt as if it was being pumped from body to body with incredible pressure from some collective muscle. Doesn't bear thinking about! I pressed my back hard against the wall of the compartment. Because I hadn't slept all night, I dropped off. When I woke up, I saw again the trail of blood that trickled unevenly along the wet floor of the wagon, like a stream threading its way between mountains, ending up between the window and the window frame, under the emergency brake. It originated from a crushed bird that had been cut in half by a sudden jerk of the window. Maybe days ago. Shut so hard, there wasn't the trace of a draft. The conductor, going by in performance of his dismal duty, had taken no notice of the dead bird. But he must have seen it. I knew that. Suddenly I heard the story of a lineman who had been asphyxiated in a snowstorm, which ended: "He never cared about anything." I don't know if it was my exterior, or something inside me, finding some expression, the aura of my thoughts, of my task, energetically preparing itself in me—but no one sat down near me, even though over time every seat became precious.

The train wheezed through the river valley. In my thoughts, I was once briefly at home. Then I was far away again, in some city I once walked through. Then I saw specks of dust on my left sleeve, which I tried to brush off with my right arm. The workers pulled out knives, and cut bread. They choked down great thick lumps of bread, and ate pieces of meat and wurst with them. Great chunks that no one would ever eat at a table. Only on their laps. They all drank ice-cold beer, and were evidently too enfeebled to laugh at themselves, even though they felt they were worth laughing at. They were so tired, it didn't even occur to them to do up their flies or wipe their mouths. I thought: When they get home, they'll fall straight into bed. And at five in the afternoon, when everyone else knocks off, they'll start again. The train rattled and plunged down, like the river running beside it. If anything, it seemed to be getting darker.

The room is as small and uncomfortable as my intern's room in Schwarzach. If it's the roar of the river that's unbearable there, here it's the silence. At my request, the landlady took down the curtains. (It's always like that with me: I don't like having curtains in rooms that frighten me.) The landlady is disgusting to me. It's the same disgust I felt when I was a child and had to vomit outside the open doors of the slaughter-house. If she were dead I would, today, feel no disgust—dead bodies on the dissecting table never remind me of live bodies—but she's alive, and living in a moldy ancient reek of inn kitchens. Apparently she likes me, though, because she lugged my suitcase upstairs, and offered to bring me break-fast in bed every morning, which is absolutely at variance with her normal practice. "The painter's an exception," she said. He was another long-stay guest, and long-stay guests enjoyed certain privileges. Even though, as far as innkeepers were concerned, they were "more trouble than they were worth." How had I happened to wind up at her inn? "By chance," I said. I wanted to recuperate quickly, and return home, where a mountain of work was waiting for me. She seemed understanding. I told her my name and showed her my passport.

.   .   .

So far I haven't seen anyone but the landlady, even though I heard a lot of noise in the inn in the interval. At lunchtime, when I stayed in my room, I asked the landlady about the painter, and she said he was in the forest. "He's almost always in the forest," she said. He wouldn't be back before supper. Was I acquainted with the painter? she asked. "No," I said. Silently standing in the doorway, she seemed to pose an urgent question, as woman to man. I was startled, and—without a word, though not without an edge of nausea—refused her offer.

Weng is the most dismal place I have ever seen. Far more dismal than in the assistant doctor's description. Doctor Strauch had spoken about it in the sort of veiled terms one might use to describe a dangerous path to a friend who has to go there. The assistant stuck to intimations. He tied me more and more tightly to the task with invisible ropes, creating an unbearable tension between him and me, while I felt the arguments he remorselessly advanced against me like nails being driven into my brain. He did at least manage not to irritate me. Confined himself rigidly to points I had to observe. I really was frightened by this landscape, in particular this one spot, which is populated by small, fully grown people whom one can certainly call cretins. No taller than five feet on average, begotten in drunkenness, they pass in and out through cracks in the walls and corridors. They seem typical of this valley.

Weng is at a considerable elevation, but still stuck at the bottom of a gorge. It's impossible to get out up the cliff walls.

The only way out is by train. It's so ugly that it's characterful; far prettier landscapes have no character. Everyone there has tipsy children's voices, scraped away to a high C, which they drill into you as you pass by. Jab into you. Jab from the shadows, I have to say, because in truth I have only seen shadows of people so far, human shadows, in poverty and in a dank tremor of frenzy. And those voices, jabbing at me out of the shadows, first of all confused me, and then drove me faster on my way. But these realizations were nonetheless sober ones; they didn't depress me. Actually all I felt was annoyance, because it was all so incredibly inhospitable. On top of everything, I had to lug my cardboard suitcase, with its contents jumbling together. The way up to Weng from the train station, where the industrial park is and where the big power plant is being built, can only be covered on foot. Five kilometers, which can't be shortened in any way, least of all in this season. Barking, howling dogs everywhere. I could imagine people being driven mad in the long run, if they were compelled to experience uninterruptedly the sort of thing I had to experience on the way up to Weng, and in Weng itself, if they weren't distracted by their work or by pleasure or other appropriate activities, as for instance whores, or church, or drinking, or all three at once. What brings a man like the painter Strauch to such a place, and to such a place at such a time, that it must be like a repeated slap in the face?

My assignment is highly confidential, and I think it was deliberately entrusted to me suddenly, from one day to the next. The assistant must have spent some time nursing the idea of charging me with the observation of his brother. And why me? Why not one of the others, interns like myself? Because I often came to him with difficult questions, and the others didn't? He specifically told me on no account to arouse the least suspicion in the painter Strauch that there had been any communication between himself, the surgeon Strauch his brother, and myself. That's why I am also to say, if asked, that I am studying law, so as to divert attention from medicine. The assistant paid for my travel and board. He gave me a sum of money that seemed ample to him to cover everything. He demands precise observation of his brother, nothing more. Description of his behavior, of the course of his typical day; information about his opinions, intentions, expressions, judgments. A report on his walk. On his way of gesticulating, flying off the handle, "keeping people at bay." On the way he handled his walking stick. "Watch the way my brother holds his stick, I want a precise description of it."

It's twenty years since the surgeon last saw the painter. Twelve years since their last letters. The painter describes the relationship as hostile. "Even so, as a doctor, I will make an effort," said the assistant. For which he needed my help. My observations would be extremely useful to him, more than anything he had yet undertaken. "My brother," he told me, "is unmarried, as I am. He lives, as they say, in his head. But he's terminally confused. Haunted by vice, shame, awe, reproach, examples—my brother is a walker, a man in fear. And a misanthrope."

This assignment is a private initiative on the part of the assistant, but I am to view it as part of my apprenticeship in

Schwarzach. It's the first time that observation has presented itself to me as work.

I had intended to take with me Koltz on diseases of the brain, divided into "hyper-activity" and "lesions" of the brain, but in the end I didn't. Instead I took along a book of Henry James's, which I had started in Schwarzach.

At four o'clock I left the inn. In the sudden massive quiet I was seized by a feeling of unease. My sensation—of having put on the room like a straitjacket, and now needing to take it off—made me charge down the stairs. I went into the public bar. When, after several shouts, no one came, I went outside. I stumbled over a chunk of ice, picked myself up, and found an objective: a tree stump some twenty yards away. There I stopped. Now I could see lots of similar stumps sticking out of the snow, as if shredded by shelling, dozens and dozens of them. It occurred to me that, sitting on my bed for a couple of hours, I had been asleep. My arrival and the new setting had taken it out of me. Must be the Föhn, I thought. Then I saw a man emerging from the piece of forest a hundred yards ahead of me: undoubtedly it was the painter Strauch. All I could see of him was a torso; his legs were concealed in deep snowdrifts. I was struck by his big black hat. Reluctantly, as it appeared to me, the painter made his way from one stump to the next. Propped himself on his stick, and then pushed off with it, as if he were drover, stick, and animal bound for the slaughterhouse, all at the same time. But such an impression faded immediately, and I was left with the question of how to get to him as quickly and correctly as I could. What should I say to him? I thought. Do I go up to him and ask him a question, in other words, do I follow the traditional method of asking about the time or the place? Yes? No? For a while I vacillated. I decided I would cut him off.

"I'm looking for the inn," I said. And that was it. He scrutinized me, because my sudden appearance was more alarming than inspiring of confidence—and took me with him. He was a long-term resident at the inn, he said. Anyone coming to stay in Weng had to be either an eccentric or mistaken. Anyone looking for a holiday. "In *that* inn?" It wasn't possible to be so callow as to fail to see immediately that that was absurd. "In this area?" Such a thing could only occur to a fool. "Or a prospective suicide." He asked me who I was, what I was studying, because surely I was "still studying" something or other, and I answered, as if it were the most natural thing in the world: "Law." That was enough for him. "You go on ahead. I'm an old man," he said. The way he looked frightened me for long moments, forcing me back into myself, the way I saw him the first time, so helpless.

"If you walk the way I'm pointing with my stick, you'll come to a valley where you can walk back and forth for hours, without the least anxiety," he said. "You don't have to be afraid of being found out. Nothing can happen to you: everything has died. No minerals, no crops, nothing. You'll find traces of this or that period, stones, vestiges of masonry, indications, no one knows what of. A certain arcane relation to the sun. Birches. A ruined church. Traces of wild animals. Four or five days. Solitude, quiet," he said. "Nature without any human interference. The odd waterfall. It's like walking centuries before human settlement."

Evening falls very abruptly here, as if with a clap of thunder. As if a great iron curtain suddenly cut the world in half. Anyway, night falls between one step and the next. The sour colors are drab. Everything is drab. No transition, no twilight. The Föhn wind sees to it that the temperature doesn't drop. An atmosphere that causes the heart to tighten, if not to stop altogether. The hospitals know all about this air current: ostensibly healthy patients, full to the brim with medical science to the point that there is hope for them, suddenly sink into unconsciousness, and cannot be reanimated by any human agency, however skillful or ingenious. A climate that engenders embolisms. Bizarre cloud formations, somewhere far away. Dogs chasing pointlessly through lanes and farmyards, sometimes attacking people. Rivers stinking of corruption all along their length. Mountains like ridged brains, overly palpable by day, blackly invisible at night. Strangers suddenly getting into conversations at crossroads, asking questions, giving answers they never asked to hear. As if just then, everything was possible: the ugly approaches the beautiful, and vice versa, the ruthless and the weak. The striking quarter hours drip down on cemeteries and rooftops. Death takes a deft hand in life. Children fall into sudden fits of weakness. Don't shout or yell, but walk under a train. In inns and stations near the waterfalls, relationships are formed that barely last a moment, friendships are struck up that never come to life; the other, the you, is tormented to the point of murderousness, and then strangled in pettiness and meanness.

Weng lies in a hollow, buried among blocks of ice for millions of years. The roadsides favor promiscuity.

Third Day

"I was never a painter," he said today; "at the most, I may have been a decorator."

There's now a tension between us that is present on the surface and below. We were in the woods. Silently. Only the wet snow, pounds of it clinging to our boots, seemed to speak continually but incomprehensibly. Breaking our silence. Inaudible words present as thought, but not as speech. He always asks me to go first. He is afraid of me. He knows from stories, and from personal experience, that young people attack and plunder their victims from behind. The bland expression conceals the presence of tools of murder and brigandage. The soul, inasmuch as someone might feel like referring in such a way to this "transgressor of all laws," because one happens to believe in it, steps out, but rationality, put together from suspicion, fear, and mistrust, makes an ambush impossible. Even though I tell him I don't know my way around at all, he makes me go on ahead. From time to time he mutters an instruction like "left" or "right" (and clears away my sense that he might be drifting off on thoughts of his own). I carry them out impatiently, and, as it were, in the dark. What was curious was that there wasn't the least light to help orient me. It felt like rowing along, in the mind as well, and balance is both effortless and impossible. What would I do if I were all on my own? A thought that suddenly presented itself. The painter walked along behind me, like some vast encumbrance on my nerves: as if he was continually studying the implications of my back. Then he got short of wind, and told me to stop. "I take this path every day," he said, "I've been walking here for decades. I could walk it in my sleep." I tried to discover more about the reason for his presence in Weng. "My sickness and any number of other reasons," he said. I hadn't expected any more detailed reply. I told him as well as I could, in brief points, the story of my life, with spots of light or sorrow, and how it had made me into what I am—without betraying to him what, at the moment, I *really* am—and with an openness that surprised me. But it interested him not at all. He is only interested in himself.

"If you knew how old I am, in calendar terms, you'd get a shock," he said. "You probably imagine I'm an old man, as young people are apt to. You'd be amazed." His face seemed to darken into a deeper hopelessness. "Nature is bloody," he said, "but bloodiest toward her own finest, most remarkable, and choicest gifts. She grinds them down without batting an eyelid."

He doesn't think much of his mother, and even less of his father, and his siblings had become as indifferent to him over time as he thinks he has always been to them. But the way he tells me, I can tell how much he loved his mother, his father, and his siblings. How attached he is to them! "Everything was always gloomy for me," he says. I told him about a passage from my own childhood. Thereupon he said: "Childhood is always the same. Only to one person, it will seem ordinary, to a second benign, and to a third satanic."

In the inn, they treat him with appropriate respect, as it seems to me. But once his back is turned, they all make faces.

"Their excesses have been noted. Their sexuality can be sniffed. One can feel what they think and what they want, these people, sense what forbidden things they are continually contriving. Their beds are under the window or in the doorway, or they don't even bother with beds: they go from atrocity to atrocity . . . The men treat the women like pieces of tenderized meat, and vice versa, now one, now the other, depending on their respective imbecility. The primitive is everywhere. Some behave as if by prior arrangement, others seem to come to it naturally . . . their too-tight trousers and skirts seem to drive them wild. The evenings go on and on: it's all too much. A few yards here or there, in or out, so as not to have to freeze . . . Their mouths are taciturn, the rest goes wild . . . day dawns, and you don't know which way is up. Sex is what does for them all. Sex, the disease that kills by

its nature. Sooner or later, it will kill off even the deepest inti-
macy . . . it brings about the conversion of one into the other,
of good into evil, from here to there, from high to low. Godless, because ruination appears first . . . the moral becomes
immoral (a model of universal decline). The forked tongue of
nature, you might say. The way the workers go around here,"
he said, "they live for sex, like most people, like all people . . .
they live to the end of their days in a continual wild process
against modesty and time and vice versa: ruination. Time
sends them on their way to unchastity with a slap. Some are
more accomplished at concealing it than others. With the
canny ones, you only realize when they're all done. But it's
for nothing. All of them live a sex life, and not a life."

How long was I proposing to stay in Weng, he asked. I
needed to get back fairly soon, to prepare for exams in the
spring, I said. "As you're studying law," he said, "I'm sure
you'll find it easy to get a job later. There are always jobs for
lawyers. I had a nephew once who was a lawyer, only he lost
his mind over stacks of files and had to quit his job in the civil
service. He wound up in Steinhof. Do you know what that
is?" I replied that I had heard of the institution "am Steinhof."
"Well, then you'll know what became of my nephew,"
he said.

I had expected a difficult, but not a hopeless case. "Strength of
character, leading to death," a phrase from a book I'd read
early on, occurred to me, and made me think about the
painter: How is it that all his thoughts circle around suicide?
Is it permissible for suicide to be a sort of secret pleasure to a

man? What is suicide anyway? Self-extinction. Rightly or wrongly. By what right? Why not? I tried to focus my thoughts on the one point: is suicide permissible? I had no answer. None. Because people are no answer, and can't be, nor is anything living, and not the dead either. By committing suicide, I am destroying something for which I am not to blame. Something entrusted to me, then? By whom? When? Did I realize it at the time? No. But an unignorable voice tells me that suicide is a sin. Sin? As easy as that? It's something that will bring the whole edifice to collapse, says the voice. Edifice? What edifice? His watchword, whether asleep or awake: suicide! It will choke him. He is bricking up one window after another. Before long, he'll have walled himself up. Then, once he can't see out anymore, because he can't breathe anymore, he'll be persuasive: because he'll be dead. I have the sense of standing in the shadow of a thought of his that is very close to me: the thought of his suicide.

"A brain is like a state," the painter said. "Suddenly anarchy breaks loose." I was in his room, waiting for him to get his boots on. "The greater and lesser assailants among the ideas" would form coalitions, only for these coalitions to be equally suddenly revoked. And "being understood, and wanting to be understood, are a deception. Based on all the errors of gender." Contraries reigned for a single, everlasting night over the day. "Colors, you know, colors are everything. Which means shadows are everything. Contraries are very highly colored." In many ways, it was like clothes: you buy them and wear them a few times, and then you don't wear them anymore, at best you sell them, give them away, let them molder away in a chest of drawers. You move them to the attic or basement. "In the evening, you may have a sense of what the morning will be like," he said, "but the morning is always a surprise." There was really no such thing as experience, not really. No continuity. Admittedly, there were ways of avoiding desperation. "These ways never existed for me." At the moment, all the things on which life insisted were losing their value. "All endeavor is riding for a fall," he said. Something was splendid, and the next thing was brutal, much more brutal than the first had been splendid. "The man who gets to the top of the tree is forced to realize there is no top and no tree. I was your age when I first grasped that nothing is worth the least effort. It both calmed me and unsettled me. Now it frightens me." He referred to his condition as "expeditions into the jungle of solitude. It's like having to make my way through millennia, just because a couple of moments are after me with big sticks," he said. He had never been short of privation, nor had he put himself beyond the reach of exploitation by others, nor could he. "I still put my trust in people even when I knew they were deceiving me, and intending to kill me." Then he had kept himself to himself, "in the way that you might stick by a tree, which might be rotten, but at least it's a tree," and heart and understanding had been dismissed, pushed into the background.

There are people in the village who have never left the valley. The bread delivery woman, for example, who started delivering bread when she was just four, and is still delivering bread now, today, at seventy. Or the milkman. Both of them have only ever seen the train from outside. And the sister of the bread delivery woman, and the sexton. For them, the Pongau is the equivalent of darkest Africa. The cobbler. They have their work; nothing else interests them. Or else they're afraid to take a single step outside. "A friend told me about the inn," I said. How did a lie like that pass my lips? It was terribly easy, as though there was nothing easier than lying. And more and more. "I like visiting places I'm unfamiliar with," I said, "I didn't think twice about coming."—"The air here has a terrible composition," said the painter. "Suddenly circumstances will start to constrain your freedom of movement." Why was it I had chosen this abode, and not another; there were other inns and pensions to be found. "And some down in the valley too. But they're probably only for transients, people stopping for a single night." It had all been my friend's idea, I lied. I had traveled here, with a couple of addresses. "And your journey was without incident?" he asked me. I couldn't think of anything that had happened on my journey. "You know," he said, "when I travel, there are always incidents, mishaps." Getting back to the village and the inn, he said: "I expect you've brought something to read, or something you're working on with you. What have you got?"—"A novel of Henry James's," I said. "Henry James," he said. "I came without books," he said, "quite deliberately. That is, I've brought a couple of little things. But really just my Pascal." He didn't look at me the whole time, his walk was remarkably stooped. "Because I've shut up shop," he said. "The way you do when you've seen your last customer out." Then: "Here, it's possible to make many observations that translate into cold, into self-loathing. If you like that: wherever there are people, you can observe them. Especially what they don't do, which is to say, what does them in." There was nothing here "deserving of the least respect." It was all so unfathomably ugly and expensive. "I'm glad you dislike our landlady," he said. "You're absolutely right." And he said nothing more under that head. Not to have any pity, but follow one's revulsion wherever it led, in many cases that was an ornament to reason. "She's a monster," he said. "You'll get to meet a whole series of monsters here. Especially at the inn." Did I have the ability to weigh up characters, a gift, "nothing to do with intelligence, which not many people have"? To imagine, say, a third character between two others, and so on . . . that was how he spent his time. "Not anymore. There is a chance," he said, "that you might be intruded upon in the night. Then don't be afraid: it will only be one of the innkeeper's concubines who's not familiar with the layout of the building. Or the knacker who seems to be night-blind. Broken bones and sprains of all types seem not to have prevented him from seeking out her bed at night." The innkeeper favored everyone, except for himself, the painter. For instance, she would change the sheets every four or five days in all the rooms, except his. She never filled his glass properly, and if anyone asked her about him, she would come out with insolent lies. Only he had no proof, and so could not confront her. I said I didn't believe the innkeeper would spread slanders about him. "She does, though," he said; "she talks about me as if I were a dog. She says I wet my bed. When my back's turned, she taps her head with her forefinger to indicate that I'm mad. She forgets there are such things as mirrors. Most people do." She watered his milk. "And not just my milk either." Quite apart from the fact that he suspected she had served him dogmeat and horsemeat for years. "She once told her children I was a cannibal. Since then her children have avoided me." She had always read postcards addressed to him, and sometimes even steamed open his letters and absorbed their contents. "Time and again, she would know things I never told her." Now he didn't get any mail anymore. "No more." He said: "Quite apart from the fact that I am made to pay for everything two or three times over, because she assumes I have money. They all do here. Even the priest suffers from that misapprehension, and is forever approaching me for donations. Do I look as though I had money? Do I look well off?"—"As far as country people are concerned," I said, "every city person comes with money, and it's their business to take it off him. Educated people especially."—"Well, do I look educated, then?" he asked. "The landlady bills me for things I never had. And she comes to me begging for money for meals for an unemployed man. Of course, I don't turn her away. But I ought to. Why don't I turn her away? She cheats me in everything. Nor am I the only one. She cheats everyone. Even her children." Cheating could be fuel for a lifetime. "Or a spur," added the painter.

"My first time in Weng, she was underage. I know she's listening at the door. If I pull it open suddenly, I know I'll see her face. But I don't." She was a slovenly washer-up. Her folded tea towels contained traces of beetles and cockroaches, and sometimes the beetles and cockroaches themselves. Even worms. On Friday nights she baked a huge cake, going back and forth between two men "she ruthlessly exploits. The knacker doesn't know that one floor down, one of the guests is getting to suck on her tits in the same dishonest way." She had recipes that went from mouth to mouth. "Dangerous and immoral as she is, she's a good cook." In her larder in the cellar and up in the attic, in among foodstuffs, sacks of flour and sugar, strings of onions, loaves of bread, piles of potatoes and apples, she kept evidence of her dissolution: men's underpants, attacked by rodents and rot. "She keeps an interesting collection of her trophies lying around at the top of the house and in the cellar. She takes special satisfaction, at times when there aren't too many men around, in looking through her collection and reviving her memories of their former contents. She keeps the keys to these rooms always about her person, has done for years, and no one but me has the least idea of what these keys are there to open doors to."

The painter Strauch spits out his sentences the way old people spray saliva in the air. I next saw him at suppertime. In the intervening hours I sat down in the public bar and watched them getting dinner ready. The painter came down rather too late for the landlady's liking, after eight o'clock; by then it was only the regular seats that had drinkers in them. An awful reek of sweat and beer and dirty workclothes filled the room. The painter stood in the doorway, craning his neck to look for a place, and when he saw me, he came toward me, and sat down facing me. He told the landlady he didn't want to eat whatever she'd cooked up that evening. She was to bring him a piece of spam and some fried potatoes. He didn't want any soup. For several days past he had had no appetite to speak of, but today he was hungry. "I was cold, you see." It wasn't cold, quite the opposite really, but: "The Föhn, you know. Inside, I was freezing. That's where it gets you, inside."

He doesn't eat like a wild beast, not like the workmen, not from out of some primal condition. He takes every morsel as a scornful remark against himself. The spam on his plate was "a piece of some carcass." He looked at me as he said it, but I didn't show the revulsion he had hoped. I do a lot of work with dead bodies, and I'm not squeamish. The painter, of course, wasn't to know that. "Everything people eat is pieces of dead bodies," he said. I saw how disappointed he was. An infantile disappointment left his face in an expression of pained uncertainty. After that, he talked about the worth and worthlessness of people with me. "The animal quality," he said, "that lurks inside people, and that we associate with raptors, waiting for a nod to leap at you, and tear you to pieces, that's the same thing as the animal we see when we cross a street, like hundreds of other people, you understand . . ." He chewed, and said: "I can't remember what I wanted to say, but I know it was something malicious. Often, of all the things you mean to say, that's all that's left, the sense that you had it in mind to say something malicious."

Fourth Day

"You just arrive in a place," said the painter, "and then you leave it again, and yet everything, every single object you take in, is the sum of its prehistory. The older you become, the less you think about the connections you've already established. Table, cow, sky, stream, stone, tree, they've all been studied. Now they just get handled. Objects, the harmonic range of invention, completely unappreciated, no more truck with variation, deepening, gradation. You just try to work out the big connections. Suddenly you look into the macro-structure of the world, and you discover it: a vast ornament of space, nothing else. Humble backgrounds, vast replications—you see you were always lost. As you get older, thinking becomes a tormenting reference mechanism. No merit to it. I say 'tree,' and I see huge forests. I say 'river,' and I see every river. I say 'house,' and I see cities with their seas of roofs. I say 'snow,' and I see oceans of it. A thought sets off the whole thing. Where it takes art is to think small as well as big, to be present on every scale . . ."

It was insecurity that drove people to extraordinary feats. People who were really not good for anything were suddenly capable of everything. Heroes had emerged from insecurity. From fear, dread, despair. "Quite apart from the creations of art." It wasn't security that held sway, it was idiocy and inadequacy—and ordinary idiocy and inadequacy, at that. He makes these remarks during lunch. He sends back the beef, even though he ordered it; he wants salt pork instead. The landlady takes the beef and goes. We have a table to ourselves. The rest of the dining room is full. You'd think there wasn't room for one more person. Chairs are brought out of the kitchen, the big bench is pulled out from under the window and extended by another couple of yards. And then there are still people hunkered on the floor, on boards put up across barrelheads. Friday, I think. Then, when there really isn't any more space, some come up to our table. The knacker and the engineer first, then workmen come and beset the painter. The landlady, bringing him his salt pork, watches spitefully as they almost crush the painter. She makes another face at him behind his back, at him and at me as well, because she's worked out that I'm on his side. That makes me suspicious to her. She sees me as another one of the same sort. Since she detests him, she must detest me too.

The knacker is a tall dark man; the engineer is a head shorter, brown-haired, talkative, very different from the knacker. "The work's dragging on," says the engineer. The work on the bridge, that is, a part of the construction of the power plant which is going on further down the valley. It was the worst time for concreting, but it had to be now. "Even overtime doesn't help much," he says. He is, as he says, "draconian." Well on top of his crews. Talks like them. Drinks like them. Doesn't stand on ceremony with them, as they wouldn't with him. He calls their names out in the dining room. Every name gets an instruction for the day ahead. It seems the engineer has everything in his head: figures, deliveries, transports, structures, not quite secured sites, everything. He chain-smokes, and his belly hits against the table when he laughs. The knacker is taciturn. The engineer seems to bring enormous strength to bear against enormity. The workmen respect him. He doesn't try to pull the wool over their eyes. "The rails need to be mounted," he says, and everyone except for me and the painter understands what that means. The painter gets up and walks out without saying goodbye to me. I'm not bothered; I'm happy to stay at the table a while longer, and listen.

The inn was one of that type where you would spend no more than a single night, and only if you had to. The painter, for some reason, had always liked it. It wasn't any amenity it had, no, it was the shortcomings of it that delighted him. A loyalty to prewar days, when the inn had given shelter to him and his sister. He had always practiced hunger and primitive living. Unassumingness. "I'm acquainted with even the most unobtrusive sounds in this building," said the painter. With the palms of his hands at night he could palp the familiar walls, whose every unevenness he knew. "I've stayed in every one of the rooms," he said. "At one time I could have bought the inn. I even had the money for it, then. But that would have been the end, you understand," he said. When he was fed up with everything, he came here. "If the walls could talk," he said. "Every room has seen its own atrocity. The war has soaked into these walls. I mean, the room where you're staying . . ." He said: "In my present mood, I don't want to say anymore. It's a matter of a decision taken by a former occupant of the room. Baffling to everyone. Godless." There were different ways of doing it, but it was all ancient wisdom. And however antiquated a man's thoughts might be, they did sometimes have radical consequences. Sometimes cold air entered the house when someone forgot to shut the windows, and everything in it perished. "Even dreams die. Everything turns into cold. The imagination, everything." Never had he had any sort of "ennobling" idea while staying at the inn. Such thoughts, admittedly, did not come to him often, it was immoral even to *want* to have them. He tended to push them away. "A man can determine the type of thought he wants to entertain." It was remarkable "how dismissive things can be when you approach them in a spirit of confidence." Life at the inn was "among the great abuses," which was where he aligned himself. Self-harm was something he had begun doing in his childhood. "It tired me out a few times. Then I caught fire." Over the years, he had taken it to the very edge of insanity. "All in all, the inn is a prosecution witness for my feelings and states. Everything says, 'This is me,' . . . there's no more virtue, no simplicity, only inbreeding to unimaginable extents."

"My time has passed as if I didn't want it. I didn't want it. Sickness is a consequence of my lack of interest in my time, lack of interest, lack of productivity, lack of pleasure. Sickness appeared where there wasn't anything else . . . My research stalled, and all at once I saw: No, I'll never surmount this wall! It was like this: I had to find a way I had never gone . . . The nights were sleepless, dull, gray . . . sometimes I jumped out of bed, and slowly I saw all thought become impossible, worthless, everything successively, logically, became pointless and meaningless . . . And I discovered that my surroundings didn't want to be explained by me."

Fifth Day

"My family, my parents, everyone, the whole world I might have tried to cling to, and to which in fact I repeatedly tried to cling, early on dissolved into darkness; overnight it just went black, withdrew from my vision, or else I'd taken myself away from it, into that dark. I'm not quite sure. At any rate, I was left on my own a lot, maybe I was always on my own. Being alone has preoccupied me, ever since I can remember. The idea of solitude too. Being shut up within myself. The way I was, I couldn't imagine being alone all the time. I couldn't get my head around that, I couldn't get it into my head, and I couldn't find a way of expressing it either." He said: "I kept going back to that point. I stood there helplessly. Stood there disconnectedly. Woke up there. Not where I should have woken up, to suit my nature. My childhood and youth were brutally alone, just as my old age is brutally alone. As if nature had a right to keep pushing me away, back into myself, away from everything else, toward everything else, but always up against the limit. You understand what I'm saying: one's ears are full of self-reproach. And if you think what you're hearing is song, some wild or domesticated music, then you're deceived: it's still nothing but being alone. That's the way it is with the birds in the forest, with seawater, lapping around your knees. I never knew what to do for myself, and now I know it still less. That's a little surprising, isn't it? I think people only pretend not to be alone, because they're always alone. If you watch them in their societies, aren't they proof of the fact: the gatherings, the meetings, the religions, aren't they all endless solitude? You see, they are always the same thoughts. Unnatural, perhaps. Too much continuity. Dilettante, possibly. If a little self-reliance is brought to solitude," he said, "that makes it bearable, but I never had the least bit of self-reliance. I didn't know how to go about anything. I couldn't cope with influences, surroundings, self. With what it was I was full of. You see. Right!" He said: "People who make a new person are taking an extraordinary responsibility upon themselves. All unrealizable. Hopeless. It's a great crime to create a person, when you know he'll be unhappy, certainly if there's any unhappiness about. The unhappiness that exists momentarily is the whole of unhappiness. To produce solitude just because you don't want to be alone anymore yourself is a crime." He said: "The drive of nature is criminal, and to appeal to it is a pretext, just as everything people do is a pretext."

He turned to face the village which lay before us: "It's not a good cast of human being here," he said. "The people are relatively short. The infants are given 'brandy rags' to suck, to keep them from screaming. A lot of miscarriages. Anencephaly is endemic. People don't have favorite children, they just have a lot of them. In the summer they suffer heatstroke, because their frail tissue can't stand up to the often fierce sun. In winter, as I say, they freeze to death on their way to school. Alcohol has displaced milk. They all have high squeaky voices. Most of them are crippled in one form or another. All of them are conceived in drunkenness. For the most part criminal characters. A high percentage of the younger people are in and out of prison. Assault and battery, and underage or unnatural sex are standard offenses. Child abuse, killings, are Sunday afternoon stuff . . . The animals are better off: after all, what people would really like is a pig, not a kid. The schools have very low standards, and the teachers are cunning and despised the way they are everywhere. Often suffer from ulcers. Tuberculosis suspends them in a milky melancholy, from which they never emerge. Gradually the farmers' sons are integrated into the urban workforce. I have yet to see a good-looking individual in this region. And yet nothing is known of the people here, or of what they think: at the most you might brush against their occupations, existences, torments, their rapid increase. Just brush against it."

As a child, he had been raised by his grandparents, and been allowed to run wild. In the wintertime, kept closely. Then he had often had to sit still for days on end, and learn combinations of words. By the time he started going to school, he knew more than the teacher did. The classroom in his country school in a quiet hamlet in Lower Austria "is unchanged to this day." On a whim, he had gone back on a visit. The same smell, he said, that had always bothered him as a child, a mixture of tar, bathrooms, corn, and apples. Now he had breathed in the smell as if it were a spring morning. He often forced himself to put together the smell somewhere, quite suddenly. He almost always succeeded. As a master every now and then will come up with a masterpiece. His whole childhood had been put together from smells; the sum of these smells had made up his childhood. It hadn't been inert, it was in continual flux. Also there were word games and ball games; fear of vermin, wild animals, gloomy lanes, raging torrents, hunger, and the future. In his childhood he had come across vermin, hunger, wild animals, and raging torrents. Also the future, and loathing. The war made it possible for him to see what people who are unacquainted with war have no knowledge of. City and country by turns, because his grandfather was restless, just as restless as he was himself. His grandmother clever, dignified, unapproachable to low-minded people. His grandfather acquainted him with landscapes, conversations, darkness. "My grandparents were masterful people," he said. Their loss was the deepest loss he had experienced. His parents hadn't bothered about him much; they were much more interested in his brother, a year older, and of whom they expected everything that they didn't expect of him: a settled future, just any sort of future. His brother had always received more love and more pocket money. Where he disappointed them, his brother never disappointed them. His connection to his sister was far too frail to endure. Later on, they took it up again over the ocean, wrote each other letters from Europe to Mexico, from Mexico to Europe, tried to parlay their mutual liking into a sort of love or dependency, in which they were possibly successful. "She writes me two or three times a year, as I do her," he said. Within him and his solitude many thoughts were engendered, which became gradually darker. Once his grandparents died, he was in "a blackness that I will never come out of."

And then his father died, and a year later, his mother. While his brother made his way, climbed up his career ladder rung by rung, to the surgeon he is now, he lost himself in the world in his head. First one way out, then the next were blocked off. Before long he was standing there, confronting ruin. There was little visible evidence of the fact: he always put on good clothes to go out in the street. But at home, in the privacy of his room, he slumped into the lowest frame of mind, into sleeplessness, into ponderings about science and art, into poverty. The more his poverty deepened, the more he shut himself away. His "artistic endeavors" didn't impress him. He could see all too clearly that the work he produced, often effortfully, was nothing for anyone to remark on, much less celebrate. What he did struck him as ordinary. Everything was crumbling. And yet occasional tricks of fate, "pure accidents," little hits of friendliness, kept him going. Where from? "Little excursions sometimes happened like a puff

of spring air," whirling him along to a little town up the
Danube, a forest village, yes, even across the border to Hun-
gary, which he had never been able to see enough of, that
"melancholy *puszta.*" But childhood was worst on that day
when he no longer had his grandparents behind his parents.
He was so lonely, he often sat on the steps in someone else's
house and thought he was going to die of misery. For days he
went around, spoke to people on the street, who thought he
was mad, unmannerly, disgusting. And in the countryside, it
was just the same: he often wouldn't see the fields and meadows for days, because of the tears in the eyes. He would be
sent here and there, and be paid for. Or they didn't pay, and
then his being away, his being there, was even worse. He
looked for friends, but never found any. It even happened that
he thought he suddenly had a friend, but then it would turn
out to have been a mistake, from which he hurriedly had to
retreat. Into further confusion, apathy, uncertainty. The dis-
ruptiveness and blandishments of sex further complicated
the situation, how to deal with forbidden sights, illnesses that
he had to cope with alone, perturbed him. How different it
was for his siblings, who were allowed to stay at home with
their parents, and "live life to the full." Since everything was
so confused, he ruined his prospects at school, with the result
that one day there was nothing left but to accept a desk job in
an office, from which he was only able to rescue himself by a
terrible scene, and then on to art school. He won scholar-
ships, and took his final exams, as required. "But nothing
came of it," he said. His early manhood was still worse. He
might have had a little more contact with somewhat like-
minded contemporaries, but "it was pretty mindless." His
early years had been hard for him. In many ways they
reminded me of my own youth. I was sad as well, but never

as bitter as he was, and at such an early age. And yet, childhood and youth were the only things in him "he found hard to say goodbye to."

Today he admitted he had burned all his paintings. "I had to get rid of those things that were a perpetual reminder of my worthlessness." They had been like ulcers, opening every day and silencing him. "I did it quickly. One day I realized I'd never make it as a painter. But then, the way everyone does, I refused to believe it, and protracted the agony for years. And then, the day before I was due to leave, it struck me forcibly."

"There was a time I would have thought it impossible for me to give in to myself so blindly," says the painter. He stops, draws breath, and says: "I could be in a good mood, after all. Why am I not in a good mood? I'm not bored, I'm not scared. I'm in no pain. I feel no irritation. As if I was someone else, just now. And there it is again: I'm hurt and irritated. Yes, it's my own doing. See: all my life . . . I've never been merry! Never joyful! Never what people call happy. Because the compulsion to the unusual, the eccentric, the odd, the unique, and the unattainable, this compulsion has wrecked everything for me, and in the creative field as well. It tore everything up, as if it were a piece of paper! My fear is rational, orderly, itemized, there's nothing low about it. I'm continually testing myself, yes, that's what it is! I keep chasing my own tail! You can imagine what it's like, when you open yourself like a book, and find misprints everywhere, one after another, misprints on every page! And in spite of those hundreds and thousands of misprints, the whole thing is *masterly*! It's a whole series of masterpieces! ... The pain rises from below or comes down from above, and it becomes human pain. I keep banging into the walls that surround me on every side. I'm a cement man! But I've often had to hold on to myself behind my laughter!"

"Do you know what I can hear now? I can hear charges being brought against the big ideas, a great court has been convoked to hear the case, I can hear them slowly beginning to arraign all the big ideas. More and more big ideas are arrested and thrown into prison. The big ideas are sentenced to terrible punishments, I know that for certain! I can hear it! Big ideas are picked up at border checkpoints! Many flee, but they are apprehended and punished, and thrown into jail! Life, I say, lifetime imprisonment is the least punishment to which the big ideas are sentenced! The big ideas have no one to defend them! Not even a wretched public defender! I hear the state's attorneys laying into the big ideas! I hear the police hitting the big ideas over the head with their nightsticks. The police were always battering the big ideas over the head! They've locked up the big ideas! Not one big idea will be left at large! Listen up! Look! All the big ideas have basically got it in the neck! Listen!" The painter tells me to go on ahead, and I go on ahead, and he drives me into the hollow with his stick.

By chance, I ran into the painter in front of the larch wood, and not down on the path where we had agreed to meet, and where I supposed him to be when I was no more than twenty or thirty paces from the larch wood, when he leaped out from behind a tree brandishing his stick, as though to cut me off. I had been singing all the way from the village, tunes I didn't know I had in me, one after the other, and he said: "I didn't know you could sing! Why do you only sing when you're alone? You never sang once when we were together. It's an odd voice you have, but by no means unpleasant." I was embarrassed and didn't know what to say. He took me by the elbow, and led me, breathing heavily, into the larch wood "Sing some more, why don't you. You don't have to be embarrassed, you've got a fine voice." But I didn't sing anymore. Even if I'd wanted to, I couldn't have produced a single note. He had decided to wait for me by the larch wood "because it's sure to be very cold on the path." We walked fairly quickly. However, he seemed to be quite tired already, and kept stopping. "The imagination is an expression of disorder," he said; "it has to be. In an ordered world, there would be no such thing as imagination, order wouldn't tolerate such a thing, imagination is completely alien to it. All the way here, I was asking myself what imagination is. I'm sure imagination is an illness. An illness that you don't catch, merely because you've always had it. An illness that is responsible for everything, and particularly everything ridiculous and malignant. Do you understand the imagination? What is imagination? I asked myself, and at the same time I asked myself whether it's possible to understand the imagination at all. The truth is you can't." He dragged his stick along a thick bough, and got us covered with snow. I had to brush it off him. "Someone who doesn't know anything, is such a thing possible?" he asked. "A man who never knew anything?"

.   .   .

By the time we got down to the station it was five o'clock. There were more people standing around than usual, and the painter wanted to barge through them, to the station buffet. I Ic put out his hand, and they melted away from his stick. I followed him at a couple of paces. In the buffet, he sat down in the corner, from which you have a view of the platform and can see the trains pulling in and leaving. Then it was too cold for him there—"a hideous draft!"—and we moved next to the stove. We each drank a couple of glasses of slivovitz, and picked out things to read from the newsstand. Weighed down with newspapers—once he's read them, I take them up to my room, to read them cover to cover—we decided to be back at the inn by seven, if at all possible. Outside the inn, while I was brushing the snow off my boots, he said: "Imagination spells a man's death . . . I had a dream last night, I can't remember the setting, but it was in some very familiar landscape; I can't remember which one. An odd dream, not one of the desperate dreams I usually have. The landscape of my dream kept changing, from white to green to gray to black, probably each time in the space of seconds. Nothing had the color we would have expected it to have. For instance, the sky was green, the snow was black, the trees were blue . . . the meadows were as white as snow . . . It reminded me of certain contemporary paintings, even though the painters aren't as radical, the painters are by no means as radical as my dream . . . it was really one of my most radical dreams. And so drastic, the landscape . . . the trees lofty, growing into endlessness, the pastures hard, the grass so hard that when the wind blew, it created a loud music, a music that seemed to be assembled from all sorts of different periods and styles. Suddenly, I was sitting in this landscape, in a meadow. The odd thing was that the people were the same colors as the landscape. I was the color of the meadow, then that of the sky, then the color of a tree, and finally I was the color of the mountains. And I was always all of the colors. My laughter caused a great commotion in the landscape, I don't know why. This pretty irregular landscape, you know, it was as animated as any I've ever seen. A landscape of people. Because the people took on the colors of the landscape as I did myself, the only way of recognizing them was by their voices, and it was only by my voice that they knew me. Such differentiated voices, you know, incredibly differentiated voices! Suddenly something horrible happened: my head swelled up, to such a degree that the landscape grew darker, and the people broke out in wailing, such terrible wailing as I have never heard. Wailing that was somehow commensurate with the landscape. I can't say why. Since my head was suddenly so big and heavy, it started rolling down from the hill where I had been standing, down across the white pastures, the black snow— all the seasons here seemed to be simultaneous!—and crushed many of the blue trees and the people. I could hear that. Suddenly I noticed that everything in my wake was dead. Withered, crushed, dead. My big head lay in a dead wasteland. In darkness. It lay in that darkness until I awoke. How is it that my dream took such a horrible turn?" he asked me. The painter took his Pascal out of his left jacket pocket, and stowed it in his right. "It's uncanny," he said.

We went to the distiller's. The way was along the whole of the forest path and beyond, where I hadn't yet been. My companion kept on stopping to exclaim: "Look, look at the silence of nature! Look, look!" He hobbled along like the hunchback I once saw in Floridsdorf. Our feet were like balls

of ice. He kept on stopping to say: "Nature's resigning!"
"Look, nature's silent now!" Yes, it's silent. "It doesn't stop, it
stops, it doesn't stop . . . Do you understand?" Thoughts, he
said, went simultaneously up and down. He pointed out animal tracks: "A stag, look! Rabbit, there! Here, a deer! There's
a fox! Aren't those wolves?" He regularly sank into the snow,
and was embarrassed because I had to take the end of his
stick and pull him out. "I'm pitiful," he would say. He listed
constellations, said: "Cassiopeia, Ursa Major, Orion." He
would disappear and then re-emerge. If I dropped back, he
would command me to go on ahead. "Always deeps and
surfaces," he said, "deeps and surfaces." Tree trunks he
described as resembling "famous judges." He said: "They
pass great judgments! Extraordinary judgments!" The distiller's was a favorite port of call for him. He always claimed
he wouldn't survive another year, "not another winter, and
each time I come, I find him." He described the distiller as the
most taciturn man he had ever met. He really didn't say one
word. The painter kept pressing us to walk faster, even
though he was responsible for our slow progress. And then
the distiller's house was in front of us. That was where he
lived, with his two daughters, as in a cave. "He sits on them,
and is afraid they might abandon him, they're afraid of him.
Before long, they won't be marriageable anymore." He
would keep staring at them, and giving them orders like:
"Bacon! Bread! Soup! Milk!" Apart from that, he wouldn't
speak all day. They obey, the way children obey. "If he's disgusted by his own daughters, he shuts them up in the attic,
where they have to spin linen. When they've finished, they're
allowed down. Not before that." The two were handcuffed,
"not so as you could see, but unbreakable."

The painter knocked on the door, and there stood a man, long and lean and somehow wooden. "Well," he said, nothing more. Led us inside. His daughters pulled up a couple of chairs, ran down into the larder, and came back with bacon and schnapps. Laid the table. We ate and drank with the distiller. Each time we finished something, he would say: "Bacon," or "Bread," or "Schnapps," and the two girls would run down to the larder. We stayed there for two hours. Then we got up, and the distiller said, "Well," when we were standing by the door, and he locked up again. We were back at the inn for supper.

"Listen," said the painter suddenly, after our walk, "listen to the dogs barking!" We stopped. "You never see those dogs, but you hear them. I'm afraid of them. Afraid maybe isn't the right word: they kill people. Those dogs will kill anything. Their howling! Their yelping! Their whimpering! Listen!" he said. "This is a dog's world."

Sixth Day

"In the summer you have to deal with millions of mosquitoes all the time. It's the swamps. Before long, they drive you crazy, and you hide out in the middle of the forest, but even in sleep they pursue you, the mosquitoes, the swarms of them. You start to run, but of course that's no use either. Every time, my body is covered with stings. You have to imagine my sister's torments, because of her sweet-smelling blood they almost eat her up. After the first few stings, you're tossing and turning in bed, making your condition worse . . . By morning you feel you've aged by several years. Your body is feverish from all the mosquito poisons coursing through it . . . and out of that terrible affliction you awaken and you realize: it's mosquito season once more. Don't imagine I'm exaggerating. As you've already observed, I'm not at all inclined to exaggerate. But you should take care not to travel here during the mosquito season . . . You won't be back. . . . All during that time, people will greet you with profound irritation; it's not possible to speak to them. I myself, as already said, wander around, looking for refuge. And then on top of that there's the heat, everything is deserted. The skies are black with mosquitoes. Probably caused by the rivers that have hardly any water left in them," he said, "the swamp." He was wearing a red jacket that day, a red velvet jacket, his "artist's jacket." For the first time, he was going around looking like you'd imagine a painter would look: mad! He appeared outside the window and pressed his face against the glass, while I was sitting in the breakfast room. Got my attention by rapping on the window frame. A large, increasingly yellow stain. He had walked out at half past four in the morning, intending "to catch the spirits of the dead."

"Horrific," he said, as he came in. The landlady had drawn the bolts for him very early, "in return for a five-schilling piece," which she then hadn't accepted. He said: "I could hear

the river from up there. No machinery. Nothing. No birdsong, of course. Nothing. As if everything had been locked
under a sheet of ice." He had found himself in "a roughly
similar condition." Had scattered malformations of ice and
snow with his stick. Spread his arms and legs and dropped
onto patches of white virgin snow. "Like a kid." Had
remained lying there for so long he thought he would freeze.
"The frost is all-powerful," he said. He sat down. Said: "Nothing is more incredible to me than the fact that I'm taking
breakfast." Early risers were in a position to admire an
implacably majestic frost, if they went out betimes. "The discovery that frost owns everything is nothing terrifying, after
all." To early risers, the world revealed itself with wonderful
clarity and distinctness. The "pitiless world of frost" contra-
dicted them, and forced them to their knees. Well-rested
early risers had a sense of the world as "safe from insanity."
He was now going to take off his artist's jacket again, he said,
he had only put it on "to give himself a morning torment."
"Naturally, in the world's eyes, it was an aberration of mine
that I put on this jacket," he said. "That I pretended I was the
man I once used to be. Now I'm another, like a man after a
further millennium. Maybe. After so many errors." The landlady brought coffee and milk, and brought a young man sitting in another corner "whole mountains of food," as the
painter put it. "A proper person, he looks to me. I wonder
what he's doing here? Possibly a relation of the engineer's.
Possibly." The landlady brought him a train timetable, which
he flicked through for a while. Was it a good idea to take the
shortcut, to get to the station, he asked. Generally it was, she
replied, but in winter, it was impassable. The stranger got up,
paid, and left. "My artist's jacket," said the painter, "is a ruin
all of its own. When I took it off, I took off the ruin too."

That was the last time he would be wearing his artist's jacket, he said.

It occurs to me that it's my twenty-third birthday today. No one, not a soul, was aware of the fact. Or if they were aware, then they didn't know where I was. Except for the assistant, no one knows where I am.

"There is a pain center, and from that pain center everything radiates out," he said; "it's somewhere in the center of nature. Nature is built up on many centers, but principally on that pain center. The pain center, like all the other centers in nature, is built up on more-than-pain, over-pain, it's contiguous, you might say, with monumental pain. You know," the painter said, "I could walk upright, but it's not possible for me. I stoop more than most people, don't I? Excuse me for walking with such a stoop. Probably it makes me look pitiful. But then you have no notion of the enormity of my pain. Pain and torment have moved in together; my arms and legs may fight back, but increasingly they're becoming relegated to the status of innocent victims. And on top of that, this wet snow, those vast quantities of snow! There are moments in which I am incapable of supporting my head. Such an exertion, ten normal people wouldn't be capable of supporting it, unless they'd had special training. So think: I have the strength of ten highly trained athletes, which enables me to raise my head from time to time. Imagine if I'd been able to develop such strength for myself! You see the way I fritter my strength on such a meaningless activity: because it's meaningless raising a head like mine. Or if I'd been able to invest one-hundredth of this strength in myself, somewhere where it might have been of significance . . . I could have overthrown every scientific idea and theorem. Reaped all the celebrity the intellectual world has to bestow. A hundredth of that strength, and I could have become something like a second Creator! Mankind would have been unable to oppose me. In the blink of an eye, I could have gone back thousands of years, and reset our development in another, healthier direction. But as things are, my strength has had to be concentrated on my head, on my headaches, and it has gone to waste. This head, you see, is useless. At the center of it there is a crude glowing planet, and everything else is full of fractured harmonies!"

"Memory is a sickness. A word pops up that reveals entire neighborhoods. Ghastly architecture. You stare into crowds of people: futile to approach them! The day is over." Ninety-eight out of a hundred people had a compulsive delusion with which they fell asleep and woke up. "Everyone is continually wading through the depth of an idea, some a long way down, others even further down. Until the darkness shows them the futility of what they're attempting; police cells with their afternoon quiet, full of sleep and the reek of prisoners. One man thinks pretty much what the man next to him thinks: the human porridge of the traffic accident, weeks ago, or years. Cornfields like whirlpools: forests, meadows, country roads, sections of fairs, torn apart by the imagination, rivers rumble in slices, workers pull long blades through the brains of paupers." There were quite literally ancient dreams, a so-called "science of simple people." A law by which all things permanently repeat themselves, while at the same time being unrepeatable. Everything at once in a cycle of permanent return, and terminally entropic. Joy attracts more joy, sins attract sins, exhibition exhibition, love love. "What connects me to myself is the thing that is furthest away from me," and "time is no means with which to engage with time," and "I am a victim of my theories, and at the same time their controller."

He asked what that was: memories, scraps of singularities that one no longer understood. Memory stayed behind and carried on producing itself everlastingly, in the same form in which, not yet memory, one had first left it behind. As on a stage, people receded. Kept receding onto one and the same plane. His head was like the wings of an infinite theater. And? The volume would diminish, and finally also the impression "that the eyes have of the thing that, years earlier, they were forced to withdraw from. Over the years, all things become air." Eventually, every so often, an image would surface out of the stream, become distinct and magnificent as the thing in which you despair. The past: childhood, youth, pain that is long since dead, is not dead, a piece of winter, a piece of spring, of summer—which summer?—whatever you loved most dearly. Gravel paths and roads, the burial sites of family and loved ones: men carrying a woman's coffin, the whole thing darkening, draymen loading up barrels, brewery employees, cheesemakers, a broken bough in front of his parents' house: the fear going down to the lake. The accumulation of coincidence turned what had been healthy into equally inexhaustible morbidity. "Everything in the world is just an essence of one's self." It was an effortless procedure for holding together a fantastic creature like a human being.

Memory was merely preference. "If not, it will destroy every-thing, even the toughest substance in oneself." Madness, joy, contentment, stubbornness and ignorance, belief and unbe-lief were at all times at its disposal. "It's pure pleasure, dis-solving even death." To stand in relation to memory as to a human being, from whom one might part from time to time, only to welcome him back with renewed cordiality into one's home, that was the thing "that benefits the memory and the man who has it, more with each occasion." Memory fol-lowed a plan that remained unexecuted. A plan. Many plans. Looking back, it seemed that, though capable of charity, it wasn't always prepared to give. Caused birthday surprises, document forgeries. Turned funerals into softly resonant afternoon ceremonials. It pretended to be deaf, just as the world was sometimes deaf, and often addressed one in unwit-tingly harsh tones, in the manner of a beloved brother, say, asking after his sister. It grew increasingly refined, between the theory and the feeling of a human being, a character, and, it appeared, "always turned up at precisely the right time." Never a lie. Calculation, yes. Not mind. Not stinting. Sunk way down in the possibilities of memory, a human being went around dumbly, deaf to everything that didn't stir from memory. It was a perpetual "thinking and-immediately-feeling-sad," not just for its own ends either: for "daily unclar-ity and daily despair."

"I have such pain today," he said, "that it's almost impossible for me to walk. Every step is agony. You must imagine: that enormous head and these tiny shriveled-up legs . . . that have to support it. Way at the top that massive head, and right down at the bottom, incessantly those frail, weak little legs.

Imagine some liquid in your head, something like boiling water, suddenly stiffening to lead and striking against the inside of your skull. Now I have the feeling this head will never fit anywhere, not even in the landscape. Only pain. Pain and darkness. I can follow your words, I can follow the sounds of your feet. Some time, I know, my head will open. I have various notions of various endings," said the painter. "If I permit it to come to a natural end; but I won't permit it to come to a natural end. Suicide: primal thing in nature, quite naturally the hardest, toughest, nothing . . . the whole of development is confined to the investigation: the generations are seated in a sort of pretrial room . . . The pains in my head, at a fixed unscientific degree of unbearableness . . . you want to see in yourself what you are capable of: on the way to extreme insensitivity and oversensitivity in graduated torments up the pillar of pain at intervals of time . . . the temperatures given in thousands of degrees . . . I'm supporting a head in which the horizons are reeling. If I could offer you a hint which is more than a hint . . . I confine myself to the cursed propensities of age; and so it is possible for me to keep step with my agonies. You see those pegs," said the painter; "I could happily drive every one of them into my brain! And my feet are hurting, my ankles. Everything. Nothing in me that is not in pain. You must think I'm a gigantic fusspot! But you can't imagine what it's like: suddenly everything swelling up and functioning on an enormous scale. Always the same roads," he said, "it drives you crazy. Freely adopted pains that I find for myself, in addition. From clumsiness or calculation. From ignorance and too much knowledge. Freeze, because you forgot to take a precaution? . . . And then an infinite amount of raw data going through my head: things to do with journeys, with business, with uncontrollable, religious schemes. You understand: everything is divisible! Just as: nothing is divisible! And the pain is driven on and up. It leaps more and more dementedly into the air. Capable of astonishing turns, it plunges down on me like a hawk. You hear?" said the painter; "you hear?" And I heard the dogs.

Seventh Day

The knacker saw the painter on the track. Hunkered down. On a root. But the painter hadn't even looked up at him as he passed. That had given the knacker a strange shock, and he had stopped and addressed the painter. "I'm working on a problem," the painter is supposed to have said. Whereupon the knacker had turned to go on, but the painter had stopped him in his tracks with the single word "ice-cold." "I'm trying out all sorts of things," he is supposed to have said, "but all my efforts fail." Then the knacker sat down with him, and began talking to him. Why not get up and go to the inn, and get the landlady to make him a hot cup of tea. The best thing would be to chase away the chill that was entering his bones with a couple of glasses of plum brandy. He is supposed to have had tears in his eyes when the knacker said, "Oh come, a painter like yourself surely won't despair."

He apparently told him once or twice more to get up, till eventually the painter saw that it was futile, and in the long term merely painful to remain sitting where he was. Then apparently he said, "It's not getting me anywhere," and got up. And they walked along the track up to the larch wood. "He crawled more than he walked," says the knacker. Then he allowed the knacker to drag him by the end of his stick as far as the inn. "I always knew there was something not quite right about the painter." The knacker says it well-meaningly, and so impassively that a great deal of feeling comes through. "That was practically suicidal," the knacker is said to have said to the painter. The observation that the painter had changed from how he was before, "when he had always been laughing, in particular when he was there with his sister," he had already made on the occasion of his previous visit. "He was here briefly in late autumn."

Earlier, he hadn't been so withdrawn, so remote. Quite the opposite: he had participated in everything, and tried to behave exactly like the villagers, be as one of them. He had gone with them from pub to pub, and had a better head for drink than a good many of the locals. "He always used to take part in the drinking on Three Kings.'" And never had he got so drunk that they had to carry him home, like some of the others, even though he had had just as much as them. "He was a great eater of black puddings, the painter," said the knacker. He had been to Goldegg for the ice-shooting, and in the Braugasthof, where they "unlock the virgins like so many wooden trunks." "Contemplative but friendly," that was how he'd always struck him before. The experience on the path had alarmed him. He told the innkeeper to put some extra wood in the painter's stove. To "warm him up, as much as possible." He had the feeling, the knacker, that if he hadn't run into the painter, he would have stayed sitting where he was, and wouldn't have made it back alive. You could freeze "between one thought and the next." You wouldn't even notice. You would go into a dream from which you would fail to emerge. The painter seemed to be in bad shape, said the knacker. "He talked about some problem. But I don't know what problem he was talking about." He, the knacker, had always got along well with the painter. And the painter for his part had always enjoyed the stories he told about the war.

He has pains in his feet. These pains in his feet prevented him from walking as much as he usually walked, and as much as he wanted to walk. "There is probably a hidden connection between the pain in my head and the pains in my feet," he said. It was well-established that there was a connection between the one and the other. "However hidden. And hence between other parts of the body as well." But between his head and his left foot there was a very particular connection. The pains he feels in his foot, and that suddenly announced themselves one morning, were connected to the pains in his head. "It seems to me, they are the same pain." It was possible to have the same pain in two different parts of the body, far away from one another, "and for it to be one and the same pain." Just as one might experience certain pains of the soul (he continues to say soul, from time to time!) in certain parts of the body. Also physical pains in the soul! Now it was his left foot that was making him scared. (What is at issue is nothing more than a bursal inflammation on the inside of his left foot, below the ankle.) He showed me the swelling on the stairs once, when it was still dark. "Isn't the swelling extraordinary?" he said. "Overnight, the malady in my head has moved down to my foot. Extraordinary." He had been walking for decades, a lot, every day. "So it can't be a question of overstraining my foot. It's got nothing to do with my foot. It comes from my head. From my brain." The swelling was an indication of the fact that his illness was now spreading across his body. "Before long, I'll have swellings like that breaking out all over my body," he said. I could see right away that what he had was a common or garden bursitis, caused by yesterday's long tramp along the path, and I told him the swelling was perfectly harmless, and had nothing to do with his brain, or the pain in his head. In medical terms, absolutely nothing. I had once had a swelling just like it myself. I almost betrayed myself. By the use of a certain expression, I would have become the medical intern I was trying so doggedly to keep concealed from him. But he seemed oblivious to it, and I said: "The formation of such swellings is perfectly ordinary." He didn't believe me, though. "You're saying that because you don't want to finish me off, at least not utterly finish me off," he said. "Why not tell me the truth? That my swelling is extraordinary? You must think my swelling is extraordinary?"—"It'll be gone in two days, as suddenly as it appeared," I said. "You lie like my brother, the doctor," said the painter. He said it with revulsion in his eyes. They flashed like cheap stones. "I don't know why you would lie to me. There's a lot of deceit in your face. More than I had thought up till now."

He scrutinized me; he reminded me of a former teacher of mine, a man I'd dreaded, suddenly returned to life: "It looks like a plague boil," he said. He felt the swelling, and called upon me to do the same, to feel the swelling. I pressed it, as I had hundreds of others before it, not all of them so harmless.

He has never seen a plague boil, I thought. His swelling has nothing, but nothing, to do with a plague boil. But I didn't say anything. I let him pull up his sock again. Feminine softness of skin, I thought. On foot, face, and neck. It struck me as morbid, I'm not sure why. Pallor, shading into gray. The cells translucent. Disintegrating in places. Splotches of yellow, rimmed with blue. The surface structure reminded me of overripe pumpkins left lying on forgotten fields. That's corruption.

"As far as the intensity of the pain is concerned," he said, "these pains in my foot stand in no relation to the pain in my head. Even so, they share a common origin. There is no help against such an illness. These two pains, in my head and foot, between them form a common front against me."

I can't say that my decision to study medicine came out of any profound insight, no, it really didn't, it came about because I was unable to think of anything I would really enjoy studying, and it came about really because I happened to run into Dr. Marwetz, who still imagines I will one day take over his practice. Even today I am unable to claim that the study of medicine is enjoyable, or that medicine itself is enjoyable. The reason I didn't change my mind—what else would I have done?—was because I was always able to get through my exams satisfactorily. Not that I even had to try particularly hard, no, I seemed to do it all in my sleep. I always approached exams in a state of unpreparedness, and the deeper my ignorance, the better my results, and some I even passed with distinction. Now I am facing some tougher exams, but I'm sure they'll be just as easy for me. I'm unable to say why. I have never been afraid of any exam. And I enjoy the internship in Schwarzach. Not least because I was able to make a couple of friends among my colleagues. Because I have the sense I am needed. I get on well with Dr. Strauch too. He gives me to understand he would like to keep me. He hopes to be able to take over the registrarship, once the current registrar goes into retirement. In two years' time. And promote me in his wake. I never thought about whether people study medicine because they want to help others. It's nice when an operation turns out well, when something you try to do for someone works out. That's really something. That puts everyone in a good mood, when something works out. And then you might run into the intern in a café or bar. My brother says it's lack of imagination that makes me want to study medicine. Perhaps he's right. But what is it really? A thing like being given the painter Strauch to observe and have its effect on me, how is that for me? Or vice versa? And isn't it more than remarkable, to go to a man, a stranger, to introduce yourself to him, and then go around with him, to listen to what he says, and look at what he does, and write down what he thinks and proposes? The assistant characterized him pretty well, only a little superficially. But if I had to say something about the painter now, I don't know what it would be. It would be nonsense. And where am I to begin, when I am asked? There's no point in writing to the assistant. I was never any good at writing letters, least of all letters like that. The study of medicine inducted me into medicine so fast that I completely disregarded the imbalance. People say I'm "getting on well." My parents are pleased that I'm making something of my life. But what am I making of my life? A doctor? That would be too peculiar.

· · ·

Once it was already dark, I paced back and forth at the station, as far as the single-story barracks with the sign "Railwaymen's Hostel." There I saw men without their shirts, bending down over dirty basins, rubbing themselves dry with gray towels, then looking at their reflections in the mirror, shaving, sitting down on their bunk beds in their underpants and eating their dinners. Black railwaymen's caps hanging on the walls, and from hooks on the doors coats, jackets, and shoulder bags with papers spilling out of them. Knives flashed through big hunks of bread, and beer bottles stood there, reflected in the mirrors over the basins.

I took a few strides back and forth, purely so as not to attract notice, but wherever there was a light I looked up. What if it was you in there, standing in front of a mirror, and chatting to others, and they didn't realize that it was you, because you were like them? What if you had changed in such a way that brought you nearer to them? If I wasn't me, I would be like them; that's where those thoughts tended. I walked along between a couple of freight trains, to the end of the station area, and then back, counting the wheels, and imagined being crushed between a couple of bumpers and squeezing into a paragraph at the bottom of the next to last page of the newspaper, the place where they itemize fatalities of slight but morbid interest. And then the men again, some already in their army-style bunks. The windows have double glazing, everything is sealed shut. So they don't freeze. There's an alarm clock which will go off with an infernal rattle at four in the morning. Then they'll crawl out of bed and slip their pants on, because it's colder than it's supposed to be, and they should already be in the train, looking to see that all the barriers are down. And then there are the first schoolkids in the front carriage, sleepy and frightened, because they're not sure that what awaits them at school isn't going to be terrible after all.

I walked down to the station alone, it just takes me fifteen or twenty minutes at a rapid clip, I promised the painter I'd pick up a newspaper for him, but the kiosk was already shut. Also, it was a day on which not too many trains passed—in the time I was down there, there wasn't a single one, apart from the freight trains thundering through. Facing the railwaymen's hostel is a sheer cliff face, there are pines and firs, shrubbery, but you can't see much of it in the dark. The river was raging, and filled everything with its roar. From the houses built on its banks, I could hear laughter, and then the sounds of an argument, but it didn't develop, but became more and more subdued, and finally stopped altogether. The lights went out in the odd bedroom, until there was only a single one left illuminated, where I saw an elderly man sitting, raising his tattooed arm to turn off the light. By now I was shivering, and I walked as fast as I could, over the bridge and up to the inn.

"Every stone here has a human story to tell me," says the painter. "You understand, I've fallen prey to this place. Everything, every smell, is chained to a crime of some sort, an abuse, the war, some piece of infamy or other . . . Even if it's all buried under the snow just now," he says. "Hundreds and

thousands of ulcers, continually swelling up. Voices incessantly screaming. You're lucky to be as young and inexperi-
enced as you are. The war was finished by the time you were
ready to think. You know nothing about the war. You know
nothing, period. And these people, all of them on the lowest
level, often the lowest level of character, these people are all
prize witnesses to the great crimes that were perpetrated.
Further, there's the fact that your regard has to break when it
comes up against the cliff walls. This valley is death to any
tenderness of feeling." Then he says: "You know, I'm an irritant, I was always an irritant. I irritate you, the way I've
always irritated people. It hurts you. I know, you're often
asphyxiated by my remarks . . . Here, I have the sense of the
dissolution of all life, of all fixity, the smell of the dissolution
of all imaginings and laws . . . And here, you see, conversations with people, with the butcher, with the priest, with the
policeman, with the teacher, with these woolly hatted
people . . . with this prototypical milk-drinker who mangles
things before he says them, with that dreadful melan-
cholic . . . All these people have their complexes. It might be a
matter of bedwetting in childhood, or the patterns of the
wallpaper in their nurseries, the rooms where they open their
eyes for the first time. All those intimidated heads," he says,
"upcountry and down. The teacher reminds me of my time
as a substitute teacher, it's enough to make me feel ill. Emo-
tional chill, yes, with the passing of the years one's conclusions become more drastic, the curlicues are omitted in favor
of a more rustic expression, in favor of forthrightness . . .
And all wartime experiences, you know, everything these
people have to talk about is to do with the war . . ."

.   .   .

Everything was "appalled." "Life retreats, and death emerges like a mountain, dark and sheer and unscalable." He could even have attained great celebrity, great fame, but that hadn't finally interested him. "I had enough talent to have become world famous," he says. "People often hang a modest talent on a big drum, and become famous. Subtlety! It's all the drum, all the big drum! I stayed aloof, I saw what the drum was, the big drum, and I was never popular. And since it's come up between us: the war is an inexpungible inheritance. The war is properly the third sex. Do you understand!" He wanted to get down to the station again as soon as possible, to his newspapers. "Those smells," he says, "the smells of unworthy humanity, you know, the smell of rot, of tramp, and the smell of the so-called wide world, the smell of leaving and being left, of arrival and the despair of having to leave. The human famishment of wanderlust has always tempted me."

I walked with the policeman a ways. He immediately involved me in a conversation. He was going on duty and no end in sight, no change whatsoever. A promotion would lift him up in the pay scale, but the work would remain the same. Initially, he had wanted to go to college. His parents sent him to Hauptschule, then a couple of years of Gymnasium, from which they withdrew him, because his father thought he might make a fool of himself. "He hated the fact that I went to Gymnasium," he says. An apprenticeship with a carpenter followed on the heels of Latin, the lathe after Greek exercises. That was his tragedy. And from then on things went downhill. From the moment he walked out of the Gymnasium, knowing: I'm never going to see inside there again. And so, by the same token: I'm never going to be able to better myself. It had all been so perspectiveless, a gray, endlessly bleak day full of suicidal thoughts, high up on the hill that rises out of the middle of the city, from which he had wanted to throw himself down. But then there was the meeting with the carpenter. The very next day he slipped into his work overalls, and for four years he didn't take them off. If it had previously been the Latin vocabulary that made his eyes swim, if it had been Livy, Horace, and Ovid, well, now it was the wood shavings, the sawdust, the presentation piece. But he went on to take the journeyman's test, and stayed another year. Then, on the basis of an ad in the paper, he chucked carpentry, "just to get out of it all," and entered the police service. He swiftly found himself in uniform, and woke up in a vast dormitory with thirty-two others, all embarked on the same course as himself. Then, after the exams, he reported for duty in the mountains. First posting was Golling. Next came Weng. A year ago, he took over from a man of forty who died of septicemia. "He scratched himself with a fawn's bone." Studying medicine, that would have been the thing for him. Becoming a doctor. That hit me unexpectedly and hard. I felt myself blushing. "Studying medicine," I said. "Yes, studying medicine," the policeman.

On his shoulder he carries a carbine, very new in its pale, creaking leather holster. What was it like, being a policeman? "It's always the same," he said. "Everything's always the same," I said. "No, no," he said. He had thought: Policeman, that would be a job with a lot of variety, with a lot of arresting and locking up and detective work. "Which it is, but it's always the same." But it was healthy, I said. "Oh, sure, it's healthy." And surely varied as well, if I think of the fights on the building site, and in the pubs. The manslaughter perpetrated by the landlord sprang to mind too, but I didn't mention that. "I want to go to the city," he said. "Oh, the city," I said. The city afforded different possibilities. There were crimes there that people in the country didn't know existed. There were major crimes in the country, but the bigger ones, the interesting ones, the ones "involving the criminal imagination," they only happened in the city. "And the rural constabulary, where I am, isn't the same as the police," he said, "and so I have to stay in the country."—"Yes," I said.

Today, when I came back from the larch wood, the postman handed me the mail for the landlady. Three letters, one of them from her husband. When I saw the handwriting on the envelope, I thought at once of the landlord, and I wasn't mistaken. When the landlady had taken the letters, she said: "Ah, one from him!" and she put all three letters—the other two were bills, something official—in her apron. At lunch, I concluded from a conversation between her and the knacker, who was helping her pour beer, that it really was a letter from her husband. He wanted her to send him some money, so that he could buy food, because the food in prison was very bad. The newspapers had recently been full of stories claiming how prisoners were living the life of Riley: from that time forth, new measures had been put in place. She should send the money to a certain individual working in the prison service, who would then act for him. I was sitting right next to the bar, and heard every word.

.   .   .

The knacker said the landlady should immediately follow the wishes of her husband, and he named a sum too, probably the one that the landlord himself had suggested in his letter, but the landlady said she wasn't about to send him anything. And what was the knacker doing anyway, telling her what to do? It was up to her, whether she was going to send him any money or not. The knacker said it was a natural thing to do. Besides, people would get to hear about it one way or another, when the landlord came out, and tongues would wag about the landlady not sending her husband any money, even though it was all "his money" anyway, all the property was in his name. It wasn't right to desert her husband in such a situation. After resisting the reproaches of her lover, the knacker, for a long time, on wider-ranging issues as well, she finally gave in after all, but named a sum that fell far short of the landlord's wishes. She said her husband had driven her "to the brink of despair" with his wildness and ill-discipline, the way he had failed to look after her and her daughter. And now he expected her to send him money, in prison? Other inmates weren't sent money. Weren't prisons there to starve and punish you anyway? You were sent there to reflect on what you'd done, over bread and water and hard labor. "But he'll never change," she said. The only reason she had married him was because she was already carrying his child. She hadn't even known there was an inn. "Only for the sake of the child," she said. The knacker was agitated. Each time she came back with empty beer glasses, he took it up again. She had always depended on him, and also the landlord had occasionally shown "a good side." Not least it had been on her account, "because that was the way she wanted it," that the landlord had been arrested and tried in the first place, and then got his prison sentence. Because nobody had been in any doubt that it had been an accidental death that had befallen the customer who had been clubbed by the landlord. She herself had pointed out to the police that the wound to the customer's head—he was a construction worker at the power plant—hadn't been caused by any fall, but had been inflicted by the beer mug with which her husband had struck the man. Since the landlord had acted in self-defense, as became clear during the course of the trial, he was sentenced to only two years. "But he wouldn't have been locked up at all," said the knacker, "he would be running around the same as ever." The landlady said back: "I can't believe it's you telling me that. When it was for your sake that I brought charges against him." The knacker didn't say anything. "Because I wanted him out of the way," she said, "because we wanted him out of the way." The knacker reckoned the landlady had been precipitate in bringing charges. The people in the village, all of them, were against the landlady, because they knew darned well that it was she who had gone to the police station to bring charges. The dead man had been in the ground for weeks already at that point. No one was talking about it anymore. Till, on her word, they got him out of the ground, and examined him thoroughly, and then started that "whole big case" against the landlord. If it hadn't been clearly proven that he had acted in self-defense—and how often it happened in court cases that the truth is unable to establish itself, yes, is somehow deflected!—the landlord would certainly have been put away for life. Did she feel no compunction? the knacker asked the landlady. She didn't owe him any reply, she said. She didn't need to defend herself. Everything had been right and proper. "It was all by the book," she said. And now, as the person responsible for his mishap, as had been shown, she didn't even want to grant him his wish for a few schillings, so that he could buy himself better food, or maybe just a little more of it? "All right," she said, "I'll send him some money." The knacker demanded that she do so right away, he wanted to send it off himself. She said her purse was in the till. Before her eyes, the knacker pulled out a couple of bills, put them in an envelope, and wrote out the address.

In the great commotion, everything full of smoke and kitchen reek, the pair of them hadn't noticed me. At a favorable moment, I stood up and went to join the painter, who was sitting by the window. "What's the landlord like?" I asked. Without stopping to reflect, the painter said: "He's bound to be a poor devil. That accidental killing business has ruined him. The landlady is the sole person responsible for his misfortune. When he gets out of prison and comes back to the inn, something terrible will happen. And of course the landlady is terrified of that." Yes, she is terrified of it.

The knacker also works as an undertaker. Now you run into him here, now there. He's responsible for burying dogs and the cadavers of cattle and pigs, but also people. When he pulled off his army uniform, they, the council, gave him his two jobs, for which no one else had applied. Since he had never learned or been trained to do anything else, it was just right for him. He didn't want to start being a woodcutter after the war, and he didn't want to work in the cellulose factory either; he was too old for the railway, the post office turned him down, and there were no other possibilities. He has quite a bit of time to himself, and is almost always in the fresh air. Once every other week he takes a trip into the city, he's the only one of all of them who occasionally sees a little bit of the world. He digs graves, and shovels them over. He removes decomposed wreaths, and occasionally he earns a bit on the side by selling the cemetery compost to one of the farmers. In the course of his digging, he often comes across items of jewelry, which it is claimed he takes into the city to sell. Summer and winter he's dressed the same, in a leather jacket and leather pants, which are tied round the ankles. During funerals, he has to stand against the church wall and wait for the ceremony to be concluded. As soon as the last people have left, he gets to work, quickly fills in the grave, which, once it's settled, he tidies up: he pours black earth onto it, and cuts pieces of turf which he assembles into a neat hill. For that he often gets whole rucksacks full of meat and butter and sausage and weeks' supplies of free eggs, which he sells to the landlady, or rather, she deducts them from what he pays on the last of the month.

Often he goes scrabbling around the cemetery for hours, lugging turf, the water-weight, and a whole set of narrow boards which he uses to measure. He makes no secret of the fact that he's often up to his knees in water, because he has to dig graves to a prescribed depth of two meters twenty. They don't believe him until they see for themselves. The clay soil, containing a lot of gravel, can no longer do anything to spoil his mood. At nine o'clock, he hunkers down and drinks a bottle of beer. When he walks out of the cemetery at five, having locked up the morgue at a quarter of, he has a tune on his lips. Everyone likes to hear his stories, even the ones he makes up as he goes along. You can see how one thing leads to another with him, the way he always comes up with something unexpected.

"As knacker and gravedigger one is an important figure, a man they can't treat like an ordinary Joe," he says. Often he has a dog that was run over by a train in his rucksack, but he might just as well pull out some completely out-of-the-way item he found in an attic somewhere, like the pair of carved wooden angels he set up in the middle of the table yesterday, to drink a toast to.

The landlady was standing in the kitchen when I went to get some hot water. She was peeling potatoes, and her two daughters were stirring the contents of saucepans on the stove, or running to the woodshed for wood and putting it on the fire, or taking out clothes and brushing them clean. The landlady wanted to loan me a winter overcoat belonging to her husband. "You must be freezing," she said, "what you've got isn't more than a raincoat. The cold will cut right through that." I told her I always wore a woolen vest, and I didn't feel the cold. "That's what you say," said the landlady. "I don't feel the cold," I said. "Well, if you keep going around with the painter the whole time," she said. "Yes, if I keep going around with him the whole time," I said. She sent her daughters down to the cellar. "How long are you planning to stay?" I didn't know. Usually, all her rooms were taken, "just not this year. Visitors don't like to come when there's so much noise. The people working on the power plant make too much noise." But she didn't make that much from her long-stay visitors. "You know, you can't ask for that much from them . . .

And then you have to have something to offer your customers in return . . . it has to be tasty, and generous portions as well . . . But the workmen, they bring in money all right." Why didn't I sit down. She pushed a chair under me. If the inn were anywhere else, she said, "but here, right where they're excavating!"

Her potato-peeling took me back to my grandparents' house, the doors that were always left open a crack, the smell, the cats that snuck around, the milk that sometimes bubbled over, the ticking clocks. She said: "It's not easy being a student either." It was something someone had said to her once, she didn't mean anything by it. She had once been to the capital, and bought herself a few clothes. "I tell you, I was relieved to be heading home." And then: "But I wouldn't mind being in the city, not in the capital, but the city." She has the legs of a washerwoman. Fat and dropsical and veined. The public bar cost twice as much to heat as it did last year. "Meat has tripled in price," she said. And then she said something that utterly distracted me, put me in mind of a lake, a forest, a house in the flatland. Winter business was just the same as summer business. She was thinking of getting the building done up, getting all the rooms painted, replacing a lot of things that had gone out of fashion, "for instance getting in a new lot of wardrobes," she said, "and new tables for the bar and new curtains and a new staircase, and the windows ought to be much bigger, I'd get the openings made as big as possible, to get some light into the place." Then she poured hot water into a jug for me. She said: "But my husband doesn't want any of that. When he gets out, that's the end of everything anyway, you know. When he gets out . . ."

The way she said it. The way she said it, I couldn't get it out of
my head: "When he gets out . . ."

When the beer deliverymen come, the landlady stands in the
doorway and sizes them up. I'm sure I'll manage to get one or
other of them into bed with me, is what she may have been
thinking to herself. The deliveries happen at three in the
afternoon, but already by late morning, she's pretty excited,
bustling about here and there, she tidies up the silverware
drawer and mixes up forks and spoons, which makes for a
little irritation at lunchtime. She sends her girls outside to see
if the draymen aren't coming. But they were always on time,
and never got there before three. "Go and see if the draymen
are coming!" she orders them. She opens the kitchen window
so that she can stick her head out, but she can't see anything,
because of the way the little hill blocks the view of the road
down which the draymen will come. She has known that
from the very first day, but still she keeps looking out. If you
ask her what she's so excited about, she replies: "What do you
mean? I'm not excited!" And she opens the main door at
eleven, and loops the handle to a hook on the wall. "We need
fresh air!" she says. "It's stifling in here. The whole place
reeks!" When the draymen draw up, she charges out and tells
them how many crates and barrels she wants. They weren't
to make too much noise, she says, she had some sick and restless guests staying at the inn. She watches the draymen
unload barrels and crates, and carry and roll them in. They
wear large, thick, shiny leather aprons from throat to way
below the knee, green caps on their heads, and keep the top
buttons of their work tunics open even in winter. She asks for
the first barrel to be lifted onto the bar and has the hose fitted

to it, and the first three, four, eight, nine glasses, sprouting
on the bar like mushrooms, all of them full of froth, she empties into a jug for the draymen, and sets out bread and butter and sausage on the table for them. She sits down with
them, and asks them questions: "What's going on down
there?" she asks.

They tell her what they know, an accident, a baptism, a fistfight at a Communist meeting, a case of infanticide, a raft on
the river, "so big it couldn't get under the bridge." About how
it's getting harder and harder to drive up the mountain, especially with the snow not being properly cleared. "But there's
no one to clear it," they say. They put away as much as they
can, then they get to their feet, wipe their mouths with their
sleeves, and go out, climb into their truck, and drive off. Then
there's nothing she can see but the brawny arm of one of the
draymen, sticking out the open window. "They have it easy,"
she says as she walks into the public room.

The landlady was an instance of someone not putting herself
out because she doesn't want to make anything of herself
beyond the ordinary, unless it were something over time horribly repulsive, which doesn't require any exertion, just a general letting-oneself-go. She sometimes appeared to him, the
painter, at the foot of his bed, in spirit, the way an image
appears, emerging from the subconscious, half dream, half
reality, something you don't like and that leaves you no peace:
when he can't sleep; when he hears noise "from down in the
public bar"; on the path, often; in the forest, then with particular roughness against the landlady and himself. The image

had become a secret enemy of his, like other images of people who one day crossed his path and have long since forgotten him, and the moment they belonged to him. By nature, she was as lonely as thousands of others just like herself. Probably with just the same gifts for this or that as those others too. But thousands craned their necks to stare at him, when she craned her neck, as awkwardly and deceitfully as she did, with her timidity and her envy at odds. "Endowed with qualities that might lead to extraordinary heights," but stifled at every turn, she lived for her physicality, for a game of hide-and-seek that she played with herself in the dark, held together by corpulence and a few simple phrases, no more than three or four.

The landlady knew what her game was. And at the same time she didn't know. "The obverse of every side appears . . . Strong-willed, but not strong, because mean." He said it as if throwing the thing he said it about in the trash. Somewhere far away. "Her knowledge is based on self-deception so primitive that it cannot be called intellectual. No different than with a dog or cat. Only more pampered. More dependent." Then he gives a brief description of once having caught the knacker getting some substantial sum of money out of the landlady. "Back of the house. First in the lavatory, then outside under the tree." Four or five hundred schillings: "Big denomination notes. I don't believe thousands, so they must have been hundreds. Which he hurriedly stashed away in his pants pockets when I appeared." The landlady said, supposedly: "You don't have to give that back to me. My husband doesn't know." When was her husband coming out of prison? the knacker then asked. "If it was up to me, he wouldn't be

coming out at all. I don't want him anyway" was her com-
ment. For nights the two of them had been together. "No
passion in it," said the painter, "purely out of shamelessness."
She, not he, was the driving force, pushing everything into
repetitions of the same collapse. "Obtuse and blind, as
women of her type always are." She had been impatient to
have her husband put away. Already when she was seventeen,
a year after the wedding, she had had enough of her husband.
Cheated him from that time forth. She always owned up to
everything, if there was anything to own up to; she didn't
bother to keep secrets. "It was always her greatest weapon,
the fact that she didn't keep secrets. And she was never short
of a little variety," said the painter. "She just went around the
corner. Straight into criminality," said the painter. "In the
mornings she would come up the mountain, at daybreak, not
at all tired, in fact quite the opposite, refreshed. I often saw
her, because there were times I would get up at three o'clock
and leave the inn, and go on long walks. If I saw her coming,
I hid. There's no shortage of places to hide hereabouts.
When she got back, her husband often wouldn't even be at
home. That suited her, because then she got to sleep in. They
must have spent years not asking one another what they get
up to, where they've been when they come back in the mornings. The children knew everything." The painter said: "In
order to land her husband in prison, she even traveled to S., to
the public prosecutor. Because the landlord was this close to
getting off scot-free." The same night her husband was taken
away by the police, she received the knacker. "He was already
waiting by the tree," said the painter. "But there were also
times when he was nowhere to be seen. Then there would
be an icy silence in the inn." Apparently, she would send
her daughters down to the village to get him. If they didn't

come back with him, they would be beaten by their mother. "Punched and kicked," said the painter. Apart from that, the landlady was "a creature that doesn't mind the odd blow, skulks in a corner, and then comes out as if nothing had happened."

For the last few years, the painter hadn't had anyone except his housekeeper. She was sufficient for his so-called "physical requirements," which others "exploited shamelessly," but which became increasingly unimportant to him. "She doesn't know the least thing about it," he said. She was a woman with the necessary intelligence for a housekeeper, dressed carefully, and took herself off the moment it was required, without anything needing to be said. Unlike most of the other housekeepers he knew, she had only ever seen him as her employer. Two days a week. He felt that to be difficult for her. She was lonely. Didn't know what to do with the rest of her time. He paid her over and above, and occasionally bought her tickets for some entertainment or other, for which she repaid him with especial care over his laundry, ironing, and keenness in the kitchen. She came from the country, and housekeepers who came from the country were always to be preferred. He hadn't had her long, two or three years maybe, because before that he hadn't been able to afford a housekeeper. At present, she was with her parents in T. The very first day after he'd given her her notice, she had driven to them. "A girl of forty-five," he said. She had mastered the art of admitting visitors and escorting them out, like a highly competent mathematician. "But I hardly ever received visitors!" he said. It took her no more than two or three days to work out what his taste was, "the way I wanted things to be." He gave her a free hand. "She brought order to the worst of my chaos," he said. "In artistic questions, she was 'well-versed,' knew her way about. Because she didn't know the first thing about art: I always got my best criticism from her." She was "equally good at polishing shoes and at the silent drawing of curtains, at smoking cigars and at puncturing the megalomania of artists . . . When she was with me, I understood what the rich were about. I suddenly understood wealth and mobility." She told him what didn't suit her more trenchantly, effectively, and agreeably than anyone had ever managed to say anything to him. "She wanted to put out flowers all over the place, wherever there was room, but I forbade it."—"I don't want hygiene to crowd everything else out!" he explained. And she got it. She opened the door for him, and closed it after him. Dusted books and walls in a way that didn't cause him to protest. Posted his letters. Went shopping for him. Did all official business for him. Brought him news he would never have discovered for himself. "She made me hot and cold compresses and said thousands of times over that I was away, even when I was in my room, in bed." He said: "Wealth is as good as poverty when it comes to producing clarity." One morning, after he knew he had a fatal illness, he locked everything up, and last of all locked out his housekeeper. "She wept," he said. "Now I won't go back there. It would be like going back to a dump. I can't go back, even if I wanted to: I'm finished." He said: "It's true, I didn't have anyone at the end except for my housekeeper. As far as everyone else is concerned I might already be dead."

The children had lice, the grown-ups had gonorrhea, or the syphilis that finally overwhelmed their nervous systems.

"People here don't go to the doctor," said the painter. "It's hard to persuade them that a doctor is as essential to them as a dog. They work on instinct," he said, "they don't like the idea of interventions. Of course." Tree boughs often broke off in storms, and came down and killed passersby. "Because no one is protected. Never. Nowhere." Death surprised you in your sleep, in the field, in the meadow. Between a "lower" and a "higher" conversation, people dropped dead. "Revert to their original condition." They usually sought out a place "to die in," where they wouldn't be found so quickly. "Outside the borders of the commune." Animals also went far away, far from their kind, when they have the feeling they're dying. "Here the humans are like animals . . . Fragments of an alien life" often fell dead at his feet. It alarmed him. In a clearing, on a bridge, deep in a forest, "where darkness pulls the rope tight." He would often stop and turn round with a sense of a voice calling him from behind—a sensation I've had as well— but not seeing anything. He explores the undergrowth and the water and the rocks and the living creatures in the water, "which can be as cruel as its deeps." He had various methods of going through the woods: with his hands behind his back, with his hands in his jacket pockets. With his hands braced protectively across his head. He often ran on ahead to catch himself up, then hung back and chased after himself again. Talked to trees "as to members of an extraterrestrial academy, like children who are suddenly overwhelmed by the sense of being alone in a destructive chaos." His powers of invention extend as far as "astonishing verbal constructions verging on the profound," which he finds in the forests and fields, in the meadows and the deep snow. Or in the hollow path where he sits: "master of contemptu mundi" is one such, "uncivil engineer" another. That craze began one summer. Once, he drowned a determinist in a hole he'd drilled in the ice crust of a pond. "Something reigns over us that, in my view, has nothing to do with us"—that often brought him up short. One might laugh about it. But it was so dangerous that "it was possible to die in it." He always rebelled against anything superior, until "there was nothing left there" for him. "Any rebellion has to get somewhere," he said. His rebellions no longer got anywhere. From time to time he saw people in whom he sees: amazing assets, inexhaustible assets, he never had such assets himself! He said: "It takes you hours to adjust to the palpitations that suddenly start going in you like drumbeats at such a sight. Nothing can stand up to it in the long run." The people here had no assets, and if they did, then they didn't have the strength to use them, on the contrary, "they fritter them away." There, "where human potential is negated." Where ugliness offered itself everywhere like "the sexual imperative." The whole region was "sodden with disease." In this valley corruption spoke "sign language so that the deaf could hear it": things that elsewhere took care to remain hidden till shortly before their objective, here showed no such fastidiousness: "people wear their tuberculosis on their sleeves. They wear it on the outside, shamelessly, so that the glacier wind can whirl them away like a pile of dead leaves."

"There are schoolchildren," said the painter, "who have a three-hour journey to school. Often enough, before leaving home—at four a.m.—they do the housework, twelve-year-olds feed and milk the cows, because no one else is able to do it, because the mother is dead or ill in bed, and the brother is even younger, and the father is in jail because he owes money at the pub. With nothing but a hunk of rye bread, they haul themselves down the mountain through the cold. There is nothing, but nothing progressive here. Storms blow up out of nothing, screams are unavailing; who would hear you. A lot of country schools have been built in mountain passes, but still children are put through the torment of a long walk to school, if they are to escape analphabetism. They have been found in twos and threes in ravines, in petrified formations, past help. The children you meet here are precocious. Cunning, bandy-legged, with a tendency to hydrocephalus. The girls pallid and scrawny and tormented by septic ear-piercings. The boys straw-blond, with shovel hands, flat low foreheads."

Leaping up and running away and sitting down again, that was really the sum total of his childhood. Rooms full of the air of dead people. Beds that, turned back, reek of death. The odd highfalutin word in the corridor, the word "never" for example, or the word "school," the words "death" and "funeral." For years these words had pursued and irritated him, got him "into terrible states." Then again, they sometimes seemed like self-raising music: the word "funeral" spreading way past the cemetery, and then past all other cemeteries as well, out into infinity, or the notion that human beings have of infinity. "My notion of infinity is the same as the one I had when I was three years old. Less than that. It begins where your eyes end. Where everything ends. And it never begins." Childhood had come to him "like a person coming into a house with old tales that are grimmer than you can think, than you can feel, than you can bear: and that, because you are always hearing them, you have never heard.

Ever." For him, childhood had begun on the left side of the road and led straight uphill. "From that point on, I was always thinking of falling. I wanted to be able to fall, and I undertook several attempts in that direction . . . but it's wrong to make such attempts. It's thoroughly mistaken." Aunts towed him into morgues on the end of their long ugly arms, lifted him up over brass rails, so that he could gaze down into the coffins. They gave him the flowers for the departed to hold in his hands, and he had to keep smelling them, and listening to them say: "What a man he was! How lovely she is! See how elegantly dressed the dead man is! Look! Look!" They immersed him "ruthlessly in a sea of corruption." In railway trains he can hear himself say, "Straight ahead." In the long nights he loved the crack of light from his grandparents' bedroom, where they are still talking or reading. Delighted himself in their shared sleep. "The way sheep sleep together" was his sense. The way their breathing knits them together. Mornings break over a cornfield. Over a lake. Over the river. Over the forest. From the top of a hill. Birdsong on the fresh breeze. Evenings deepening in rushes and silence, into which he intones his earnest prayers. The whinnying of horses plucks apart tufts of darkness. Drunks, carters, bats all terrify him. Three fellow pupils dead on the street. A capsized boat that a drowning man failed to reach. Cries for help. Enormous wheels of cheese with enough force to crush him. Hidden in a brewery cellar, he is afraid. In between gravestones a game is played where figures are tossed from one to the other. Skulls glimmer feebly in the sun. Doors open and shut. Vicarages are the scene of meals. Kitchens of cooking. Abattoirs of slaughtering. Bakeries of baking. Shoe shops of hammering. Schools of teaching: with open windows, fit to scare you. Processions show colorful faces. Baptismal infants with feeble-minded grins. A bishop greeted with noisy cheers. Railwaymen's caps are mistaken on an embankment, which causes men wearing workpants and nothing else to laugh. Trains. The lights of passing trains. Beetles and worms. Brass-band music. Long streets full of grown-ups: a train that makes the whole world shake. Groups of huntsmen take him with them. He counts partridges, chamois, deer. Fallow deer, red deer, the hair-fine distinctions! Snow falling on everything. His desires as an eight-year-old, as a thirteen-year-old. The disappointments sopping into the bedclothes. Floods of tears when confronted with something so baffling. Not even six, and so much pitilessness already!

Cities, bubbling up against their inventors.

"Childhood is still running along beside us like a little dog who used to be a merry companion, but who now requires our care and splints, and myriad medicines, to prevent him from promptly passing on." It went along rivers, and down mountain gorges. If you gave it any assistance, the evening would construct the most elaborate and costly lies. But it wouldn't save you from pain and indignity. Lurking cats crossed your path with sinister thoughts. Like him, so nettles would sometimes draw me into fiendish moments of unchastity. As with him, my fear was made palatable by raspberries and blackberries. A swarm of crows were an instant manifestation of death. Rain produced damp and despair. Joy pearled off the crowns of sorrel plants. "The blanket of snow covers the earth like a sick child." No infatuation, no ridicule, no sacrifice. "In classrooms, simple ideas assembled themselves, and on and on." Then stores in town, butchers' shop smells. Façades and walls, nothing but façades and walls, until you got out into the country again, quite abruptly, from one day to the next. Where the meadows began, yellow and green; brown plowland, black trees. Childhood: shaken down from a tree, so much fruit and no time! The secret of his childhood was contained in himself. Growing up wild, among horses, poultry, milk, and honey. And then: being evicted from this primal condition, bound to intentions that went way beyond himself. Designs. His possibilities multiplied, then dwindled in the course of a tearful afternoon. Down to three or four certainties. Immutable certainties. "How soon it is possible to spot dislike. Even without words, a child wants everything. And attains nothing." Children are much more inscrutable than adults. "Protractors of history. Conscienceless. Correctors of history. Bringers-on of defeat. Ruthless as you please." As soon as it could blow its own nose, a child was deadly to anything it came in touch with. Often—as it does me—it gives him a shock, when he feels a sensation he had as a child, provoked by a smell or a color, but that doesn't remember him. "At such a moment you feel horribly alone."

He had had "the worst education, the worst imaginable education." The seeming advantage he had drawn from the fact that everyone ignored him later turned out to be a "catastrophic misjudgment." Basically, they hadn't given him a thought, right from the start. "But that doesn't help a child get an upbringing. They took trouble, yes, but about my shoes. Not my heart. About my meals. But not my mind. Later on, but even then much too early, when I was thirteen, I may say they stopped bothering about my shoes and my meals as well." I think, what sort of upbringing did *I* have? And was it an upbringing? Not just a growing up? Growing wild? The way stubborn plants grow wild in a garden full of weeds? Was I not always made to rely on myself? Care? Advice? Where? When? From the age of fourteen, I had to negotiate everything myself. Everything! Intellectual things too. Impalpable things. But it was never so terrible for me as it was for the painter. It was never so bad for me. I'm different; not so agitated. He's all agitation and irritation. I'm not always agitated and irritated.

Often he had asked himself: "How will I get out of the darkness? My head enwrapped in darkness, swaddled in darkness, I always tried to put the darkness behind me. Signs, yes, signs of idiocy . . . The darkness reached the pitch of insanity. At twenty, thirty, thirty-five. More and more ruthlessly with the years. I tried to get about: it seems important to me to alert you to this idea . . . I favor very simple explanations: a bend in the river, you must know, is like a bend in the human spine, glistening, sparkling, glistening in the afternoon sun, part of an unending spine curving over the horizon: that's it . . . Under some circumstances, it's enough to kill off the darkness in one's own head—because it's only inside one's own head that there is this darkness—with the darkness in one's own head. Mark you: the darkness is always a matter of one's own self-contained, severed head.—The people, forced back from their own personal darkness into a more general dark-

ness, continually forced back, you understand . . . Like
myself, once, leaning in my parents' house with bare torso, in
the darkness. In front of me: a bicycle wrapped in the wind,
two dancing schoolchildren. A smell of raisins. And in
between, the dullness that cements foundations. The face,
clipped from the newspaper, of our math teacher, who confronted us with the achievements of Voltaire. The outline of
Homer . . . dinned into my brain, in the dark, phenomena
and epiphenomena, notions of time, and sub-notions of
time. Riddled by all these. To all the questions of old age, no
answer. The general bitterness proceeds with deadly precision: a dog writhes on the grass. It might be a dog, or a mole,
or just some dirt that you suspect of wanting to exist . . . you
dance over the abyss in which every day you smash your
pains, and the pains of your pains."

He gave me an account of how he formed relationships and
broke them off. He didn't think of telling me. Telling is
reserved for other characters. Not him. How he planned
journeys and went on them, or planned them and didn't go
on them after all. How he discovered his capacity for pleasure
and enjoyment, and how he took these to heights that were
beyond the common man, or forbidden him. He mastered
collapses, everyday, all-round, personal failures. He accused
himself many times of lying, and applied the criteria of
incorruptibility and precision in the establishment of facts
against himself. Ruthlessly, one would have to say. Undefined
things struck him as too vain for him to want to approach
them. Oceans appeared to him as dark lunacy in front of his
eyes, drawing a line that mocks infinity. Mountain chains glit-
tered in prospect. Abysses, black and hostile, causing a ripple

down the spine. The air often atremble with distant thunder. Before long, the looming outlines of southern limestone cliffs. All stunned with lightning. Cities assembled on uncertain coasts. Notions like "pride," "abandonment," "strictness," and "deadly solitude" were formed from his unconscious gestures. Memory, which can be as clear as the air on an August day in eternity, spurred him to astonishing mental feats and an astonishing understanding of the world. History investigated him, and he returned the compliment— and there was harmony. Nothing was so clear as through his registering of it, his senses must be the purest imaginable. From infancy, schooled in heaven and hell, and the kingdom in between. But they were only moments that, to him, are native to every human being and then one day, as on command, cease to come. He was leery of opposing the "destroyers of his senses" with force. He cursed them, and they prevailed. There lay on the ground the thing that he hoped would heal him for ever. At his feet was "the kingdom of possibilities, which is blameless." The way he learned to deal with people in the same way as with stones, with news as with antique objects. The way he found out what thoughtlessness is, how it makes one dull, lonely, desperate. The way he was able to unite future, present, and past in himself and developed a game in which he would occasionally lose himself. The way he learned to switch off his body by purposeful calculation, and his mind as well, forcing it in a direction that was then fixed, "the only direction," an orientation that took him maybe a fraction of a second. The way he learned to live, though surrounded by the dead, the abdicated, the eliminated, the deposed, the fallen. As though in a never-ending tunnel, he lived on in himself in his darkness. He thought back on a youth that was restless but, as he now saw, stalled.

· · ·

In the course of the night, the wallpaper pattern in his room became more and more of a hell, full of terrible scenes of disfigurement. It finally put him under toward daybreak. And that was the time when, out of exhaustion and revulsion against everything and himself, he fell asleep. But no. Masks approached him with accusations that shredded his brain. Human detritus. Voices grew loud, but made no sense. "And all they are is ornaments formed from primitive cactus designs. I expect I look for horror every night, here as everywhere else. That's my only way of accounting for the fact that it comes out at me every night. The whole room is coated with these scenes. You know, they even do their writhing and wallowing on the ceiling. I have to get up periodically. To check the door's closed. Locked. I was surprised here once before. And that's so much worse." Lurid pictures would assail him "from behind" if he tried to lie on his front, so as not to have to look at the wallpaper pattern.

He spoke while we were sitting downstairs in the public bar. There was nobody else there. The landlady had gone to the village, to order beer from the brewery. Last night, she ran out of beer, because there was a colossal bout of boozing and guzzling, which drained every last drop from her crates and shelves and displays. It was all gone. There wasn't so much as a slice of bread left over. Until three in the morning, the whole building was shaking with the men's laughter. If we went out, we had to leave the front-door key on the left window seat, hidden behind the beam. The cold has got worse.

In the morning, the windows were white and opaque. Flowers and faces had formed on the panes, "masks of destruction," as the painter called them. We couldn't see out. Hundreds of dirty glasses, jugs, and bottles had been scooped onto the bar. A few items of clothing forgotten by the workmen were left hanging on the door and the wall. Shabby. Containing crumpled bills, handkerchiefs, photographs, and combs, as we were later to discover, the painter and I, when we went through them later on.

The smell of the booze-up, whose occasion remained obscure, was still hanging heavy in the bar, in the whole of the building. It was too cold for anyone to think of airing the place out. In the kitchen, there was utter chaos. Suddenly, the windows trembled, the walls twitched from an explosion down in the valley that felt like "a smack in the face of the air." "They're blasting a great hole in the mountain," said the painter. "They're making a second reservoir."

There was construction going on down there on such a scale that you couldn't say "how it was possible." The engineer had told him some numbers. Dates. Dimensions. "Staggering," said the painter. "Over a thousand workmen are crawling around like ants down there." And indirectly the work would occupy and pay the wages of tens, of hundreds of thousands. "The money invested here goes into billions." The state knew how to exploit its sources, and apply its science. It was "glorious." But down there, "and not just down there either, there is a development in progress that will turn everything upside down." Technology was continually revolutionizing itself. "Come on," he said, "let's step outside. Perhaps we'll be able to see something."

We went outside. But there was nothing to be seen but a thickening pall of gray in front of our eyes. "I want to see the funeral today, from my vantage point over the pass," he said. "They're burying the grocer."

Eighth Day

Today I cleared the path of snow from the inn to the road. The landlady called me a "kind gentleman," and she twice brought me large glasses of slivovitz when she saw me leaning on my shovel, resting. She said: "I would never have thought you were so strong." I said I was used to physical work. Circumstances had repeatedly led me to perform physical work. Doing physical work, so as not to go out of my mind over my studies, that was something she could well understand. "It hasn't snowed as much as this in years," she said. She pointed south toward the mountains, which were obscured by clouds. She went in, and came out with a salt beef sandwich. "If you work, you're going to need something to eat," she said. She was pleased I was clearing away the snow, because she wouldn't have gotten around to it. "That would be a pity," she said. When she saw the painter coming out of the inn, she left me alone, and went in past him. It looked as though she wanted to avoid him. She didn't want to be standing there with him. That was how it appeared anyway.

It was unbelievable what I'd managed to do in such a short space of time, said the painter. He had been watching me from the window. "If you hadn't volunteered," he said, "no one else would have done it." Unusually, he had slept that night, he said, and he stood behind me, which bothered me. "Unusually, I slept. 'Sleeping' with me means merely that I don't go pacing my room all night!" From the degree of his morning pains, he could predict the pains of the evening to come, and the night. "It will be a terrible evening, and a godawful night. But it can't go on much longer, I'm sure of that." Decades ago, in the capital, he had "belonged to a snow-clearing troop. Three schillings eighty per hour, under a carbide lamp." My snow-clearing reminded him of those bitter times. "The time I was more dead than alive. I was often on the brink," he said. "But what a wonderful time that was, compared to today . . . at least, soon to end in my death." I barely listened. He felt like going to the café in the afternoon. "Will you accompany me? Down to the station? There are new editions of the weekly magazines."

Then he briefly described how he had once met himself as someone else. "Have you had an experience like that, ever?" he asked. "When I went up to myself, I naturally wanted to shake my hand, but then I suddenly pulled it back. And I knew why." I cleared the last of the snow, and took the shovel back in the house. The painter waited outside for me. When

I came back, he said: "The young man just has to pick up a shovel to feel alive. But what does the old man do?"

Life was like a forest: you kept finding signposts and markers until, all at once, there weren't any. And the forest is never-ending, and hunger only ends with death. And you keep walking through clearings, you can never see past those clearings. "The universe can feel oddly constricting, under certain circumstances." But to show someone the way to where he was now, if the person didn't happen to know it already himself, that was something he was no longer prepared to do. "I work with my own notions, elaborated by myself out of chaos." One would have to understand what he meant by "bitterness," by "fundamentally," by "light" and "shade," and "poverty *tout court*." But who understood. And yet, one might sense what sort of areas he was in. What was causing him grief. Perhaps more than he realized. "Knowledge distracts from knowledge, you know!" People in uniform bothered him. "I hate the police, the rural constabulary, the army, even the fire brigade." All of it gave him a sexual stimulus that he preferred not to entertain. He can't deal with any of it, whether it's railway employees, or actual soldiers. Officers disgust him. For their inhumanity, "which is bred into them to exacerbate it." But they repel him as much as they attract him. "Yes, they attract me too. I've told you why. Problems that are stifled in the smell that makes way for the images." Then: "In the age when I was susceptible, women tended to attract me more by their defects: older ones, ugly ones." He had always been stirred anyway by absence, it drew him with an infantile, forbidden passion. He had never been clear about anything. "Clarity is something more than human."

He seeks and propounds simplicity, and detests it at the same time: always wanted to break clear of it. The certainty with which he devotes himself to quiet is no less than that with which he espouses disquiet, without him being able to tell you why. He decided: and also for the obverse. And yet it's always him as well. Perfectly circumscribed by what defines his point of view. "Is that mad?" he asks, after explaining a certain set of affairs, as if it had been a room in an infinitely large building. "Incompleteness always makes what I wanted to reach fall in on itself." To put the ground under his feet behind him, he walked, he moved, no matter where, no matter how: "but I can't put the ground under my feet behind me." It was a law of nature . . . sleeping and thinking and all the things in between, pushed in between, extruding from between—they were all distractions from himself. And yet there was no method for distracting him from himself. "Of course it's all sterile because it's all been mapped and well-established; and what I say is so basic as well." The place where you see that it's all ridiculous keeps recurring, each time you looked out the window, or looked into yourself. Wherever. "And then one time you pull off your great coup: you end it!"

"When they present themselves, everyone I know looks the same. What's within them looks the same too, whomever it belongs to. Everyone has the same. I find that repulsive. When I say 'dismiss,' a smell remains that darkens everything." He said people were, initially reluctantly, later without any objections, bearers of various occupations, holders of opinions with varying top speeds and fuel-efficiency quotients. "A simple country girl as much as a CEO." Of limited feeling and mind, the individual no longer mattered. "What's the point if the most cunning, not the wisest, get the best seats? If they take out insurance policies in the millions? Future prospects worth millions? Hearsay? Hairsplitting? Balderdash?" We were preceded by a reputation that killed us.

"Many ideas turn into lifelong disfigurements," he said. The ideas often surprised one years later, but sooner or later they would always make the one who had had them look ridiculous. The ideas came from a place they never left. They would always remain there, in that place: it was the place of dreams. "The idea doesn't exist that can be expunged or expunge itself. The idea is actual, and remains so." Last night, he had been thinking about pain. "Pain doesn't exist. A necessary illusion," he said. Pain wasn't pain, not in the way a cow was a cow. "The word 'pain' directs the attention of a feeling toward a feeling. Pain is overplus. But the illusion of it is real." Accordingly, pain both was and was not. "But there is no pain," he said. "Just as there is no happiness. Found an architecture on pain." All thoughts and images were as involuntary as the concepts: chemistry, physics, geometry. "You have to understand these concepts to know something. To know everything." Philosophy didn't take you a single step nearer. "Nothing is progressive, but nothing is less progressive than philosophy. Progress is tripe. Impossible." The observations of mathematics were foundational. "Oh, yes," he said, "in mathematics everything's child's play." And just like so-called child's play, mathematics could finish you. "If you've crossed the border, and you suddenly no longer get the joke, and see what the world's about, don't see what any-

thing's about anymore. Everything's just the imagining of
pain. A dog has as much gravity as a human being, but he
hasn't lived, do you understand!" One day I would cross a
threshold into an enormous park, an endless and beautiful
park; in this park one ingenious invention would succeed
another. Plants and music would follow in lovely mathemati-
cal alternation, delightful to the ear and answering to the
utmost notions of delicacy; but this park was not there to be
used, or wandered about in, because it consisted of a thousand and one small and minuscule square and rectilinear and
circular islets, pieces of lawn, each of them so individual that
I would be unable to leave the one on which I was standing.
"In each case, there is a breadth and depth of water that pre-
vents one from hopping from one island to another. In my
imagining. On the piece of grass which one has reached, how
is a mystery, on which one has woken up, and where one is
compelled to stay," one would finally perish of hunger and
thirst. "One's longing to be able to walk through the whole
park is finally deadly."

I met him behind the hay barn, huddled on a plank of wood.
It was already dark, and he said he had heard me approaching
from the pond. "I know your walk exactly." People like himself, who generally kept their eyes closed—"in itself another
preparation for death"—had an extraordinarily keen sense of
hearing. "You were still a long way off, but I could hear you.
You slowly approached my grumpiness. Did anyone ever tell
you you don't walk like a young man?" It must strike me as
odd to find him here behind the hay barn. In fact, he was dis-
playing one eccentricity after another. "True, isn't it, everything I do is eccentric? I hunkered down here, because I could

no longer stand. I'm afraid your suggestion of the compress"—it seemed to me he said the phrase with a certain relish, and repeated it several times to himself, as if poking his head out of a foxhole—"your suggestion of the compress was a poor one. My swelling is still there. I was right, it can only be a matter of the worst case. Before long, I won't be able to walk at all. I hope you've revised your opinion that there was nothing to it?" He lapsed into a long disquisition on his illness, which was spreading "in positively philosophical fashion," between his brain and his foot. Essentially, it was an affirmation of a "holy science."

He had walked through the larch wood and then to the pond—"there are only two walks here, the one or the other"—and had actually been meaning to go down to the station, to supply himself with newspapers and "give himself a fright. Newspapers are the only luxury I have. What human beings no longer are, what nature never was, newspapers now supply me with: a little variety, a little distraction." In the newspapers, he found confirmation of many of his theories. Newspapers constituted, effectively, the world, all of it, the world and the cosmos, in every issue he opened. "The world isn't the world, it's a zero." Every day, through the agency of the newspaper, he was compelled to open the argument with himself. "In terms of the discomfort they provide to many, with every reason and justification, the newspapers are the only comforters of mankind." Newspapers were to him what brother and sister and father and mother had never been. "What the world never was for me. Often the newspaper was all I had, for days, weeks, months, only the newspaper, it told me that everything still existed, everything, you know, all around me and within me, all those things I thought were gone."

On the slope, under the big linden tree, where the humming of the telegraph wires is loudest, a few paces from the big power mast, he had been taken with a sudden nausea, and had hurriedly turned back. "It's my foot." He had had to drag his foot after him like a lead weight. "I had the feeling it was about to snap off." At first he had tried to get to the inn by the shortcut, but then he had broken down, he said. With the last of his strength he had taken refuge in the hay barn, where he had hoped to be able to shelter from the wind. "Behind me I have warmth, the hay, you see!" Then, while thinking about his sister—"a very sad thought!"—he had been made aware of my approach—"that oddly crumbling sound." "I'm happy you came along. Is it by chance, or did you happen to see me?" It was chance, I said. "As soon as I sat down, the pain in my foot eased. It moved up, to be closer to my brain."

He's forever complaining about the pain in his foot, "which is always at its worst when the pain in my head eases." He had followed my advice that he should put his foot up at night, on a pillow, but "as you see, it was no use. Quite the contrary. The swelling has grown. It's as though it was sucking up everything that's in my body. The same sucking feeling, by the way, that I have in my brain." He's right, the swelling has grown. Because he's walking the whole time. It's maybe twice the size of what it was the last time I saw it. But no discoloration. His anklebone has completely disappeared. "The best thing you can do for your foot is not walk for a day or two," I said to him. "So it's as simple as that, you think, to fight such a terrible illness?"—"I'm sure it will have gone in a few days," I said, "disappeared."—"Here, on my arm, you see, there are signs of swelling too," he said. He pointed to a spot on his forearm, where there was supposed to be swelling, but I couldn't see anything. I palped the spot, but couldn't feel anything untoward. "Surely you can feel something's on the way. You can't have any feeling for illnesses." His head was full of "indescribable conspiracies." Pictures he sees, just as anyone does, suddenly spun round, were torn apart "in little scraps, you know. But I'm quite reconciled to the fact that everything about me is diseased. In the grip of illness. I don't think the illness I have is infectious. As soon as I discovered it, I had the feeling it was incurable. Incurable," he repeated, and stopped. We were walking in single file, as ever, me first, him following, first up to the village, then to the inn. "A patient recognizes an incurable illness right away. Usually he keeps his knowledge to himself. It looks quite different from anything curable." His blood was full of so many poisons that you could "wipe out whole sections of cities with it." These poisons kept forming little concentrations under his skin, anywhere they could find. "Hence the swelling on my foot," he said. "Just as there are hulks of ships on the banks of great rivers, so there are poison deposits on the banks of my arteries and veins. Death can only mean the cessation of all my pains. Death means being rid of everything, and most of all, of myself." There were no more issues to be settled between himself and his death. "The arrangement I have come to with my death is mutually advantageous."

.   .   .

If the villagers could do what they wanted, they would spend their lives guzzling and boozing. You'd have to fear for their jaws, even now alarming quantities of food and drink dribble out of the corners of their mouths. The landlady sics them on her tripe and onions and boiled beef and steins of beer, it's like siccing dogs on something you're not quite sure about. She provokes. The painter is disgusted by the food and drink that the engineer and the knacker hurl themselves upon. Those who have sung, now wail. The engineer says something against the church, the knacker about an infected ox that some people in the village had chopped up and eaten. It so happened that yesterday once again he had been forced to go down the gorge and up the shady side to find a dead dog. People seemed not to be able to bury their own pets. They gave him a tip, and asked him questions. What was the origin of this or that. How did you get here or there, and what was it like. How you got out of there, they didn't know either. "Yes, mysticism," that's the only thing the knacker knows to say back, "mysticism." Or: "mystical influence," and the now drunken engineer says: "The scholiasts!" and fiddles with a bone. The landlady can't keep up with the orders, she struggles, kicks out at people under the table; either they don't notice, or they misinterpret it. The ones who take a kick as a secret summons to join her in bed at such and such a time, they get it right. She's sweating, and her chin glistens like the sausages she shoves in front of the policeman's uniform, causing him to scoot back, and study his belly. "No, no!" says the engineer, "not the least idea!" He knew how to tackle granite, what to do with intractable people. "But I don't use my fists!" he says, "I don't need to do that. No, no!" And then there's such a hubbub in the room that you can't make out a word. The landlady's daughters are slithering from one man's knee to the next. "An unpleasant odor," says the painter, but he's apparently still too weak to get up. "I just want to finish my drink," he says. "It's always the unforeseen that occurs—a party!" says the engineer. The less-well-off were jealous of the better-off, he says, and no one knows who's in the box seat and who's not. But in heaven there was enough space "for the last snotnose."—"Oh, yes," says the knacker, "there's always room in heaven." Sometimes he felt like a horseman trying to continue to ride without his mount, says the engineer, almost exploding with heat, "you hang in the air for a while, and you continue to make progress. But the moment you start to think you're in midair, you go crashing to the ground, and everything's gone to pot." Then, when the plates have been taken out, they sing "Zu Mantua in Banden," at a volume to shake the walls. The painter makes his way through the racket up to his room. It's not till two in the morning that there's any peace. Before that, there's a lot of merriment and squalor and the great futility of everything.

Ninth Day

"Did you hear the drunks? Did you hear them after midnight?" he said. "I lay awake all night. Walked up and down. I even opened the window and let the air pour in, that terribly cold air. But it didn't do any good. I thought I might go down and complain. But there's no sense in that. I'd only encounter incomprehension. The thing that makes me most indignant is that incessant door-slamming. Like continually being beaten about the head! There's nothing worse than incessant door-slamming in a house. People slam doors without the least thought. It's a trait of inferior humanity. Habitual door-slamming is even capable of killing someone. My whole day is wrecked if someone slams the door. But here they slam them all the time. Imagine yourself forced to live somewhere where they continually slam the doors! A place inhabited by habitual door-slammers! You're up against it, I tell you . . ." He says: "Look at my little shoes, my little tiny shoes!" and he presses on one of them with his cane. And I look at his shoes. "My head is so swollen, I can no longer see my shoes. I have infinitely tiny shoes, and very rickety legs. Infinitely tiny, infinitely minute shoes! And what these legs have to endure, when I think of my head! I look like some sort of grotesquely swollen insect! My head is so heavy, a dozen strong men wouldn't be able to lift it . . . but my legs, those tiny little legs, they can manage it. I always take a footbath in the evenings now. That helps. I can't see anything with my head. It's all gray. And yellow. And then the colors start to run, and I see nothing but pain."

If he ran into a tree with his head, it felt like a swollen hand. "Do you hear? There's a chainsaw installed in my head. That saw makes so much noise it could kill me! Great planks of wood are forever getting jammed in my head, I'm not exactly able to say where: way down, or right at the back . . . and then it's the waterfall that's making me black out. I can hear your voice, but only at a great distance, as though through a wall. Of course I know you're walking along beside me. But it's as though you were walking beside me a great distance away. I can hear you. You're tramping through the snow as I am. You drag me after you. You force me to walk with you. Force is what it is . . . Youth is always painless," he said. We were between the church and the village. Sometimes we could see neither church nor village, because great swaths of fog were rolling through the valley. "Youth is barely acquainted with grief. Or oppression. Or hopelessness. But what I'm saying is wrong. When you're young, everything is so much worse. The oppression is worse. The hopelessness. The pain. In fact, youth is inaccessible. No one can get at it. Not at real youth. Real childhood. No one can get at it. Is that true? Do you think I should give my coat a brush?" he asked. "You speak so softly. We are in a swampy landscape here, you must know. If it was summer, we'd already be finished. But what can kill you in summer, drag you down, it's all frozen over now." We reached the hay barn and sat down on the wood plank where he had squatted the day before. He said: "By nature, you might call me ideal." As soon as he'd recovered, we got up, and walked back the way we'd come for a little stretch, but then turned off it, to get to the inn quicker. "Once we're back at the inn, you should look for something for yourself. Anything. Whatever you like. I'd like to make you a present. Choose something in my room. You know, you don't attack me. Everyone else attacks me."

"What do people say about me?" he asked. "Do they say 'that idiot'? What is it they say?" He wanted an answer. "I'm an irritant, that's what it is. My head was always an irritant to them. Now, in my sickness, there are further traits emerging in me that were formerly hidden. That hadn't got as far as my head. It's true: sick as I am, it's no longer possible for me to suppress anything. Not a thing. You see, this is the way I am, it's nothing bad. They laugh at me because I wear puttees. Also because my stick is an ornamental cane to them. And that's just the beginning." Then: "On the one hand, I should like not to be all alone; on the other, they all disgust me. Everything disgusts me. It forces its way into them, and into me, aversion and intolerance. No dealings. No. Should I sit down with someone? No. With the engineer? With the knacker? With the landlady? With the priest? With one of them? No. At one time, it might have been possible. Now I'm a long way from there. But of course I'll give it a go. So as not to sink. Or perhaps because I want to sink." He said he might have made some sort of scientist. "But I am deeply incapable, deeply deeply incapable." The unusual qualities of many people were barely worth remarking on. "But I am nobody."

For days now, there have been no other guests at the inn. Only the painter and I. Between meals, it's as silent as the grave. "Our grave," the painter suddenly said today. He raised his stick at something I couldn't see, and repeated: "Our grave." Then he cut round the inn, and vanished into the dark shadows of the trees. For the first time, for some reason, he wanted to be alone. That gave me the chance to go up to my room. At first I thought I might write a letter home where I would mention my mission, where I was, what I was doing with the painter. A few details established themselves in my brain. Then, no sooner had I written three or four sentences, I dropped the sheet of paper in the stove. I read my Henry James book, and drank a glass of beer I brought up from downstairs. "The doctor is the helper of mankind," I thought, that pronouncement that always provoked me in the most idiotic way. Helper of mankind, I thought. Helping and mankind, the distance between those two terms. I can't imagine myself ever helping anyone. When I'm a doctor . . . a doctor? I and doctor? The whole thing feels to me as if I'd just woken out of a dream, and now I'm to go about in a white coat I've got on for some reason. The "helper of mankind" flitted through my brain, and gave me a headache, my first in a long while. I don't understand anything.

With my head full of those thoughts, I wasn't able to make any progress with my Henry James either. I closed the book and slipped it into my coat, put another big log on the stove, and left the inn, heading for the village. In less than a quarter of an hour, I was at the cemetery, which was where I thought I might find the knacker. I would have loved to talk to him, teased one of his stories out of him. But he wasn't in the cemetery. A few local women were carrying paper wreaths into the chapel. There was a rattle in the bell tower, and at that same instant, a chunk of ice came off the church roof and fell at my feet. I stopped in alarm. One more step, and . . . I remembered how once, fifteen years ago or so, an enormous icicle flew down, brushing my sleeve, and the air pressure alone was enough to knock me over. Back then, I hadn't been able to sleep for many nights because of the excitement, and I went on wetting my bed for weeks afterward. Disappointed not to have seen the knacker, I walked along by the children's graves, this way and that. But before long, my walking struck me as pointless, and I couldn't bear it anymore, and ran into the nearest pub on the village square. I sat down in a corner, from where I could watch the farmer's lads playing cards in the other corner, drank a couple of glasses of beer, and didn't get up until I was fairly drunk. I stumbled into the ditch a couple of times, straightened myself out again, laughed into space, and didn't get back to the inn until much later.

In the public bar, the engineer said the construction of the power plant was the largest such project ever to have been carried out. Even now experts were arriving from all over the world on a daily basis to have a look at the thing. "But can our state afford such a large project?" asked the painter. "Oh, yes," said the engineer, "the state is rich. If only it would always put its money into such large and useful and universally admired projects. But unfortunately the state wastes most of its money!" Billions disappeared every year without a trace. It was known where the money had disappeared to, to ministerial villas and ministerial factories and into the nationalized enterprises, which were so badly run that it was completely pointless putting any money into them. All those businesses ran at big losses, which had to be made up from the public purse. "But most of it goes on representation," said the engineer. And the painter said: "There's no other country like ours, where the ministers have a choice of twenty official cars; if there were, they would all go down the drain."—"Back where we came from, in other words," said the knacker. "Yes," said the painter, "we're bankrupt." "Bankrupt," said the knacker.

The engineer, who had ordered us a liter of wine on his tab, then said: "The power plant will supply electricity to the whole of Europe. No layman could even begin to imagine a construction like it. I only know the very broad outlines, and have detailed information about a few parts of it. Everyone has his own particular area for which he's responsible. The real achievement belongs to those scientists who designed it. I am only responsible for the building of it, and the building of a small section. If you think that a cubic meter costs about as much as a village to build, and not a small village at that, then you can begin to imagine the scale of the investment. But really it defies the imagination." The painter says: "But the landscape will be wrecked by it. The more such power plants are built, and I'm not arguing about the need for them, or that they're not incredibly useful, they're the best thing we could build here, I'm really not arguing about that, but the more such power plants are built, the less beautiful country-side will be left. Now, this valley is ugly anyway, and it can hardly be disfigured more than it is already, one ugliness more or less hardly matters, but in beautiful landscapes, and our country largely consists of beautiful landscapes, in such landscapes power plants can have a devastating effect. Half the country has already been wrecked by the building of power plants. Where there used to be flowery meadows and rich farmland and first-growth forests, there are only these concrete lumps now. The whole country will soon be paved over by power plants, and before long it will be impossible to find a spot where you won't be bothered by power plants, or at the very least by telegraph poles."—"Yes," said the knacker, "that's true."—"The great rivers are being destroyed as well," said the painter, "because people build dams at those points where they flow most beautifully, and through the most beautiful scenery, and break their flow with ugly power plants. Not that I'm an enemy of the new architecture, quite the contrary, but a power plant is always a thing of ugliness.

There are already thousands of them up and down our country." The engineer says: "Why shouldn't we use the energy that is ours to exploit? All the other countries are building all the power plants they can. Electricity is a precious commodity." And moreover power plants were by no means as ugly as the painter claimed they were. Because they were built as simply as possible, they often fitted into the landscape as if they had always stood there. "In many places, reservoirs come into being that actually constitute an improvement on what was there before," says the engineer. "Ugly villages and swamps and useless waste ground could all disappear underwater overnight." The painter says: "But dams are continually being breached, and then the waters inundate the quiet fertile lowlands, and hundreds of people are ruined, I'm forever reading about such incidents."—"Yes," said the engineer, "you're right there."—"And the people don't know what they've done to find themselves exposed to such a constant danger. Because there's really nothing much that can be done about a dam breaking, is there, Engineer?"— "Yes, we're pretty helpless if it comes to that." But dams were only very rarely breached. And those occasions were generally from natural causes, outside human forethought. "There, you see!" said the painter, "you see!" The engineer says: "Dam bursts are so rare, and the resulting losses, in terms of human lives, I mean, are so small, that they don't really impinge on the calculations . . ."—"Oh, they don't impinge?" says the painter; "they don't impinge?"—"No," says the engineer, "they really don't impinge. Not if you think of the colossal advantage of having the power plant there."—"Oh, the colossal advantage of having the power plant! And you think a hundred thousand deaths are any different from a single death?"—"How do you mean?" asks the engineer. "Ah," says the painter, "now, you see: how do you mean?" And then the engineer says: "The danger of human fatalities exists everywhere. And in fact people are killed everywhere. A very few in power plants. Workmen, yes. But workmen die everywhere, you get deaths on any building site. If our country hadn't built the power plants it did build, never mind under what circumstances, then it would be a poor country." Whereas now, whatever the abuses and the corruption, it could still claim to be a prosperous country. "The more power plants are built, the more fortunate our country." Everybody was agreed about that. Only the painter didn't say anything, just: "Yes, power plants."

"The engineer was in the Klamm valley," said the painter; "if I'd known he was going to the Klamm valley, then I'd have gone with him. He could have given me a ride in his car as far as J. It's ten years since I was last in the Klamm valley. You must know, the waterfall there is quite thunderous. Well, the engineer half froze to death in the Klamm. If he'd asked me, I could have told him what to put on, if you're going to the Klamm!—'The Klamm is an experience,' I told him, and he said: 'But what about the wild boar!'—'The wild boar?' I ask, 'the wild boar? You didn't believe that rigmarole about the wild boar, did you?' 'Rigmarole?' he asks. 'Yes, the rigmarole!' The thing about the wild boar is a rigmarole. The knacker tells everyone going to the Klamm that there are wild boar there who will attack humans, you know! But the thing about the wild boar is an absolute rigmarole! 'A rigmarole!' I say, and the engineer says: 'I've heard them!'—'Heard what? The wild boar?' I ask. 'Yes, the wild boar.'—'The wild boar? If you heard wild boar in the Klamm valley,' I said, 'then you never heard a wild boar, because there aren't any wild boar in the Klamm valley. None!' I said definitively, and the engineer: 'So you think the knacker was pulling my leg?'—'Yes, the knacker pulled your leg,' I say, 'the knacker pulls the leg of everyone who goes into the Klamm valley.'—'But they were wild boar!' says the engineer, refusing to be convinced by me. 'All right, then they were wild boar,' I say. 'Only a fool can fail to distinguish between wild boar and a fox or a deer. Those were foxes or deer.'—'No, they were wild boar,' said the engineer. And I turned and walked off. You know," said the painter, "there haven't been any wild boar in this part of the country for hundreds of years. Not up here in the mountains; down in the flatland, that's another story, they wreak all kinds of devastation there, nibbling corpses, and barging open the doors of people's houses, and surprising them in bed. But here there are no wild boar. 'You should have put on your fur hat,' I say to the engineer, 'and you should have wrapped your feet in puttees.' Yes, that's what he should have done, he saw that too. But he believed the rigmarole about the wild boar."

We walked past the pond. The painter said: "People have vanished here, and never been found; nothing more was seen or heard of them. I could give you several instances of people vanishing here. Most recently, the butcher's girl vanished. Without a trace. The evening before, she was in her bed. In the morning she was gone. Once and for all. That such a thing should be possible," said the painter, "it suggests there's something to the supernatural, doesn't it? Or don't you think it's supernatural if a person simply vanishes? Without a trace? Leaving nothing behind but a wardrobe full of clothes, a couple of pairs of shoes, and a prayer book? And even after ten years nothing has been heard of them?"

I stay downstairs in the public bar, because the people create a bit of warmth. Up in my room it's cold, the fire has gone out, and I don't feel like trying to get it going again. I can't sleep in a warm room. I've got a small cast-iron stove in my room. It quickly becomes red hot, but just as soon goes stone cold. And the room is like the stove. Down in the public bar, I join in their card games. I go and sit with them once I'm sure the painter won't be back down. He wouldn't like to see me playing with them. Or should I just tell him? Why don't I tell him? I shouldn't let him boss me around. But sometimes he stays sitting there himself, and asks the engineer something to do with the construction of the power plant, or the knacker about some detail in one of his war reminiscences. "Was that in Poltava?" he asks, to test out the knacker. And he says back: "No, it was in Odessa," and if, as the painter recalls, he said, "in Odessa," weeks before, at the same point in the same story, then he knows that the story is truthful. The painter likes to ask these trick questions. If the knacker had said: "Yes, in Poltava," then that would have been proof that the story he told was not a truthful one. Or the painter says: "The girl remained faithful to that man to the end, didn't she?"

Many times I have to fetch the beer-warmer from the kitchen for the painter. But then he leaves it in the glass for so long that the beer becomes undrinkable, and then he says: "I can't drink this!" and pushes it away. He orders one glass of beer after another, and leaves them untouched. If he steps away, the engineer drinks it off, or the knacker, or whoever else happens to be sitting nearby. Sometimes he takes his Pascal with him on walks, and suddenly pulls it out of his pocket, opens it up at a certain page somewhere, and says: "That's a great thought!" pretends to read a section, looks at me, and returns the book to his pocket. "Blaise Pascal, born 1623, the greatest!" he says. It might be two o'clock before I get to bed. In the end, it's still the engineer and the knacker sitting there, and the landlady and me. Now the cards are on the table, now they're in our hands. The landlady keeps record of who wins. The wall clock ticks. Outside, the world shrivels up with cold. "Up until six months ago, I kept a dog," says the landlady, looking out the window. And seeing nothing but fear. The light is dim, and my eyes hurt as one o'clock comes and goes. Up in my room, I suddenly feel terribly alone, without knowing why. It takes me hours to get warm.

"I'm standing in front of the tree," I say, "but I don't know what that is, a tree. What is it? And there's a human being standing there, and I don't know what that is either. I don't know anything. Now it's high up and now it's cold and now it's dark. Do you know?"—"Me?" says the knacker, "why me?"—"And you're looking up at the blackness, and those are clouds, aren't they? And then you walk into a building where it's warm. And there are people sitting. And there are some in the cemetery too. Do you know what that is?"—"No, people," he says. "Yes, people." And suddenly it feels cold, and I'm shivering, and I ought to hurry back, the painter's waiting for me. I told him I would be back soon, he asked me to get him some shoelaces in the village. I went to the cobbler's, and bought him the shoelaces. And then I went out, and stood in the village square. Well, so it goes, I said to myself. And then: "Shoelaces." And then I go round to the cemetery to ask the knacker something. Once I'm up there, I can't remember what it is I wanted to ask him. He is standing in exactly the place where in my memory—or even in my dream, if you like—I thought of him standing. He is wearing what I supposed he would be wearing. He climbs out of a grave, and I put the painter's shoelaces in my pocket. "I wanted to ask you something, but I can't remember what it was," I say. "I've forgotten it."—"Ask me something?" he says, and descends into the grave again. I can only see his head, and I take a step forward, and now I can see his back as well. "A grave," I say. He says: "How do you mean, a grave?"—"It is a grave, isn't it? A deep grave."—"A grave, yes," he says. "Why?"—"Do you know why? How deep a grave can be," I say. People walk around on the planet for a while, which looks to them like the sort of place where you can walk around—who says that?—and then they fall into a grave like that. Who had the idea of letting people walk around on the planet, or something called a planet, only to put them in a grave, their grave, afterward? "That's a very old tree," I say to the knacker. And he: "Yes, it's a very old tree." And after a while I say the same thing about a person, without realizing I'm saying the same thing, I say: "He's very old, isn't he?"— "Yes," says the knacker, "he's very old!" And then: "What's it like in the parson's house? Cold?"—"Yes," he says, "very cold, *very* cold." And I say: "How are things in the city? A lot of people, I expect?"—"Yes, a lot of people," he says. "And what's tomorrow's weather going to be like? Can we hope for something pleasanter?"—"Hope?" he says. "Yes. We can hope."—"And why does the grave have to be dug today, when the burial's not till the day after tomorrow?"—"Why? The burial's the day after tomorrow," he says. "The afternoon of the day after tomorrow."—"Yes, the afternoon of the day after tomorrow."—"It must be cold, down there," I say. And he says: "Cold. Yes, it must be cold, down there." What do we know about it all. Was he going the same way as me, I asked the knacker. Yes, he is going the same way. I wonder what he has in his rucksack, I think. We take the shortcut to the village. I wish I had stout shoes! The knacker says: "In the war, there was no lack of criminality here. And even after the war, when I was back home, people were brained over a bicycle or a piece of bread. And imagine this: the French let the convicts out of the prisons, and they flooded the entire country; every little place saw killings over a blanket, or an old horse. Not to mention the acts of vengeance!" said the knacker. "Did the painter not tell you about any of that? During and after the war, he was in Weng with his sister. The farmers did not treat him at all well." The painter had been forced to sleep in an attic of the inn for a while, "because the rooms were all full of soldiers." They had arrested the landlord, and put him up against the wall to shoot him, "no one knows why. But at the very last moment they didn't shoot him." During the war years, the cellulose factory had "worked exclusively on producing munitions." Attempts had been made to bomb it from the air, but the planes had crashed in the mountains, or had been forced to turn back because of poor visibility. As a returning veteran, he had been forced to lie low in hay barns for weeks. "I spent many days sleeping in cornfields. The corn was high. I ate fresh baby beets and corn," he said. "It was very quiet down in the valley." Here and there, he had heard the sound of gunfire. No trains. Nothing. "The bridges had all been blown." Chunks of rock lay across the tracks. "Sentries had been put out in front of people's houses." When they were finally withdrawn one day, he left his cornfield, and went into the village. He got himself some old pants and an old jacket, took off his uniform, and got into the pants and jacket. Then he went round to the mayor's office, where they were pleased with every man jack. They were looking for someone to bury the dead. "I was engaged on the spot."

He became knacker a week later, when they stumbled across two hundred shot horses in the larch wood, which for several days had been spreading a nauseating smell that they hadn't been able to trace, because the wind must have come from the opposite direction, otherwise they surely wouldn't have been able to tolerate the stench. "I had to work day and night. To separate the shot soldiers from the shot horses. The horses we simply burned. A great big bonfire," said the knacker. "The soldiers we buried in big pits. Some hundred or so young men who had come from somewhere or other on those horses. We don't know where from, and we don't know who shot them either. People seem to think it was French machine guns . . . that's what they think." When I said goodbye to him in the village square, he said: "All full of cadaver smells!" And I went to the post office.

Tenth Day

For the first time, I had a dream about Strauch; following this dream, or perhaps even during it, it occurred to me that I hadn't dreamed for some time, certainly, I can't recall a single dream I had recently, though that must be a mistake, one of those "mistakes that distract us from death," because there is no such thing as "people who don't dream," our nights are dreams, nothing but dreams, which we are unable to see, though we are aware of them, even if this awareness takes place without consciousness. Be that as it may, I dreamed about Strauch for the first time. I was in a clinic in a city, a building put together from all the clinics I had ever visited and worked in, and I had the rank of doctor, I was, as I was being told on every side as I walked through this big clinic, a "highly regarded doctor," even a "renowned doctor," a "specialist," as they told me on every side, I heard the word "specialist" from all round, from every direction, everything was buzzing and hissing the word "specialist" at me, sometimes also "medical specialist"; my progress was a tormenting fording or crossing of this concept, I ran, but I couldn't run, after all, I thought, a specialist doesn't run, I didn't have to control myself, but I was controlled: I walked through enormous wards, where crowds of patients had been waiting for me, and were bowing to me, their heads curiously low to the ground, so that I was unable to see their faces, I saw only their long, bony, fleshy, fatty backs, I saw those backs and the feet of these people, oddly I was able to give them all their names, and some of them I called out, and it was a torment when those I called emerged from the mass of the patients and told me their medical histories, really only by a variety of hideous facial expressions; behind me I had a line of doctors, among them the assistant, also several faces of specialists who had marked my exams, and who would mark my future exams, all were behind me in a horribly stiff gaggle of doctors, as if "condemned to medical anonymity," they were all responding to me, to everything I appeared to be expressing; I said: "Of course there are certain constellations which prohibit life!" (I remember that sentence particularly clearly); to that sentence they responded as follows: they simply denied that those patients who seemed to demur against my sentence possessed the faculty of thought, they shouted them down; those patients who refused to be shouted down were *removed* by them, made invisible, made invisible for me; the doctors burst out in a gale of laughter at that. I said: "Life forbids individual lives!" whereupon they threatened the patients with grave punishments should they offer a response to my second sentence; the doctors themselves laughed even harder; when their laughter became unbearable, I fled into another room, this one was a white-tiled, abattoir-like room, completely empty, where the doctors let me go all alone. I could sense, however, that they were standing by the door, which had closed behind me. All at once, I saw an operating table in the middle of the room, which at first had been empty; suddenly I saw Strauch strapped onto the operating table. Suddenly I had a collection of instruments floating in front of me ready for use. Strauch lay immobile and strapped to the operating table, which was moving in a semicircular rotation. The ghastly thing was that the operating table *con-*

tinued to move; each time I approached it, it moved, and I saw that I wouldn't be able to work at this operating table. "No!" I screamed. The doctors, standing outside, burst into further laughter. They chanted: "Operate! Operate!" and they laughed. In the midst of their laughter, I kept hearing the assistant say: "Make an incision! What are you waiting for! Make an incision! You have to make an incision! Begin! Don't you see you have to make an incision? You owe *everything* to my brother!" And then I began to operate; I don't remember what sort of operation it was, I was performing a whole series of operations: a spleen-kidneys-lung-heart-head operation; and all on the continuously and irregularly gyrating operating table. Suddenly I saw that the body, on which I had thought to perform certain precise operations, had been completely slashed to ribbons. The body was no longer recognizable as a body. It was like a piece of meat, which I had radically, impeccably, and completely insanely cut up, and was now as impeccably and crazily stitching together again. All through these operations, which followed the very *strictest methodology,* I was regaled by the laughter of the medical retinue, which was waiting outside, apparently following everything I was doing in the operating theater, annotating every single cut with a puking gurgling laughing display of technical superiority. Finally they thought the operation had been *brought to a successful conclusion,* whereas I myself was of the view I had merely "ripped and cut open and completely wrongly stitched back together." They surged into the theater and yelled that I had performed a great feat, the greatest-ever feat in medical operational terms, they cheered and finally they lifted me shoulder-high, they all wanted to shake my hand, or kiss my hand, they had broken out into the most appalling cheering; held aloft, I looked down from close to the ceiling of the operating theater on a heap of mutilated flesh that, under the application of electric current, seemed to move, to twitch, a heap of minced meat that spastically discharged blood, incessantly discharged blood, vast quantities of blood, slowly inundating everything in blood, everything, the doctors, everything; also the cries of the assistant, those awful sentences, drowning in the vast flows of his brother's blood: "Don't worry, the operation has been a success! This is your brother, I'm your brother! Don't worry, the operation has been a success! . . ." When I awoke, I had to open the window and put my head outside. I had the feeling I was going to suffocate. But outside, there was the moon, and the stars looked like sheet anchors. The doctors in my dream, some of whom were familiar to me, but then it turned out I didn't really know them at all, had children's voices. You have to picture these doctors to yourself, men of all ages between nineteen and seventy, often with big bellies and round swollen doctors' heads, all yelling and laughing like three- or four-year-olds, or like thirteen- or fourteen-year-old kids!

In the Poorhouse

"I'd like to take you along to the poorhouse once," said the painter. "It might be a good thing for someone like you, without much experience—that is the case, isn't it?—" he said, "to take a look at one of the most pitiful and oppressive institutions there are, a collection of infirm old people, incapable of doing anything beyond mumbling to themselves. I don't think it'll shock you to such a degree that I would have to smack myself on the wrist and say: I really shouldn't have done that, taken that fellow in there, made him acquainted with the hydrocephalic, with the alcoholic, with the swollen smoker's leg, with the senility of geriatric Catholicism. The old just want to eat," said the painter, "the old men are guests of the devil, the old women suck on the tits of heaven! And all without self-defense! That smell," said the painter, "when you set foot in the poorhouse, you don't know if it's apples or the rotting breasts of old grocers' wives. You want to hold your breath," said the painter, "hold your breath to everything with the impertinence to lie ahead of you! But already your chest is full of rot. Suddenly you can't even manage to exhale anymore, can't exhale so much filth, so much age, the stink of so much unbelievable redundancy, that dull melancholy stink of ichor. Yes," said the painter, "I'll take you along there. I'll show you the place. You'll curtsey to the mother superior. You'll tell her your little story, the little story of your life, and you'll get one or two back! You'll be torn apart! The old are the grave-robbers of the young. Old age is graverobbery. Old age gets its bellyful of youth," he said. "So I come into the poorhouse once," said the painter, "and they bring me bread and milk, and they want me to drink schnapps as well, but I say I don't want any schnapps, no no, no schnapps, I say, under no circumstances, and I refuse and resist, but they pour out a glass for me anyway, and I don't drink it, and I say, no, I'm not drinking this, and the mother superior pours the schnapps back in the bottle, and I know she's after money, the whole village is after my money, all of them, they all want a piece, they all take me for stupid, basically they all think I'm stupid, limitlessly stupid, because I've been feeding them all, feeding them all for years, with advice, suggestions, tips, help, support, yes, even money, I've stuffed so much money into this rathole . . . so, I come into the poorhouse," said the painter, "and I refuse their schnapps, and I listen to their begging, listen to them saying I should give them a subvention, 'a very small subvention,' which 'the Lord' (what Lord) will 'give me credit for,' and I listen to it all, and I look at the mother superior, and I hear her feet working the sewing machine treadle, she works the treadle while she pulls a ripped old man's shirt under the needle at her breast, and then a jacket, and I look in her face, her wide, puffy face, her swollen hands, her square dirty fingernails, I look under her bonnet, her snow-white bonnet, I think: Ah, so this is evening in the poorhouse, which is always the same evening, for a hundred years, for five hundred years, the same evening as this one, sewing together and drinking together and eating together and praying together and lying together and sleeping together and stinking together; it's all this one evening, I think, which no one is thinking of changing, and no one is thinking of, period, it's the evening of loathsomeness and rejection by the world. If you must know," said the painter, "I'm sitting there for an hour and I say I'm prepared to pay a supplement for an old man, a cooper, if you must know, in leather leggings and a loden coat, in a canvas shirt, and with a fur cap on his head, I say I'm prepared to purchase a Severin calendar from the mother superior, one of those loathsome productions of clerical idiocy, and then I notice there's a man lying on the bench by the wall, completely motionless if you must know, with the Severin calendar on his chest; the man is lying behind the mother superior, and I'm thinking surely he's dead, the man must be dead, and I give myself a nudge, and I think, the man must be dead, so this is what a dead man looks like, old and dead, and I wonder how it is that I've not noticed this dead man lying there all along, with straight thin legs that look as though they've been stuffed into the craw of eternity. But there can't be a dead man lying here! Not here! Not now! In the dark, I failed to notice the man the whole time I was here, also because the mother superior was claiming the whole of my attention with her nonsense about the Severin calendar. 'Our Severin calendar,' she kept saying the whole time, 'our Severin calendar benefits the poor in the Congo, the poor in the Congo . . .' I've been listening to her say that for fully an hour, I think to myself, and I want to jump up and go over to the dead man, but then I see the man start to move, suddenly the man on the bench is moving, and he pulls the Severin calendar up from his belly to his chin, so that he can read it. So, the man isn't dead after all! But even so, I think to myself, he looks like a dead man, dead people don't look any worse, in some sense this man is a dead man! I watch him move his arms, how he leafs through the calendar, avidly leafs through the calendar, but his body is completely motionless, and once again I think to myself, yes, he is dead! But then I hear a breath, the first 'breath' from this dead man. I feel alarmed, alarmed mostly at myself, because I hadn't noticed the man all the time I was there. The mother superior hadn't mentioned to me that there was a man in the room with her. In the darkness I wasn't able to see him. Suddenly, after an hour, I saw the body, the head, perhaps the legs as well, because, I don't know why, imperceptibly, for some reason, it got a little brighter, even to see the man by, perhaps because my eyes suddenly got used to the darkness (your eyes don't work, for a long time, if you must know, your eyes don't work, then all at once your eyes start to work). Suddenly my eyes saw the man, my eyes saw this dead man. He was lying there like a piece of wood. And then this piece of wood started to breathe, it breathed and it started to flick through the calendar. Then I said to the mother superior: 'There's somebody lying there!' But she didn't react at all. She was reattaching a sleeve she had previously cut off. 'There's someone lying there!' I said, a bit louder. Without looking at me, she replied: 'Yes, a human being.' It was terrible, the way she said it. I wanted to say, 'He's lying there just like a child!' But instead I said: 'He's lying there just like a dog. What's he doing here?' Someone like that isn't going to be able to listen, I thought, and so I could speak about him with the mother superior quite uninhibitedly. 'He's reading the Severin calendar,' I said, 'even though it's dark, even though it's almost pitch-dark.' 'Yes,' said the mother superior, 'he's reading the Severin calendar.' I had to laugh! I started laughing, I burst out laughing, most of all because I recalled that I had taken the man to be dead, taken him to be dead the whole time, and in fact I said: 'I thought the man was dead.' I had to get up in order to stop laughing. I had to walk up and down. 'Dead!' I exclaimed, 'I thought he was dead!' Then I was suddenly alarmed, you understand, by the face that was lying in the dark, lying as if above the surface of a dirty pond. 'This man is reading in the dark,' I said. The Mother Superior said: 'He knows everything, he knows everything in the calendar. He's learned it all off by heart,' she said. She didn't stir, and kept pushing the treadle of her sewing machine. 'He gets frightened when he's not here with me,' she said, 'then he shouts and turns the whole house upside down. If I let him stay here with me, everything's quiet, and he's quiet as well. It won't be much longer before he finally moves off.'—

'Finally moves off,' she said. She wanted me to pay for a couple of yards of flannel shirting for the old man, but I said I needed to think about it, I'd consider it. I thought it was an impertinence on her part, trying to hang a couple of yards of flannel shirting on me as well. Then, sitting impassively at her machine, she described her childhood to me, if you must know. I always like to hear about that. Her father was crushed by a tractor, if you must know, her brother, a sportsman's guide, put a bullet in his brain because he hated the world. Commonplace destinies. She's a prolix, dropsical type," said the painter. "But I haven't told you the most important thing: there I was, sitting there, thinking I should say goodbye, when a dreadful noise made me jump to my feet. The old man had fallen off his bench—dead. The mother superior closed his eyes, and asked me to help her lift him back up on the bench. Shaking, I did so. I thought, now I'm breathing in the dead man's air, and I went. All the way home, I thought: my lungs are full of dead man's air. I hadn't been mistaken, I'd been right all along, the man had been dead the whole time. Perhaps the movements I saw were just fantastic inventions on my part, he was dead all along, just dead the whole time the mother superior was repairing his jacket and his shirt, because they had been his jacket and his shirt that she had pulled this way and that under her needle, with an irritated expression on her face, with an expression of appalling irritation on her face. And he was dead long before I ever came along, I'm convinced of that." The painter took a step back, and drew something in the snow with his stick. I soon saw that it was a sketch of the mother superior's room in the workhouse. "There's the bench where the dead man was lying, whom I failed to see for a whole hour, even though he was close enough to reach out and touch, here is the sewing table, here is the mother superior, here's her wardrobe, if you must know, there's the bed of the mother superior, and there's her chest; here, you see, is where I sat down; this is where I came in through the door, and greeted the mother superior, I went up to her, and she immediately started trying to interest me in a subvention, in a Severin calendar. I knew I would part with the subvention and purchase the calendar, but I drew the whole thing out. I thought I was alone in the room with her, the way I had always been alone in the room with her, who could ever have supposed there would be anyone else in the mother superior's room anyway, but I had a strange feeling as well, a feeling I can't describe. Then it got brighter, and all at once I saw the stiff contours of the old man. Also I had said 'like a dog' to the mother superior. She even repeated it after me. The idea that the man couldn't hear anything made me burst out laughing. Here, you see," said the painter, and he drew a circle between the bench and the sewing machine, "right here is where the dead man lay when we picked him up. The whole thing is quite extraordinary and not at all well described; but the only reason I'm telling you about this incident is because, however incompletely, it does give a picture of the mysterious lack of accountability in the world. On one of the next few days," said the painter, "we're going to the poorhouse. A young person must see what suffering is, what suffering and dying are, what it is to rot away." We walked quickly home. The painter suddenly ran away from me, with an unexpected turn of speed for one of his years. "Wait for me!" I called after him. But he didn't hear. He disappeared in one of the many dips in front of me.

Eleventh Day

People like the landlady didn't understand values like respect
and awe. She goes to church, but only because she doesn't
want to be rebuked. Because otherwise she would be
destroyed, living among people who have got it into their
heads that you have to go to church. Drowning among country people is a miserable way of drowning. They calmly
watch their victim resisting, and the waves closing over their
heads, as if it was the most natural thing in the world: letting
an evil person, someone who doesn't belong in their world,
simply sink. Someone who didn't take instruction from
them, wasn't persuaded by what they told him. Someone
who struck them as odd from the outset, and therefore
unworthy of sharing their lives with them: "The landlady is a
stranger," said the painter. She was always strange to them
all, because her father came from a different region, a valley
nearer the Tyrol. They describe someone like the landlady as
vermin. The farmers do. And the farmers still rule here, even
though their influence has been pushed back. Even though
the proletariat has attained privileges that, three or four years
ago, would have been unthinkable. The proletariat: all the
people who, in the last three decades were washed into the
valley, to service the cellulose factory, the railways, and now
the power plant. "There are still the Corpus Christi processions," said the painter, "and Ascension Day parades, but how
much longer? Catholicism is on the wane. At least here.
Communism is on the march. In a few years' time there will

only be Communism. And then agriculture will be a dream. No longer leading anywhere." He said: "But the landlady goes to church, because she still depends on the farmers. And she attends the Communist meetings, because she's compelled to do that too." But for her, the inn would surely have changed hands before now, because "her husband is a drunk who drinks more than he brings in, unless she slaps his wrist." Always drunk, he lives the life of a "slimy bloated newt, from time to time lashing out." He often lay in the garden with outspread arms, gaping mouth, and rolling eyes, as if he was dead, and merely swollen with schnapps and beer. Often he would call the cab to get a ride home instead of walking. He knows she holds everything together, that everything depends on her, and that it's up to her whether she takes the thread he's dangling from, and simply and brutally snips it, so he doesn't send her away anymore. Rather, it's she who can do as she pleases. If anything, it's he who has to worry about being sent packing. But the property belongs to him, and that keeps her from putting her most radical plan into effect: to throw him out once and for all. Cannily, because he's not stupid, he's steadfastly refused to make over the property to her, as she's often expressly called on him to do, he even refused to cede a part of the property consisting of the real estate, the hollow, and the inn, to her. So she's probably always going to have him to deal with. "Often they dragged him over from the shady side," said the painter, "where he was drinking on credit." Every three weeks she went the rounds, to pay his tabs at all the places where he drank. She begged the landlords, her competitors in effect, to no longer serve him. But they always ignored her wishes. Any landlord has got to be pleased about slowly wiping out a rival. They even egged him on. And when he gets let out of prison, it'll carry on. Often, when she paid his bills, she would get to hear about other women who had eaten and drunk at his expense, and who "themselves had been rather generous"; but she was used to that, and of course she compensated. She is the daughter of a road worker, who, when he died, left just enough to cover his funeral expenses. Aged fourteen, she went to a dairy farm as a maid. She was always a good worker, and that was what got the landlord's interest, and prompted him to bring her to the inn.

The painter Strauch is one of those who turn everything to liquid. Whatever they touch dissolves. Character, solidity, stability. "No one can see me, because no one can see anything," he has said, and: "The principles that put millennia on the skids." Or again: "Any activity is predicated on another, any meaning, any style. Wisdom on nonsense, and vice versa and simultaneously." Breakfast is "way too ceremonial" for him, "it feels absurd to pick up a spoon. Meaningless. A sugar cube is an assault against me. Bread. Milk. A catastrophe. The day begins with insidious sweetness." He hunkers down on his chair, which is far too low for him. But even there he towers over me. He looks down at me, his eye piercing. "To allow ingratitude to develop within one," he says, "only to take note of a thing once one is certain what a terrible thing it is. Facts pile up, terrible facts too, and before too long you're just the miserable little wretch trying to push the table back, which gets you a clip around the ears from above." So great was reason that it too was "condemned to fail." "Those two notions of mine, trotting along side by side like a couple of dogs, barking at everything." Wanton destruction, to make contemplation a little easier. He whispers, and listens to the

walls shaking. "There is an obligation toward the depth of
one's own inner abyss," he says. He pulls himself together,
and it takes the brutality of simply getting up to bring him
back to himself and out of himself. To some expression, like
"It's so utterly ghastly here!" He is dominated by himself, as
by a lifelong injustice. By his destructive apparatus.

"There is little else but corruption," he says, "but it's impossible to eradicate. Opposition, a general opposition, a sign of
youth, is growing weaker. The forces are shrinking. Everything is concentrated on getting through its allotted time . . .
That's got nothing to do with intelligence. In general, people
on a lower level find it easier to deal with their surroundings.
By and by it comes to your attention: the world around you,
nothing but corruption, colossal misrule. On the whole the
fools who can't see that are small in number. One's fellow
humans? No more than a list of professions. What time is it?
Half past four. Getting some air before going to bed is
another sacred error. A smart observation: 'the round fat face
of the landlady, which has bounced off the engineer.' Ah, the
engineer," he says. "You know, frost disfigures all men. Frost
and women are the death of men. In the morning he sits over
his blueprints, and doesn't go mad. They're all sitting around
now. All these men sitting around will have to be paid: this
sudden cold snap will cost hundreds of thousands! And no
improvement in sight! If you ask me, I rather like cold, sharp
winter days."

The way he compares the inn with an Alpine village in
Carinthia, and with a ballet dancer who has had just one

appearance in the opera and whom he describes as "a natural talent, but very dangerous," is very illuminating. Or a vegetable trader who once gave him a smack because he thought he was stealing his tomatoes, with Napoleon III. It seems to me that even as he's speaking about the woodcutter he watched dying, he's already thinking about the tragedy of the four hundred mountain people who were abruptly killed in catastrophic storms. And then always himself. A sudden blast of wind forced him to the wall, and put him in mind of a celebrated acrobat. "He performed four somersaults between the backs of two galloping horses." When he says "London," he envisions the outer suburbs of Budapest. Sections of the lower Danube he attaches quite effortlessly to the upper Rhine. He swaps one delta for another. "In fact, that's my sense of color," he says. Certain mixtures of aromas play a part here. I can readily imagine him as a thirty-year-old, crossing the swollen plazas, and despising the dead, megalomaniac capital of the country. Anything provincial and dilettante as much as the "truly great" and the untouchable. His self-contempt is not based on ignorance; after all he was a city-dweller. Miles ahead of him he sees a lost thought return to him after years away. "Murder has a taste of honey," he often thought. While his mouth talks about the ways of making paper, his hands are burrowing in his jacket pockets. He sees images faster than his body can catch them. "Every street debouches in my brain," he says. He has turned a vast system of beginnings and significations into an edifice of thought where he tries to order the extraordinary chaos of history. "For decades, I've suffered from the most extreme attention, do you have any idea what that means?" If he talks about a tragedy, he shows no signs of the tragedy in his expression. When was it? "I've invented a notation of my fears," he says. Of the three who go to make him up, he doesn't know which one he is here or there, when and where. "Being on the lookout doesn't imply ill intentions, you know." Everything was morbidly affected by the horrible, and "harmlessness has taken on all the tasks of destruction, do you see?"

He had been walking in the defile. At first he had found it difficult—"it took all my shattered strength"—to make his way up through the deep snowdrifts. "Branches leaped at my face like wild animals, you know!" But then he had moved almost at a jog, as before his illness. "I couldn't stop. My head took control over me, if you must know!" Darkness had brought him to the defile. "I could have walked on, to the hay barn and further. But no, I had to walk up the defile. The defile that starts exactly where I saw the churchgoers emerge the day before yesterday. They were people such as I have yet to meet, from the shady side, as it seems to me, people from an era that ended millennia ago, great people, striding as if they walked past everything. Past a world that struck them as petty and spoiled. Past a later man, of whom they must have been warned. They reminded me of deer, so gigantic, so kingly, in the way they loomed up ahead of me. I ran into the defile, because I thought that would change my ideas," said the painter. "With the help of the defile, I thought it would be possible to get some other ideas. I wanted to change the direction of everything, everything that had been as sad all day as episodes from my childhood, inaccessible, because you can never get out of them." But he had been disappointed. A sudden snowfall surprised him in the middle of the defile. Then he sat down on a tree stump, "a quite rotten little stump, just big enough for me," to wait for it to stop snowing. "But how can you wait for it to stop snowing? And why?" Immediately persuaded of the stupidity of waiting for it to stop snowing, he had leaped up, and crawled back down the entire defile. "On all fours, like a wild beast that lives in the dark, in the gloom." He had managed to get out of the defile in pretty quick time. "Even as a child, I used to be frightened of defiles," he said. "While I was sitting on the tree stump, I had the feeling I was going to sleep, drifting off, you know." With that feeling, he had been very happy. It mastered him, and he supported it, so that it got stronger. "Pleasure," he said. "The way you can just fall asleep after a great exertion, the way great cities seem to shrink back as you dash through, or the claws of caged lions and tigers." The way someone settles to sleep, all animal, he too had settled. And then he had suddenly become aware of the foolishness of waiting for it to stop snowing. And he had jumped up and away, first in quick bounds, then ever more slowly, barging through snow with his chest. "It would have been my grave," he said.

He thought he had left his jacket behind in the public bar, and went back down to look for it. I saw him come down, but for some reason I couldn't ask him what he was doing downstairs, having already once said goodnight. I could have asked him: "Do you need anything? Are you looking for something? What are you looking for?" But he was already at the foot of the stairs. "My jacket must be hanging in the public bar," he said. I went into the public bar, and looked for the jacket, but couldn't find it. I asked the landlady and some of the customers, but no one had seen his jacket. The painter stood in the doorway, observing me. I had the feeling he was directing me to look for the jacket here and there; pushing me down to the floor, pulling me up to the great beam between the stove and the wall, from where you have a good view of the whole bar area. I didn't see his jacket anywhere. The public bar was packed. A few other people helped me look. I saw a lot of new faces. The entire construction crew for the power plant seemed to be there: thousands of them! I felt I was drifting through a sea of fog. Individuals looked at me out of some rotting vegetation, it seemed to me. Like a jungle. I looked along the walls, but didn't find any jacket. I wanted to be thorough, and looked on the floor again. The jacket might have fallen down, after all. The landlady stooped as well. "No, there's no jacket here," she said. I checked among the many workmen's clothes hanging up on the walls. But no painter's jacket. When I got back to the corridor, where I thought I'd find the painter, he had disappeared. Did he go up to his room? I wondered. But: he wouldn't be able to get up as quickly as that. "Herr Strauch!" I called. No answer. Then I noticed that the front door was half-open. The painter was sitting on the bench outside. "I'm ignoring the cold," he said, and disappeared further into his jacket, which it seemed he was suddenly wearing. "Where I found my jacket?" He had hung it on the front door when he returned from his walk, and forgotten about it. "Were you looking for my jacket the whole time?" he asked. You absentmindedly hung or left something somewhere, forgot all about it, and got into a terrible state as a result. "I think about what will be once everything goes black," he said. "When there are no more colors, only black." Then he pointed out a lot of stars to me, up there in the night sky, more stars than he'd seen in a long while.

Twelfth Day

In the morning he surprised me with the news that the swelling on his foot had gone. "There's no sign of it," he said, "it's retreated, no doubt only to pop up somewhere else. You'll see." As he was standing in my doorway, I asked him inside. "If you don't mind an old man fouling your room," he said. He crossed my room to the window, and looked out. "You've got the same view as I have: darkness! Doesn't it depress you? All these days? People like you spend years, decades, on the brink of depression. Then suddenly you fall in. Head first." He sat down on my bed. "Lawyers make nothing but confusion," he said. "A lawyer is an instrument of the devil. In general, he's a fiendish idiot, banking on the stupidity of people much more stupid than himself, and by God he's always right." He felt through his pockets again. "Jurisprudence creates criminality, that's a fact. Without jurisprudence, there would be no crime. Did you know that? Unlikely as it may sound, that's the truth of the matter." He set his stick against my jacket, which I'd laid over the chair back, speared it as with a fork. "Youth is an ornament," he said, "and ever more an ornament, and is always in any case refreshing." He left my jacket alone. "Youth has no ideals; nor any masochistic notions, which will come later. Then, admittedly, with lethal effect." He was still able to imagine what it was like, being young. "One imagines it'll be better later on," he said. "When everything isn't ebullience, isn't confusion, isn't cerebral. When everything is as distinct as the shadows inside you, with their hard, silent edges." There were many mistakes he had only made because he was young. "Youth is a mistake." The mistake of age, on the other hand, was see ing the mistakes of youth. "It can happen that a young fellow can cease to be young in the midst of his youth," he said, and then: "Do you believe in Jesus?" which, he said, was much like asking: "Do you think tomorrow will be even colder than today?" He was going, he said, to take a walk down to the station. "First along the shady side. Then to the newspapers. Then the café. Let me think: couldn't we visit the parsonage? Or the poorhouse? No, no, not that. But anyway, you're coming. Aren't you?"

He listened to me a long time today as I told him about home. About how I had often gone on trips to the mountains, the lake, the cities. Also that I would read to them all from the Bible, father, mother, siblings—that seemed to make him sad. That we had trees in our garden that we had planted ourselves, cupboards and wardrobes where we keep early treasures, candles and baby clothes, pinecones from a cold and happy winter. That we always wrote each other letters, and worried about each other. That we knew of houses that were never locked up. Also forests, beaches, sled hills, known only to us. That there were beds turned back for us in heated rooms, and books, and that we love music which brings us together when it's dark outside. And how storms suddenly wreck things that have been conceived to last for eternity, and were loved by everyone. He listened to everything I had to say, without a single interruption, even up and down the many detours and byways I took, where there was talk of security and being together and being alone, of lack of self-confidence, of trust, and rebellion and distinctions, of suddenly stopping and going back, of fear and reproach, of love and torment, of deception and self-evidence, where clouds rose up, and heavy snowfalls darkened town and country, where people continually renewed each other, where there was grief after days of exuberance and rivers dragged their courses, where you gradually forgot how to live and found again what had been lost, where silence alternated with excitement, stimulating modesty here and brutality there—things that didn't resolve themselves, how people walked past each other, not recognizing themselves, fell into silence, and the sayings of sadness, where nights were uselessly waked through and a thousand important days were slept away. It all made him very sad, but he was quite without bitterness. "Fascinating," he said after these morning hours in which I kept saying, well, that was about the way of it, to myself and to him, who was so taciturn, "It's like listening to my own life story. I can see it all before me with my own eyes, and I know that's how it was." And after a while: "Of course we see everything under false pretenses."

I attempted a description of my room at home. Forced myself, step by step, to see everything in my room, along the walls, back and forth, to notice the sounds that came in, barged in, at various particular times of day. Began with the door, with its deep keyhole, through which you came into a sort of cavern, back out a little, past the hinges to the corner where dust always settled, got damp, dried out, and finally formed a solid mass, further bound together by fly droppings. Then on, along the ceiling, drop down to the floor, onto the carpet, take in the ornaments, Arabian window casements, potpourri, staircases, views onto the temple and the sea, immobilized by heat. Through the keyhole into the chest, half-dead with the smell of the summer clothes jammed into it, looking for a way through the dark and the soporific smell, out and onto the window seat over the garden. Then the picture of the beautiful city, lying there in autumn, in wild brown colors. The mountain scene, with the walkers emerging into a river valley. Along the gilded frame, from one carved heart to another. Grandfather's picture, then grandmother's. The letter from my brother, covering over a third of the hunting scene, showing a hunter playing a bagpipe, and calling several other figures to dance. The copper engraving of an old castle in the flatland. Then the table and bed and chair, the floorboards, the cracks in the plaster. And all the connections between everything. The copper engraving and the castle, the castle and the lake, the lake and the hills, the hills and the mountains, the mountains with the sea lying below, the sea and the people, and their clothes and the summer evening, the air over the river that has our boat bobbing on it, long past midnight. Or grandfather's picture with a room in a brewery, with a suicide, with a fisherman dragging a pike out of the rushes. I said: "Each item takes you to all the others. It's a proof of all of them." But the painter didn't reply. Suddenly I noticed that he hadn't been listening to me, that what I had been thinking and trying to say hadn't interested him at all, because he said: "It's too bad that I am compelled to take my meals down in the public bar. That the landlady won't bring them up to my room. Send a child up there. It's a torment for me to sit in that public bar. But then I suppose I'm looking for things that will irritate me. The smell," he said, "makes me ill. The smell of workmen has always made me ill. And always attracted me. Yes, it's true. If I come down sooner, the food isn't ready, if I come later, there's nothing left. As if they were all equipped with trunks and claws when they eat," he said. "The inns in the valley make even more of a profit, those inns make an immense profit. Only undesirables make their way up the mountain. Those who are heavily indebted, and can't show themselves in the valley anymore. For whatever reasons. They cook in vast cauldrons down there. And all of them with the very cheapest fats and oils. Not our landlady! Even though she too, as I've already intimated to you, uses dirt, and works with dogmeat and horsemeat. I've always hated human gatherings."

"In the morning, I was just cleaning my boots—they don't clean your boots properly here, you always have to go over them again with a rag yourself—I saw the landlady hitting her elder daughter. Suddenly I heard it. She must have struck her with a hard object on the head, because I saw her running downstairs, bleeding. She collapsed under the chestnut tree, holding her head in both hands. I expect she spent half the night among the railwaymen. In the snow I saw traces of blood when I went out later, because I couldn't stand it in my room anymore. Scraps of words came up to my window. They were already on their way to the post office, but I caught everything. I jumped up and ran to the window. The whole scene was squalid. Presumably the girl spent the night with the son of the crossing-keeper. 'Whore!' I hear. 'Whore!' The landlady must have thought I was out, because otherwise she wouldn't have lost control in such an abject way. The girl was contorted with pain under the chestnut tree. She's not even fourteen. You've probably seen him, the crossing-keeper's son, a big young fellow. He works in the cellulose factory. He only ever visits the inn when the landlady's away. I haven't seen him for many days now. Back when the knacker was singing with the engineer, he was there: dark, and solidly built. I'm sure you must have seen him. At lunchtime, I heard the girl has moved out. She was in a train with her lover. It made a terrible impression on me, the girl's helplessness I found especially alarming. The landlady lashed out with the poker. With the poker, if you must know. She lashed out at her like a butcher."

Down on the building site, I remembered the time I used to go over the big bridges in blue workmen's clothes. The air was fresh, and the noise wasn't roused yet. Morning came down off the mountains into people's houses, where they were saying their goodbyes for the day. Quickly they gulped down their coffee, and on the street chewed the bread that their wives had spread for them, or they didn't eat anything at all, and started work on the building site on empty stomachs. The first shovelful took away your nausea. With my twenty years, I was stronger than the others, and I never really got tired. A big concrete mixer and a digger with the words "Zwettlerbau A.G." loomed over us as we stood in the excavation. They were chilly days of autumn, but in a short time we were stripped down to our pants. And at noon we meandered over the road into the beer garden. It occurred to me that for a while I was perfectly happy with my life. To carry on in the same way seemed quite natural to me. In my family I had always heard about men who set out in construction and ended up in the gutter. They weren't the worst. For weeks I felt so happy in my work that I forgot all about my studies. But I passed my exams. As if in my sleep. I don't know how I did it. I expect I was lucky. The rest of the world that wasn't working on building sites struck me as crazy, and those people who weren't standing in holes in the ground I looked at with sympathy. My evenings didn't get so long, I was dog-tired, it felt sensible to collapse straight into bed, I didn't even unpack my work things, I just left everything in my rucksack, and dropped into a deep sleep until half past four in the morning. The evenings came with the smell of the river drifting through the vegetation in the beer garden. There I would drink a beer with a couple of the guys, sometimes four or five beers, and we didn't say much, but I liked what we did say. I was never able to speak to anyone else later as well as I did with my buddies from the building site. They didn't say where they came from, and what they wanted to do with their lives. Probably they didn't want to do anything particular with their lives. What should they have wanted to do with their lives? Did I want to do anything with my life? Probably the name of some young woman, a single mother, cropped up from time to time, or the name of a brother, and occasionally some town or village, where people wake up and go to sleep; I peered into kitchens and hallways, into garages and cesspools, and signalmen's cabins.

And then I was a driver for an iron firm, and things got even more taciturn. And when we stood in our twos and threes on the big bridge over the big wide river, looking down into the water, then I wouldn't think about countries and continents. The ships traveled down to the Black Sea, through the Iron Gate, through the various capital cities, and I was happy. But

I'd been spoiled, and I had my head full of something that only half convinced me, and I picked up my wages, and, come October, I went back to my school desk. I suppose I became unhappy again then, but in the long run even if I'd stayed on the building site, that might not have saved me from unhappiness. Who knows?

I too regularly felt drawn to the simple people, I told the painter today. Where all you see is the wheelbarrow going back and forth on a plank over a ditch with someone standing in it. Where all you see is clumps of earth being tossed up in the air. Who by? Well, you don't know. Down there where they're building the power plant, they stand around at nine o'clock and light their cigarettes and empty their bottles of beer and gesture with their fingers how many days till they're due a holiday. But what will they do with it? Go away somewhere? When they've got the money to afford it! But where to? And isn't it just too exhausting? They stay home, and just play cards a little later into the evening, because they don't need to get up early, they go to the cinema, they write a letter that's a year overdue to a brother, a sister, a mother. They balance across the rushing river, and those are the tricks they perform, life-and-death tricks, when they're employed to slot in a section of a bridge. From six thirty in the morning to four thirty in the afternoon. Nine hours, because one is for eating and resting. Sometimes they shout across to each other, as if it was something essentially important, and not just a rope that needs tightening. The voices are used up. The crane swings across, now this side, now the other, and the mechanical digger at the end of its wires bites into the earth. Spits out great chunks of earth between the men. The hydraulic drill might have driven them crazy twenty years ago, or at least one or other of them, but now no one is driven crazy by it. The trucks drive up from the railway station, sometimes they appear, sometimes they go again, and they go very close to the edge, and they need to be filled by the men. They wind the one rope ever tighter round their own necks. Most of them have never done anything else anyway but load and unload, standing in standing water in their gumboots and knocking in bridge piles. The fact that they're used to it gives those people a pretext who never had to load and unload, never stood in standing water in gumboots, knocking in bridge piles; the pickaxes come whistling down on instructions given from the bank. You can climb around on the dirt and quiz the one or other of them without saying a word, without him saying a word either. If you watch, you have to be careful no one sees you, because otherwise you'll be suspected of thinking about something you should have been thinking about all along. What is it these men slip into when they slip into their blue jackets, that, when the sun comes out, are hung up all over the place, on tree branches and on balanced shovel handles? Often the whole valley rings with their hammering and drilling. Then they detonate another big chunk out of the mountain into which they're fitting the power plant, and the air pressure smacks against the cliff face.

Today they got a couple of people out of the Klamm valley on a sleigh. Two strangers, who wanted to spend the weekend high up in an Alpine hut. But they didn't even get as far as the glacier when they took their fall. As if by a miracle, they were almost unhurt and managed to stay warm all night under the branches of a broken pine. Even so, they were so weak come morning that only the elder of the two—they were both students—was able to crawl down to the valley for help. When the men, who apparently initially refused to go to the aid of the one lying up on the mountain with an injured leg, and for that reason was also unable to move, finally went up to help, they found the student unconscious, half in a stream. Only the fact that the rescue party reached him soon after he'd fallen into the stream saved his life. It was further miraculous that the students survived their initial fall relatively well; it was a ridge that had already claimed a lot of lives.

The engineer, who saw the students being taken down out of the Klamm valley, says the locals abused them to their faces, because they were forever having to deal with climbers, who, either out of ignorance or inadequate preparation and equipment, fall or lose their way, or get into some sort of scrapes. They should just leave them up there, they say. Why should their menfolk risk their own lives for the sake of "city showoffs"? What on earth were they doing, going climbing in all weathers, risking death by exposure, in a storm or rock-slide? The city-dweller had no idea of the force of a storm suddenly breaking loose at altitude. The vehemence with which trees are uprooted, with which a gale smacks into a sheer face, causing the rock to tremble. Nothing of avalanches, or numbing frost. Nothing of the darkness that suddenly extinguishes anything that might offer sanctuary or support.

. . .

"Every year there are a couple of hundred who lose their lives in the rocks somewhere," said the engineer. "The Klamm is dangerous, unless you know the footholds." Even today there were people lying around there with smashed limbs in the Klamm, who couldn't be brought out, because it was too inaccessible. "Actually, it's a mystery what brings all these thoughtless city-dwellers to the mountains." The two students had been put up in an inn by the station. They were given warm beds and an earful of abuse. The engineer saw to it that they were made to pay for all the expenses resulting from their foolishness. "It seems they planned to kill themselves," he said, "up in the hut."

We know a thing or two about that in Schwarzach as well, the numerous tourist tragedies, from straightforward to complicated breaks, which develop into brain paralysis, to those cases where we get to the waterfall too late, or a wayside hut, where they simply lay them out, cover them with a canvas groundsheet or a piece of cardboard or some branches, and wait for the intern to issue a death certificate for them. Those are the city boys' stunts, so they can impress their dubious friends for another year, and get their names in the paper, because they've been up a 2,500- or a 3,000-meter peak. What is it with climbing anyway? What's the difference whether I'm three hundred meters up, or three thousand? It's simply that the one is more dangerous than the other, the one isn't a stunt, but the other is supposed to be. I've often seen young people snuffed out, just because darkness has fallen all round them. And how do we benefit from standing around there clutching our rolls of bandage in hope, and the priest already on his way?

Or else we manage to get them into the hospital, and I'm sitting next to a lad or lass who doesn't yet know that he or she will never walk again, will remain stiff as a board to the day of their death, and I hold their hand, and I say something in the ambulance that's a flat-out lie. I might say: "You'll be on the mend soon!" or: "It'll take care of itself!" and I'll only be struck by the horrendousness of what I've done at night, when I'm lying in bed. Then, in hundred- and thousandfold voices I hear their "No! No!" What it means to take the legs off a young man who's a truck driver by profession. Or a newspaper delivery girl, or a student who was planning to go to India! They rip downhill on their skis and wrap themselves round a tree, that happens every day. Almost all the wards in the hospital are full of tourists who've met with accidents. You have to say they have only themselves to blame, they should never have gone up the mountains in the first place! But they are drawn up there, to the summits, up the slopes; whole school classes are found frozen, along with their teachers. If you ask them how they came by their frozen leg, which we've had to amputate, they say it was for a bet or showing off that prompted them to go on a climb; and that's where it happened, most times nowhere near the peak. Once we had a boy in the hospital who survived for four days in a crevasse that already had three carcasses of mountain goats in it. It was only weeks after they brought him down that he got sick, and slowly lost his memory.

Thirteenth Day

"You only need to hear a certain name, and you start to make your excuses. Then someone is presented to you, and you've already closed the file on him. He can say what he likes, he'll never get out of the oubliette we dropped him into, he'll never get clear of it. Everything this person then does will look like the shameless self-promotion of an undesirable, of someone utterly unappetizing. That," said the painter, "was how the engineer was for me, when he was introduced to me, I was immediately revolted by him, and I dropped him through the trapdoor, into the oubliette, as described. The first time I heard his name, I was almost sick. The idea of that name produced the most appalling impression of the person that went with the name. And when I met him face to face, I wasn't disappointed. You're never disappointed when you meet the person who goes with a name that you've chewed over and spat out." If you met people before learning their names, the name, when you were told it, always fitted them. "Most people, all you need know of them is their name, you know." The name contained everything you needed to know about them. It was mostly the names that prompted one to get to know someone. "The person who goes with a certain name never lets the name down. There are names that, when you hear them, give you a stronger feeling of nausea than the worst lack of appetite you can imagine. For instance, when a friend tells me the name of a friend of theirs, whom I haven't

yet met. Have you not come across that phenomenon yourself? The name makes the man."

I completely forget what I'm here for. That I have to make
my observations. I think of it suddenly, when I'm in the larch
wood possibly, when I notice something particularly striking
about the painter, in the middle of the street, in the public
bar, when he suddenly takes a great gulp from his glass of
milk, like a healthy person, and then immediately wishes he
hadn't. That suddenly comes to mind, when I'm lost in trains
of thought that took their starting point with the painter,
when I'm far away from myself, separated by ranges of
strange speculation. And I know that nothing but what I see
will come to me. I intimated something of the sort to the
assistant in the letter I wrote today. And that it's so gloomy
here, always gloomy, gloomy even on fair days. How a word I
say sometimes pains me. A word that's said to me. That can
happen as well. I walk all alone through the village, and stick
to the views of people, that's what I do. And to the sky, which
borders on nothing, and so doesn't exist. In fact, I'm in hell,
and have to keep quiet. The painter says it's all incomprehensible because it's human, and the world is inhuman, which
makes everything comprehensible and terribly sad. He lets
the words hang there. "Terribly sad" is what he says, and the
way he says it, it must pierce the hearts of everyone. Beauty
was a danger for itself, just as darkness was "independence of
desire." Or I walk over to the hay barn and imagine how he
quells me with a mere look. And then I think of my task.
Really, I ought to have a plan, or a table perhaps, where I can
organize all the information I gather, add in the new data
from above, and from below, so that whatever's come in too

high can be reduced, and whatever's too low can be added on to. But perhaps it's all physical evidence that's incapable of being ordered. Why is there no organization? In my observation of the painter, I mean to say. Am I in fact observing him? Am I not just looking at him? Am I observing him when I look at him? Looking at him when observing him? Then what? I'll be pretty stumped when I next sit across the table from the assistant. He imagines I'll come back to Schwarzach after a while, and spread out everything I've observed in front of him, and say: This is how it is! That's the way he said it! That's exactly how I made my observations! No possibility of error! His sadness is unlike any I imagined, but that's how it is! Do you understand? No. I'm sure I can't even string two or three words together coherently. Even though everything is perfectly clear. And how! And then there's silence, nothing happens that would be pertinent. And how differently everything will present itself when I pick it out of what I've written. Completely differently. Because what I've written is wrong. Nothing written is right. Has any claim to rightness. Not even to precision, even though everything is set down conscientiously, with the view of knowing something about a distinct set of affairs. At best, less wrong. Still wrong, though. Of a different wrongness. Untrue.

I opened the door of his room, and saw him engrossed in his newspapers. That is, I saw—because he was sitting behind his bed, in front of the picture whose landscape I hadn't yet discerned: a brown picture with large black stains that might be houses, but might equally be trees—I saw the newspaper, but behind the newspaper was him. Without putting the newspaper down when I stepped in—he didn't look up at me—he left me to sit down where I was. "You find me reading an interesting article about the imperial palace in Persia," he said. "You know, those people must have quite unimaginable amounts of money. By the way, I've read a report on the meeting between the French and Russian foreign ministers. A very odd affair, that, indeed. Are you interested in politics at all?"—"Yes," I said, a young person's perfectly natural reply. "I'm really not interested at all in political wheelings and dealings, not anymore. But there was a time, not all that long ago either, when I was always hungry for news of political developments. Politics is the only interesting part of human history. It offers substance for anyone's meditation. Evidently! Now, as you know, I've withdrawn, and follow things in a more casual manner. But the report on the foreign ministers' conference, that's something you have to read. Plus, if you feel like it, and I would urge you to, as you're still young, and still have everything to learn, the article on the imperial palace in Persia. I take it you're familiar with the history of the Peacock Throne?"—"Yes," I said. "There are some passing references to it here." Newspapers were the greatest wonders of the world, they knew everything, and only through them did the universe become animated for their readers, the ability to picture everything was only preserved by newspapers. "You still haven't been to pick up the last few issues. Would you like to take them with you now?" It was all but dark in the room, and the air was barely breathable. I decided to go right away. "Of course, you have to know how to go about reading them," said the painter. "You mustn't just gobble them up, and you mustn't take them too seriously either, but remember they are miraculous." To this point, I still hadn't glimpsed him. "The idea that you get information about the whole world from a few little pieces of paper," he said, "and are able to feel involved with everything, without taking a single step, even, if that's your preference, from the vantage point of your bed! A miracle!" he said. "The dirt which people hold against newspapers is just the dirt of the people themselves, and not the dirt of the newspapers, you understand! The newspapers do well to hold up a mirror to people that shows them as they are—which is to say, revolting." Sometimes, in effect everywhere and always, "the beauty and the greatness of human beings" could also be gleaned from the newspapers. "As I say, reading the newspapers is an art, the mastery of which is perhaps the most beautiful of all the arts, you know." Then he folded the newspaper up on his knee, but I still couldn't see him, because it was suddenly completely dark.

How he once spent four months painting a hand, he told me today. Then, at the end of four months, he fed the painting to the flames. "Not a bad picture. But the hand didn't work. Later, I painted in a completely different style." Unlike other painters who have to work in brightly lit studios, he could only work in darkened rooms. "It has to be dark, that's the only way I can paint. In complete darkness. Not the least light should be allowed. But now I don't paint anymore." Before he began on a picture, he would tramp all over the city for days, from one café to the next, one neighborhood to the next, often riding for hours on streetcars and subways, on buses, from one terminus to the other, going on long marches in shirt and pants, mingling with workers and market stallholders, from time to time eating a meat sandwich somewhere, then sitting in a café again, moving on, past long gray enclosures thrown around pieces of waste ground, through viaducts and playgrounds, to dairies and parks. "I often used to have a rest in a washroom somewhere," he told me. "Changed my clothes. I changed three or four times a day, I always used to carry three changes of clothes in my briefcase with me, so that I could change whenever I felt like it." He spent whole afternoons hanging around stations, watching people and trains. "Stations, and especially ugly old stations, have always been an experience for me, from childhood on." Then he climbed into his elevator and rode up to his studio, straight into the darkness. While he was painting, only he could see his picture, because it was so dark. Before beginning, he disconnected the doorbell, locked up whatever could be locked up, stripped to his shirt. "The picture painted itself through my art," he said. He didn't go to bed for days, only loafed around on his two big sofas. Never knew if it was dark outside or not, lost all track of the date. Didn't know if it was spring or summer or winter. When he thought his picture was done, he drew back the curtains, so abruptly that the light blinded him and he couldn't see. "Only by and by could I see that it was no good," he said. "That once again it was just a shot at something that had treated me like a dog, and it was nothing, nothing, nothing, nothing!" All these paintings he ended up shoving behind a wall where friends of his—"friends?"—would occasionally pull out one or other, to transport it to a dealer, or have it photographed or written up. "My paintings were always well reviewed, except by myself," he said. "Basically there is no criticism, and the people who busy themselves with art are as uncritical as at any time in history. Maybe it was the lack of criticism that irritated me, and that's why I never became a good painter?"

"You know," the painter said, "that art froth, that artist forni-cation, that general art-and-artist loathsomeness, I always found that repelling; those cloud formations of basest self-preservation topped with envy . . . Envy is what holds artists together, envy, pure envy, everyone envies everyone else for everything . . . I talked about it once before, I want to say: artists are the sons and daughters of loathsomeness, of paradisiac shamelessness, the original sons and daughters of lewdness; artists, painters, writers, and musicians are the compulsive masturbators on the planet, its disgus-ting cramps, its peripheral puffings and swellings, its pustu-lar secretions . . . I want to say: artists are the great emetic agents of the time, they were always the great, the very greatest emetics . . . Artists, are they not a devastating army of absurdity, of scum? The infernality of unscrupulous-ness is something I always meet with in the thoughts of artists . . . But I don't want any artists' thoughts anymore, no more of those unnatural thoughts, I want nothing more to do with artists or with art, yes, not with art either, that greatest of all abortions . . . Do you understand: I want to get right away from that bad smell. Get away from that stink, I always say to myself, and secretly I always thought, get away from that corrosive, shredding, useless lie, get away from that shameless simony . . ." He said: "Artists are the identical twins of hypocrisy, the identical twins of low-mindedness, the identical twins of licensed exploitation, the greatest licensed exploitation of all time. Artists, as they have shown themselves to me to be," he said, "are all dull and grandiloquent, nothing but dull and grandiloquent, nothing . . ."

In the store I suddenly realized that school has started again. The whole of the gloomy store was full of schoolchildren, buying books and textbooks and pencils, and grown-ups were looking for pens and ink and drawing paper for their first-graders, and issuing threats and making jokes and laughing and throwing piles of loose change on the counter. The little girl in the black dress, the daughter of the proprietress, couldn't manage to keep up with counting all the loose change, which the children had probably been hoarding for the past half a year or more. "And another pencil!"—"And another pen!"—"And another pad, just the same!"—"No, not a ruled one!"—"No, I want a red one, not a blue one!" I wanted to buy a pencil and barged forward, but in the end I didn't care about waiting my turn. How the sweet and the repulsive odors of the children and the grown-ups mingled in this small, almost pitch-black space! Right at the back is the peephole through which you can see out to the snow. I took my pencil, and went outside. There I ran into the knacker, who was dragging a large cowhide behind him. The butcher had given it to him, he said, and he was taking it home and then he would get it tanned, and use it as a bedroom rug. "A cowhide makes a particularly warm bedroom rug," he said. In the morning he had been down on the construction site; he had arranged a meeting with the engineer, who had given him a tour of the site. They had gone to the canteen together, and eaten a particularly good meal. "It's much cheaper than the inn as well." He wanted to ask me whether I thought the

painter was strange. "No," I said, "he's a man like any other."
I could be right. He thought the painter was crazy. Something was wrong with him, on this visit anyway. "It's as
though something happened to him in Vienna," said the
knacker. "Yes," I said, "he's unusual, but not particularly
unusual." He had seen the painter sitting in the church yesterday, "in the front pew," shaking his head. The knacker
hadn't drawn attention to himself, so that he could go on
observing the painter. The painter had taken a couple of
quick paces to the altar, and raised his fist against the monstrance. "Then he walked out of the church, and went down
to the pond." The knacker said: "And the business in the
ravine was crazy as well." I let him move off with his
cowhide, which left bloodstains on the snow, uneven bloodstains, and I went to the baker, who changed a hundredschilling note for me, with which I paid for the beer I'd drunk
over the last few days. Outside, I ran into the painter, who
was wearing his artist's jacket. "I want to give myself a fright
again today," he said. "Give myself and the world a fright.
When I wear this red jacket, I feel like the biggest twit of all
time. And people believe I am the biggest twit of all time.
Come along, let's go and get some supper."

In the evening, once the painter had gone upstairs, the
knacker sang songs with the landlady. With an animal undertone, the knacker sang:

> Through mouth and anus
> the devil pulls his rope
> the beast so pulled
> can give up hope.

And he sang:

> Morning, noon, and evening . . .
> What says the night,
> the gloomy gloomy night?

During supper, the painter had suddenly said: "Listen! Listen!" In the dreadful sausage-eating, beer-drinking din, he said: "Listen, the dogs." I couldn't hear them. But he wouldn't give up, and without the others sitting at our table noticing, the engineer, the knacker, the landlady, the policeman were sitting there as well, the painter said: "Listen, the dogs! Listen to that barking." And he got up and walked out, and went up to his room. When I followed him out into the entrance hall and stopped, I could hear through the half-iced-up open front door the long-drawn-out howling of dogs, and sometimes their barking. The endlessly drawn out howling, and the sound of barking biting into it. In front of me I heard the barking and howling, and behind me the laughing and vomiting and smacking of playing cards. Ahead of me the dogs, behind me the customers at the bar. I won't be able to sleep tonight.

Fourteenth Day

He, the assistant, obviously thinks I can perfectly well carry out an assignment like observing the painter Strauch without taking any harm from it. "Harm! How could it harm you,

observing a suffering human being?" he said. So he understands that his brother is suffering. Not the *extent* of his suffering, which he is unaware of. Because the suffering of the
painter exceeds the capacity of the assistant to imagine it.
How deep are the painter's sufferings? Is it possible to determine how deep someone's sufferings are? And when they are
at their deepest? The assistant sent me here thinking I would
be able to keep off influences that might be bad for me. Yes,
and of course that's something one has to be able to do, to
keep off the so-called bad influence of the people one is in
contact with, forced to be in contact with, so that it doesn't
affect one. Deal with it, however difficult it might suddenly
turn out to be. Keep your eyes open, you won't ignore it, you
won't ignore the danger, but will meet it with the correct
defense. In the company of the painter, I am of course continually exposed to bad influences. But I can see them, and I
can distinguish the point where the bad influences begin, and
where the bad influences are not good, because it is also possible for bad influences to be good. Presumably, this
encounter will only take its full effect on me much later. Not
now. Just as childhood influences are only now unfolding; the
experiences you have at eight or nine suddenly shape the
thirty-year-old. In the same way as a dye might gradually
spread through a body of deep water—water which, further-
more, has always been a tad murky anyway. Is that right? The
painter gives me many bearings. He is by no means hermeti-
cally sealed away. There are a lot of access points to him, but
even so one often finds him where one hasn't been looking,
hasn't suspected he might be. "I have a rigid conscience," he
says. What does he mean by that? Or when he says: "Reality
is incapable of empathy," saying it to himself, it would
appear, with no connection to what he said before or after, I

don't see what he means. His best ideas come to him while walking. In the fresh air. In the inn, or indoors in other places, he retires into himself, and you can sit with him for hours without getting a single word out of him. Now, silence and a gift for listening, even if no one is speaking, are both things I was born with. At home, sometimes no one would talk for days, at the most someone might ask for a plate or a pencil or a book. I no longer find it so difficult walking at the slow pace the painter likes, though I'm used to going quickly from one impression to the next, rather than stopping all the time, as he does, to sit down and rest. For me, the painter is a big problem I somehow have to solve. A task, in fact. And for him?

What sort of language is Strauch's language? What can I make of his scraps of thought? Things that initially struck me as disjointed and incoherent, actually possess "truly immense connections"; the whole thing is in the nature of an enormous transfusion of words into the world, into humans, "a pitiless proceeding against stupidity," as he would say, "an uninterrupted, regeneration-worthy backdrop of sound." *How* get that down? *What* notes? Schematic or systematic to what point? His outbursts descend on me like rockfalls. Abruptly, things he says detach themselves from the explosive guffaw of ridicule which he reserves for himself "and the world." Strauch's language is the language of the heart muscle, a scandalous "cerebral pulse." It is rhythmic self-abasement under the "subliminal creak" of his own rafters. His notions and subterfuges, fundamentally in accord with the barking of those dogs that he drew my attention to, with which he "scattered me to the air." Can it still be described as language? Yes, it is the false bottom of language, the heaven and hell of language, the mutiny of rivers, "the steaming word-nostrils of brains that are in a state of endless and shameless despair." Sometimes he will speak a poem, and then tear it apart, reformulate it as a "power plant," "a barracks for the raw philosophy of a wordless tribe," as he says. "The world is a world of recruits, it needs to be brutalized, you need to teach it to shoot, and not to shoot." He rips the words out of himself as from a swamp. This violent ripping out of words leaves him dripping with blood.

The war had left its grisly traces up and down the valley. "Even today you keep encountering skulls or entire skeletons, covered over by a thin layer of pine needles," says the painter. In the forest over toward the Klamm valley and behind the lake, also in the larch wood, disbanded regiments had been starved to death. "And then they froze. A few were able to get away, but only a very few, the others were already too weak to reach the villages. And the soldiers didn't think of murder," murder being a preserve "of the dark elements out of the East." The convicts from the nearby prison had also wrought considerable havoc, and a lot of missing men who had broken out and never returned were found dotted about under bushes and rocks. "Often, it was children out blackberrying who would suddenly scream, and drag their mothers over to some spot overgrown with snakeweed. There they'd find a human being, naked, the clothes ripped from his body once years back. Hunger turns people into animals." At the end of the war, the forests had been full of war gear; tanks and armored cars and cannon and motorbikes and cars had been junked among the trees all over the place. "Some exploded when they were touched. Often the tanks contained the bodies of their crews, huddled together with torn lungs. People who opened the hatches made some grisly discoveries," he said. "By and by people dared to disassemble the war gear, and they also started burying the dead soldiers—on the spot, because they didn't want them in their own graveyards, they were too alien for them. When they touched them, the bodies disintegrated, they had decomposed in the air. In the hollows, children found bazooka shells, which tore them apart. There were little scraps of children, you know, hanging off the trees. You could find men in their prime ground up under the wheels of field guns, in the ravine there was a group of grenadiers with their tongues cut out, and their penises stuffed in their mouths. And here and there, there might be shot-up uniforms in the trees, and stiff hands and feet poking out of the pond. It took years before the locals straightened out the forests and the countryside as a whole. At first they only went out to collect foodstuffs they found in the tanks, and various other useful objects, uniforms, as I say, which they adapted for themselves and then went around in for years; and only then to bury the dead, or what was left of them, the remains, as they say, and finally they turned out with rakes and shovels to wipe out the traces. But the traces of the war are not yet wiped out," said the painter, "this war will never be forgotten. People will continue to encounter it wherever they go."

"What do you think the painter Strauch said to me today?" With this question that wasn't a question the landlady surprised me in my room, having knocked and entered to make the bed. So doing, she picked up the pillow, tossed it up in the

air, and caught it a couple of times. She shook out the feath-
erbed at the open window. "What do you think?" she asked,
having made the bed, and as she wiped down the washstand
and filled the ewer with fresh water, and my glass on the bedside table. She drew everything out that she did, so as to be
able to tell me finally what it was that the painter Strauch—
"still in bed, not yet dressed, even though it was nine o'clock
already!"—had said. "He said he would surprise me one day
by lying dead in his bed." She had laughed and supposed the
painter was having a bit of fun with her. But then she had
seen from his expression that he meant it. "You know, I can't
be doing with that in my establishment, a corpse," she said.
And then she left my room, but came back in right away and
said: "I forgot to close your window." She closed the window
and then stopped in the doorway, as though looking to me
for some sort of explanation. "Isn't it funny to try and
frighten someone like that?" she said. "The painter's a bit odd
this time, I find. What's the matter with him? Do you know?"
I didn't know, I didn't have any idea. The painter was worried
about something, but I didn't know what it was that was worrying him. "He's a different man from what he used to be,"
she said. "But I'd be sorry if he was ill or something," she
said. And then she finally left my room, I heard her shouting
for one of her daughters down in the passageway. When I
went down later to stretch my legs, just once round the inn,
because I had the feeling I wouldn't be able to sleep at all
unless I got some fresh air, and suddenly feeling tired, I
wanted to lie down for an hour, so as to be refreshed for when
the painter came for me later, when I was downstairs I went
into the kitchen under the pretext of having to get a glass of
water, which was fresher from the kitchen well, and there she
was standing there in just her skirt, and hearing me coming,

she hurriedly tucked her undershirt into it, and I said, while I drew a glass of water from the well, which is a draw-well of the sort you generally only find on the outside of farm-houses, and not inside a kitchen, I said: "Did he talk about suicide at all?"—"About suicide?" she said. "No, not about suicide. That would be still worse. He only said I'd find him dead in his bed one morning. Perhaps he has the feeling he might have a stroke. He always used to worry he might have a stroke."—"He was worried that he might have a stroke?"— "He surely wouldn't kill himself in my establishment? I think he was just having a bit of fun with me," she said, and, feeling sure he wasn't having fun at all, but merely stating something I got to hear from him quite regularly, I drank my glass of water, and set off outside.

On the way to the church he kept stopping and drawing my attention to the fact that he was an old man, and I shouldn't wait for him. "I don't mind. Quite the opposite." After he'd said that four or five times, the last time in a sharp tone of command, I simply left him standing in the middle of the slope, by the big tree stump that marks the boundary between two fields, and ran up as quickly as I could. I enjoyed the feeling of suddenly being free. Like a dog that's slipped his leash. Up at the top I stood in such a way that he couldn't see me, but I had a good view of him laboriously making his way up. It seemed to me he rested more frequently than the day before, when we had taken the same walk, and he had asked me the following question: "What sort of person are you? I can't make sense of you. Tell me what you think. What you're doing meeting me all over the place, and accompanying me! Going around with me! Have you at least enjoyed a bit of a break? It's the tension that's the mystery. You're a mystery to me, even though you're a very natural and uncomplicated type!"—Watching him now, I thought a little puff of wind would be enough to knock him over. When he stopped, he marked the ground with his stick, Indian signs, he told me, that are incomprehensible to me. Some of these signs remind me of animals, a cow for instance, a pig; others are shaped like temples, or the courses of rivers. Circles. Other geometrical forms. Even up where I was, I could hear him muttering to himself. Like an old general talking to himself, and then turning to the army that will always be there in his imagination. And he looked, too, like someone bending over a staff map, with everything on it down to the least detail depending on him. He was talking in foreign languages as well, Asian words and scraps were flying through the air. The whole scene, with him the focus of it, reminded me of a painting I saw years ago once in the Kunsthistorisches Museum in Vienna; I can even remember the room it's hanging in: a river landscape by Breughel the Elder, where people are trying to find distraction from death, in which they are successful, but only, as the picture seems to be saying, at the price of infinite torments in Hell. The black of the tree stump, which shaded into the black of the painter's jacket, and the black of his pants and his stick, was finally picked up by the black of the mountain peaks. When he was no more than a few feet away from me, standing on one of the last steps going up to the church door, I was afraid of him. I imagined him coming up to me from behind, and clubbing me over the head with his stick. When I looked in his face, that idea left me. Even though nothing about his face ruled out such a possibility. "If you like, we can go in the church," he said. And immediately after: "No, you go by yourself. I'll wait for you outside." I went into the church and sat down in a pew with a good view of the altar. I picked up a prayer book that was lying on the pew next to me. Leafed through it. Found a psalm. Read the psalm: "Asperges me, Domine, hyssopo, et mundabor: lavabis me, et super nivem dealbabor. Miserere mei, Deus, secundum magnam misericordiam tuam. Gloria Patri!" And then: "Me expectaverunt peccatores, ut perderent me: testimonia tua, Domine, intellexi: omnis consummationis vidi finem: latum mandatum tuum nimis. Beati immaculati in via: qui ambulant in lege Domini. Gloria Patri." I read the whole thing through again. A second time. And a third. But it was unbearable to me, I could make no sense of it at all, and I had to get up and leave the church. As I crossed the soft carpet to the door, I saw angels' faces of incredible ugliness, and the nearer I got to them, the more fearsome they grew. When I stepped outside, the painter had disappeared. He had in the meantime made his way round to the laying-out chapel, which was attached to the rear of the church. From there, standing in deep snow, he called out to me: "Stay where you are, otherwise you'll have a fright!" I didn't know what he thought would give me a fright. Then it occurred to me that the chapel was used for the laying out of corpses from time to time. "There's a dead man in the chapel," he said, and raised his head up past the windowsill, which caused his hat to slip back over his neck. When he returned, he said: "A painted corpse. They have the most gruesome way of painting corpses here." He wondered what had prompted him to go to the chapel at all. "It's not curiosity," he said. We were late getting back to the inn; it was one o'clock.

. . .

Strauch the painter is shorter than Strauch the surgeon.
Strauch the painter is one of those cases where there's nothing to be done with hammer and crowbar, with knife and saw
and pincers and scalpel. So let the thoughts of modern science take their way, the inventiveness of many sleepless
nights. Because this is a case of an error purchased and now
almost entirely paid off by Death. Yes? A consequence of
development which is no development, a consequence of
matter. Of movement that is no movement. Something
organic that isn't organic. A point of departure that is no
point of departure. Can't be. Of an incurable illness. He continually scents danger. It's clear that he continually feels himself under threat. Continually on the alert, in the same way as
the world about him seems to him to be. So what is the
organism? What is the contrast? Body and mind? Mind less
body? Body without soul? What then? Under the surface?
Above the surface? And on the surface? A shy destiny coming
to an end, and what is it? But there are illnesses that are completely unrecognized. They have always existed, and always
will exist. If one becomes curable overnight, another may
become incurable overnight. One fewer is one more. Why?
How? Is the causation any indication?

The painter said: "The priest is a gravely ill man. Yesterday,
before coming back to the inn, I spoke to him. He asked me
for money again. For the poorhouse. For the sacristy, you
know. He is very well aware of my views on the church. He
likes to walk in the snow for an hour. In summer, he sits by
his pond, and catches nothing in two weeks. The church is

not overly generous with its employees. The church in the countryside is something like folk poetry. You see it on the trees and in the cellars and on the potato fields. Going around with children. Its laughter has a fiendish rhythm. It's afraid of all ceremony, in particular it's afraid of the bishop. You know, there's something poetic about that. If you suddenly hear a man sobbing, then it's the priest. Incidentally, he has an excellent library. Doesn't know any sermons. He is so timid, a bird is enough to give him a fright. But if need be, he'll go to visit a dying man at night, in the pitch dark, alone, with a lantern. Often to remote farmhouses, far up in the ice and rocks."

"Enormous amounts of timber," said the painter, "vast quantities of valuable wood go to waste up there. Thousands, hundreds of thousands of trees. The cellulose factory gobbles them up. By the time it reaches the valley, that's all they're good for. This whole landscape," he said, "used to be simply a wild, wonderful biotope . . . Come," he said, "I'll show you a few types of tree that are particularly common here . . . Here is the spruce, picea excelsa, first and foremost, then the Scotch pine, the fir, the larch. The odd cembra pine. Come along, I'll give you a few details, on broad-leaved trees, angiospermae, and conifers, the gymnospermae . . ."

At the outset it amounted to something, but even then it was already seeking to cause pain as soon as possible, the relationship between two young people who, short or long, but in any case suddenly, had come together, said the painter. "Before it turns into anything," he said, "that's when it's beautiful and precious." Youth somehow "pulled off the stunt of fooling the world for a brief moment," and for a few days and nights everything bore the appearance of happiness. I was thinking of S. and wanted to write her a letter at once, and just at that moment I also wanted not to write, and I tried to think of something other than her, but I didn't manage, not till I was out of the village, not the whole way up the path, not in the ravine, and not in the inn; I said to myself: What was that anyway? Didn't it finish long ago? What happened? And how and why was it suddenly over? At first not a day without her, then almost not a night without her, and then everything started to crumble the way it always crumbled, withdrew in two directions from two people, and was gone. And where did it go to? Often I woke up at night, in alarm. And followed a trail that suddenly ended somewhere in the forest, by a river, in a fire. I often, often asked myself what it is that creates the conditions that make two young people unhappy. I'm so young, and yes, it's over! There was a coming and asking and establishing, and that's how pitiless it was: the end. If I were to write again, she thinks, then it might start over. But it can't start over, it mustn't. "It's a lie," said the painter. I know what he meant: there's a lie founded on another lie, and looking for refuge in a third: which is to say, bang in the middle of another person. I hadn't thought of her in weeks. I went away from her as one might walk out of a shop, with the firm resolve never to go there again. OK. The painter said: "Then it's like a couple of mountains that are separated by a rushing river." Suddenly I noticed I had been singing, the whole stretch of the way to the cornfield. I was singing to mask over what I was thinking. But thoughts don't leave when you ask them to, you can't just usher them out.

On the contrary: it's then that they really take root in you, and start to produce reproach and irritation all the way to infinity. If the afflicted one gets into this destructive process, he can become powerless whatever he does, wherever he goes. The painter said: "The most beautiful flowers are cut first; what help are clever gardeners then?" He pulled me further and further into gloomy thoughts that finally, mad as it seemed to me, as the noose tightened around me, prompted me to tear myself away from him. I ran off without a word to him, and then waited by the hay barn. I apologized. He was quite unfazed.

Between the larch wood and the hay barn, where they allegedly found the butcher's big dog, "frozen, having fallen asleep under the boards," the painter draws my attention to various trees, some in a group, others standing on their own. "Here, you see," he said, "the spruce, *Picea excelsa*, the aristocratic sister to the spruce that is called the spruce fir, wrongly also silver fir. The fir . . ." He steps up to the fence and says: "Here, you see, the oak . . . This one is a durmast oak, this one a pedunculate oak . . . The oak has a growing season of two hundred years. The name is derived from the Old Indian word *igya*, which means, roughly, veneration. But you will also find ash and alder," he said, "and even sycamore. And down there, you see, that yew that I told you about on the day of your arrival here. It's a majestic holdout from primeval times . . ." As we walked along the larch wood— I had the feeling of walking in my own footsteps of the day before—he said: "This is a moment of demonic quiet. A phenomenon still too little investigated by science." It really was quiet, not a sound from the work down in the valley. Nothing. "The world still entertains a very primitive understanding of such quiet. All my life I've thought of it as an illness in an exhausted nature, as hideously ripped-open abysses of feeling. To nature, this quiet is horrible."

Of course it's not possible to have an insight into everything, but I think he is depressed by not receiving any mail. "Since no one knows where I am, no one can write to me either. But nor do I want anyone to write to me," he said. "I don't write any letters, so no one knows where I am. I don't think I'll ever write another letter." In his condition, he's not up to writing in any case. When he sits down to make some notes in some "logbooks of inventions" that he started many years ago—"at the instant when I begin to go into myself"—his headaches worsen to the degree that he is forced to stop, to abandon a thought halfway, to shut his notebook, and lie down. And he really doesn't want to write to anyone either. For him, that's all in the past, so far that it's all unavailable, out of reach, "not one person, nothing." He regularly thought of himself now as drifting under water, and then frozen somewhere into a world of irrelation. "If you can't open your mouth, you can't scream." Time went by, or then again not: "Sometimes it's as though it stood still." How it will end, "seeing as it will end," I'm not sure. The worst case might suddenly come about, I know that from experience. I don't believe in miracles, at least not now. I can imagine him killing himself. But it might take a long time till he does. He might wait for spring, and then summer, and then next winter, and so on. But it can't be a matter of decades. Not with him. Not even years, because

he is ill and will soon die anyway. There's activity in his subconscious, even if everything's been switched off on the surface. A great-uncle of his killed himself, by the way: he was a
gamekeeper. Apparently because he was unable to take "any
more human misery." They found him in the woods. He had
shot himself in the mouth. If you inquire, you will find sufficient cause in every individual. But, as the assistant says, his
brother had "suicidal inclinations" from the outset. Suddenly
he starts talking about his disease again, which is "completely
asymptomatic." At night he gets to the root of it, but then at
the critical moment, it all recedes again. Only the pain was
left, "a pain that is incapable of passing its apogee . . . At
first," said the painter, "I was told there was a treatment for
my head, an approach, a method. But suddenly I looked
behind the scenes of medicine: they know nothing, they
can do nothing! I rejected all their methods. Doctors are
just quacks, you know! Mechanics. It's true, they can't tell
their patients immediately that they're hopeless cases . . .
that medicine is just a superficial calmative for body and
psyche . . ." He said: "Another pillow to prop my head up at
night? I've tried that, and I've tried no pillow at all. The pain
comes when it pleases, and the illness suits itself, it's completely ununderstood . . . you know, one would have to investigate the extremes of pain in all their gradations, trace the
whole architecture of pain! Well, enough of my illness: illness gets people talking, whether common or refined . . . You
want to know whether the other fellow is suffering as much
as you are . . . you talk because you want sympathy. You hear
about the catastrophic abuses in medicine: catastrophic coin-
cidences, the feebleness of the so-called doctors, the many
botched and bungled operations, incidents, and so on and so
forth . . ."

"One might go to the bakery, perhaps," he said. "But did you know the baker has tuberculosis? All the people here run around in a highly infectious state. The baker's daughter has tuberculosis too, it seems to have something to do with the runoff from the cellulose factory, with the steam that the locomotives have spewed out for decades, with the bad diet that the people eat. Almost all of them have cankered lung lobes, pneumothorax and pneumoperitoneum are endemic. They have tuberculosis of the lungs, the head, the arms and legs. All of them have tubercular abscesses somewhere on their bodies. The valley is notorious for tuberculosis. You will find every form of it here: skin tuberculosis, brain tuberculosis, intestinal tuberculosis. Many cases of meningitis, which is deadly within hours. The workmen have tuberculosis from the dirt they dig around in, the farmers have it from their dogs and the infected milk. The majority of the people have galloping consumption. Moreover," he said, "the effect of the new drugs, of streptomycin for example, is nil. Did you know the knacker has tuberculosis? That the landlady has tuberculosis? That her daughters have been to sanatoria on three separate occasions? Tuberculosis is by no means on the way out. People claim it is curable. But that's what the pharmaceutical industry says. In fact, tuberculosis is as incurable as it always was. Even people who have been inoculated against it come down with it. Often those who have it the worst are the ones who look so healthy that you wouldn't suspect they were ill at all. Their rosy faces are utterly at variance with their ravaged lungs. You keep running into people who've had to endure a cautery or, at the very least, a transverse lesion. Most of them have had their lives ruined by failed reconstructive surgery." We didn't go to the bakery. Straight home instead.

THE DOG BARKING

"I could say it's the living end," said the painter, "but it's the end of life, by turns low down and high up, low down, then all around, it smashes its head against the snow blanket, it crashes incessantly against the awful iron in the air, the iron in the air, if you must know, that's where it gets shredded, and you have to breathe it in, breathe it in through your ears, till you go crazy, till the noise shreds you, till your earlobes smash brain and muzzle, muzzle and brain with the limitless naïveté of destructiveness. Listen to it, stop and listen to it: that yapping! It's not possible to eradicate it, all you can do is push it back, push it back with your brain, push back the yap, the bark, the ghastly godawful yowling, you can press it down, but then it comes up worse, it will crush flesh, soul and flesh, it's established itself like maggots in space, established itself everywhere, in the shattering fat of history, in the quarterstaves of the insoluble diluvia . . . It makes no sense," said the painter, "to try and hide in the dog barking, it will find you out, and then even your fear will be chewed up . . . Yes, I'm frightened, I'm frightened, everywhere I hear: fear and fear, and I hear fear, and this ghostly trauma of fear will ruin me, drive me mad, not just my illness, no no, not just my illness, but the illness *and* this trauma of fear . . . Listen . . . how the barking organizes itself, how it makes space for itself, listen, it's the cracking of canine whips, it's canine hyperdexterity, canine hyperdespair, a hellish serfdom that is taking its revenge, taking its revenge on its grim devisers, on me, on you, yes, you too, on all limitless apparitions, on all limitless, terrible, basically cut-off apparitions, on human organs, which are the organs of heaven and hell, on the infernal organs of the heights and the celestial organs of the depths, on the jailbird unhappiness of all tragedians . . . Listen, these tragedians, listen to them: that stubborn deafmute breed of snakes' tongues, listen to them: the monstrously unappetizing republic of all-powerful idiocy, listen to them: this unsolicited shameless parliament of hypocrites . . . There are the dogs, there is their yap, there is death, death in all its wild profusion, death with all its frailty, death with its stink of quotidian crime, death, this last recourse of despair, the bacillus of monstrous unendingness, the death of history, the death of impoverishment, death, listen, the death that I don't want, that no one wants, that no one wants anymore, there it is, death, the yap, listen, the unlawful drowning of reason, the refusal to give evidence of all supposition, the spastic smack of soft brain on concrete, on the concrete floor of human dementia . . . Listen to my views on the yap, listen . . . I want to try and plumb the thinking of the infernal tempest, the confusion of eras, Cambrian, Silurian, Carboniferous, Permian, Triassic, and Jurassic, the monstrous Tertiary and Quaternary, the monstrously meaningless rejection of the great floods licking up from the depths . . . Listen to me, I am going into the yap, I go in and I smash their fangs, I yell at it with the thunder of my unreasonableness, I scramble its processes, its mendacious propaganda . . . Listen, stop, listen, the sweating stupid slavering dogs' tongues, listen to the dogs, listen to them, listen to them . . ." We were standing on the spot from which you can see down into the Klamm. "Wolves," said the painter. "From here you can see straight down the throat of all wolf science." He was exhausted. I could hear the dogs. I could hear the barking and yapping. I was exhausted too. I was stunned by the painter's outburst, my body felt crushed as though by a rockfall; "and then I found him crushed on the road, below me, at my feet," the painter was saying. I immediately organized the painter's outburst. I'm astonished, I need only to push the button on my listening machine, and the outburst passes over me. But I'm exhausted. I'm utterly exhausted. "Listen," said the painter, "it's the yapping of the end of the world. Quite manifestly it's the end of the world in person, in this yapping. How sternly and implacably it's proceeding in people's faces, in people's faces, in the face of thoughts, in the face of reason, against all ridicule." He said: "I'm afraid. Come. Let's go. Let's go to the inn. I can't stand to hear any more of that yapping." Never had the dogs barked like this without interruption all day and all the previous night. "What else could this yapping portend," said the painter, "as we know everything and understand everything, if not the actual end of the world." He lengthened the words "end of the world" across his tongue like a priceless delicacy, and like a "sinful pleasure" he pulled the words "end of the world" across his tongue. Then we were silent. In the ravine, he said: "Infamy! Don't you see what it says up there, high up in what we flatteringly term the mother of heaven: it says: Infamy!"

Before he retired to his room, "not to sleep, but to howl to myself in the silence of horror," he said: "How everything has crumbled, how everything has dissolved, how all the reference points have shifted, how all fixity has moved, how nothing exists anymore, how nothing exists, you see, how all the religions and all the irreligions and the protracted absur-

dities of all forms of worship have turned into nothing, nothing at all, you see, how belief and unbelief no longer exist,
how science, modern science, how the stumbling blocks, the
millennial courts, have all been thrown out and ushered out
and blown out into the air, how all of it is now just so much
air . . . Listen, it's all air, all concepts are air, all points of reference are air, everything is just air . . ." And he said: "Frozen
air, everything just so much frozen air . . ."

Fifteenth Day

"Diseased," said the painter, "everything in the countryside,
and most particularly here is diseased. It's a grave mistake to
assume that people in the country are of greater worth:
country people, ha! Country people are the underclass of
today. The underclass. And the country is degenerate,
debased, so much more debased than the city! The last war
has been the ruination of country people! Inside and out!
Country people are just trash! And tell me now, what was
ever so great about country people, about farmers? Were
they so incomparable? Soil and inheritance, was that it? No, it
was just gossip! Gossip, you hear? Gossip! Country people
might be more reserved, but that's the breathtaking, the dis-
reputable, the heinous thing about country people! That
whole simple, pitiless world of thought, where simplicity and
low-mindedness get hitched and ruin everything . . . ! Nothing comes from country people! Villages, morons in short
sleeves! Country churches, moronic. Listen: I'm talking

about the infestation of the country. The country is repulsive! I've never had any regard, not the least regard, for farmers. Perhaps you have a different view. As far as the future is concerned, the rural population is without significance. And the rural population! The country is no source anymore, only a trove of brutality and idiocy, of squalor and megalomania, of perjury and battery, of systematic extinction! Not even a monopoly of quiet anymore! There is, as I see, no crasser mistake than to assume that everything in the country, and in our countryside in particular, is roses, and to imagine it has something to teach us, that there is something philosophical about the way of life there, and that it is any better than in the cities! Well, it's quite the opposite!

"Out where the world collides with itself, there's welfare. Here there's no welfare. Welfare can't get into this valley. It's too tight and too squalid and too ugly. The cliffs block its path. In the darkness it would lose its way in no time. Welfare only reaches the edges of the Alps. Whereas here, it's dark. Here is work and poverty and nothing besides. Here it's the noose or the river. The unions have plenty to say. The parties have plenty to say. And nothing changes. At forty, these men are washed up. Finished. You can see them a while longer, and then you hear they've fallen off a rock. They hang themselves in a storehouse, in power-plant outbuildings, in the cellulose factory washroom. Thinking of them often disturbs the women giving birth, you know. The electricity lines drive them all crazy, and the river roars like a cow with its throat cut."

. . .

In the winter, it was naturally hardest to make any headway with building work, says the engineer. We are sitting down in the public bar, and the painter pretends the engineer's words are of the greatest interest to him. He has a bad headache, but he doesn't let on, drinks wine like the rest of us, and sometimes makes a move as though to check that his Pascal is still in his coat pocket.

"When we're expecting a frost, we can't do any concreting at all," says the engineer. "But there are other things we can do: right now we're sinking a bridge support. That's not without its dangers."

The painter says: "Isn't it very cold over the river? It makes me cold to look at it, what can it be like to stand over it all day and give instructions."—"It's not cold," says the engineer, "it's just important to have a head for heights. If a man doesn't, he'll fall head first into the water before he knows where he is."—"Is the water deep at that point?" says the painter. "Not right there," says the engineer, "but the current is very powerful. Even if you happen to be a good swimmer, and physically strong as all our people are, you'll have a job to get out, because it'll just wash you away, and in a few seconds you'll be at the old weir, and you'll meet your death."—"Ah, right," says the painter, "there's the old weir as well. Won't the old weir be destroyed when the power plant is finished?" "Yes," says the engineer, "then it'll be redundant."—"Of course," says the painter. "How many people have you got working for you at present?" he says. "Two hundred," answers the engineer, "but there are never that many at one time, some will be off for the day, some others will be sick. On average it's a hundred and eighty."—"A hundred and eighty!" says the painter, "that's a lot of men!"—"It's important to know where to assign them. What the most suitable occupation for each individual is at any given moment. Of course that's a continual headache. But that's what I do at night. At night I think about how to arrange things for the next day."—"Do you write your ideas down?" asks the painter. "No, I never write anything down," says the engineer, "I keep it in my head. In the morning when I drive down to the site, I issue the instructions I think up overnight. Or sometimes I tell the people who are eating and drinking in the inn to pass them on. That saves me no end of running around on the site. Getting from one work group to the next can be time-consuming. Often the different groups are working a long way from one another. One group might be working on the bridge, another will be loading and unloading on the road, a couple of hundred yards away, and a third will be over by the waterfall." The painter says: "And where do you eat lunch?"—"In the canteen. Everyone does, except one or two who have time off and go up the mountain to eat at the inn, where the food's better."—"But then the canteen's probably cheaper than here?" says the painter. "Cheaper, but not so good."—"And what happened at Christmastime, did everyone go home?"—"Only a very few went home. Most of them haven't got a home. We celebrated Christmas in the canteen. Me as well."—"And does the contractor pay a Christmas bonus?"—"Yes," said the engineer. "A generous bonus?" It was fairly sizable, says the engineer, "building firms are not mean when it comes to Christmas money." In fact, the workmen did fairly well for themselves. A temporary worker on the site could reckon to pick up his three thousand schillings. "That's more than a middle school teacher," says the painter. "Of course, there's no comparison between the work done by a laborer down there and a middle school teacher."—"Of course not." The knacker says: "And some do overtime, and they pick up four thousand and more."—"True," says the engineer, "but they're working themselves into the ground." It was no secret that they get lung disease, and often collapse and have to spend weeks in the hospital. "The contractor's not happy to see too much overtime being worked. Because they know they'll have to offer sick pay for weeks and months." But for the amount of work they did down there, "they're not overpaid." Anyway, they needed the money, because they have to eat properly, and drink as well, so they don't get depressed after work. "It's the bachelors who do best for themselves. They're usually young and strong, and can put a bit aside. After a couple of years, standing in the dirt, they often start their own business or something, the ones that know how." He himself had once stood in the dirt like that. As a young fellow he had paid his way through college by temping on building sites, just as I had done, well, he had done it too, standing around in puddles and ditches, and worrying about getting through his eight cubic meters of earth per day, or risk getting fired. "I've done it all, and I know my way around, and the men know that, and that's why we're on such good terms." There was no other engineer on the site that they got along with as well as with him. They had confidence in him, for instance when it came to representing them with the contractor. "As soon as the first warm days come along," he says, "then we'll start to make some headway."—"I expect you're pretty well paid yourself," says the painter. "I've heard that construction engineers are among the best paid people in the country."—"Yes," says the engineer, "true enough, but I could have gone to India and made more money. But then I didn't go to India, though I can't say I wasn't tempted."

Suddenly I thought of the bustle of the capital, where between twelve and half past one everyone who is anyone walks along the Graben or shows themselves on the Kärntner Strasse, as in a display window several hundred meters long, from the point of view of the businessman, from the point of view of the manager's wife, from the point of view of the attorney's wife, and from several hundred other points of view, as for instance the chartered accountant's wife or the woman with the fruit stand, who's come up from the Naschmarkt, to be there as well. And I think how I fit into the scene with my books and papers under my arm, how I pick up snatches of conversation, a greeting or a goodbye, or even just swearwords or complaints. There I am, suddenly in the fresh air, which seems to have come down into these streets from the outlying hills, and I don't know what to do with myself this lunchtime. My friends are all gone, headed home, eating lunch with their girlfriends or their brothers or their aunts from the provinces, and I'm all alone. I ponder which is better, to take in the words of the self-important and the curious passersby, or to go and sit in a park, of which there are many in the capital, one more beautiful than the next, and finally I decide on the latter course, and I've already turned down the Albrechtsrampe to the green island, where day in, day out the birds sing and the children play tag. That's where the secretaries sit eating their sandwiches, and the milk women have a break here, and the occasional doctor of philosophy with no better option sits on some stone step or pedestal to dig into his salt beef, carefully wrapped this morning for him. It smells of jasmine and hard-boiled eggs, and there's the periodic rustle of dried leaves being pushed by one of the innumerable attendants from one end of the park to the other. A look at my watch tells me I have two hours till the next lecture. I put my books down on the top step of the staircase that leads up to the rather pompous Greek Temple of the Muses, and before long I'm stretched out in the sun, which seems to be almost setting. Before long, October's finished, and there are no more leaves on the trees and no more humans in the park. Before long, the first snowflakes will fall on my shoulders, and my sandals will be replaced by shoes. But even in winter the Kärntner Strasse is so thronged with people that it feels warm, even when it's thirty below. And the Graben is lit up at Christmastime, and people bump into each other, and everyone feels glad to be alive. Sometimes you might shiver a little to be standing all alone in the midst of so many people, but then you think of your bed, and you don't feel sad anymore.

Today as I was sitting in front of the window, I had the idea that I ought to do something about my future. At least the immediate future. About what would happen once my internship in Schwarzach is finished. How will I get ready for my exams? I don't have the sense that I know enough to even attempt them. And here I'm not even able to do anything to prepare. There's no time. Because I'm altogether under the painter's thumb, I have to go where he goes, although that's not really it: I can't help going with him wherever he goes.

Even if he didn't ask me to go with him, I'd still want to go. They are always the same walks. They aren't really walks at all. Just tramping through the snow, the wind, the forest, the cold. Sometimes I'm on my own. After lunch, when he goes back to his room, to lie on his bed—"Don't imagine I'm sleeping!"—when he suddenly sends me packing, like he did the day before yesterday. Then he looks at me and taps me with his stick and says: "Now go back to the inn. I want to be on my own." Then I leave him, but even then I'm still with him, in my thoughts, which are forever circling around him.

I ought to write home, at the very least I ought to tell them where I am, so that, having heard nothing from me in two weeks—I bet they've asked in the hospital if they know anything—they know what's going on. But they would think it was strange if I wrote and told them I was here to observe someone. Observe someone? They wouldn't understand that, they can't imagine what it is to observe someone, I'm not sure I know myself what it is. The assistant's brother? Well, why? Because he's very ill? Mortally ill? But they don't even know the name of the illness? Something in the brain? Something in the head? Someone who's not quite normal? And they expose you to him? On the assistant's say-so? And with the agreement of the registrar? A recognized surgeon? A danger like that? Such a young person? Who doesn't really know what he's about himself? A painter, with confused ideas? Someone who's perhaps utterly confused? Someone altogether abnormal? But that could have a terrible effect on our son and brother and nephew! Better, then, not to write.

After all, what are two weeks! I've often not been in touch for longer than two weeks. Sometimes not for months. They're used to me turning up and disappearing again and not being in touch. And if they think I'm at the hospital, where they know I'm very well looked after, they won't assume anything too strange merely if I don't write to them. My future's like a stream in a forest, of which there are many precise descriptions, but nothing more; the forest is endless and as dark as only a childish notion of a forest can be, on the edge of gloom, and about to turn into utter gloom. The future is a long way off. And yet it's at the door. Go through the door? How? How to equip myself as I pass through the door, into the dark, or even down into the dark? I'll go home, shut myself in my room, and study the skin and the liver and the pancreas and "hearing tests." I will study coldly, implacably. The window will be closed, maybe it'll already be snowing outside, I'll have to turn everything else down, I won't come down for meals, not even join the others for breakfast; they'll call, I won't answer. Then, one evening a walk through the forest and back, along the stream, past the mill, sit on the bench with a wide view over the countryside.

Then set off on my journey. Back to my room at the hostel, with no light and no sunshine. I'll fix myself something to eat, look at my watch, lie down and not be able to sleep, I'll pace up and down the street, and open my books again. And what about the internship? What will it bring me? How much longer will I be at Schwarzach? What if the assistant is dissatisfied with me? If he thinks, oh dear, I should have given someone else the task, not him? And will I get five hundred schillings, as I do every year? Even if I've been gone quite a long time? Wonder whether the matron knows? Yes, of course, she'll be reminded of the fact that I'm not there at every mealtime. Now I think of the ghostly atmosphere in the staff room. There's a radio there that hasn't worked for years. A clock that ticks, but tells the wrong time. Vases with flowers that are long since dried out. A gray oilcloth spread over the long table, tacked down. Paintings on the walls, scenes from village life, done by a rather fetid academic painter. Books from the nineteenth century, unopened for decades. There I see down one side of the table the registrar, the assistant, the assistant's assistant, the bonesetter, the pediatric surgeon. And on my side of the table the other two interns, the Greek doctor, the new med students. They eat in silence, and sometimes they draw a complicated fracture of the ulna on the table, or the position of an embryo, and the sister who carries in the food then wipes everything off once they're all gone. I walk down the long passages, get lost at the end, where all the doors are suddenly locked and you can't remember which way you came, I bang on a door, and already I'm thinking I'll have to spend the night there, in that room, surrounded by locked doors. I hear footfalls, and I bang on the door with my fists, and the door opens, and the sister says: "Why, doctor, what are you doing in here?" And the sound of that "doctor." Sounds how? And then I try and compare a human being with another human being, both with the same illness, and reacting to it differently. One dies, the other survives as if nothing had been the matter. And both had the same illness. I read, it's almost dark, but I read in my Koltz, a section which explains about diseases of the brain, but the disease the painter has, which is a disease of the brain—what else would it be?—doesn't appear anywhere in

Koltz. And we're talking about a very new book, by a leading authority, just imported from the States.

And then I go to the chapel, only a few yards, because the chapel is built onto the hospital, or is it the hospital is built onto the chapel, I don't know, both of them are several generations old, they have the same thick walls, and both give off the same chill. And then I cross the bridge, and I sit in the café, and I pick up a newspaper. And later, in the middle of the night, I am woken up, because "for you, doctor, an interesting case," there's a new admission. "A fractured atlas, with paraplegia." I pull on my white coat, and follow the nurse who woke me down along the long corridors to the operating room, where the assistant is standing ready, just one or two preparations, and he makes the first incision. "There's almost no light," he says, and the operation gets under way. And continues perhaps until morning, and there's no time to go to the staff room for breakfast. A head needs to be raised a little, a leg wants to be reset, a camphor injection is required, and a blood transfusion. The sisters perform astonishing feats. Never get to bed before eleven, and are back from church already by five, having been heard singing there at half past four. Everywhere, the great white tulips of their bonnets, which manage to flower where everything is dark with despair, where everything else is bleak and bare and inimical. The relatives of the patients who died overnight are standing between the elevator and the bathroom, holding in their hands the last possessions of their brother or sister. About to be dispatched to the cemetery administration. And the smiles of the young nurses put all sadness to flight. What will my future bring? What awaits me? Tomorrow! The day after! I don't want to think about what might be. What will be. What's the future anyway? I don't want to think!

I quickly took a letter to the assistant to the post office. There was the postmistress, a relative of the knacker's, with her back to me, writing something in a ledger. "The painter," she said, taking my letter and stamping it, "the painter hasn't been by in a long time." Earlier, he'd used to get mountains of mail, the postman had had so much to carry for him. And now nothing. Not one letter in all the weeks the painter had been here this time. "He doesn't look well," she said. "Yes," I said, "he's ill."—"Ill?" she said. What was wrong with him. "I don't know what's wrong with him."—"Something serious?"—"Yes," I said, "something serious."—"But why doesn't he get any mail?" That was nothing to do with his being ill. She seemed to think if someone is ill, they will need letters, more than if they're healthy. What else does a person need if he's got his health, she seemed to think. I don't know anything about his postal arrangements, I said. Of course, I couldn't help being struck by the fact that he got no mail. But I didn't want to continue the conversation with the postmistress, and I went out.

Outside the post office, I thought: It must be a terrible thing for his housekeeper, not to know how he is. Where he is. And then I hurried across the village square. I climbed up the steps to the cemetery. There was the knacker, up to his belly in the earth. I had just come from the post office, I said. It was so quiet today, why was that. "I've never known it this quiet," I

said. "Yes," said the knacker, "it is quiet. There's no wind."—
"No," I said. And then I thought of something: "The landlord . . . How did the manslaughter case come about? You
know, that business at the pub," I said. "The manslaughter
case?" he said. "Yes, the manslaughter case. What sort of man
was he?"—"What sort of man?"

He had sat in the inn for a couple of weeks, but got rowdy
every night, and often called for more to drink at three in the
morning. And once the landlord had refused. Then the workman had lashed out with his fists. And the landlord with a
beer glass. "It happens," said the knacker. "They usually get
up afterward and sit together and have a drink and get to be
friends. Didn't happen on this occasion," he said. "But at first,
people thought it wasn't a crime?"—"Yes," said the knacker,
"at first."—"Then how did it come up?"—"Yes," said the
knacker, "how did it come up?"

He picked up his shovel again, and went back to work. I went
over to the children's graves and looked at the photographs
on the tombs. Whey-faces, I thought. Puffy faces. Dead faces.
Faces attacked by birds of prey. When I went back, I passed
the knacker again, and he stopped digging. "Isn't it strange," I
said, "that it's so quiet today?"—"Yes," he said, "it often gets
so quiet, you can't hear nothing but your own heart beating."
I went down to the rectory, and headed off to the larch wood,
away from the village.

. . .

Nothing, not one thing, was mute. Everything continually expressed its pain. "The mountains, you see, are great witnesses to great pain," said the painter. He walked toward the mountain: "People always say: the mountain reaches up into heaven. They never say: the mountain reaches down into hell. Why not?" He said: "Everything is hell. Heaven and earth, and earth and heaven, they're all hell. Do you understand? Above and below are hell, here. But of course nothing reaches into anything else. Do you understand? There is no adjacency." The newly arrived Föhn showed up details on the shady side that normally were not seen. "You see?" said the painter, "all those shadows? They're mountain goats, look!" He drew me closer. "Look!" he said. But I didn't see any. "That mountain always put me in mind of a gigantic catafalque. See!" It's true, the mountain does have the outline of a gigantic catafalque. "In summer I sit here for hours, and study it all," he said. "Insight? I don't think so. I just look at everything. So that it doesn't kill me." He now went on ahead. "Death doesn't want us to occupy ourselves with it," he said. "Come along, you go first. And that's why I continually occupy myself with death!" Was I not cold? Was I not shivering? I wasn't shivering. "In the Föhn, nothing seems to make sense. Everything you say seems nonsense. Religions dupe us about the fact that everything is nonsense, you know. Christianity is nonsense. Christianity. Yes. Prayer is a false state of consciousness. One that turns everything into nothing. Prayer. Absolutely." But the human animal liked to live in such a false state of consciousness, with misleading impressions, "that pressed his head down to the ground. Suddenly, one renounces all falsehood. Renounces unchastity, chastity, weakness, the opposite of weakness, renunciation itself. Then everything comes clear. There have been such dark moments in my life that left me unable to speak finally, and that are killing off and will kill off what existed in me, and exists in me, and will never exist again.

"I often tried to come closer to the truth, to this understanding of truth, even if only through silence. Through nothing. I didn't succeed. I never got beyond the attempts. There was always an ocean in the way, my inability to tie her heart, as people say, to mine. Just as I never succeed in coming into harmony with the truth, so nothing in my life succeeded, except my dying. I never wanted to die, and yet never tried to compel anything more rigorously. To make the world die in me, and myself die in the world, and everything to cease as though it had never been. Night is much darker yet than any notion of night, and day is just a gloomy and unbearable interval." He wanted to go home. We walked up the ravine.

"The policeman is another one enjoying carnal relations with the landlady," he said. "I have made some observations. They fit my theory. I get up and go to the window and see the policeman. I hear a conversation outside, which woke me. An exchange between the landlady and the policeman. At first I thought the policeman was on duty. That maybe the landlady got him to come for some reason. But then I could see from the state of his clothes that he had spent the night with the landlady. His uniform was partly unbuttoned. He walked back to the village with his rifle on his shoulder. I noticed once before a certain tension between the policeman and the landlady. I wasn't mistaken. The disordered clothing and the policeman's whole manner indicate that something tran-

spired between himself and the landlady that night. I'm a
light sleeper, I wake up at the least sound. That's why I see
more than others do. It's not pleasant. My suspicion is confirmed: the policeman stands in for the knacker, when the latter is away. It's strange the people that come together. One
would have thought they must be mutually repellent, but no,
they attract one another. The policeman is very young.
Younger than you." When we stood outside the inn, he said:
"I had thought of asking you up to my room, but I won't
now. Perhaps we could put it off till tomorrow." He opened
the door and with his stick pushed me into the public bar,
where a lot of people were sitting. It was twelve already.

"The walls are hollow. Even soft rapping will make itself
heard down into the foundations," he said. Since there was a
rushing stream a hundred yards further on, the inn was subject to a continuous, but therefore all the more dangerous
shaking. "The plaster in my room is crumbling," said the
painter. "The stucco rose pattern is cracked from top to bottom, and way beyond. There are great patches of damp. If
you lay your hand on them, you will feel cold. The cowbells
in autumn are said to have a deleterious effect on the fabric.
You hear the water barrels down in the kitchen with a noise
like thunder. Not to mention the beer barrels when they are
trundled inside. Of course the termite labors day and night.
But I like all that. It doesn't scare me. Quite the contrary. I
have the feeling I am at home."

For the painter, everything is terrible. "Every so often new
tunnels through the walls are completed, and then there's a

trickle of sawdust," he says. "If there's a break in the cold, then the window frames creak, and the floorboards, as if they were exhaling." Down in the cellar there was a crack made by an earthquake once. Clocks and paintings had rattled against the walls. Lamps shattered, some floorboards had to be relaid. Carpenters and masons were kept busy for four or five days. Apparently, Weng was situated on the eastern extremity of a fault line that came up from the south to the northern foothills of the Alps. In the vicarage cellar there was a rock split in two that one could view. "For the earthquake, it was the work of a single second," says the painter. The rock had split asunder, the vicarage itself had sustained no damage whatsoever. Since that time, various stories had circulated about the "earthquake rock" in the vicarage. "Every place has its miracles. Did you know I once found a pair of blackbirds in the attic, dried and pressed together? A pair of blackbirds. Fossilized. As if their song were still filling the air." Summer was "warm and full of apprehension." Winter "cold and strange." An elderberry bush had suddenly pushed through the rear wall of the house. "A jolt in the night. As if a hand had suddenly moved everything by one handbreadth . . . I was here once, it was the end of October, when I had the sensation that the song of birds that had been there all spring and all summer had frozen in the air. And was waiting for deliverance. For the first warm days . . . Profound shadows" were often projected by the inn. Just as the whole depression in which the inn is situated is fertile ground for dowsers.

There are many reasons for the painter to be in Weng. A sudden gust of an ill wind was enough to set him down here. The inn has always disappointed him. As he says, "It disappoints even the undemanding guest." It was a nook "where an existence can knit itself together." He often thought of it as resembling a cemetery like the one at San Michele in Venice, "where the dead are stacked in layers . . . Have you not noticed the way people live in cemeteries? That big cities are big cemeteries? That small towns are lesser cemeteries? Villages yet smaller ones? That a bed is a coffin? Clothes are graveclothes? That everything is a readying for death? The whole of existence is a trying out for laying out and burial." The idea of situating the inn on this deadly spot, "where nothing has ever stood," was inexplicable. The landlord's father was effectively given the site in the hollow. He won it in a bet. No one remembers what the bet was about. Leftover railroad ties were used in the construction of the house. Old bricks, laboriously tapped clean by the builders themselves. "Cement they stole from the storehouses of the cellulose factory." They had the inn ready in four years. Three days after it was finished, the builder died. "Isn't it always the way that people die when the house is finished? Or perhaps a little before? But always on the summit, or just below?" The landlady had been unable to pay for the railroad ties in ten years. "But when the state's your creditor, you take your time," he said. "The walls are so thin, you can hear people's thoughts through them." Their bad consciences. Upstairs and down. "The landlady sometimes goes around and swills out the dirt with bucketloads of water. Also the traces of slaughtering days at Christmas and Easter . . . Fresh coat of paint every fifteen years . . . The wallpaper patterns go from room to room." Electric light had been introduced shortly before the last war.

.   .   .

"Another reason I'm here is the abattoir smell that lingers over the village." He went around in that smell with his pants belt pulled tight, as if to cut it off. "Sometimes my methods get to be too much for me." There were a thousand references to the torment, the myriad awfulnesses, from the second you awoke in the morning. "The damp, infertile soil that the inn stands on . . . All imaginable diseases are continually germinating in this soil. It's not possible to be so healthy that being here won't cripple you inside and out."

Among other things, he had occasionally worked as a substitute teacher, teaching at various elementary schools. "Conspiracies against myself." Since, as was known, there was a monstrous shortage of teachers, he had always been able to find employment. It surprised him that he had never been called upon to take any sort of proficiency test, "not one." The very first time he had put himself forward as a substitute, he had found himself hired. "I was hungry, I thought I would try and get something at a school I passed every day. They wanted to put me in a classroom right away, though they didn't know the first thing about me. I said I hadn't even written out an application. They didn't want to let me go. Can you understand that? There were loads and loads of schools then, and no teachers. Far too few teachers. I handed in my application to the official in the local education department, who processed it immediately, in my presence. The official should have presented it to several other officials in the ministry, before it went to the highest authority for approval. In the event he took it up to his superior himself, who immediately gave it the nod. That same day I went back to the school, and was taken on. I was given a classroom in the school basement, with electric lighting on all the time. I moved schools several times a year. In between times I didn't work. For as long as possible. As long as I wasn't compelled to have any dealings with the art world. Sooner go back to school than have dealings with the art world. Sometimes I needed support from my brother, who always had extraordinary ties with extraordinarily influential individuals. He was useful to me, even though I never approached him for help. Of course, I never told him about being a substitute teacher. But as you know, word gets out . . . It's impossible to do anything without word getting out, without it becoming public knowledge. Public knowledge in particular in those circumstances where what you most fear is something becoming public knowledge . . ." In fact, he had no aptitude for dealing with children, he was incapable of teaching them anything. "But the school authorities never asked me about any of that. They took me without a single question. Asked me only whether I was happy with the money I would have earned, had I decided to stay. The children bossed me . . . The tragedy of it was that the children bossed me from the start. Even though they were frightened of me. Of course the relationship between teacher and pupils is far from ideal," he said. "Children are monsters . . . Powerful and cruel, like monsters." The only way he had been able to restrain them had been by showing them from the outset how unpredictable he could be. "I beat them too . . . But it hurt me. It hurt me so much, I was frightened of myself." His way home after class had been "paved with fear." In spite of which, it had been the best thing for him, being a substitute teacher. Rather than using his art to pay his way. "I always hated the art world." Accusations against the world around him had always really been accusations against himself. "Everything is

your own fault. The things that make you suffer are your own
fault. You can always make an end. If you don't make an end,
you suffer. Suffer horribly. Stop suffering, and make an end,
why don't you?" he said. During his lessons, "which might
have been taught by anyone who could count up to fifty, and
speak and write three correct sentences, for instance the sentence: 'I leave home with my father, and come back alone,'
or: 'My mother is kind to me,' or: 'The days are bright, but
the nights are dark,' I read my Pascal all the time. You know
Pascal! Even then I read nothing but Pascal!" It was a remarkable thing that he had only ever taught in ancient, dilapidated, already half-shut-down schools. "Even the way I spoke
should have warned those responsible against taking me on,
against getting involved with me." But one shouldn't over-
estimate substitute teaching either. It was basically "a martyrdom which I suffered in patience, because everything else
would have been much worse." There had been frequent
complaints from parents to the headmaster. "They complained about all kinds of things. And the heads had no
option but to have me transferred. To request a transfer for
me. Then I would be transferred." After two years he might
find himself back at a school which he was all too familiar
with "from many fits of weakness." "But basically they just
used me as a stand-in for sick teachers."

"Substitute teachers have no rights," he said. "And they only
make about two-thirds of what a regular teacher makes."
There was admittedly a trade union for substitutes. He had
never joined this union because he had never in his life joined
any organization, group, or collective. "It would be doing
such violence against myself, it would no longer be me," he

said. The substitute teachers' union had kept trying to force him to join. "Even though I was only an occasional substitute . . . Just imagine, they sometimes waited for me in the street. They made threats against me." But they didn't know how stubborn he could be when it came to sticking up for one of his principles. "In addition to the substitute teachers' union, there was also a 'substitute teachers' association,' which was an informal initiative on the part of the substitutes. They meet every Saturday afternoon. Apparently they pass resolutions. What resolutions? I have no idea what resolutions. How they mean to oppose their union. How to support their union against other unions. How to oppose the school authorities. The state. Their enemies. Anyone they feel is doing them wrong." Apparently, there was also a "substitute teachers' fund," for the support of the widows and orphans of substitutes. "I've got nothing against such support . . . But basically I don't care how worthy a cause can be, I'm not joining . . ." He was already disgusted when the journal *Substitute Teacher* occasionally peeked out of his mailbox. "They sent me that twice a month. Whether I wanted it or not. I never paid for it. I never ordered it. And I've never read it." To his pupils—"they all had the same face"—he had always been presented as "the new stand-in." "Psychologically, it was a smack in the face for me . . ." The first thing he had said to his pupils had always been: "Fresh air! Open the windows, let's get some air in here! This classroom needs air! Windows open, open!" Then he had asked them to say their names. When a name was incomprehensible to him, he asked for it another time, "better articulated," and written up on the board. "Most of the pupils weren't able to write their names." He had always taught first grade. "On one occasion, a second grade. But that made me ill." It had been irresponsible on the part of the school authorities to put him up in front of new first-graders, as their first teacher, because "the first teacher you have is the decisive teacher." In fact, he had never hated anything in his life as much as classrooms, and the teachers in those classrooms . . . "But that's what you must do, those things that you always loathed, those things that always repelled you." His most worthwhile hours as a substitute teacher had been spent taking his classes to a park. "We are instructed to go to a park with our classes once a week, and explain to them everything that grows there: flowers, trees, shrubs . . . to tell them the country of origin of the respective flowers and trees and shrubs. I never told them the name of one single flower or tree. Nor gave them one country of origin. Not of a single flower or tree. Because I am opposed to the enlightenment of children where plants are concerned, in fact, where nature is concerned. The more you know about nature, the less you know about it, the less worth it has to you. The keen ones, who came to me with the names of flowers and trees and the names of their countries of origin, I simply told to shut up." He had always sat down on a bench and immersed himself in his Pascal, and let the children do as they pleased. "I just had to be sure no one got hurt. Or lost." The summer months had been the most pleasant. "I also liked going to the swimming pool with my children . . . At the time I was reading a lot of Maupassant and Poe and Stifter. If they got too loud, I shot them an angry look. Threatened them with punishment. Mostly, the look was enough. They were scared of me, even though, as I've already said, they bossed me about. Most of them were spoiled, and I tried to unspoil them. I tried. But there's not much you can do in such a brief time as I tended to spend in my schools . . . The system needs to be changed. Turned on its head. Do you know that our schools are among the most antiquated in the world? It's a scandal! Take the appearance of our schools, crumbling, neglected, dilapidated, well, that's what they're like on the inside as well. We should really be concerned about the sort of kids that come out of them!" The parents' complaints that were regularly sent to his various headmasters generally referred to his "offensive opinions," which he was accused of "ramming down the children's throats," like "medicine." "'Offensive' didn't mean anything indecent or anything. They just used it to refer to anything they disagreed with." They complained that he talked to his classes too much. "Then others complained I talked to them too little." He had never been opposed to children's jokes. "But they never made that many jokes in my classes." In the first year of elementary school, the children were usually even more apprehensive than the teachers. "A large proportion aren't really at school at all, they're in a state of terror . . . School buildings are just premises of terror for them. The fear of school is the worst fear there is. Most people are ruined by it. If not in childhood, then later on. It's still possible to die from fear of school at sixty." He had imagined, when putting himself forward as a substitute teacher, that he would escape from his solitude, which he had been simply unable to master. "But in front of my classes, I was more alone than ever . . . Thoughts of suicide came to him once in the middle of a lesson. I still remember the classroom and the circumstances. I remember the children. As a substitute teacher I had the advantage of a certain sum of money that was paid to me on the fifteenth of every month . . . But of course a life as a substitute teacher is simply atrocious."

· · ·

The landlady now puts a compress on his swollen ankle. I finally induced him to allow it. "As hot as possible, and about a quarter of an inch thick," I said to the landlady. "You sound as though you know what you're talking about," she said. The painter just mocked me. He only put up with the compress so that I would leave him alone. "It's the first time I've allowed such a young person to tell me what to do, and agreed to such a senseless procedure." And he laughed. It was the first time I had seen him laughing. He was like someone who hadn't laughed for years. For decades. Someone who's never had anything to laugh about. He's laughing now, I thought, for all those years. His laughing tired him out. It was as strange to him as an incision in the belly is to most people. "What are you doing with me?" I stand by his bedside and watch the landlady smear the blackish-brown ointment on a rag of linen. Quite proficiently. She lifts up the painter's leg, and wraps the rag around it. "Not too tight," I say. "What a palaver!" says the painter. The landlady says: "Now you've got to lie there and be quiet, Herr Strauch!"

The painter asked her what there was to eat. "I can't eat that!" he said when she told him. I look at his room. It's so dark, it's almost impossible to see anything. When the landlady goes, he sighs very loudly. His room is bigger than mine. Much gloomier. That's because of the drawn curtains. Which I took down on my first day. "I always keep mine drawn . . . If you like, you can borrow my book. Borrow my Pascal!" I say I have my Henry James. "Ah yes, your Henry James." He lies there like a corpse. "Are you interested in poetry?" he asks me. "Not really," I say. "I'm not interested in anything made up," he says. There's a clock ticking somewhere. I look for it, but can't see it anywhere. It must be in the commode. Smell of the washstand. The stove is glowing, but it's not creating any heat. "I'm always cold," he says. "What is it that makes pain unbearable? What is pain, if not pain?" It's so quiet, his breath almost bursts the window. I look at his yellow face in the dark, now not saying anything anymore, so I say "goodnight," and go.

Sixteenth Day

I want to make a record of the fact that Strauch had a dream last night, "a dream," he said, "a dream that had nothing in common with all my other dreams. I have to tell you, it was the dream of a terminal unhappiness, a dream of ending, of a simply overwhelming ending. I dreamed of a color, which doesn't distinguish this dream from others, my dreams, I may say, all begin with a color, I assume a primary color, one of the three or four—are there four?—primary colors; thereafter, the dream mutated rapidly and extremely purposefully into the relationship between colors, where all colors have the same significance, all of them still toneless, into the darkness of the colors, into their blackness and their luminosity, toneless, soundless, then suddenly, accelerating into a sound, a solitary linear sound, and then: the sounds gained as the colors receded, suddenly this dream, profoundly unlike all my other dreams, was only sound, not to say: music, though that is inapplicable in this instance, misleading, distracting. There was a sound, it appeared, with no beginning and no

end, it was there, and it developed into an ambitious, an infernal sound, I can think of no other way of saying this, I don't
have the words, you understand, even though I strain my
memory I haven't the words, a sound, and then a monstrous
noise, such a monstrous noise I could no longer hear anything: in this space, which was and is an endless space, one of
many such endless spaces (a notion that always means to
destroy me!). In this space, in which black and white were
spoiled, brutally spoiled by an amusical-celestial force roaring
and shrilling, two policemen were tumbling, tumbling as if in
space, suddenly there were three of them tumbling, I can't
really say they were floating, actually they were tumbling
as in the clutches of a fantastic, all-embracing, immodest
rigging-loft in a theater, in the immodest, fantastic, all-
embracing theatrical rigging-loft of infinity . . ."

Toward evening, there was a blizzard, and I watched waves of
snow blow against the window. While the window had initially darkened from the approaching blizzard, once the snow
started to fall, sheeting against the inn, it grew very light. I
was reading in the newspaper about people who were
demanding this or that, or who knew this or that, and some
others who neither demanded nor knew anything, of cities
that were sinking, and heavenly bodies that were no longer
far away.

The landlady was home, and her two daughters were doing
their homework in the kitchen.

.   .   .

The knacker is doing his rounds, I thought, the engineer is issuing orders across the river.

The rector is sitting in his rectory, and the butcher in the pitch black of his abattoir.

The cobbler is running his thumb along a seam.

The teacher is drawing his curtains, and feeling afraid.

They are all afraid. I thought of Schwarzach.

All at once, I'm standing in the operating room once more, and lifting up a dead head. I take the elevator down into the basement to pick up a pair of crutches, and then back up to the third floor, where someone wants the crutches.

I think of my mother. She will be wondering: why isn't he writing? They will all be wondering why isn't he writing. I don't know the answer. I can't write to anyone. Not even the assistant!

I look out the window again, and see nothing. That's how violent the snowstorm is.

. . .

Then I hear voices in the hallway, the first of the workmen, brushing the snow off their clothes, stamping their boots so hard the whole building shakes.

But it's still much too early to go down for supper. When I hear the voices, I picture the men, I see their faces, though some remain dark for me, and don't acquire definition.

I read my Henry James, without understanding what I've read: I seem to remember women following a coffin at a funeral, a railway train, a destroyed town, somewhere in England. The noise of the customers slowly transfers itself from the hallway to the public bar. Now everything sounds a little more muffled. A door is yanked open, falls shut. Then it sounds as if a barrel is being rolled somewhere. A couple of men are laughing while they wash and brush up in the kitchen, where the landlady always leaves a jug of water and a towel out. The blizzard is unremitting. I get up and go downstairs.

In the hallway I run into the painter. No sooner had he got out of the village than he found himself caught up in the blizzard. Suddenly he hadn't been able to see anything, the snow had wrapped him up like a bunch of rags, "rags of snow . . . During the blizzard, I had such thoughts, no, not thoughts, but access to thoughts, access to some mysterious, usually

unavailable landscape . . . Lots of closed doors, you understand . . . I knocked on them, and shouted and yelled, and
finally pounded them with my arms and legs. These scenes
and the concomitant facts, this dereliction . . ."

He was very agitated. "Unworthy, you know. I'm unable to
explain myself, the truth, the propensity for the truth is so difficult, that human faculties aren't sufficient . . . it's all a matter of fragments, suggestions, all of thought is just one never
experienced clarity . . . for nothing. So much material. Those
vast proportions! This unworthy orientation . . . all human
misery struck me as luminous enough! A blizzard is certainly
a deathly process . . . but what is a blizzard? How does it
come about? A mutiny, miraculous . . . my account is nothing
but fear, nothing but a child's fear of an uncommon spectacle . . ." The engineer had come upon the painter lying on
the street, and lifted him into his car, and taken him along.
"But for the engineer, I would have lost my life in the blizzard," he said.

The policeman had got to that point where hormones suddenly grab hold of the entire organism, and youth vanishes in
the flashing of an eye. "This fine face," said the painter, "how
much longer will it remain fine? Will it be spared the general
disfigurement of all life? No. Some bestial quality makes its
way across such a face by night, and leaves its marks on it:
first of all dimly, then unignorably, and finally remorselessly.
In the end, we will turn away from such a face, because we
are unable to bear it anymore, and we will search for another
one, not yet disfigured, still beautiful. Then we will be simi-

larly fascinated by this new face, until it takes the same course as its predecessor. And so on with all faces. Incidentally, the policeman has many of the same traits as you. But I'm sure that's just youth, just generic youth." Then: "When I was your age, I had already seen a lot, and had more or less withdrawn from everything. By the time I was twenty-three, I was pretty much done with everything. That's an alien feeling to you, I can imagine. You haven't yet withdrawn from anything, not conclusively. Nor has the policeman either. I'm discussing a juncture, a block, a barrier for certain pursuits . . . a moment of the sort I mentioned earlier in our discussions . . . where everything falls apart, you know, where your voice is sodden, and the pee soaks into your pants, even when you don't want it to . . . The policeman's just as quiet as you. Always was. How do you get to be a policeman? How do you get to be something so revolting? A uniformed official. How? Just by slipping into the uniform? Slipping into the loathsomeness? At first reluctantly, shall we say, but then habitually, and finally with something mechanical and everyday about it, even with a feeling of belonging? Belonging to what? The people at the inn are poison to that policeman. But he's long infested anyway. He's given up reading books, given up anything that's nothing to do with the police. Grubby characters are forever trying to sully the others, that's what makes them grubby; and sooner or later they always succeed, as we may see with ghastly clarity. Just as I'm going around with you now, so previously, a year ago, or earlier this year, up until a few weeks ago, I was going about with the policeman, but now he's withdrawn, doesn't often come to the inn, at night, and I know what he's come for, but you only ever see him stepping out of the shadows, only notice him once he's given you a fright. I think he's lost, well lost."

. . .

He explains how memory shifts from unconfined joy to sorrow, and light turns into darkness, just as morning becomes noon, noon afternoon, and afternoon evening. How homecoming comes to feel like escape once did. How neglect and incapacity make for torment, bitterness, and despair. "What's the danger?" he asks. Putting it to use? Putting what to use? A man watches a woman who only lately was delighted with herself, with him, now falling like a stone into the wretchedness of pregnancy. Her voice is suddenly tired, and her heart jaded, she just wants to be left alone. Strength of character starts to fade, there is nothing left. Antipathy hurts quite amazingly. Serenity becomes disfavor, then open hostility, then killing and letting live. The jolly climb to the peak ends up in the inn in the valley with aggravated assault. A happy, enchanting turn of phrase suddenly brings about a quarrel. It's the machinery that thinks and that governs the man. Admiration turns into reproach, character swiftly and reflexively into lack of character. Dreams turn into the destruction of dreams, and poems turn into piles that are driven home. He knows how morale comes to grief, and primal happiness turns into a lie. How a mean instinct finds its way into a million receptor centers, and wipes them all out. "Who knows anything about the moment, but everything shrivels up in a moment, the extinction of everything is the work of a moment." He explains the air to me which drowns one color, and allows another to climb into the unbearable. "With my grandparents," he said, "where happiness came and went, and often stayed for hours, unobserved of course, there we could marvel at the way a filthy mood suddenly took control, which froze everything that made up this mood, and finally ensured that it was forgotten: the walk in the woods, the sleigh ride over the frozen lake, the reading aloud, the clean pure water. A hand moved, and there was no contradiction." Just as crimes and accidents were brought on by great happiness. "The result of thoughtlessness, which can be so beautiful, it can move mountains. Compared to a wind, which will suddenly expose a tree. With the sea's rough justice. It's baffling how everyone calls for a lasting happiness," he said. "Since all anything has is resale value." Ornaments that charmed entire Sundays would suddenly turn into grotesques, just as people turned into animals and vice versa, enough to put anyone to flight. Blue went black, and black to blue. Top turns to bottom. Just as a street turned into another street, no one quite could say where. "A man never knows the decisive moment." Everything flowed like rivers which were condemned by nature to carry greater or lesser quantities of water.

During the blizzard, a fire broke loose in the neighboring village, which turned a large farmhouse to ashes. The site of the fire is five or six miles' distance from Weng. A lot of people ran over there, even while the blizzard was still raging, fires exert an irresistible pull on people. They leave everything standing and have nothing but the inferno in their heads. When I met the painter in the entrance, he said: "Did you see the knacker charge in here? He says the fire was started by an electric spark. Did you see him giving his information? He plunged in the way a herald in Greek tragedy does. Typical of people," he said, "both dementing and demented, just as they both govern and are governed. The knacker and the landlady, they're both good examples of fires as they go through the

people. You see," he said, "on the one side there's the bearer
of news, on the other the receiver of news, the astonished,
the sensation-hungry. It takes the landlady to give any importance to what the knacker has to say. Then the landlady takes
over the knacker's role, and then others take her role, and
his, and eventually an entire population is busy with the
news . . ." The fire had cost the lives of hundreds of pigs.
Men with cloths wrapped round their faces had tried to rescue the pigs who had broken loose, but then the pigs had run
back into the flames, cows as well, ducks, all the poultry had
gone up in flames. Everything burned or choked in the fire.
The fire engines completely helpless, because all the wells are
frozen, none of the streams carry any water . . . In the space
of a few seconds, huge flames had sprung up, which were
kept down by the clouds. There had been a flickering in the
sky that they all had seen. Albeit, there had been nothing to
see from the inn. You can't see anything from here. You can't
see anything from the hollow. "A terrible fire! The Weng fire
brigade have come out, didn't you hear?" I didn't hear anything. "No one in the inn heard anything. Nothing is heard in
the inn, everything passes overhead. You have to imagine the
dry wood, the hay, the straw barn was like a glowing cube of
fire, as it finally broke apart. Hoses without water, fire chiefs
standing by helplessly, their crews unrolling the hoses, and
then no water . . . Where was it going to come from?
Unimaginable, people are so helpless. A colossal scene as the
roof frame comes crashing down! I saw such a thing once
before, in a Bavarian village, when I was walking down the
road, completely blinded by snow, trying not to suffocate in
it, when all at once sparks were spinning round my head,
more and more sparks, not just white flakes, but red also; I
ran in the direction from where the red flakes seemed to be

blowing . . . Left of me, up on a hill, I saw a burning roof frame behind the wall of snow. The whole horizon was on fire. Perhaps I was thinking of rescuing someone or something, but the spectacle was ringing in my ears and warming the soles of my feet! As I soon saw, I was the first person to discover the fire. Great waves of heat washed up to me. I was still a hundred yards from the fire when I heard creaking and groaning and breaking and finally also screams, and then suddenly alarmed people were running around, *out* of the fire, or *into* the fire. Picture it to yourself: it was night, people were in their beds, they ran as they were, in their nightgowns and nightshirts in the snow, burning torches falling down in the snow, it hissed the way it does when you extinguish a burning candle in snow, you know, and then the roof tree came down! At first it seemed to buckle, and then it came down with a tremendous crash. And then there was the bellowing of the cattle that weren't able to get away, because the doors were all pinned shut from the incredible pressure from above. The whole thing happened very fast, in under twenty minutes. The firemen braved the flames, pulled people out, but they were already half-dead, or fell down dead in the snow. It was pure chance that I saw it at all, it was because I was late getting home, from the house I was living in at the time I wouldn't have been able to see anything, it was built in a hollow, like the inn. As it transpired, the owner of the house and his wife both died in the flames. And another three or four other people as well, who were working there. A couple of the servants were taken to the hospital with burns, and received treatment for months, and in one case, as I learned, for years. Their lives, of course, were ruined. When the knacker came dashing in, I immediately remembered that fire, I've never forgotten it. Then, as now, there were rumors of arson. Now, as then, poor people set off for the site of the fire with their rucksacks, to try and pick up pieces of beef and pork and scraps of poultry. Emergency slaughters were carried out on the spot. You know, anyone's allowed to help himself to a burned carcass. Whatever was there to be picked up, people picked up. There are people who are just waiting for a fire to break out, and then head off there immediately, sometimes in cars, to try and loot whatever they can. They turn up with slaughtering tools, with axes and knives, and they chop everything into pieces. A fire is an extraordinary spectacle! A grotesque spectacle!" At ten o'clock, I was still sitting in the public bar, because the knacker couldn't stop talking about it, he kept starting over afresh, all the while missing tricks he could have picked up, because he had a king or an ace or whatever, and then the engineer came by, he had been at a dance somewhere, and he reported it was arson. There were people being questioned already. A group of police and court investigators was at work, and would be at work all night. A large insurance deal that had been concluded only the day before was almost certain proof that the owner had set fire to his own house.

Seventeenth Day

It was arson. But it wasn't the farmer, as everyone supposed, who set fire to the house, but one of his farmhands, who didn't know the insurance was in place, and who wanted to damage his master. It is known why: there is talk of a "relationship" between the farmer and the farmhand, of which the farmer's wife, who also died in the blaze, was informed. And so the farmer stands to receive a large sum of money. Apparently, he wants to invest it in a factory in a Tyrolean valley, and not have anything more to do with agriculture. They found his wife at the back of the house, crushed by a falling beam. The assumption is that she ran back into the building to find her little boy, but the little boy was faster than she was, and got out of the room by himself; then, as she rushed back out of the house, having avoided the flames and smoke, the beam fell on her head. In the dark they clambered over her body several times without realizing it, they supposed she was in the building, under the wreckage, among the animals that were burned to charred ruins, blackish-brown lumps of matter, with horns or hooves protruding from it in some cases, looking as stiff and rigid as cast iron, and giving off a frightful smell, which I now seem to remember having smelled around the inn as well. Our policeman had to force people away, strangers come to loot, with his rifle butt, and even hit the odd one a blow over the head, when they refused to do as they were told. A doctor had arrived, but too late. They were able to save the tractor, on which the farmer had driven clear of the burning house. The landlady is going to the wife's burial, she knows the family. "A large farm," she said. As a girl, she had once been employed there, with her sister. "The whole of one summer." Now they are looking everywhere for the farmhand who started the fire. The policeman duly went up to the inn early in the morning to ask questions. But no man who answered the description of the wanted man had ever shown his face in her inn, the landlady said. The arsonist comes from Carinthia, "where all bad lots come from," as the landlady says, and had only been working at the farm from late fall. The police think he may have gone home, but they want to keep an open mind. It was his day off, and he was wearing his Sunday best before leaving the house. Afterward, during the fire, the farmer had recalled that he had taken his little suitcase with him as well. Generally, such people, once they have perpetrated their crime, tend to turn up at friends' or relatives', and are found by the police. They would see where they found him, if they found him at all. But usually they find people like that in a matter of days, if not hours. Because they won't have gone very far, they don't have the means. Or the courage either. They will hide out in a hay barn or a wayside hut and will be found, half-starved or completely starved. If the farm had burned down just a day earlier, the farmer wouldn't have stood to get a single cent for it. Whereas now he'll receive an enormous sum. The fire-setter must have miscalculated by just one day. "You know," the painter said, "the whole country, as you see, is full of criminals. Full of murderers and arsonists."

"It's oppressive," said the painter, "really oppressive today. The smell of the fire is everywhere. Do you feel like going up and having a look? I don't myself. If there were a sleigh, but there aren't any sleighs. It's too much trouble." He had sat in the kitchen of the poorhouse and talked with the mother superior, and some of the kitchen women. "They make soup from potato peels," he said. Gypsies had passed through the village, and been given a hot meal at the poorhouse. "They came with a horse and cart. Part of a larger group that stopped down at the station. From Croatia. The mother superior gave them all bread and a medal. The Gypsies are left over, left over from a world that's sick of itself. They wanted to sing, but the mother superior didn't want any singing, and so they didn't sing, and they packed the bread in their cart, and drove off..." He said: "And then I went through the village. But the weather, as the teacher likes to say, is stupid. The newborn are dying all over the place. Emergency slaughterings are undertaken every day. I've heard the butcher giving out orders nonstop. His wooden clogs against the aluminum tub of blood. The glistening of the calf's intestines as he pulled them out. The warm, sweet smell of them! You know, they still brain them here, they refuse to shoot them, the way they do everywhere else. One man grabs hold of the ears and tail, the other clubs it down. I expect you're familiar with the sound of an animal collapsing onto the cement floor of an abattoir. The mountains are suddenly so near, you think you'll hit your brains against them. The whole village is littered with tufts of hair and scraps of hide. I tell them to tidy them away, and shovel snow over the puddles of blood, but who listens to me. In the countryside, the paths are always sodden with blood. I went into the butcher's and told him he should get his apprentice to sweep the hair away from the entrance to the slaughterhouse, and cover over the bloodstains, and then I didn't leave till the fellow had swept and covered it. The butcher said there was going to be a big lavish affair in the next village because of the farmer's dead wife, they had come and placed orders with him. And that was why he had been doing some fresh killing. He needs to supply them tonight." They had a sledload of meat to deliver to the community center in O.

We had reached the place where the Klamm suddenly opens out. It was a long way round, but Strauch was dead set on going there. I had read him a sentence from my Henry James book, and he interpreted it in the most wonderful way, this incomprehensible, to me incomprehensible sentence, which kept me awake all night (I have to say, I was never in all my life afflicted with this restlessness, I had gone down from my room into the public bar, and then walked out of the house into the cold air, into the "graveyard chill," I wandered into the ravine, I had thrown a jacket over my nightshirt, slipped into my trousers, and was walking "into the unconsciousness of things"; but I am unable to explain any of it, I can't write anything down that happened, neither of that nor of anything else)—when the painter interpreted this Henry James sentence to me, and the Klamm lay in front of us, the snowed-in approach to the Klamm, he stopped suddenly and told me to stand two paces behind him. He didn't turn to face me, even though he suddenly started talking to me. "You see," he said, "this tree comes on and says the line I told it to say, an incomprehensible line of poetry, a line that will turn the world on its head, a so-called line against God, you understand me! This tree walks on from the left, the cloud comes on from the right, the cloud with its softer voice. I view myself as the creator of this afternoon drama, this tragedy! This comedy! Now listen, the music has come in right on cue. The music plays on the difference between my words and all others. Listen, the instruments are perfecting it, my tragedy, my comedy, the instruments, all the high-pitched and low-pitched instruments, music is the only mistress of the double killing-ground, the only mistress of the double pain, the only mistress of the double forbearance . . . Music, you hear me . . . language approaches music, but language hasn't the strength to circumvent music, it has to directly approach music, language is nothing but weakness, the language of nature as much as the *language of the darkness of nature,* as the language of the depth of leave-taking . . . You hear me: I was *in* this music, I *am* in this music, I am made of this language, I am contained in the quiet poetry of this afternoon . . . Do you see *my theater?* Do you see the theater of apprehension? The theater of God's un-self-sufficiency? What God?" He turned to me and said: "God is a cosmic embarrassment! An immense embarrassment of the stars! But," he said, and set his index finger against his mouth: "let's not talk about that. I want the tree to finish its lines, I want the stream to finish its lines, I want the sky to finish its lines, and I want Hell to master the rationale of its fires, to the very end. I want these fires, you must know. I want these shadows, I want these shadows to kill . . . to kill each and every thing . . . I have compassion with this tragedy, with this com- edy, I have *no* compassion with this tragedy, this comedy, this self-invented tragicomedy, with these self-invented shadows, with these torments of shadows, with these shadow tor- ments, with this endless sadness . . ." He said: "Such a spec- tacle is a product of absurdity, of divine absurdity, such a spectacle, you see, you must know, is nothing but laughter . . . And now listen," said the painter, "the world arises into the air from its own dark, just as air, just as the water in the air, the relation between the air and the other air . . . Yes," said Strauch, "and now I'm going to clap my hands, quite simply clap my hands, I'm going to clap my hands and bang my head against the most sensitive point of the universe, and the whole thing was just a specter, just a specter of a ghost, you understand, just a ghostly specter." We walked into the village. He said: "Sometimes exhaustion comes into my head like a self-dispersed theater, like some- thing endlessly musical-demoniacal, and destroys me. It destroys me on the way to inability to be myself, on the way to the smallest, most remorseful tranquillity in my memory, and my ravaged heart." He said: "For me it might have been enough simply to say, tree, forest, rock, air, earth, but for you, and for the world around, that's not enough . . . You suddenly find yourself manufacturing a trauma, a drama, a comedy, a worm's cast of a comedy . . . And sometimes nature will wring one's neck, *nature without simplicity,* and then you see: the endless complications of terrible nature. Then, finally, everything is incomprehensible, ever more incomprehensible! All I had wanted to say was: 'Here comes the tree . . .' Nothing more. 'The air is learning its lines . . .' Nothing more. Come on, let's go, and let's not be scared anymore."

"The depredations of the forest are spoiling the balance of nature," he said, as we were standing by the edge of the larch wood, there where you can plummet down vertically into the river, opposite the "sarcophagus." "If these human assaults continue in their present exploitative fashion for another hundred years or so, then wherever we look in the world, we will only see these ghastly scenes of dying forests." He said: "Each time I look at it, this landscape looks uglier to me. It's ugly and menacing and full of wicked memory particles, a landscape that can really dismember a man. With its glooms and its savage herds and its accumulated devastation where the workers are being put upon. Unexceptionally malignant ravines, cracks, stains, disheveled shrubs, split trunks. All hostile. And regardless. On top of everything else, infested with the stink of cellulose. The birds fly up completely helplessly in summer, not knowing where they're going, and then there's the darkness of the actual rock face: you'd think you were suffocating. Nowhere is the cold so great, nowhere is the heat so unbearable. This thinking that it's all death, you know, this gloom, the monstrously generic nature of it all . . . without question, death is the limitless, the most successful moment is death . . . All future hope is in death." Then: "What is the mass that misunderstands death? What are the crowds that foolishly antagonize it? The crowd is always there, and moves into itself, into its restricted districts . . ." He went into the larch wood, and told me to go on ahead of him. "I have often seen policemen gallop up on tall horses, and rain blows down on the masses: it's a recurring image: the way they lash out at unprotected heads with clubs and rifle butts. The way the crowd closes ranks, shows first horror, then fight. How, only lately dominated by the police, they now dominate the police, who are still raining blows on them, you understand . . . The crowd is a phenomenon, the phenomenon of the man in the crowd has always fascinated me. The crowd exerts a morbid pressure on the individual to want to join it, to have to join it, you know . . . Disgust at being a part of it, disgust at not being a part of it. Now it's the one form of disgust, now it's the other . . . But people are always the crowd, always the mass. Every individual is the crowd and the mass, even the one who's pinned between tall cliffs, who'll never get out from between them, who'll always remain high up and out of it . . . But this mass man, this crowd man, you know . . . It's extraordinary to be part of a crowd! To know that that's what you are: part of a crowd!" He said: "Shouldn't we go to the curling arena? The people here have three passions: curling and whoring and playing cards. Did you understand the point of the game yesterday? You were freezing. You should have worn a thicker scarf.

Don't you have a proper woolen scarf?" He stomped over to a pile of brushwood, and motioned to me to follow him. "Look!" he said, and he lifted up the brushwood. There lay four or five deer, pressed together, frozen, with glazed eyes. "You'll find refuges like this all over the place, they are always death traps when it's as cold as it is this year," said the painter. And I remembered the time when spring came, and I dragged together lots of deer carcasses with my brother in the great forests, and buried them. Often they were half eaten by foxes, and only their heads and skeletons were left.

Today there was a letter from the landlord. Probably his letter was to confirm the receipt of the money that the landlady, on the insistence of her lover, the knacker, had sent him, I thought. Then I went around a long time with this letter, and kept wondering what would happen if I opened it and read it. But that would be a crime. So I didn't do it. The landlord's handwriting made me think about him and his life a lot. I felt that everything that went on in this person is doomed to be unhappy. And I can imagine him getting driven ever deeper into his sadness and his hopelessness, like a boat with an unconscious man in it, being pushed by the current ever nearer to the brink . . . At first I was unable to account for the way the knacker supported the landlord, by almost forcing the landlady to send the money he asked for, and how he keeps on supporting the landlord, even though the landlady is his mistress . . . Now I probably know why, though I'm not able to express it. I keep hearing how nicely the prisoners are doing in prison, but they can't be doing so nicely that they don't find it a terrible affliction, wherever they are and whatever they're there for and under whatever the circumstances are, to be locked up . . . That handwriting shows you the whole misery of that condition, you can see it right away . . . I kept looking at the handwriting, and went round and round the hay barn. I wonder whether the landlord has another request now? I thought. What will he have to write to her about? He surely can't know what she thinks about him, and how she opposes him, acts against his interests, quite apart from her unfaithfulness, which he knows about. And about the knacker too. It's a terrible situation. In my agitation I go to the cemetery, to look for the grave of the workman whom the landlord killed. I walk up and down, and then I'm standing in front of a snowy mound, with a cross stuck in the earth. But no name. Nothing. That's surely it, I think. I stand there and I feel like crying. In fact, I did cry. And then I quickly went into the chapel, but it was so cold in there, and so stupidly quiet, that I could get no peace, and I went out into the cemetery again. Roofs all round. Houses, with smoke pouring out of them. I felt utterly miserable. Then I ran into the knacker, coming over with his cramp-irons and shovel from the rectory, walking through the graves toward me. He must have seen me. What was I doing there; it wasn't usual to find a person in the cemetery at this time. I wasn't doing anything, I said. Nothing at all. I was bothered. I couldn't ask him whether that mound was where the workman was lying. "No," I said, "I'm not doing anything." I must have struck him as very disturbed. I was disturbed. Then with the letter in my hand, I ran to the inn, and gave it to the landlady.

I saw the landlady preparing food in the kitchen, bacon and sausage and apples and coffee all piled up on the sideboard. In between times she went to the stove and the public bar, and she kept going into the pantry, because she'd forgotten something that she could bring out and lay on the sideboard with the other things. There was a blue bag of lump sugar. I stood in the kitchen, because I was waiting for water, which she'd put on the stove to heat up especially for me. Then she disappeared into her bedroom for a little time, and when she came back she had a pair of her husband's warm woolen socks, which she set down next to the food. "Your water will be hot soon," she said. Then I watched her pack all the food things in a big cardboard box. "Did you see the knacker anywhere?" she asked. "No," I said. "He said he'd come and take the things down to the post office for me." She wrapped the cardboard box in a big sheet of brown paper, and tied it up with thick twine, perhaps some old washing line. "That has to go out today," she said. "It's urgent." She had the makings of lunch in big saucepans on the stove. She stirred one, then another, with a big wooden spoon. She fed the fire with more wood. "If it goes to the post office now," she said, "it'll go on the mail sleigh." Would the parcel cost a lot to send? "No," I said, "it won't be very much." The postmistress had used to be a friend of hers, and had spent years eating in her pub. "But our husbands forced us apart," she said. She had divorced the postman, and married a worker at the cellulose factory, five years ago now. "It was always going to go wrong," she said. "I would never have married him!" Then the knacker came in, with his rucksack on his back. It was good that she had got the parcel packed and ready, because he was just on his way to the post office. "I can't send him any more than I've got here," she said. He seemed very surprised that it was such a large parcel. "I put his warm socks in there too." She went into the pantry and came out with some bacon, which she cut up and laid on a piece of bread. That was for the knacker to eat. He ate up the bread and bacon. To me she said: "I'm sure your water's hot now." I had forgotten all about the water. I took the jug off the stove, and went up to my room. I thought the landlord probably wrote and asked for some more food. And for some warm socks. I was sure there had been dissent between the landlady and the knacker before the making up of the parcel. The knacker had a lot to carry.

Eighteenth Day

"I could drill through my boots, you know that? I could. But I don't want to. I've got the strength. But I'm not going to drill through my boots. It would be a pointless waste of strength." We walk on. He says: "The whole world consists of pointless wastes of strength. I'm waiting for the end now, you know! Just as you're waiting for your end. Just as everyone's waiting for their end. Only they don't realize they're waiting and waiting for what I've always been waiting for, namely the end!" He reminds me of a church singer, who is suddenly called upon to *speak* loudly into the nave. "My end frees me! Me and my person. All the things that only exist in and through me!" His sentences echo back, as from the walls of a church. "That's the extraordinary thing!" Then: "Vague, always vague! But I don't intend ever to express myself with precision. I can imagine it must be difficult to make anything of these connections, omissions, sins of omission, accumulations, obligations, verdicts . . . No, I don't demand that! I no longer demand anything. Anything. Nothing from any- one! . . . A situation like the one in which I find myself is completely unimaginable. Of course, I don't know anything either. That's true. I'm a burden on you . . . I know your life can't be easy for you either, but it's a good deal easier than mine. To begin with," he said, "you have all sorts of possibili- ties. You are able to enthuse about all sorts of things. The most banal things! You develop an array of gifts, of the sort that many people manage to develop, canny people, brutes, and then timid like wallflowers. You can do this and that and the other thing, and your head is stuffed full of all sorts of plans and future directions. All in all, you think you might want to do pretty much anything and have it in your power to do so. You think you're in a circus, and because you're so gifted and so popular, you can do anything in the circus that takes your fancy: any stunts, even the hardest, any tricks, even the meanest. You think you can walk on a tightrope, high over a drop, where the air is already thin . . . you think you can ride, put your head in the lion's mouth, and take it out when the beast roars . . . acrobatics . . . stunts . . . you think you can do anything, and you also think, and you're completely persuaded of that fact, that you can be the direc- tor as well . . . the circus director: fine, there are no limits, because you see none. It's all unlimited, and that deadly subconscious feeling of being able to turn your hand to absolutely anything . . . till one day your first idea comes to you, and then a second, a third, and a fourth . . . one after another . . . finally hundreds and thousands, thousands of ideas: those are the painters, the newspapermen, the prison wardens and the prisoners, the policemen, the philosophers . . . heir, cow, tail, minister, director, you understand . . . till you end up not being convinced by anything . . . that's what it is . . . Because you have your moments of this and that, and no character . . . how soon everything turns into nothing, unemployed, unskilled, mad, unemployable, manifesting the signs of idiocy . . . But all that's just a point of view," he said, "no deeper and no less deep than the crassest error."

Existence was well used to torrents, but sometimes it tended to forget that, and was carried along: "But it's always an existence," says the painter. Years ago, he had been in Weng with his sister once, "in spite of herself. She hated the region. In wartime." More and more, the valley became a sort of refuge for the pair of them. "Unlike then, I'm unprotected now." His sister's baby, "back then, behind the church wall," she was pregnant by an apprentice well driller, had died in its infancy. "No one knows why it suddenly died." That fact, and the fact that his sister had had no objection to having the baby—"to her it was a happy and unlooked-for chance to find herself, as it were, overnight, in a state of expectancy—she never got over it. After conceiving, she came to me with friendly traits she had never had previously. Suddenly my sister manifested a sort of previously repressed wildness. At mealtimes. When I met her for walks. In the dark sometimes. When she said 'goodnight,' you could see it. The precocious father of her baby became a jailbird. Involved in several rapes, in the end he was unable to avoid the scaffold. He was from Goldegg. At the time, he was just fifteen. But powerfully built, like all the young fellows here. Come over the mountain, and punch six bells out of all and sundry. It was a warm spring day. My sister was walking in the graveyard, as she often did. You could hear the war from over the cliffs. The workhouse drew him in, the clogs of the prisoners at Garsten jail were like a marching band. I've got a photo of him. Over the years I managed to find out quite a bit about him, for instance that he fathered five children, who are all running around somewhere, living on farms. In workmen's hostels. Who knows. Sometimes nature wants nothing but to test her strength on two people who don't know what brought them together, why they belong together: there's a sudden violence, favored by the climate in these parts, that switches off logic and emotion and thought for the duration. Often, it's just an animal cunning that gets its way."

His time as a substitute teacher came up again. "All my life, I've never hated anything as much as I hated teachers. Those teachers who always struck me as the embodiment of stupidity, the stupidity was drilled into their underpants. Also the generally dangerous ridiculousness, which further makes huge claims. For, as you must know, teachers make huge claims which take precedence over other claims. I so detested the teacher's life, that I simply snubbed fellow humans whom I had known for some time but who had gone to become teachers. And there I was suddenly overnight becoming a substitute teacher. And on my own initiative! Just imagine my extremity! But I got out of that disgrace . . . A teacher is the mouthpiece of an entire generation. And you see: teachers make for calamities. Injustice and war. Of course, I was not a regular teacher, and I wasn't on a regular pay scale either. Not a teacher in the strict sense. Only an occasional substitute teacher. So I wasn't involved in that ghastliness."

He had suddenly found himself a substitute, a sort of casual teacher, just as others, and he himself in past years, were casual laborers. He doesn't see much of a distinction between casual teaching and casual labor. The principal difference being that the casual laborer is generally in the fresh air, whereas the casual teacher is always in stuffy classrooms. The casual teacher feeds the children with figures and signs, and the casual laborer feeds the cement mixer with buckets of water and sacks of cement. The casual teacher has to be careful he doesn't fall off his little classroom platform, and the casual laborer that he doesn't fall onto the pavement from the third or fourth story of a building. "The casual teacher is so pathetic that regular teachers look the other way when he walks past them. They stand around in the corridor with their hands behind their backs, and form up into a solid phalanx, so there's no room for the casual teacher in their midst. If the casual teacher has a question, he has to go to the director, because the regular teachers won't give him an answer. 'I'm going away,' the regular teachers tell their classes, 'and a casual teacher is coming to fill in for me.' They don't say: 'You're getting a new teacher . . .' And thereby they spoil everything for the casual teacher. For instance, casual teachers are not allowed to wear the white coat of regular teachers. At the most, substitute teachers are allowed to wear sleeve protectors. Of course I would never have worn a teacher's coat in any case. Much less had recourse to sleeve protectors . . . Nor do substitute teachers qualify for a training supplement." He had never known what to do with himself in the breaks, because the regular teachers all snubbed him. "The substitute teachers' trade union wants to improve all the conditions that the substitute teachers are exposed to.

But the more it does, with its clumsy methods, the worse things are for substitute teachers. It's a fact that the regular teachers' union has much more influence."

Today I wrote my fourth letter to the assistant, even though I haven't had a reply from him to the first three. I drew a comparison between the painter Strauch and the surgeon Strauch. Inside and out, the two belonged to two quite opposed worldviews. They are two opposed worlds. Just as his brother and I are different. Different, not made of one and the same substance. The surgeon, who aims at a successful career. Who is either unfamiliar with despair, or else won't have it anywhere near him. Only at a distance, where it can't hurt him. Concerned, true, about the condition of his brother. But only out of his guilty conscience. He is not *quaking*.

An activity that fills his days and nights, to wit, surgery, which has also given him local celebrity, won't let him think any more deeply, as humans can and sometimes desire to do, when they are basically unemployed, and therefore only concerned with themselves. In the operating theater, there is no thinking, only doing. After that, there is eating, and then sleeping, at the most there might be a little distraction in between times. Hardly any conversation. Hardly any variety. No moodiness. No melancholy. No troublesome memories. No women. The football pools. Down on the courts, a spot of tennis to counteract the unignorable signs of middle-age spread. No writing letters. No reading, with the exception of the specialist literature, as for instance the book *On the Etiol-*

ogy of Smegma, or *Cancer Research in America.* The envious, the imitator, and the admirer are zealously kept at bay. The subjects of conversation are cancer, lung disease, wasting sickness, cramps, embolism, sites of infection. Wine is drunk. There are whispered meetings with nursing sisters. Interns and surgical nurses are ordered around, suddenly in the middle of an operation, bodies are sewn up, rolled out, "they wash their hands of them."

It so happens that a condition is fatal that was not thought to be fatal. It happens more frequently than one might imagine. Outside the hospital walls. No news leaks out that would have serious consequences. He, the assistant, knows how to talk to people: to the consultant, to such and such, to the patients. He is free with the *Du* form, but it doesn't mean a great deal. He is said to have a steady hand. Even by his helpers during the operation. Defter with his scissors than with needle and thread. Bold. Decisive, where others dither around. If someone dies, the reasons for it don't greatly interest him. A devotee of the chase, he has no interest in the twilight world of art. The things his brother used to do were always repugnant to him. The academic side of him has gone on developing. He hates aesthetics. Also dreams. He appears never to have suffered. One can observe an athletic arrogance in him as he strides out of the hospital. On Sundays he goes to church. He is careful not to believe any more than is prescribed. Communists approach him, because he has never mocked Communism. He has a reputation for "textbook operations," of the sort that is useful to every doctor over time. The scuttlebutt is that therapy is no longer a labyrinth to him. During the operation he exerts a magnetic pull on the instruments. The registrar has already designated him his successor. He is kind to me. Why? But then again, the way he deals with the scalpel seems highly artistic. Not just artful. He takes patients' notes up to his room with him, the light is still on at two in the morning. He's up at seven. You hear him. His footfalls in the corridor. Remarks have been attributed to him like: "Source the fantasy in the delusion . . ."—"Groundless screams" or "the word gentleness, which keeps recurring." Not an enthusiast. Not a spoilsport, because not a player. A rock? For me, yes. Places where no one has yet been, where nothing has lived. Vistas that lie open. The surgeon, the competent one. The painter, his brother, the incompetent, I think.

When he took off his hat, I saw he had a wound on his head. He had lost his bearings at night, and hit a beam. "I crawled along the floor, not knowing where I was going. Then I tried to get up, and smashed my head against a beam." I couldn't have the least idea of what the night he had spent had been like. The fear of being "completely mad" had sent him plunging out of his room, "between three and four a.m., in blank despair." Half-dressed, he had first gone downstairs, into the kitchen, then the public bar, where he had looked for something to drink. "But she keeps everything under lock and key." Because beer bottles and juice often went missing, the landlady had taken to locking up her supplies. Guests at the inn had even tapped the barrel, and let half the beer run out. "I didn't manage to find anything. Not in the kitchen, and not in the public bar," he said. Then he had thought of the cellar, but on the way he had remembered that she always locked the cellar too. "As you know, she always keeps the key to the cellar on her person." Then he had gone back, and abruptly lost his orientation. "I didn't dare turn on a light. If I turn on a light, I'll wake everyone up. I didn't turn on a light. . . . I expect I crawled around in circles." The wound to his head had happened very suddenly. Suddenly he felt warm blood on his hand, and smeared his clothes with it. "On the floor as well . . . In the morning, I was the first one downstairs, at five o'clock, and wiped away the bloodstains I left behind. Even the doors were smeared. And the walls too." How he'd got back up to his room he couldn't remember. "I fell into bed when I was upstairs. So I was lucky I woke up before five o'clock, so that I could straighten everything out. Just imagine if the landlady had found my bloodstains everywhere! . . . I originally went upstairs to wash. Since I'd lain down in my bed in my clothes—I was simply too weak to get undressed—I got the bed all bloody as well. But that's not unusual. I dabbed the wound with cold water, which felt good. Then I put my feet in the basin too. The pains relented. The burning got less." That night, he had had the feeling the whole time that he had to hide "from something terrible." He had gone over to the window and opened the curtains and looked out. "It was as if I were in an aquarium where the water had frozen. Everything in the aquarium was frozen. The trees. The bushes. Everything. Coated in whitish ice that was so clear, you could see the rocks beneath. At the least movement, for instance if I breathed, tens of thousands of cracks would form in the massive ice block that the world had turned into." He had been stunned by the sight. "I had to turn away, it was so fascinating . . . I went back to the wash basin, and dipped my towel in the water, and tied it round my head. When I returned to the window, the scene had changed. No ice. No rigidity. Suddenly everything was living and moving. And that was even stranger." Then he sat down on his bed and, to distract himself from what he had seen, he tried to think of something in the past—"something jolly. A good moment, a single beautiful moment. But I could find none. If only I could have been able to watch a single amusing figure go by, in my memory! But no, there wasn't the least thing to distract me. I was only able to muster a few shallow breaths," he said.

By morning, the wound to his head had healed. I looked at it when he sat down to breakfast. It was healing, as if on a healthy person. Closing, as if drawn together with an invisible thread. He had reflected about himself all night, and come to various, "albeit unsatisfactory," conclusions. There were so many ways in which one might look at oneself. From the surface. From the deep interior, "from way underneath." From a thousand acute or obtuse angles. What one saw was so wretched. And simultaneously frightening. "A man writhing like a worm in all the mirrors he's forced to look into." The head wound, from which he had now almost recovered, had compelled him to reflect on human diseases. The human diseases of the body and the human diseases of the other thing. "What constitutes a disease in the first place?" he asked himself. "Do they even begin? Are they not perhaps there from the beginning? Where do they come from, if they weren't always there? At what point can one say that they are perceptible? When are they imperceptible? When, where? In the place where they suddenly break out? What does 'from the beginning' mean? When would that be?" He had walked across the cornfield a ways. "I had the feeling my wound was electrically charged," he said. "I was thinking about the connections between pains. All the way, I was working on that one thought. But I suddenly didn't feel like it anymore, perhaps because such horrible insights were coming to me, quite against my will. And getting stronger all the time. Suddenly wiped me out. Once again, I saw how pointless it is to pursue a strain of thought utterly, in the belief that one wouldn't perish in it, as in a tunnel. Not suffocate in it."

"As if doors were opening all over the place," he said. "People and the likenesses of people, my whole defeat approaches me from all directions. I am continually repelling intrusions. Scraps of memories from the time I pursued my experiments, which were eclipsed by the comparable but more thrustful experiments of others. I thought quite a bit about my painting today. I attended exhibitions. I leafed through catalogs in my memory. Friends came to call. Sat with me for an hour or more. The studio suddenly appeared. The ghostly conversations. Suddenly all that nonsense—particularly attractive to women, who crouched on my chairs. Young men in tight trousers sprawled in the dark. Oldsters who wanted to buy into respectability in the form of art. The world is straightforward. I saw my windows blocked up with the rottenness of people who didn't know why they were there, what they were about. Idealistic vaporings flattened themselves against my windows, while the cigarette smoke twisted upward. Those evenings still disgusted me years later. Those mornings. Those nights that lay between the evenings and the mornings like static orgies of philosophizing. Flesh against flesh. If I intervened, everything flew apart as if putrid, scattered like dust. I mustn't give offense. Young people came to inveigh against the old. Old people came to inveigh against the young. Everything came to me like a whirlwind that left behind only despair. I suddenly saw the detail of a landscape I painted the summer before last: a green establishing itself against blue. The forcefulness of it. Everything struck me like feral horses, after decades of domestication. And then a hand that wouldn't do what it was told. Didn't want to live, even though, finally, it *had* to live. Everything very spiritistic, you understand. The smell of coffee and the winy sentimentality that came with the private views. Incapable of anything more. Exhausted, even with sleep. 'A masterpiece!' they exclaimed, and that was it for a second or two. But only for a second or two, you understand: a river landscape, devastation, a city of martyrs. One celebrity betrayed the next, to eyes that saw more clearly than was good for them. Ghostly too, because the unattainable was so effortlessly reduced. Disparaged heroics, you understand. Snobbery just barely adjusted to mendacity. The most unprepossessing prepared to pass judgments only a king should pass. I had assembled a whole generation of usurpers about me in the form of those three or four or five or six people, who like me in their quest for scale had plunged into the poverty of their emotions. Rome was bandied about as if it were a mug of beer. The idea of fame was connected to the feebleness of the world around, the size of other shrubs bred behind high garden walls, so that they had to see what grew there and how to destroy it: to be capable of anything in the starred world. And then suddenly the people disappeared, art disappeared out of me, out of the studio, the studio itself disappeared, everything disappeared, and left me calmly striding out, if only for a few moments at a time, when I can take fifteen or twenty paces by myself. Without disgust."

Nineteenth Day

"The qualities of youth and the qualities of age are the same qualities," said the painter, "but the effect they produce is entirely different. You see: the qualities of youth are not objected to in the young, but the qualities of old age are objected to in the old. A young man may tell lies without someone wringing his neck, but an old man who tells lies will have his neck wrung. A young person will not be condemned for all eternity, but an old person will be. A young person with a squint can appear droll, an old person with a squint is repulsive. In the case of the young person, they say, there is the hope that he may one day be cured of his squinting. In the case of the old person who squints, there is no hope of his ever being cured of his squinting. No, no possibility. A young person with a deformed foot excites our sympathy, not our disgust, but an old person with a deformed foot only excites our disgust. A young person with sticking-out ears may make us laugh, an old person with sticking-out ears embarrasses us, and we think: how ugly this person is, who has had these ugly sticking-out ears all his life. A young person in a wheel-chair moves us. An old person in a wheelchair plunges us into despair. A young person without teeth can strike us as more or less interesting. An old person without teeth makes us ill, makes us feel like vomiting. Youth," he says, "has it all over age, and it can do what it pleases. Its stupidity doesn't repel us, its shamelessness is bearable. Old age meanwhile cannot afford to be stupid, without risking its neck, and the shamelessness of old age is, as we know, the most loathsome thing there is. With the young person, they say: Oh, he'll grow out of it! With the old person, they say· He's too old to ever change! Whereas in fact the qualities of youth and the qualities of old age are the same qualities."

In his time as a substitute teacher, he devised a method to counter his solitude and loneliness that turned out to be very efficacious. "I used to take sleeping pills," he said, "and slowly boosted the number of pills I took. In the end, they had absolutely no effect on me, and I could have gulped any number of them, and still not have got to sleep. I repeatedly took such high dosages, I should have died. But I only ever vomited them up. Then I would be unable for days to pursue the least thought, and it was precisely this inability to think that got me through long periods of complete horror . . . You have to be careful you don't end up living for longer than your natural lifespan," he said. "Life is a court case which you lose, whoever you are, and whatever you do. That was decided before any human being was even born. The first man fared no differently from us. Rebellion against this only leads to deeper despair," he said. "And no more distraction. From the age of thirteen, no more distraction. After the first sexual experience, no distraction. Do you understand?" The only variety was thunderstorms, "and lightning the only poetry." He said: "Seeing as you're locked up, locked up in solitary confinement, you're increasingly thrown back upon yourself." The questions one asked oneself slowly became one's death. "But you know, we're all dead anyway from the outset." There were simply "no more forms of assistance."

One lay on the floor of one's cell, along with the shattered limbs of past millennia. "Deceits and subterfuges," he said. Just as the handling of facts injected insignificance into the brain, whatever question one asked oneself. "Every question is a defeat." Every question wrought devastation. Disinclination. With questions, the time passed, and the questions passed in time, "so meaningless that everything is just ruins . . . There, you see," said the painter, "it's quite black down there. Last night, I dreamed the workers climbed up the mountain, and flooded the village and the inn and everything. In their thousands and tens of thousands, they swarmed up here, and whatever didn't belong to them, they trampled underfoot, or it was suffocated in their blackness. How calm it is now! Listen!" The butcher greeted us, and we greeted him back. The houses of Weng seemed jumbled together, as though crushed at the foot of the cliff. "Earlier," said the painter, "I used to have no pity for human frailty. Any pain seemed to me unnatural! Suddenly I saw myself confronted with an abundance of frailty." He said: "Will you be playing cards tonight? The knacker is a good cardplayer. The engineer as well. They're all of them good cardplayers. I don't know why I've always had such an aversion to cardplayers." He muttered something about cretinism in the mountain valleys, in the high Alps. And then: "Our Father, who art in Hell, unhallowed be Thy name. No Kingdom come. Thy will not be done. On earth, as it is in Hell. Deny us this day our daily bread. And forgive us no trespasses. As we forgive none of those that trespass against us. Lead us into temptation, and deliver us from no evil. Amen. That one works just as well," he said.

· · ·

Today, I was to collect the painter from the vicarage, where he was paying a visit. "Just ring the bell and wait," he instructed me, "I'll come down right away." He didn't say I was to go into the vicarage. He visits the vicar from time to time "to discuss his black cat with him, because it's not possible to talk to him on any other subject. But he has such excellent wine that I never refuse his invitations," said the painter. Accordingly, I crossed the cemetery, and walked to the vicarage. In the cemetery, I read the names on the children's graves: here and there, the parents had had their deceased children photographed, and had these photographs displayed on the tombstones. There were many instances, though, of graves with no names on them, without any reference to the child buried there. I was struck that the path that ran through the section of children's graves to the big compost heap had no footsteps on it. No one had been to visit the children's graves, certainly not for a long time. There were no candles of the kind that all the children's graves had back home in L., usually burning. I rang the vicar's bell, and waited. It wasn't long before a window opened above me in the second floor, and I took a step back and saw the thin face of a young woman. The vicar's cook, I thought. And then I heard the sound of footsteps coming down a flight of stairs. Just inside the door, the painter said goodbye to the vicar. He would certainly come again before long, and he thanked him for the refreshments. Then the door opened, and the painter emerged. He took me by the arm, and pushed me along the vicarage wall out into the open, where the ash trees stood. The vicar had told him of great upheavals that were in progress within the "vast Church apparatus," and of the great impetus coming from the person of the new pope. "But of course," said the painter, "whatever the Church does, it is

a completely illegitimate organization. Particularly as
church." Then he complained about an "agonizing headache,
that had already set in when I reached the vicarage, they
seem to come earlier and earlier, but without losing any of
their ability to get worse and worse." The vicar's cook had a
relationship with the chimney sweep, he said, but she was so
loyal to the vicar, her brother, that he couldn't get by without
her. "The vicar is a farmer's son from the Lungau," said the
painter, "and completely unable to cope on his own." He
admired his simplicity, and he was "absolutely a good person," albeit, as already said, "incompetent in the most basic
things. Not to mention such things as archiepiscopal visits,
where he falls down utterly." Well, the vicar knew his position with regard to the Church. And he didn't make any
attempt to work on the painter with anything that he was less
than completely convinced by himself.

Suddenly we saw a group of power plant workers ahead of
us, on their way to the inn. They walked in silence, and then
greeted us, because they knew us, as we them. "You see," said
the painter, once they had passed, "those men are on the
right road, they are good men." He watched them go, passing
under the juniper bushes, and then disappearing. "You see,
there, on the opposite side, on the shady side, that's where
they're going to dig the second underground reservoir," he
said. "It's quite easy to discern the lines of the whole thing.
The road which you see in front of you was built by the
Energy Ministry, and it is immensely profitable to the farmers on that side, because it goes straight past their farms.
They were only required to pay a minimal subsidy, those rich,
well-off farmers. A laughable supplement, a sum half of

which was paid on their behalf anyway, by the Ministry of Agriculture. Before that, there was only a very narrow rutted cart track leading up to those farms from just behind the station. You see: this is the point where the river will be dammed and put to work, as you see, the power plant itself will have to be built partly in the river and partly into the mountain, on the other side. In the three and a half years that they've been working on it so far, eighteen men have lost their lives here, meeting their death either by crane, by water, by rockfalls, or under the wheels of trucks. If you take everything into account, it's not even a terribly high price! You can see the difficulty of the whole undertaking: it's not a propitious region for building in!" Getting a job down there was next door to kicking off. "In practice, everything is that much worse. The men remain tired out for the rest of their lives, and unfit for any higher task. But then, what might that be! I'm afraid this anthill is nothing but an earth-mover, on the vastest scale, for a project priced in billions."

"You have to wonder whether you should really see them as human at all," he said, "those people who come limping along at five to twelve, limp into a hut, or into a canteen, or an inn. The workers have their particular smell, and the building site has its particular smell, and the cellulose factory; each smell is woven in with the others. And in the cellulose factory, as you know, the work practices have remained unchanged for decades. The work premises have remained unchanged too. High windows which it's impossible to see out of, because the dirt on them is inches thick. Mind you, with that machine noise going on, you wouldn't want to look out anyway, where would you look out to? Into blackness.

Into cold blackness. First, the power plant people tried to recruit workers from the cellulose factory for their project. They set up a recruiting office, and offered signing-on bonuses. But very few went over, because they didn't need to be told that the power plant would be finished one day, in a year, or two, or three, but the cellulose factory will just go on forever. At least, as far as anyone can see. The cellulose factory is an incredibly certain proposition for everyone. In the end, the power plant will end up as a huge source of labor for the cellulose factory. Almost all the workers there are Communists. Communism falls on fertile ground here. Here, up in the Alps, where you wouldn't think it at all likely. Everything down there is Communist. It's an area that might have been made specially for Communist infiltration. Communism, as you might not know, is at least the intermediate future for people all over the world. Communism will rule everything, even the remotest valley in the world. Even the most obscure corner of the last winding of a brain opposed to it. Communism is something that thrives on dirt and stench and harsh contrasts. Well, if Communism comes, all that can take a running jump! And behind it Moscow stands and supervises, the way it stands and supervises everywhere." He said: "And yet, this was originally an ancient Christian valley. But, tell me if you can, where does Catholicism, where does Christianity have its roots nowadays? Where?" We were standing in the middle of the village square.

"Were you ever happy? And did you know then what happiness was? And in a situation you never thought you'd leave?" He said: "I don't want an answer to my question."

After we ran into the knacker, who was in conversation with the cobbler in a doorway, we walked to the vicarage, and from there, through the garden of the poorhouse, back to the village square. "Do you hear it at night when I open my window?" he said. "I often get up and open my window. Walk back and forth, back and forth. But it doesn't settle me at all. I think I'm going to suffocate: but when the cold air streams into my room, my head feels even worse. I think the cold air will get me going again, like winding a watch. But that's an illusion. The effort and the deviousness I need to get myself going seem to be getting more and more demanding. It is like with a watch, yes. Even if that's a very simple comparison, but then I'm in favor of using only very simple comparisons in speech, like handholds, to give support . . . You're probably a stranger to insomnia. At any rate, I haven't heard you complain of insomnia. Everything torments me now. I'm like a man tormented by a river he can look at without being able to jump into it. Disgusting points in relation to people and the human past. I see nothing I like." And then, when we're in the larch wood again: "Is everyone waiting? Is everyone waiting as I am waiting for something that will alter, shred, conclude everything? To continue it on a completely different level, or way down?" Then we run into the postman coming out of the inn, and he greets us by touching his hand to his cap. Silently. When he's at a sufficient distance, the painter says: "He's another one with those dog movements that most of them have here, those dog-paw gestures. He hates his wife. Hates his children. Drinks. Shirks. Man is an ideal hell to his fellow men. And everything gives him phenomenal grounds to be the way he is." We pass the hay barn. And then quickly into the inn.

In the night it approaches him like a whole mountain range to torment him. Only began to recede as it got light. Long-extinguished memories were reawakened in him: war, hunger, hatred. The attempt to wrestle sorrow into reason was futile. The futility of creating anything, a picture, a thought, entered the world of his cells as it grew dark, and fled into its hiding places with the returning light. "The day has different pains. I have a brother who's a doctor," he says, "you know, but that's not enough. Anywhere there's a doctor, there's a lot of damage." He mentioned his headache again. In very early childhood he had had a headache, once only, very suddenly "terrible pain behind my frontal bone," on the edge of a forest. Then not again, not for decades, not till *the onset of this illness.* But "many in our family were destroyed by these headaches, I know that. That dam-bursting and incessant nonsense that crushes words in its path," he said. "Pain can be an obligation." And: "Even against my will it can reach its objective. It keeps reaching it." One had to adopt the pain "like the mirage of a bridge you don't know where it leads." Then he started to talk again about the sleigh ride we had gone on the day before. Down to the station. Should he ride in front or in back, his hesitation delayed our departure by fifteen minutes. That sleigh ride reminded me of episodes from distant childhood: winter landscapes. I remembered the form and the color and the breadth and depth of sleigh traces, and the sensations I felt while looking at them. I adeptly put all the windings of the road behind us. "Not so quickly!" I heard from him a couple of times, he drilled his head into my back, and clasped both arms around me. At the bottom, in front of the station, he was sweating. We went into various shops, bought things, talked to the people behind the counters. Then I went to the apothecary's for him. He was waiting for me at the station with a thick pile of newspapers in his arms. The mayor picked us up on his horse-drawn sleigh and gave us a lift to Weng.

At the station he was overcome by a great impatience, a sudden disgust, as it seemed to me. "These people who don't know what to do with themselves," he said. Stations were "centers of far-reaching lunacy. There you can study brutalism." Asked about the seven or eight newspapers he had in his arms, he said: "I am principally interested in new ideas. Less what makes the world hold its breath—that'll be forgotten by the morning. But new ideas, *what will come tomorrow*, the future." The way he stood all alone in the station hall in front of the ticket counter, he looked like someone for whom nothing is more than a child's brief game, which will end in death. No. He was just scraps of words and dislocated phrases.

The engineer says that starting tomorrow they will have to work through the night to finish in time. Almost all had volunteered for the night shift. For an hour at night you got three times as much as an hour in the daytime, and today they put up floodlighting to light the site at night. The works management clearly expected the local people who lived along the river to complain about the extra noise. But "their

complaints will be rejected, that's already been agreed with
the mayor." Of course the crane makes much more noise at
night than by day. All sound is louder at night. Now, when
they're knocking in the props for the extra bridge, it will be
particularly loud. But if they don't work at night, the whole
thing will take an extra year. And that would be one in the eye
for the management, and cause vast losses for the companies
involved in the construction. What was quite astounding was
that the union had no objection to the proposed night work.
The engineer reckons the only reason it was keeping quiet
was that it had some stake in one or other of the companies.
And so it said nothing about working on Sundays and holidays, let alone on Saturdays and afternoons. "From now on
we'll be working through," said the engineer. "I haven't been
able to sleep for a long time anyway. I might get to lie down
a while, nothing more." There were continual disputes
between the different departments within the project. There
was disagreement as to which firms should pick up contracts.
There too, everything was political. Often components of
inferior quality were ordered because the firm supplying
them was more acceptable to the board than another firm
whose goods were of higher quality. It was another draw-
back, the engineer said, that no temporary housing had been
thrown together for the wives and children of the workers.
"The upshot is that they have to travel forty or fifty miles by
train in the evening, and the same coming back in the morning." That sapped the energy of the workforce. Individuals
who weren't living on-site were noticeably weaker. And they
were more expensive too, because the management paid for
their rail tickets. Nor were such men suited for night work.
Or for work on Sundays and holidays. "But if they have their
families on-site, then they'll agree to work at night and on

weekends." He, the engineer, would improvise several more temporary accommodations for wives and children in the course of the day. It was worth it, even now. It would also cut down on the amount of association that went on between married men and local girls and women, and less friction. Because it often happens that married men here on their own would drop into the station buffet "just for a glass of beer," that turned into four or five, and at the end of which it no longer occurred to them to go home, but instead they picked up some railwayman's girl, and disappeared with her behind a hay shed, or into a quiet room in an inn somewhere. And then they don't go home till they've had enough, which might be three or four nights. And then the wives turn up and complain to the management, which is completely in the dark about everything. "Now, if you set up accommodation for the families, all that could be avoided," said the engineer. "At least, the trouble could be reduced to a minimum." One couldn't hope to eliminate it altogether, anywhere conditions were primitive, there would always be drunkenness and excess. "Anywhere you have a lot of workers, you'll get a lot of pregnancies," says the engineer. They'll make a baby with any girl or woman that strikes them as suitable for the purpose. "What do you think's on their minds, once the shift's over?" The knacker grins, and with one gulp empties his half glass of beer. "I've witnessed scenes, I tell you, scenes in my own office," says the engineer, "that no one would believe." The wives too had a completely false sense of their husbands, but a man was really not cut out for marriage. A woman, yes, but not a man. The night shift went from six in the evening till five in the morning. There were meal breaks at nine p.m. and at two a.m. But he, the engineer, would have to be on his feet day and night, at least some of the time. "I have good foremen and overseers and good masons and concreters," he says, "but still you always have to be on the lookout." He wasn't petty or mean. When one of the workmen's wives had come to term recently, he had picked her up in his own car and driven her to the hospital. "Little kindnesses like that win you sympathy," he says. The knacker asks how deep into the riverbed they had to drill. "Twenty meters," says the engineer. And had they completed the relaying of the rail tracks. "Yes," says the engineer. They had had to blast twenty thousand cubic meters of rock out of the mountain to relay the tracks. "That wasn't in the original blueprints," he says. "That alone added a couple of million to the costs." In such a way, construction projects, whatever their scale, always ended up costing you more. "Generally, with building projects, you should double your estimate," says the engineer. "It's easy to get in too deep. Believe your figures, and you get burned." A lot of projects were standing around half-built, and falling down. "To be certain of completing a project, a private contractor should have at least double the budget in the bank. Only the state can build as and when it pleases, and be certain of completing it, because only the state has the funds, and the ability to raise more."

There's a kind of twilit zone between me and the painter. What he says is like a distant rain, the settling of clouds over a far landscape, sending their shadows over everything. He says: "The nearness of a person produces in one the desire to know him to that point where he ceases to exist for oneself. That's how it is with people." Then he comes round to our walk the day before, when it occurred to him that the distance from the moon to the earth is less than that between the human head and heart. "You always wander around in your own heart, and agreeable as it is at the beginning, so horrible and destructive it gets to be later on." In the beginning was the end, everything for him proceeded from that sentence, that and: "a table is also a window, and a window is also the woman standing beside it, a creek bed is also the mountain reflected in the creek water, and a city the air above it." Tangled up with himself as he was, "a man was lost . . . refuges?" No reply. Breathing made him nauseous. He says: "I'm sure your head is bursting with ideas. With opinions." Then: "At first I thought I'd ask you up to my room, and we could talk there. But I'm too tired. Youth is aggressive against age at the point when it starts to draw in its horns. Has long ago drawn them in. One is also continually exposed to individuals who hate anything in the least intellectual. I've had to fight all my life. Particularly against women. My conclusion, coming at the end of an extensive landscape of ideas, would be: beware of women, but most particularly beware of the feminine part of your own nature, which is set on destroying you. The liking to have things easy, the need for warmth, the hunger for ornament, all these essentially feminine attributes, are inimical to the male. Woman—and the feminine in general—knocks a man down to his anti-male feelings. I could name you any number of outstanding men who were ruined by their wives. Persons of great talent, and the most impressive scale. The feminine is treacherous by its very nature. It undermines and hollows out. It's poison for the masculine brain, for the brain as a whole, for the masculine. If it's a matter of taking a man apart into his components, and not bothering to reassemble him . . . In scientific terms, a woman is a sort of effigy of a man . . . The hereditary enemy of thought . . . I mean, they don't even let their husbands read newspapers . . . Yes, the man who keeps them is not allowed to think . . . Woman is a destroyer, she's not capable of friendship . . . They're made for marriage and children, the only moment they stop lying is when they're giving birth . . . Women are for bedding, and nothing more. A woman has no sense of humor. She's the devil's tool, and she's responsible for the tragedy of humankind."

That night, because I couldn't sleep, because I was thinking about myself, and could find nothing to deflect my thoughts, I got up and went over to the window to look outside. But I could see nothing. It felt unbearable in the room, so I slipped on some clothes and shut the door behind me and went downstairs. There was a dim light on in the hall. I thought I might step outside, and perhaps walk up and down the street a ways. A long time ago, when I was a child, I had often woken up in the middle of the night and gone for a little walk, along a pier, through a piece of forest, and felt afraid; but it was me who was responsible for that fear, and that was the state I wanted to induce this time as well; maybe the larch wood? I thought. But as I made to open the front door, I saw that it wasn't locked, the bolt hadn't been thrown, and then I spotted a light coming from the public bar onto the opposite wall; there was a light on in the public bar, maybe someone had heard me, but I couldn't think who would be in the public bar at this hour; I didn't know what time it was, but it seemed late enough for me to assume that everyone would be in their beds. To begin with, I didn't want to go in the public bar, then I gave myself a little talking-to, and I opened the door. There in the corner, next to the bar, in the place where I myself liked to sit, I saw the knacker and the landlady sitting together. It looked as though they were having an argument, but I wasn't taken in by that, in fact they had just slept together, as I could tell by looking at their rumpled clothes, and their faces, which were ashen and drained. On the table stood some half-empty beer glasses and scraps of bread. The knacker's boots were on the table. He must have pulled them off when they lay down on the bench together, I thought. The landlady was disheveled. All this I could see at a glance. I didn't want to linger there, but the knacker asked me to sit down with them. They had been having a conversation about the situation with the inn, he lied, and took his boots off the table, and slipped them on, and the landlady sat up straight and picked up one of the glasses, and drank some beer. Sometimes you just wanted to stay up all night, said the knacker, at night you had wonderful ideas sometimes, and conversation was easier as well. Would I like a glass of beer, he asked. I sat down at the table. It was cool in the public bar, and I suddenly felt chilly. The knacker stood up and drew me a pint. He set it down on the table, and sat down again himself. The landlady was thinking of selling the inn, said the knacker, while her husband, who, as the painter would probably have told me, was in prison, was opposed to the idea. The landlady wanted to leave the region altogether, where, not least on account of her husband, she was not well-liked. Her children didn't have an easy time of it either. If it was up to her, she wouldn't stay there a day longer than she had to, and she wouldn't mind if she never saw the place again. But that, apart from the fact that the landlord is opposed and always will be opposed to the idea, was "unlikely," said the knacker, and apart from that it was hard to sell *such an inn*. It had nothing appealing about it, and wasn't in good condition either. "Quite apart from its location," said the knacker. "The landlady is chiefly concerned with the future for her children, which looks pretty bleak in Weng. And above all she's afraid of her husband returning from prison, and picking up his life where he left off, where he had to leave off." He had written her that he had every chance of being released in the next couple of months, "for good conduct," and that he would then "straighten out" the inn. The family, the knacker said, was in a rather wretched way; no one understood the others. Nor was the landlady the sort of woman her husband needed. She would be destroyed by such a man. She was continually sending him food parcels, the knacker said, and he didn't even thank her for them properly. "But you have to help someone like that, who's been taken out of society, and held up to all as a criminal, don't you?" he said. Yes, I said, you had to help someone like that, never mind what he'd done, what his present situation was, what he had on his conscience, and even what he might have done with you or to you. You always had to help prisoners. Not point your finger at them, but help them. You always knew what you could do to help. The landlady had sent her husband woolen socks, for instance. But "she's as certain as she can be of anything that once her husband is released and comes home, he'll do something awful to her. He's going to kill her," said the knacker, "not least because he knows that she gave evidence against him that landed him in prison." Anyway, once the power plant was up and running, and no more construction workers came to eat and drink, they might as well shut up shop, because the locals don't come. Previously, wedding parties and funeral feasts had been held here, as in other inns in the locality, but all that was finished now. Not one farmer came here anymore, and not their sons either, who, as was understood, weren't so put off by "that kind of thing." "When the power plant's finished, we'll be finished here as well," the landlady said. But the landlord didn't want to go. "It's where he's from," she said. She'd like to chuck the trade altogether, and maybe move to the city. She would make her way there. You could always find a job if you looked. There was more work available than ever. She had never felt at home in the valley. She had come unwillingly in the first place, and then only because she had a bun in the oven. All of which wasn't quite true, but it sounded persuasive enough, and I listened attentively. The knacker said: "In the city, a woman can find a type of light work that doesn't take it out of her so much. A factory job, for instance. Something like the cellulose factory in the valley, where the women don't 'overdo it,' and get decent enough wages. You can keep a couple of children on the money." Anyway, she was over the worst with the children, and before long, one or other of the girls would find herself a husband. Everything would be fairly straightforward, without the girls' father. And with that they got to the sentence that, once the landlady had said it, froze the atmosphere, the sentence: "Oh, if only he weren't around anymore." The knacker tried to draw attention away from the horror, and said: "They've introduced a bonus system at the cellulose factory"—and had I heard anything about it. But he could see I hadn't followed him. In the end, he said: "It's pretty hard for a woman to have to live with a man who's inclined the way the landlord is." Yes, it was hard, I said. The landlady now got up and went into the kitchen, and came out with a big cake she had baked, that was still warm. "I'll cut it right away," she said, "this is an occasion." And she cut the cake and said we should each take as much of it as we wanted. "It's better with raisins," she said. In the evening, she had been very tired, after washing up she had had to sit down for a while, and during that time she must have dropped off, but only for a little while, ten or fifteen minutes, then her daughters had woken her, and she had had to go round the back of the inn to take a look at a snowman they had built. But the snowman had given her a fright, and she had run back inside. "The girls didn't understand why I got such a fright," the landlady said, "but it was a terrifying snowman. The girls didn't know what they were doing." Then there had suddenly been some custom, a couple of workmen had come in, already drunk, who "had poured as much beer into them as they still had room for," then the policeman had shown up and scared them off, but then some others had come, and a couple of strangers after midnight, it was one o'clock "when the last of them was gone." And then she suddenly felt more awake than she had all evening. And so she and the knacker had decided not to go to bed at all, but to sit up in the public bar till morning. "Yes," I said, "it can be a helpful thing to spend a sleepless night." And with that I stood up, and they said they would stay sitting there, as they'd said, until morning, and I went up to my room and fell asleep immediately.

Twentieth Day

I get up at six, as I am used to doing, and light the stove. I always prepare the fire the night before. It's still dark, but light enough to wash. The cold water is very invigorating, and I feel like taking a walk right away, into the village and back, or up to the church and back, or only as far as the larch wood. But if I did, I know I would wake everyone in the building. The landlady would forbid it. So I sit at the window and look out, and see nothing but a tree trunk and the snow and in the snow the tracks of deer and dogs and chickens, and I read my Henry James, which is good distraction for me. Then, when it's time for breakfast, I head downstairs to the public bar, and wait for the painter so that he doesn't have to eat breakfast by himself. I am always hungry in the mornings. The landlady runs back and forth and hurries her girls off to school. When they've gone, the engineer and the knacker, who both stay on the second floor, leave the inn. Often guests appear by eight whose arrival I missed the night before, arriving late and moving off early, tramps and traders and other restless individuals, who've turned in for a night's sleep; usually they're badly dressed, wearing some cheap suit material, with no mittens, often they only have summer shoes, but some others pay with big notes and order up a breakfast I would never dare to for myself, with eggs and bacon, and they even order a glass of wine to go with it, and they pull newspapers out of their pockets, and lean back, and look every inch the well-informed citizen. Sometimes I see women too, yesterday for instance, relatives of people in the village, who can't stay over with them, because their relatives don't have enough beds for them, and they go out right away on an empty stomach, into the village, where their breakfast will be waiting for them.

After breakfast, I go out to the village with the painter, we buy something, and we stand around in the square, and decide where we'll take our walk later in the morning, and where in the afternoon: "Shall we go up to the church?" I say, and the painter says: "The church? But we went there only yesterday." Then I say: "Let's go to the larch wood then!"— "The larch wood?" he says. "But we were in the larch wood only yesterday."—"Then why don't we go down the ravine. Or to the station, even!"—"Yes, let's go down to the station," the painter says then. "The station is the only place there's any point in going to, because they sell newspapers there. If any place has any point to it, if there's any point to anything. Is there any point?" Then we're standing in front of the cobbler's window, and looking in, and thinking how cheap the shoes are here. "But they're not worth much," says the painter. "See, they're not even real leather!" Then we go over to the village hall, where the painter is greeted nicely. "Everyone knows me here," he says. "And they're nice to me because they're hoping for further sums of money from me. But they're not getting any more money from me. The vicar maybe, but not the parish. They don't even put up new public benches." The old benches are worn out, but the community won't put up new ones. Then we're between the two oldest buildings, the schoolhouse and the butcher's shop, and looking down the valley: "See," says the painter, "this is where you have the worst ugliness in front of you. Look at those railwaymen's cottages! Look at the power plant! Look at the cellulose factory! Look at the people running around this way and that, like vermin! Look, there's the doctor's house. The architect's house. The brewery! The railway station. Look!" He's tired. He says: "Do you know what's on the lunch menu? No?" And: "You should have seen me on these mountains ten years ago. I was so limber. Up that one! Up that one! See that white speck up there, right at the top, that's a chapel, I climbed up past that chapel all on my own, over to the Hochkönig, that range you can't see from here. But from the distiller's house on fine days, then you can see all the jags of those limestone peaks."

We eat lunch together. Then the painter goes for a little nap, and I take out my Henry James. I often read for several pages, without understanding what I've read. Then I read them again, and see that what I read was good. It's all about unhappy people. I shut the book and go over to the window and make notes, I write down whatever comes into my head in whatever way, then I hear the painter emerge from his room downstairs, and call me. I go down, and before long we're on the way to the larch wood, or the church, or already deep in the ravine. The painter talks, and I listen. I understand little of what he says, often he speaks too softly, as if talking to himself, or else I don't understand it because it doesn't seem coherent, or else because I'm too stupid. How am I to understand a sentence like this one: "The earth might be clear, I feel myself stuck between its hinges, without regard to myself, you understand!" Many times he stopped, because what he said had exhausted him. From time to time he asked me something. For example: "How do you find boredom? What do you think of the state? What's the difference between me and you? Is it scale? Will you be staying here long? Is there a difference between you and me? Do you believe in the miracles of mathematics? What do you do when you go to your room? Do your parents have a large garden? What plants grow in it? Is it cold where you live? What do you do in the evenings? Is your father a reader? How can you think of contradicting me? Oh, I know you didn't mean to contradict me! Do you pay as much for a glass of milk as I do? Are you surprised the landlady didn't ask you where I was

yesterday? How often do you think I've been to Weng? Did
your father say that? And you like the city? This book? Your
sister, you say? Not the theater? And the earth, you think, will
remain undiscovered? Are you afraid? No? Yes? Humanity?
An idea?"

THE STORY OF THE DEAD WOODCUTTER

He says: "That grisly experience, you know, I wanted to tell
you about it last night, but you were already gone. The business with the dead man. Now, remember, I'm taking the
shortcut. I walk for some time. I'm in a fairly good mood. I
stop by the fence. I get to the tree, and I see a couple of
people turning to look at me, and I see them just as I turn
round myself; maybe I turned and saw them because I felt
them turning to look at me. But it seemed odd to me that I
didn't notice them pass me. Because they must have passed
me, otherwise they couldn't have found themselves at the
spot where I saw them when I turned round. Do you follow?
I must have been lost in thought when I passed them, quite
oblivious to their being there. They were strangers. It seemed
to me, not well equipped. Not for this type of country. Probably trippers from somewhere. Maybe they had come up
from the city. Their jackets were city jackets. They seemed
very 'cultured,' that was my impression. Anyway, I started to
wonder about those people, and then I thought whether I
should take the ravine, or the road, that is, if I was going as
far as the road. No, I'm not going to turn back here, I said to
myself, I'll take the next shortcut, which leads down from the
other side of the larch wood to the river, and I walk at a fast
pace, and come out behind the station. I intended to go to the

café. First of all, though, I think, I'll go to the station and pick up the newspapers. Dusk was falling. I walk up to the bridge, and see this man in big boots, you know, one of those wood-cutters, who are everywhere to be found at this time of year, with their shining boots and their tight leather caps on their heads, their woolen mittens, and the terrible incessant crack-ing of whips. One of those knickerbocker types with a horse-drawn sleigh, laden with fir logs. In the first week, they drag them down the mountain streams, and in the next, they get them to the station, or to the sawmill, or to neighbors. I look across to him and am just thinking along the lines I told you about just now when he asks me the time: 'Half past four,' I say. I still see him clearly before me: a young face, but already chewed up, pale, streaked with the cold. I ask him where he's from, where he's going, and he tells me. He's from the shady side, he says. I say: 'Aha, from the shady side,' and I make to go on. And in the way that you promptly forget some people that you meet, I promptly forgot all about him. I want to get over to the station quickly, and all at once—I'm at the end of the bridge now—I hear a sound I can't describe to you; but the sound is such that I find myself running back in the direc-tion of the sound, and I see this man I was just now talking to, this young lumberjack, only now he's lying under his sleigh: he moves his hands a couple of times, his legs are already stiff. Dead. Now people start arriving, from the rail-waymen's cottages, from the station, from down in the vil-lage, before long there are lots of people clustered round him. I bend down to him, and I see he really is dead. He already has that color in his face, yellow, yellow-black, and rigor mortis. On the ground I spot a pool of blood; the people want to drag the sleigh out of the way, but I stop them, because you're not supposed to tamper with anything at the scene of an accident: 'Get back!' I say, and I brandish my stick at them. The horses were quite calm. I see the boots gleaming, because of course the lamp is swaying over the dead man. You know, just a moment ago I was talking to him . . . 'Half past four' . . . Then a doctor came. They carried the dead man into the village a ways, and laid him on a garden wall. Then took him into the house. Went back to the sleigh to pull it off the bridge, and into the village. Then they spent a long time standing around the pool of blood, as the temperature fell. On the river, you know, in the middle of the bridge . . . When I came back, with my newspapers under my arm, they were still standing around the pool of blood. He had skidded, and the sleigh had run him over and crushed his thorax. I couldn't get rid of the smell, the smell of death. And you know, by the time I was back up through the larch wood again, at eight o'clock or half past, under the full moon, I saw those people again that I saw on my way down to the station earlier. They were in the same place. When I looked across at them, they were laughing to themselves, as if they were cold. It felt eerie. Especially after the episode with the dead man. I had to go a long way round, so as not to encounter those people. Terrible people, you know, in their city clothes, and stubbornly continuing to laugh."

It starts to get dark at three o'clock already. The light leaves the east, and moves across the sky, till it goes out there too. Turns black almost. In the ravine, the painter often starts to skip. I notice canine qualities in him. For example: he sometimes turns his head like a big dog whom his master has told to sit. Twice I spent an afternoon on my own, went to the village, then down to the station, and around the cellulose fac-

tory. I tried to find the shortcut in the dark, but didn't manage, and had to retrace my steps up the road. I was relieved to
see the first lights, and then to find myself back in the village.
On the way to the inn, I felt scared. I don't know what of, suddenly there were people standing in the road, walking up to
me, but they didn't address me. The previous afternoon,
which I had again spent alone, because the painter had stayed
up in his room—"I want to try to write something!"—I ran
into the landlady. Walked with her up to the hay barn. On the
subject of the painter, she said she had known him "to dress
with more elegance before." She wanted to know whether I
didn't find anything curious about "artist Strauch." "No," I
said, "he doesn't strike me as being at all curious. How
come?" She didn't say anything, and walked over to the farm
where she got milk. Supper doesn't take long, it has to be
bolted down before it gets cold. Also because they're waiting
in the kitchen, to be able to wash up the dirty plates and cut-
lery. During supper, I think over everything that happened to
me today. I also think about how I ought to write to the assistant. But there's nothing more difficult than that. I'm unable
to express myself as I would like, in my head everything
looks different from how it is on paper. On paper, it's all so
dead. I run up to my room, and write down this and that, but
it's as though I were killing it all in writing it down. There's
nothing left of it.

"Terminal illnesses compel their carriers to acknowledge
them. I have had many occasions to observe this for myself,"
says the painter, "and the medical-scientific literature bears
me out. The terminally ill patient enters his terminal illness,
first with astonishment, then with meekness. A terminal ill-

ness gives the sufferer the illusion of being a world unto himself. Terminally ill patients fall for this deception, and thenceforth live in the deception, live in their terminal illness, in the illusory world of the terminal illness, and no longer in the world of reality." The illusory world of a terminal illness and the world of reality were contrary notions. The terminal patient no longer trusted the real world, but entered the illusory world of his terminal illness. Terminal illnesses "are rhythmic religious conveniences. People enter them as they might enter an unfamiliar garden. You know, in terminal illnesses there is often a protracted process, a sort of institutionalized terminal feeling in the patient—and then, suddenly, dramatically, *there is death.* Terminal illnesses are like exotic landscapes. An internal process of the inner egoist." He says: "There are very eccentric valleys here, and these valleys contain manor houses and castles. You visit these manor houses and castles, and you tell at a glance: the world you come from has no business here. You have to picture it to yourself as profoundly unreal, *like the deepest reality.* Doors open on people sitting in exquisite costumes, people enthroned, as if cut out of an imaginary painting, and when you make a move toward them, to touch them perhaps, they suddenly come to life. If you're addressed by one of them, you have the sense of never having heard a human voice before, never a language, having always been ignorant of the art of listening to someone speaking, of saying a word or two yourself, basically you don't know the first thing about words. And you don't speak, you are just astonished, and you listen: everything is made useful and conformable, there are no errors, chance and evil are eliminated. Simplicity like a clear blue sky arches above one's thoughts. Nor is there anything fantastic, even though everything is sprung from the imagination. Simple wealth, human warmth without a trace of criminality. Of dispute. Continual ongoing closed season. Cool reason and well-situated concepts and heart. Solid faces, built to last. The air lucid with thought, and competence exclaims: 'My God.' Gradually the turns of phrase and expressions reach a climax, the cleverness giving you pause. Laws apply here, intellect and character are pleasantly conjoined. Logic is converted to music. Old age is suddenly capable of beauty, youth feels like a row of foothills. The unfathomable truth lies on the bottom."

Twenty-first Day

His sentences are oar strokes that would propel him forward if it weren't for the powerful current. Sometimes he pauses, falls silent and listens, as though to check whether his present situation might not have been replaced by its successor. "It's impossible to direct anything." Things still in the future and the distant past all pull on one string with him, sometimes ten times in the space of a single sentence. He is a man who thinks continually of great losses, without any detachment. The sea surfaces in him, and in the sea is a boulder, part of an enormous sunken city, the end of an unanticipated story, far in the past. Death knots his net . . . Colors that are nothing but extrusions of flesh narcotize him philosophically . . . The adducing of extremes, so as to be able to spit them out. Tensions between eerie subaquatic scenes. The word "yoke" occurs frequently. The word "true"—but also "untrue" and "unreal." The word "ear of corn" may acquire the same meaning as "the whole of our welfare state." They are his eyes that speak, they enact his thought, they pitch wildness and quiet alternately at the disquiet of others. The painter is such an oddity, I think, that no one understands him. Not a type. Always reliant on himself, and always rejecting everything coming at him, he has taken advantage to excess of all possibilities. To look at him is to look at the millennia. "Mountains, you know, can serve as telescopes, through which one can see into the future." Or "inhumanly human." He is able to irritate people, where there are no people. To suppress effervescence, where there is no effervescence. "Isn't that an animal speaking? Am I not vermin?" Everything purposes the acceleration of his decay. Everything indicates a decisive childhood which was soon injured, a "stung nerve center," an organically fertile double significance of insanity.

I met the painter in the company of the policeman. When I said I felt like a walk in the ravine, and the painter felt like accompanying me, the policeman took his leave. He stamped through the cornfield toward the curling rink, where children were playing. The policeman was telling the painter that at Wagner's pub the previous night there had been a fistfight between locals and some showmen. The showmen had had a lot to drink, and not wanted to pay, they had tried to slip out through the back door, but were caught and finally overpowered. The policeman, who had happened to be at Wagner's at the time, threatened them with his gun, and then they allowed themselves to be captured. One of the showmen managed to escape in the direction of the larch wood. Another was found near the pond. In the course of the fight, a couple of farmers' boys had received head injuries, and the policeman had been kicked in the stomach, which still hurt. Now the showmen were sitting in the lockup, and they will be brought to trial. For stiffing the barman, and several counts of grievous bodily harm. During the burial, they had had to take the cobbler's apprentice to the hospital. He had been floored by a punch. The doctor, who had traveled up to the village to see to the injured, diagnosed a serious concussion, with fracture of the skull, and spinal injuries. No mention of any possible paralysis, thank God.

It had all started with singing and dancing, said the painter. Then there had been a sudden exodus from the bar, and the farmers' boys had only needed to look at one another to understand "what was afoot." They left by all the different exits, to block off the escape routes for the showmen. "The showmen have parked their trailers down outside the railway station," said the painter. The police sealed and confiscated the trailers. They wanted to go down to Carinthia, where they came from. Deformed women and deformed animals were their principal objects of display. Cows with six legs, or two tails, of the sort you got sometimes. "That always brings in the public," said the painter. "A woman with two noses, irresistible!" Now the animals and the women have to be looked after at the public expense, because the showmen are behind bars and are therefore unable to look after them. Also, fires needed to be lit in front of the trailers, to keep the women and animals from freezing to death. The trailers were under strict guard, because it was feared the escaped showmen might try to move them. The showmen had gone to Wagner's with the explicit intention of not paying their tab.

At first they had bragged about the money they all claimed to have in their pockets. Some of the farmers' boys had been under the impression that they had seen the showmen with money. The policeman, however, as he had said, had been on to them from the start, and with rather more than the usual suspicion one perforce entertains of showmen and artists and people like that. He had had his eye on them the whole time, even while they were dancing and singing, but not seen any grounds to intervene. Not until they left the bar. "Lucky," the policeman said, "that the farmers' boys didn't pull their knives. Otherwise there could have been a massacre." But as it was there had only been fists and boots, whereas stabbings were very often fatal. "Every one of the farmers' boys has been involved in a stabbing before now. It was a miracle that none of them pulled their knives. Maybe they thought they could polish off the showmen without recourse to knives." And they were proved right. "The one who comes out of it worst in the end is Wagner, the landlord," said the painter. "The showmen didn't stint themselves, they ate and drank of the best, and they ordered whole rounds for other customers as well." Wagner might confiscate their trailers, which would be "scant recompense" for his losses, and even then the police don't think he can expect to be awarded them. He thinks, if he has the animals slaughtered, he can make up his losses. The trailers were only good for transporting hay, you couldn't load wood on to them, they are too rickety for that. Anyway, the policeman reckons the trailers plus contents will fall to the state. They're considering what to do with the three disfigured women, probably they will send them back to Carinthia, where they come from, tomorrow. And now of all times, when there are so many burials going on, this matter with the showmen! The policeman says they are being fed from our inn. They shout and make noise so that they can be heard all over the village. The children go and make faces at them in the village square. "Tomorrow they're being taken to be arraigned," said the painter. The policeman had hand-cuffed one of them, the others had had to have their hands tied with clothesline. There had been a huge stir in the village. All of a sudden all the lights had come on, and "people had gawked out of the windows." A second policeman had been sent for from the lower guard post in the village. "Now the two of them have to sleep in the passage in front of the cell," said the painter, "though of course there's not much hope of that, given the way the arrested showmen are drumming away on the door."

We were already deep into the ravine when we decided to turn back. He had had a pain-filled night, said the painter. "Each time I try to do something to diminish the pain, I end up making it worse. The unendurable doesn't really exist," he said, "because the unendurable would have to be death, and death isn't unendurable. Do you understand."

THE STORY OF THE TRAMP

In the larch wood he ran into a tramp. His first thought had been that it might be the escaped showman, but the tramp was nothing to do with that. Not at all. The painter had been startled, because he had failed to see the tramp, and tripped over him. "Like a corpse lying in the middle of the road," says the painter. A hypothermia victim, he had thought, and taken a step back. From the man's clothes, he could tell he wasn't from here. Where is he from? "Striped pants, you know, the sort that circus people wear, particularly circus directors." Assuming the man was dead, he had tried to flip him over with his stick so that he could see his face, "because the fellow was lying facedown. It's natural to want to see someone's face," said the painter. But no sooner had he applied the stick to the "dead man," than he had emitted a scream and leaped to his feet. "Oh," the tramp is said to have said, "I was just playing dead, I wanted to see what happened when someone comes across somebody else, lying flat on his front like a dead man, in the road, in the middle of the forest and the middle of winter." With those words, the tramp had got up, and brushed down his pants. "If you think I'm the escaped show-man, you're mistaken, I have nothing to do with those show-men. You don't have to worry about that. Let's shake!" He held his hand out to the painter, and introduced himself. "He gave me such a complicated name that I was unable to remember it," said the painter. "Then he buttoned up his coat, which must have come undone. A dignified but com-pletely reduced appearance," said the painter. "It could just as easily have been a trap, I mean, God knows whom I could have encountered." That was no one's idea of a joke, the painter had said, one did not simply play dead, that was a prank, a silly prank of the sort teenagers might indulge in, to give their parents a fright. "Just imagine if the shock had given me a heart attack!"—"Then I would have run off," the tramp is said to have replied. Anyone could have a heart attack at any time. "Yes. Of course."—"No involvement from any other party would have been suspected," the tramp is supposed to have said. "Of course not," the painter. In any case the road was full of tracks, who would have taken the trouble to trace all the different footwear. "No, of course not.

If you should happen to be in financial straits," the painter is supposed to have said, "then I must point out to you that I have no money. I am a poor man, and my situation is miserable."—"Oh," the tramp is supposed to have replied, "I've got enough money." He was amazed that the painter should take him for a robber, was it perhaps the fault of the circus pants he was wearing. "Oh, no," the painter is supposed to have said, "I'm an artist myself."—"It's remarkable how little understanding is displayed by people one would expect to have a lot of understanding," the tramp is supposed to have said. Besides, he did not dislike the painter. "When I heard someone approaching, I lay down in the road. It was just an experiment."—"An experiment," the painter is supposed to have said again. "Yes, an experiment. And what happened is exactly what I thought would happen. I listened to every step you took. The way you walk, it's as though you were on deer hooves," the tramp said. "I had a fantastic image of you in my head as you approached. A completely fantastic image of you!" His pronunciation was a little northern, it might be that he was from Holstein or Hamburg. "A deer is coming to present itself to me," he said, and: "That was pure poetry." The painter: "I understand." What profession did the tramp pursue, inquired the painter. "I am the owner of a movable theater," he is supposed to have replied. "The way you're dressed, one would have thought you'd just come from some rather dubious society piece," the painter is supposed to have said. "You're not a million miles out there," the tramp: "I appeared in this costume three hundred times in Frankfurt am Main. Till I could stand it no longer, and ran away. You should try playing the same part in a play three hundred times, and a pretty boring play at that, a so-called George Bernard Shaw play, and you'll go crazy too." But he was surely a man who could live by his jokes. "Oh, I should say so too. I have always lived by my jokes."—"And how do you propose to continue now? Since, as I am forced to assume, you are pretty much at loose ends, drifting here and there? How do you mean to continue?"—"I never asked myself that," the tramp is said to have answered. Since he, the tramp, the theater manager, the director of a so-called movable theater, had no children, it wasn't so very difficult to live "unto the day." But was that entirely realistic, said the painter. Men of his (the tramp's) type had freedom, disrepute, and humor written in their faces. "I am said to have picked up a few magic tricks from my father," the tramp is supposed to have said, "that everyone likes. For instance how to make my head disappear. It's very easy." He could do a demonstration, "if the gentleman cared to see," and the painter did care, and the tramp duly made his head disappear. "The man only extended as far as his Adam's apple. What I say is true. It may strike you as thoroughly implausible, but it's as true as the fact that I'm standing in front of you now. The whole appearance of that tramp . . . And just imagine this whole scene taking place in the middle of the larch wood, where we take the fork down into the ravine . . ." Then, in a trice, the tramp's head was back in its original place. "That's just a simple trick, making my head disappear," said the tramp, "what's harder is playing ball with your own legs." Of course the painter wanted to see that magic trick as well. And suddenly the tramp's legs came down from the sky, and he hunkered down on the ground and played ball with them, kids' ball games. While he was playing, he said: "I'll stop right away if you feel scared." The painter could feel a shiver, but he still said: "No, no, I'm not scared." He was, as you say, astounded by what was put on for him. "I have never seen such consummate magic tricks," he said. "Now I'm too bored to go on," the tramp is supposed to have said, and he stopped. "The thing with the head was as baffling to me as the other one, with the legs," the painter said, "can you imagine it? Of course, as with everything, there must be some sort of knack to it!" All Paris had lain at the tramp's feet, and if he felt like it, it would lie at his feet again, only he didn't feel like having Paris lying at his feet again. "I'm bored." In London he had been presented to the queen. If the gentleman would like it, he would be happy to give him the address of his movable theater. "It's small, but exquisite," he is supposed to have said, "and it can go into action anywhere you require." It was the most exquisite of theaters. The most exquisite theater in the world. But one day he was fed up with magic tricks—"it's so easy to get fed up with magic tricks"—and had turned instead to pure, true art, the sort of art that isn't dependent on magic tricks. Now, he was sure the gentleman would love to know which was harder, to perform magic tricks of the sort he had just performed, and which were unquestionably among the best in the world, or else to act in straight theater, to put over a true art form, then, as exemplified by the theater, an art without tricks, as for instance, "playing King Lear." They were both equally difficult, one was harder than the other, but it was a better thing to act in a play than to perform tricks, he personally found acting far more satisfying, and for that reason he had magicked up his movable theater "out of thin air," as he said. "Though, of course that too was a stunt, a sort of trick," said the tramp. Acting, moreover, was highly intellectual, whereas performing magic tricks wasn't intellectual at all. Only the trick itself was. "Of course it always comes down to the audience." And he said, supposedly: "The audiences for my magic tricks are a thousand times dearer to me than the audiences who watch me acting." The audiences for his tricks would know right away what it was that was so astounding to them, whereas the audiences for his acting never seemed to know. "Theater audiences are invariably disappointing. Audiences for magic tricks never are." And yet he would rather act, even though he was better suited to doing tricks. "Theater audiences don't make me any happier than magic-trick audiences," he said. "Audiences for magic tricks are as they are. Theater audiences are never as they are, they are always as they ought not to be, they want to be as they are not . . ." The audiences for magic tricks were never so stupid that they failed to realize how stupid they were, but theater audiences were, if anything, more stupid. "Most actors are so stupid they don't even notice how stupid the audiences are. Because in general actors are even more stupid than audiences, even though an audience is infinitely stupid." Why did he not demonstrate any more magic tricks, the painter wanted to know. "Magic tricks of themselves are not satisfying," the tramp is supposed to have said, "but a play can be satisfying in itself." He didn't know, anyway, why he now preferred acting to demonstrating magic tricks. Right at the moment, he wasn't doing one thing or the other. "But I will demonstrate my magic tricks again!" he is supposed to have said, "and Paris will lie at my feet again!" Then he supposedly asked what the quickest way down to the station was. "Go down the ravine," the painter told him. Then: "I'd like to know at what age magic tricks of themselves are no longer satisfying." The tramp reflected briefly and said: "That's different in each performer's individual case. But often the magic tricks are no longer satisfying, even before they have been mastered," he is supposed to have said. The painter offered to accompany the tramp part of the way down the ravine. "I know my way around here," he is supposed to have said. "You lose your footing somewhere, and you'll break a leg. Come with me!" Before they parted, the painter asked him: "What was it that prompted you to try that silly nonsense out on me?"—"Silly nonsense?" the tramp is supposed to have answered. "You mean, playing dead in front of you? That's a passion of mine, that's all." And then he suddenly disappeared. "He was as supple as you'd expect a performer of magic tricks to be," the painter said. "I've never met anyone like that, who claims to be the proprietor of a 'movable theater.' Or do you think I've made up the whole story?" I think it's true myself.

Twenty-second Day

That night, I made a grisly discovery that confirms something the painter merely assumed. After the building had been in silence for several hours, I suddenly heard the knacker under my window. A guest had moved into the room next to mine, who was gone in the morning, and I thought he would have heard the noise the knacker was making outside the landlady's window and get up, because I could hear him stirring, I could hear it through the wall. But then there was quiet in the room next to mine. I went over to the window, and I could see the knacker outside. The landlady had opened her window to let him in, and helped him get inside. Then he reached down, and hauled up the rucksack, which he had left outside in a heap of snow. I had the sense he might have a car-

cass in the rucksack. The thought that he might have a carcass in his rucksack would leave me no peace, and I decided
to go downstairs and listen outside the landlady's door, and,
perhaps, I thought, hear something from her conversation
with the knacker that would either reinforce me in my suspicion that there might be a carcass in the rucksack, or alterna-
tively might set my mind at rest, because there would clearly
not be a carcass in the rucksack. I don't know why I was so set
on knowing. There would be nothing unusual about the
knacker carrying carcasses about with him in his rucksack,
it's part of his job. I slipped into my pants and vest, and went
downstairs. I had to exercise care. The painter was asleep.
The new guest was asleep too. Everyone was asleep. I could
hear the knacker in conversation with the landlady. He had
been delayed at the crossroads, he was saying, by a certain
party well known to them both from earlier times. This man
had drunk away all his money, and now asked him for the
train fare home. The knacker's passing this way was a sign
from heaven. "Just like that, in the middle of the night," said
the landlady. "I expect he was at the Oberwirt's," said the
knacker. I was afraid the door might open, and they would
see me standing in the doorway. The landlady said: "So he's
back in the area now!" And the knacker: "No, he won't be
back again!" The man had said he would pay him back by
mail. "He'll not pay you back!" said the landlady. "Not him.
What was he doing here anyway?" He couldn't tell her, said
the knacker, it sometimes occurred to a man in the middle of
the night to go back to a region with which he had had some
previous association. "He's to blame for everything," said the
landlady. "It was him who turned you know who into a criminal." She meant her husband. "Even when they were at
school together, he was working to turn him to the bad. He'd

better not show his face anywhere I can see it." Then she suddenly asked whether the knacker had brought what he had said he was going to bring. "Yes," he said, and behind the door I could clearly hear the smack of the carcass on the floor. "Such a beautiful dog," said the landlady. I was appalled. She would clean it right away, she said. Then I heard the two of them go down to the kitchen together. I went straight up to my room. Was unable to sleep, though. Now I know she cooks with dogmeat, I thought. The painter always said so. And he's right.

In the morning I wasn't sure I might not have dreamed the whole thing with the dog's body. But no, I really had heard what I thought I had. I shuddered to think of it, but at the same time I resolved not to tell anyone this story, which still struck me in the light of a dream. It would be grist to the painter's mill if I told him. Even the fact that I had heard the knacker making noise outside under my window, and got up, and went over to my window; if I had told him the whole story of this nocturnal experience, and my sensations in the course of it, it would have confirmed him in much, not just his theory that the landlady had been using dog- and horse-meat in her kitchen for a long time. So the knacker takes carcasses round to her inn. Probably infected pigs too. Things have lost their power to disgust me. But I'll be sure to look closely at the landlady's meat dishes in future. I won't eat minced meat in any form, or sausages, or stews; larger pieces of meat that are whole on your plate are easy to identify as pork or beef or veal. It would be a calamity if I told anyone of my observation. Presumably the landlady pays the knacker a pittance for the meat in his rucksack, but maybe, and this is perhaps likelier, she doesn't pay him a penny for it. She has a lover, then, who is at the same time the cheapest imaginable supplier of meat. The painter was always struck by the fact that the landlady's butcher's bills were so low. And this is the answer to the riddle. I must on no account tell the painter of my nocturnal experiences. Looking back on it, I was quite transformed by what I saw and heard that night. Had I ever before got up at night and gone to the window, to investigate sounds whose provenance I knew, and knew to be harmless? And then putting on clothes, and going downstairs! And eavesdropping at the bedroom door! Taking risks that only a madman would take! I really was scared of being found out, too, as I stood listening at the landlady's door. That such things are possible in dreams, even in the dreams of otherwise sane individuals—in dreams, all things are possible—I know; but this was no dream. All morning I was agitated, and the painter detected my agitation, on the walk to the village and in the cemetery, it wasn't his story with the tramp, those "bewildering instances of endless eccentricity" were confusing to me too, but they were not the spur—it was the story of the dog's body. I ate nothing at all at lunch. I only drank a glass of beer, and the painter asked me if I was ill. "No," I said, "I'm not ill."

"One keeps descending, among the low," said the painter, "then lower and lower, far lower than them. What I say is true: the finer traits of humans have always been repugnant to me: I have had to brush them away, I never wanted to come in contact with them. Periodically, throughout my life, I have descended into the low, squalid world. I always felt I belonged there. And so I remained there. And the low world, you know, isn't low, and the squalid world not squalid, at any rate the low world is never as low as the other, nor the squalid as squalid. Hence too my preference for poverty, for rejection, you must know. Because when I was poor, I was also a man who seemed to have some value to myself, even if I walked in filth, and was filthy myself . . . But that's just something I say to myself . . ." He said: "Imagine a tree that you expect to bear fruit once again, and that disappoints you by not bearing any more fruit." Almost all lives had been disappointing in such a way. "Wherever you look, trees that no longer bear any fruit." The human race was the unfruitful thing, "the only unfruitful thing in the whole world. It serves no purpose. It can't be made into anything. It can't be eaten. It isn't a raw material for some process outside itself." He was a pessimist, which was something ridiculous, something finally much worse. And beyond that, more ridiculous still. "The brain says one thing, and the rest of the body says something else, and what ends up happening is something that neither the brain nor the rest of the body is happy with." From out of himself he had gone into the world, and been through the world back to himself. "It's in myself, as I know, because it's deeper than the world." The knack of switching himself off was something he had often managed to achieve between opening his eyes and closing them again. "Too much respect at the beginning, and too much hatred and revulsion later on. First of all the drive to get to know certain cities, and then the drive to forget all those cities again. Men like rats, chopped up by street sweepers' shovels. Too many negotiations with humans have done me in." Unusual interests: "Investigations, the ideals of investigations, the ideals of friendships followed successively by being delivered of the ideals of investigation, being delivered of the investigations themselves, of the ideals of friendship, and finally of the friendships themselves." For years, it had all been nothing more than "eavesdropping on suffering." In split seconds, eternities of disappointment. In his permanent condition of dupe, the human was relegated to being his own arena.

Earlier he had been able to catch charmed words like balls, the word "creation," first off, then the word "chemistry," then "instinct," "painting," and last of all "murder." The ruin of mankind had been a child's dream. And everything settled then. Father and mother exemplars of unhappy, irresponsible, no longer amendable actions on the part of instinct, emotion, the devil. "In winter, pain falls in the form of snow, did you know that?" Songbirds sing pain. "The weak man has no law that will protect him."

The landlady was astonished at the numbers who turned out for the funeral of the farmer's wife, who, as the fire was destroying her house, was crushed by a falling roof beam. From everywhere, from the remotest valleys, they came, relatives and acquaintances and the merely curious. The funeral procession had been so long that not all the mourners had got into the graveyard. A number had had to wait outside on the cemetery steps during the service, and in the square in front of the church. Never in her life had she seen so many flowers and wreaths. She had been most interested to see the widower, but had only caught sight of him once everything was over, and managed then to exchange a few words with him, having once been in service to him. "He's much more dignified than he used to be," she said. As there were so many relatives around, she had to move off. But she was invited to the funeral meal, which was taking place in three inns at once, because one wouldn't have had enough room for all the guests. The food had been better than for any corpse she could remember. The band, having just played a funeral march by the graveside, had struck up in a rather more cheerful vein outside in the square, which had been "heaving with people." In the cemetery itself, the mourners had trampled on all the graves, they had pushed their way forward to the grave itself, so that they could peer down into it, but no one had been able to see anything worse than a plank. "The cemetery in S. is three times the size of the one in Weng," she said. Of course a lot of people from Weng had been to the funeral as well, especially "money people." Because she owned no black coat, only a gray one, she had been a bit embarrassed to begin with, but later she forgot all about it. "I was the only one in the place who wasn't wearing a black coat." They had loosed off rounds while the coffin was being lowered into the grave, just like at New Year's. The vicar and the mayor had made speeches, but she hadn't been able to hear a word. Her daughters had pushed their way in among the black-clad people through to the open grave, and mingled with the relatives of the dead woman, which earned her some furious looks, even before she left the cemetery. The revels went on till five in the morning, till everything had been eaten and drunk. But she had set off for home at eleven. "I was pretty drunk too," she said. The knacker had taken her back in his sleigh. I heard them, how he unloaded her, and how she tried to detain him, but he left anyway. Last night she had gone down to the station for a bunch of immortelles which she left on the dead woman's coffin, once there was no one around to see. What had been of most interest to her was the food the various landlords had prepared, for the most part following *her* recipes. Their vicar had joined in the dancing, and been pretty free with suggestive remarks as well, she had been surprised to see a vicar, "a man of God," carrying on in such a way.

"People need to taste the whip," said Strauch, "the knout of the executioner." He urged me to put on sturdier shoes, he found it unbearable to see me in such "luxury items" as the shoes I had on every day. But I have no sturdier shoes. I own just two pairs, a pair of boots for the winter, and a pair of ankle-high shoes for summer, which I left at home. "Things change here very quickly," said the painter, "quite without notice. Suddenly it's so cold, it can freeze your sinuses. A sudden blow, and you go from one thing to the opposite." He didn't think it would snow any time soon, but there would be an iron frost. He could tell by all sorts of things, by plants, by everything, that a frost was in the offing. "A terrible frost. You can see it in the trees and rocks. You can hear it, when you hear the animals." And one day everything would freeze, "and be dead. The world as presently constituted. Even the air will go rigid, and the snowflakes in the air." When he was walking out of an inn once, in the Tyrol, where he used to go at times, "into the clear country," as he says, he suddenly jammed his stick into a pig that had frozen solid. He had wanted to drive the beast on, but the stick was caught fast in the pig, as if it had been made of snow. When he pulled out his stick, the pig made a squelching noise, which disgusted him. "The frost eats everything up," said the painter, "trees, humans, animals, and whatever is in the trees and the humans and the animals. The blood stalls, and at great speed.

You can break apart a frozen human like a piece of stale bread." He said: "Did you notice that country people never wear a coat, no matter how low the temperature? At least not here, in this region. In the flatland, yes, but not here. In the lower Alps, but not in the Alps proper. The men put up their collars, the women come down from the mountains in their folklore outfits. Even at twenty below zero." The cold drew people together as much as the beasts in the sty, around a dish or a book. "Cold is the most sharp-witted state of nature," said the painter. Schoolkids usually got no further than an outcrop of rock, and then they turned back, for fear of freezing to death. Or the schools were closed on account of the low temperatures. People died in midsentence. In the middle of a cry for help. The stars flashed like nails driven into the night sky. "Air composition that makes reason ring out like the tongue of a bell."

Had I ever had a frozen limb or digit, he wanted to know. "There are many men who have been marked by frost."—"No," I said. "In the war, I should tell you, men had the feet freeze off their legs, and the ears off their heads. By thinking on a certain subject, a condition that may be thousands of years away, or at the very least a beautiful memory, it is possible to generate warmth in oneself, even heat, but only to a certain, finally unsuccessful, degree. Even those soldiers who burned with homesickness during the Russian winter campaigns were not enabled to survive by their homesickness." He said: "When the days get that cold, I sit in my bed, and stare at the frost flowers on my window, that in a succession of miracles evoke landscapes from painting, from nature, from inner despair, only to crush them again, and to draw from them such truths as, to my conviction, are dispersed in their hundreds of thousands and their millions in our lives, and portray more than an intimation of a world that lies alongside our familiar world, a universe we have failed to recognize."

Then, in front of the trunk that looms out of the middle of the pond, he said: "We all live the lives of death masks. Everyone who is really alive has taken his off at one time or another, but as I say, people don't live, it's just, as I say, the life of death masks." There were no real humans anymore, just death masks of real humans. And the whole thing was so grotesque precisely because it amounted to a vast "crippling by reason," spreading from our brains to those of friends and neighbors. "A seeming life, no longer capable of real life. Cities that are long since dead, mountains too, long dead, livestock, poultry, even water and the creatures that used to live in the water. Reflections of our death masks. A death-mask ball," he said. He became agitated when I told him I didn't believe in his "death-mask ball." "You young people don't believe," he said. "The whole world is nothing but a death-mask ball." In accordance with its development, and the development of the cosmos. "The influence of the stars, the astral bodies is not open to doubt." He said: "What I tell you is intellectuality pondering logically." What is that? "Nothing you can touch, nothing you can think, nothing apparent, nothing real, as we have come to refine the idea, nothing we can 'deal with,' nothing for Pascal, nothing for Descartes. Nothing for humans. Nothing for swine. If monstrosity could breed in one man's head, where would that get us," he said. "The incomprehensible is our life. Nothing else.

That sometimes finds form in humans, just as swarms of birds take to the air and turn it black. The incomprehensible is the miraculous. The un-understood world is the world of wonders, the one you understand has no wonder in it." Each step toward knowledge was a step away from wonder. "Science of course claims the opposite. But just as any science always claims the opposite of any other science." And then things weren't quite that simple. For: "Science lies, that's its principle, it destroys, and makes megalomania possible, and the miraculous. What science wants is to stop being science, at a certain point it wants to select. That's its endeavor. And that's worthy of our support." A man was never in the way of science at that point where it was seeking to emerge from itself, and go back to humans. He said: "Then, when science has achieved its end, the death masks will become human beings again."

Pub gardens in summertime were often full of people who clearly "take themselves to be the center of the world. They draw attention to themselves immediately. Go up to a table in the deepest shade (or, in the present season, we would say: next to the open fireplace!) and that may have been reserved for them. What goes on in a brain that conceives itself to be the center of the world. Millions of lights going on and off in millions of centers! That's the world. That's all it is. The ordinary sits at a table with the extraordinary and drinks a pint of beer, or eats a plate of scrambled eggs. Plays chess or a game of cards. Each ordinary and extraordinary individual that makes up the world. But what is ordinary? What is extraordinary? In the summer heat (as in the winter cold), humans are less confined, because more helpless. They pull on ropes, and

pulling on the other end is the world: 'my world.' That's
where they think it is, or that's where they think they are.
And that's how they come to think of themselves, sitting
there with head erect, as being what they claim to be, the center of the world. 'When I'm dead, the world will die' is what
they think." He, the painter, thought of humans as "aborigi-
nal outgrowths, bordering on the unfathomable, but only
bordering on it." His picture of pub gardens in summertime
enabled one to follow the trails of humans in their greatest
folly. "To identify their world. To identify the world. Tactics?
Where vulgarity carries its head as high as royalty. Brutality
wanders along like the epitome of gentleness, celebrated,
ethical, inimitable. The thought of a glass of beer leads to the
wildest overestimates and thoughts: the world is what I am!
Begins where I begin. And ends where I end. Is as bad as me.
As good. No better, because me. No question, me. Likes to
drink. Likes to eat. Doesn't know one percent, because I
don't know one percent either. Famous? Well, yes and no.
Too much, that would mean knowing more than me,
wouldn't be good for it, because that would mean I was sick.
Without appetite. That's the world: confined to a head of cattle, confined to roast beef. A human will never go beyond
where he thinks the world will go. His personal edge is also
the edge of the world. Its defeat is his. In a pub garden in
summertime, the world is confined to the hunger and thirst
of the world. Of each individual in it. Each single individual.
'A beer, please,' means the world is asking for a beer. It downs
it, and after a while, it feels thirsty again."

Women were like rivers, their banks were unreachable, the
night often rang with the cries of the drowned. "Living

together as husband and wife, you know, that's the same as
unjustifiable torment till the end of the marriage. When the
states of two individuals are pushed together into unbearableness like seams of rock. Then black ceases to be black,
and a child is no longer a blessing. Everything turns into its
obverse. You know, poverty looks quite different, wealth
turns out to have been a deception, ahead of a further, catastrophic deception." It soon turned into a stagnant pool,
where the two partners stared emptily at one another. Each
of them destroyed by figures and calculations. A head full of
shame and waste, that was marriage, for man and woman
alike. "They walk in through the church gates, and walk out
through the brothel door. There are mirrors where you can
see everything to the point of cruelty, to the deadly thumbs-
down." And it was all an immutably fixed underground
process. Why? Waking dreams suddenly come out, supposi-
tions turn into bitter truth. Blows, received in a dream, send
you reeling. The frustrated fantasy dreams of travel, of
returning to a solitude that wasn't solitude at all. In the middle of the city, there's a sudden gust of wind you thought had
long passed. But you can no longer shake the tree to bring
down the overripe fruits. No. A dog runs against your shin,
and you wake up feeling embittered. There's a bricklayer
hunkered down on some scaffolding planks, there's a railwayman standing looking at his watch because he's tired, there's
someone walking along a roof carrying a sheet of glass for a
window . . . Removal men with weight lifter belts are good
for hefting tables and crates about, you think, and you feel
like the saddest man on the planet. And the world is miles
away from the spectacle that abandoned it, as ruthless as a
bad mother, running after her lover. Strauch said: "The truth
is like some crazy gardener, uprooting cabbages and letting

them lie. It's a spree." The man walks beside his wife to the edge of town where the factories are and the mines that feed him, with his child by the hand, he walks into an endless unhappiness. And it must often come to him, the glib saying that thousands of people are used like pieces of sacking, and then discarded. And he thinks of words such as "added" and "subtracted" and "oppressed" and "beaten." And wherever his wife looks, she sees only addled faces. And the scabies on her daughter's face. Whatever it is you might want is not on the menu. To walk together till it means falling together, till it means murdering each other together. "If at all, then take the child as well." And he: All he proposed was the effort to get crushed. To the rail embankment. Just a few yards off. Oh, yes. But brutality always intervenes, everywhere. The thing that glistens softly over the rooftops, well, it might be warm air, but actually it's the beginning of the end. And the creaking tree: malign, the blackness of its trunk. And still, everything takes its usual course. No one says anything. Which makes everything even worse. The child is put to bed, and then you dread everything ahead of you. The one lying beside the other in bed thinks everything that is so terribly evil could—an ill spark crosses the other's face—be the truth. And even if it's not, it still hurts.

To-ing and Fro-ing

I have to say, there was a real to-ing and fro-ing today.

We came out of the larch wood, making for the village and beyond into the deep forest. I was leading the way. The painter followed me, all the time I had the sense he's about to lay into me, he'll attack me from behind. I don't know what prompted me to think that way, but I was unable to lose the fear that was oozing out of me. From time to time I picked up a word he was saying, it was completely incomprehensible to me, I couldn't answer him when he asked me something, because really he was only asking himself. He growled at me: "Kindly stop when I ask you a question!" I stopped. "Come here!" he commanded. Suddenly I realized (it was in his tone, and I felt only I was in a position to realize this) the resemblance to his brother, the assistant. He said: "The air is the only true conscience, do you understand me?" I replied: "I don't understand you."—"The air, I say, is the only true science!" he repeated. I still didn't understand, but nodded anyway. He said: "The gesture of the air, the great aerial gesture, you understand. The nightmarish sweat of fear, that's the air." I told him that was a great thought. In my opinion it was even poetry, to me what he had just said was the distillation of all memory, of all possibility. "Poetry is nothing!" he said. "Poetry as you understand it is nothing. Poetry as the world understands it, as the poetry hound understands it, is nothing. No, this poetry is nothing! The poetry that I have in mind is something else. If you meant *that* poetry, then you'd be right. Then I'd have to embrace you!" I said: "What is your poetry?"—"My poetry isn't *my* poetry. But if you mean *my* poetry, then I'll have to admit I'm unable to offer you a description of it. You see, my poetry, *which is the only poetry,* and therefore also *the only truth,* just as much as *the only truth* that I find in the air, which I feel in the air, which is the air, *this poetry of mine* is always generated at the center of its own thought, which is all its own. This poetry is momentary, is instantaneous. And therefore it isn't. It is *my* poetry."—"Yes,"

I said, "it is your poetry." I had understood nothing of what he had said. "Let's go on," he said, "it's cold. The cold is eating into the center of my brain. If only you knew how far the cold had already advanced into my brain. The insatiable cold, the cold that insists on its bloody nourishment of cells, that insists on my brain, on everything that could make anything, could *become* anything. You see," he said, "the brain, the skull and the brain within it, are an incredible irresponsibility, a dilettantism, a lethal dilettantism, that's what I want to say. One's forces are attacked, the cold bites into my forces, into my human forces, into the lofty muscle power of reason. It's this ancient tourism of cold, billions of years old, this exploitative and pernicious tourism, that penetrates my brain, the entry of frost . . . There is," he said, "no longer the category of 'secret,' it doesn't exist, everything is just *frigor mortis*. I see the cold, I can write it down, I can dictate it, it's killing me . . ." In the village, he popped into the abattoir. He said: "Cold is one of the great A-truths, the greatest of all the A-truths, and therefore it is all truths rolled into one. Truth is always a process of extermination, you must understand. Truth leads downhill, points downhill, truth is always an abyss. Untruth is a climbing, an up, untruth is no death, as truth is death, untruth is no abyss, but untruth is not A-truth, you understand: the great infirmities do not approach us from outside, the great infirmities have been within us, surprisingly, for millions of years . . ." He says, staring through the open abattoir doors: "There it is clearly in front of you, broken open, sliced apart. And there's the scream as well, of course! If you listen, you'll catch the scream as well. You will still hear the scream, even though the facility for the production of the scream is dead, is severed, chopped up, ripped open. The vocal cords have been rendered, but the scream is still there! It's a grotesque realization that the vocal cords have been smashed, chopped up, sliced apart, and the scream is *still there*. That the scream is always there. Even if all the vocal cords have been chopped up and sliced apart, are dead, all the vocal cords in the world, all the vocal cords of all the worlds, all the imaginations, all the vocal cords of every creature, the scream is always there, is always *still* there, the scream cannot be chopped up, cannot be cut through, the scream is the only eternal thing, the only infinite thing, the only ineradicable thing, the only constant thing . . . The lesson of humanity and inhumanity and human opinions, and of the great human silence, the lesson of the great memory protocol of the great being, should all be tackled through the abattoir! Schoolchildren should not be brought to heated classrooms, they should be made to attend abattoirs; it is only from abattoirs that I expect understanding of the world and of the world's bloody life. Our teachers should do their work in abattoirs. Not read from books, but swing hammers, wield saws, and apply knives . . . Reading should be taught from the coiled intestines, and not from useless lines in books . . . The word 'nectar' should be traded in forthwith for the word 'blood' . . . You see," said the painter, "the abattoir is the only essentially philosophical venue. The abattoir is *the* classroom and *the* lecture hall. The only wisdom is abattoir wisdom! A-truth, truth, untruth, all added up come to the vast abattoir immatriculation, which I would like to make compulsory for humans, for new humans, and those tempted to become humans. Knowledge in the world is not abattoir knowledge, and it lacks thoroughness. The abattoir makes possible a radical philosophy of thoroughness." We had gone into the slaughterhouse. "Let's go," said the painter, "in me the smell of blood turns into *the extraordinary*, the smell of blood is *the only parity.* Let's go, otherwise I should have to uproot the possibility of new intellectual disciplines from my own thinking materiality, and I don't have the strength for that." He took large steps, and said: "The beast bleeds for the human, and knows it. Meanwhile the human doesn't bleed for the beast, and doesn't know it. The human is the incomplete beast, the beast could be fully human. Do you understand what I mean: the one is disproportionate to the other, the one is massively dark to the other. Neither is for the other. Neither excludes the other."

Twenty-third Day

"I find the inn insufferable, you must know," he said. "But I have an instinctive yen to expose myself to it, to expose myself to everything that is directed against me. Where there is putrescence, I find I cannot breathe deeply enough. I always want to breathe in the odor of humanity, you understand." He had always been at pains to strike up a relationship with the world around him, "which is a deeply contemptible undertaking, of course." To stay close to the things he hated had been his endeavor from the start, "to wander around like a dog among human legs, perfectly meaningless, surrendering to my sense impressions." Then, like a dog, they had always kicked him. "It's true," he said. "Always drowning in the midst of people, but never going down. Wherever there are people, the necessary sweating out of lust!" He had always told himself: "I keep steering clear of murder, homi-

cide, suicide. It drives me crazy." The sound of the workers
eating their soup was for him "a dull, distant ringing of bells,
portending nothing." Each time he set foot in the inn, he felt
disgust. But then he raised his head, "far beyond himself," so
as to beach himself "like an ocean-going vessel onto the
desert of humanity. Like a sportsman, I show off my injuries," he said. "I settle down between walls of meat that
warm me. Then the unbearable turns into something physically soothing for me." He thinks he is successful in passing
himself as being like everyone else, but he is not successful.
He thinks he is unobtrusive, but that makes him all the more
an alien in their midst. "Do you see the big chunks of bread
floating in your soup? I am reminded of the end of the world.
A grand vision, you know, is founded on a very small observation."

"You are molested wherever you go," said the painter. "It's as
if everyone had conspired to bother you. An instinct that
rages through them all like a wildfire. Against you. You wake
up, and you feel molested. In fact: *the* hideous thing. You
open your chest of drawers: a further molestation. Washing
and dressing are molestations. Having to get dressed! Having
to eat breakfast! When you go out on the street, you are subject to the gravest possible molestations. You are unable to
shield yourself. You lay about yourself, but it's no use. The
blows you dole out are returned a hundredfold. What are
streets, anyway? Wendings of molestation, up and down.
Squares? Bundled together molestations. And all that inside
you, you know, not at some distance from you! And all for
some insane purpose! And you're not able to cling on anywhere for assistance. The whole of life, put together from

cries for help, an interminable thought, interfered with by happy humans, workmen, simple housewives with shopping baskets, you know! The begetting of children goes to your head! Women's desire to conceive? The molestations are so grave, you do nothing but hold your hands over your head. There is no protection for the human. Questions only aggravate the situation. In an emergency, questions might save you from punishment, but only for a time. Honest, open faces turn out to be traps, spring landscapes turn out to harbor plagues. You have already inhaled too much poison to hope to be able to escape. There is no help, you know, there are no untried means, not 'art,' not 'obsession,' nothing. Insomnia might be a mitigating factor, except that it produces the same consequences as dull-wittedness. You see: I simply have the thought that I was such and such, and that burdens me. Seeing the inn burdens me. Seeing myself. Seeing you. Because that means playing a part, and that burdens me. But kicks are not merely inventions of a shared external world. No. And darkness is often a flowering ceremonial, processions of morbid beauty flit across it, a dizzying arrogance . . . I suffer at the hands of the above-average, you must know. From the objections of nature, from rights that are anathema to me. I always draw the short straw."

"And then this alternation between absolute sluggishness and the disappearance of my process into an unplumbed, bottomless region only available to the insane . . . And yet, I have to say I have never complained, never complained . . . even the most intractable situation I have successfully negotiated by obstinate refusal. Sometimes I have even succeeded in returning from such straits into health. Now I no longer believe in such a solution: it would simply kill me from behind my back. The inn is dark, and the humans go around in their terrible fevers, sunken, mysterious, unable to die, you know, while things outside are even darker. While everyone in the inn is asleep, the pressing hostility outside increases. I am of the view that there are no extraterrestrial influences involved. It's an appalling thing to me to know that I may be infecting you with my illness, and just as appalling to feel how necessary you are to me . . . and since I am, as you know, a master of restraint, and have always been able to confine myself to the tiniest limits . . . now do me the favor and tell me what you think of me, I mean, tell me the truth and don't leave me in this ridiculous torment . . . You can go your ways, I don't want to claim ownership of you, I don't want you to be irritated with me . . . The pain, you know, the pain in my head drags my earlobes down to my knees."

"The tragedy" was not always tragic, wasn't always perceived as tragic, "even though it always is a tragedy . . . The world isn't moved by tragedy. *Nothing is tragic.*" The ridiculous was "more omnipotent than anything else." Within the category of the ridiculous, you might find "tragedies like mine shafts, when you didn't have a light." There was despair in the ridiculous. "It is," said Strauch, "as if the terrible thing *were true.*" He dropped his stick, and I stooped to pick it up for him. "Everything always strikes us differently on every occasion. Frost for instance," said the painter, "in one man it's chilblains, in another it's a little town in summer . . . And finally, as we know, frost may also signify the *end of a world empire.*" It strikes him as practical to wear puttees, and he says: "Why did people ever stop wearing puttees? You can't buy puttees anywhere nowadays. And ordering them made costs a lot of time and money and nerves." Every new acquisition was such a problem for him that he ended up not acquiring it after all.

"It's a monstrous thing that tragedies always contain monstrous tragedies within them." He says: "What is a state of panic? Is a state of panic when something is approaching that you know very well or that you *don't know at all,* and are afraid of for that reason?" The word "monstrous" sounds quite hollow the way he uses it. Sometimes he uses the word "morbid" as he comes after me. "Isn't monstrous misery the same thing as monstrous happiness? The monstrous vulnerability of connections in the brain . . . ?" Man was "in his fact," and: "There are only bailiffs and those who are afraid of bailiffs and who would like nothing better than to become bailiffs . . ." and: "The sky would get goose bumps if it knew something we didn't. Eerie? That's the many-dimensional darkness in the evening between the cliff faces." When he stops, and laughter spills out of him, then everything is indeed eerie. When, as he does today, he jabs his stick into my back, and says: "Now walk down into the hollow! Walk!" And I suddenly see the lights of the inn ahead of me, no more than a dozen paces away.

Tomorrow is the funeral of the woodcutter who was run over by his own sleigh. The landlady got a death announcement from his family. Here, fatalities are announced on *parte* slips, which are pinned up on doors. Where the deceased are local people, you often see these *parte* notices on every door, as now, when the *parte* notice of the farmer's wife and the crushed woodcutter appear on every front door. They are big cards, edged in black. On them, it says when the deceased was born and the day he died. Whose child he was, and who his next of kin are. Where he is buried, and where a mass is being read for him. His line of work is also given. All the relatives are given with full names. The woodcutter has been laid out for days already in his parents' house on the shadow side. The landlady got herself ready bright and early, and went down the ravine across to the shadow side, to pay her respects to the parents of the dead man. He was engaged, and in another three weeks, he and his fiancée were to have married. It was all prepared. But not the funeral, which needs to be arranged hastily and very differently. His bride was spending night and day kneeling at the bedside of her fiancé. Just praying, wouldn't eat anything. The landlady had spoken to the boy's parents. "A young man in the pink of health," she says. The dead boy's parents had asked her to stay for lunch, but she had to be back at ten, to start cooking. A lot of blood had flowed out of the corners of his mouth, she says. "It was thick and brown." The loss wouldn't have been so grievous, "if he hadn't been the only son, now lying dead in his room, under the shroud that his mother sewed and decorated for her own use at some future date."—"When an only child dies, then it's as though the parents are dead as well," the boy's mother is supposed to have said. The young deceased was said to have been cheerful "and better educated" than most of his age. Had even read books that no one else had read, and the bride was prettier than all the other girls. His father had forbidden him to drive up to the clearing again, but he wouldn't be put off. Now the father was blaming himself. "I should have forbidden it flat" were his words. The woodcutter lived to be twenty-two. Each time someone dies who's younger than yourself, it's a frightening thing. Why? They wondered whether to bury him in a black or a white coffin, in the end they settled on a black. All at once. They still lay his place at table for him, where he would have eaten if he'd got back alive. The landlady said: "I don't suppose there'll be as many people at his funeral as there were for the farmer's wife's funeral."

Twenty-fourth Day

There were a lot of people at the burial of the young wood-cutter. The landlady had got a good spot, and stood and wept in front of the open grave for the duration of the ceremony. "I like a good cry," she says, "when I'm at a funeral." The woodcutter's coffin was shouldered by four of his erstwhile school friends. The preacher said something about "a short but God-pleasing life." His fiancée stood between his parents, all three of them veiled. Everyone filed past the open grave, swung the holy water sprinkler, only the painter and I remained at a suitable distance by the wall. Before the relations could approach us, we left the cemetery by the front steps, and stood to one side of the village square. The band was playing a march, and the feeling was that of all country funerals that don't pass off in silence. Even while the burial was in progress, we could hear through the open windows and doors of the restaurant the clinking of pots and pans for the funeral feast. Barrels were tapped. The ham steamed as the rind was pulled off it. I thought how back home in L. funerals pass off in exactly the same way. Maybe things are even a bit more pretentious, because they have more money there. And then I remembered the way it was when some poor devil died. Someone from the poorhouse, or down on the building site, or in one of the railwaymen's cottages. Someone who "doesn't belong"? I've seen one, and even if I hadn't, I could have imagined it easily enough. Then, with a minimum of fuss, and with no printing of any *parte,* because there's no money for any *parte,* a pine coffin is stained, and the dead man is pulled out of bed, and nailed into the pine coffin. There's no thought given to possibly laying him out. Where would they lay him out? In the poorhouse? In the railwayman's cottage? In the power plant canteen, even? In the main office of the cellulose factory? No, he's hurriedly nailed into his coffin, even before the preacher's informed, if indeed he is informed at any time, because often enough they don't think of the preacher, and why should they? and the knacker digs a hole, probably it's two meters twenty deep, because those are the stipulations, and at seven in the morning, the coffin is lugged to the hole by the knacker and the sexton, and no one is in attendance except maybe a few people who happen to be up and about, and then it's lowered into the hole, and covered up right away. A workman has to reckon he wouldn't get so much as a dog attending his burial. Unless it's a case of a regular industrial accident, then part of the crew would attend, and the engineer would say a few words; but if he dies on his own time, outside of office and factory hours, no one will bother about him. And if he's married, then his wife will stay home, because it's too cold for her, or the kids are sick. And why should anyone come out for a burial at all? "A big burial," said the painter on the way home. "Strange, I was the man with whom the woodcutter had his final conversation. No one knows that."

I shivered.

During the burial, I remembered the man the knacker met at the crossroads, probably where the road from the larch wood branches off down to the river. I imagined the man as in something of the same predicament as the landlord. Probably he too has been locked up several times already. Neglected from childhood, perhaps an orphan, abused by older children, beaten by his teachers, exploited by the tradesmen he was apprenticed to, and finally made a monkey of by landlords. The nature of his relationship to the landlady is not certain. No doubt, she knows him pretty well; the way she responded to everything the knacker told her about him, she must have "loved" him at some time. Didn't the knacker mention some "act of vengeance" that will prove ruinous to the suddenly reappeared man? He had only loaned him the money because he talked fairly convincingly about a job he had started. A job in a railway foundry, thirty kilometers upstream. The knacker remarked on his poor clothing. From something he said, I was able to deduce that the man is unmarried. He must have had a hundred jobs in the course of his life. Bedridden for years from a bullet wound incurred during the war. "So he's hanging around here again!" the landlady said, and: "He's the one who turned him to the bad!" Those are serious allegations. While the cemetery was heaving with people, pressing us, the painter and myself, back against the wall, I saw a man who "knocks on all doors, and isn't admitted anywhere," till he's completely plastered, when they scrape him off the roadway like a mole. I could ask the painter whether in addition to the landlord and the landlady and the knacker there isn't a fourth party involved somehow. Then the painter might say that he's the principal figure in the whole drama, where these four people are tangled up for better or worse. No, I don't want to get him onto that. And maybe the painter doesn't know anything about anyone who's "to blame for the whole thing," and "should take care never to show his face around here again." The painter pushed me toward the exit, and with his stick propelled me down into the village square. "I've just been thinking about a line in Pascal," he said: "It's the line, 'our nature is motion, complete stasis is death.'" He said: "When I come out of that sentence, I'm completely disoriented." When the funeral people came down from the cemetery, the painter wanted to stay in the village square. He felt like hearing "one or two pieces of music" that were announced by the band. It's very cold today, and we had to keep stamping our feet on the ground to keep them from freezing. "Actually, it's a nice custom to leave the dead behind to the sounds of music. To shake them off with a funeral feast." The band played, and the sounds of firecrackers rent the air.

Then I remember about the knacker and the dog's body in his rucksack. My behavior that night was more than peculiar. For days I tried to account for it to myself. I had been in a state of extreme agitation that I now find difficult to imagine. Everything has gone, and all I know is that it was once a certain way, and I am left with a feeling of revulsion for the food served in the inn. The following morning, I really could smell dogskin in the air. Because I knew the landlady was on her way to the cemetery, I went into the kitchen and the pantry, which unusually was not locked, but I didn't find anything. Everything was neat and tidy, which in itself was unusual. She will have stashed the meat and the hide in the cellar, I thought. And the cellar was locked. As the painter says, she always carries the key to the cellar on her person. The thought of what things she might keep lying around in her cellar filled me with fresh revulsion. But then the painter called for me, and, keeping a couple of steps in front of him, I set off in the direction of the village, in the direction of the cemetery. Lots of farming people. Once again, I had occasion to observe that the men did not wear coats, just suits or jackets and pants made out of various puke-colored materials. A fully occupied sleigh overtook us. I thought about the game the landlady was playing with the knacker, and the knacker with the landlady. I said to the painter: "How old do you think the knacker is?" I couldn't imagine him being any particular age. "He's a man in his prime," said the painter. "In his prime, then," I repeated, and simultaneously asked myself what that meant: "in his prime." When is your prime? "Is he forty?" I asked. "He might be forty," said the painter. "Why are you so interested in the knacker?" It had just occurred to me to ask him what age the knacker might be, I didn't especially know why. "Something suddenly occurs to you," I said. "Curious that I was the last person to speak to the woodcutter," said the painter. "He was an ordinary-looking man. And so many people are going to his burial. His boots were shining, because the lamp was directly above him. It had been dark for many hours."

. . .

While the burial was in progress, I several times thought of the noise that the dog's body had made as it landed on the bedroom floor.

On the way home, he got going on the state and the government and neutrality, provoked by an idiotic remark of mine. The state was the state as conceived by Plato, or it was no state at all. "There is no state. The state is impossible. There has never been a state." As far as our own state was concerned, then, aside from the fact that it wasn't a state ("no longer a state!"), it was something as ridiculous as a "squeaking little rhesus monkey in a big zoo," in which, naturally enough, only the well-fed and beautiful specimens of lions and tigers and leopards attracted any interest: it was their roaring. Only roaring counted, squeaking was ridiculous! It was "only the great roaring" that counted! The squeaking would be roared down! The great roaring will roar down the ridiculous squeaking! Our head of state was a "co-op manager," our chancellor "a market-day brothel attendant." The people had the choice of butchers, apprentice electricians, dully blown-up waistcoat wearers, between grave-robbers and grave-robbers' assistants. Democracy, "our democracy," was the biggest swindle. Our country sat heavily in Europe's gut, completely indigestible, like an "ill-advisedly swallowed clubfoot." Even "our dance is dead, our song and dance is dead! All repro! All frippery. The whole thing scandalously destructive frippery. The nation is really a national disgrace! You know, this squeaking, which, faced with the roar, the big roar, should just shut up! Nothing but squeaking! Ridiculous, high-pitched, dangerous squeaking! Folly and megalomania are now partners, squeaking partners, you know, hand in hand dancing their way down into the abyss, perfectly common or garden-variety squeaking partners, delusions born of feebleness, delusions born of repugnant squeaking!"

"Everything is barbarous kitsch. Yes," said the painter, "the state itself is cretinous, and the people are pitiful. Our state is ludicrous. On top of everything, the pretense of musicality. Petit bourgeois sordidness . . . it's too revolting: a layer of scum on top, and the general, galloping dullness of the population . . . we are at a stage of absolute degradation. Our state," he said, "is a hotel of ambivalence, the bordello of Europe, enjoying an excellent reputation, especially overseas."

The extent of his misfortune, he said, had suddenly revealed itself to him, "on a day whose date I could tell you now, and also the persons with whom I had contact on that day; city-dwellers, metropolitans, all of them with strong roots in whatever it was they did, in a factory, or a profitable art gallery, or in the backwash of some invention they made, and that earned them large sums of money, or people who were just happy, and didn't especially know why, and didn't care either, it didn't occur to them to wonder why, people with whom I stood in eventually abrasive and stultifying and repugnant relationships, that by and by degenerated; I would spend whole nights at the homes of these people, they showed me mountains of photographs, emptied brains full of dirty jokes at my feet, and I had to laugh, and I did laugh, and I drank and laughed and slept, often on their floors, and then I once more had to invoke the name of art, and I was so pitiful that it seemed to draw them to me, this pitifulness that showed itself in me drew them to me, they took me here and there with them, and they wanted to weld me to their lives, till the moment happened, on that day when I saw I would have to stop, not turn back, because there is no turning back, but I stopped, I quite simply stopped, and far away from those people and their habits and their possessions and their opinions, far away from their world, which didn't fit with my world, I began to go forward by myself on a different plane, from one hour to the next, when I clearly saw I didn't belong anywhere, not in the place I had just fled, for good, and not where I came from, and not where, without exactly knowing why, I wanted to get to, in the direction of which I was moving, like an escaped convict I ran off, I zigzagged away so as not to fall into the hands of my pursuers . . ." It had been his misfortune not to belong anywhere, "no longer to have anything at all."

"You know," he said, "when you're suddenly walking through the streets, from one meaningless thing to the next, through streets all of which are black, and the people are black, and they float as quickly and darkly and clumsily as yourself past you . . . You are standing in a square, and everything is black, suddenly everything inside you and outside you is black, no matter where you look at it from, black and stirred smooth, and you don't know what stirred it, and everything is broken . . . You still recognize an object here and there, but everything is broken and smashed and ripped; for the first time you prop yourself on a stick, which you've only ever used as a weapon before against humans or dogs, but now you prop yourself on it, and you seem to be floating in a sea of lead, and here and there you make out some new, further blackness . . . people don't know, is it the coming of spring, or is it the end . . . the great letters on the department stores coming toward you, having joined forces against you in a great rabble, a great rabble of a revolution, they ruin everything in you, where nature and creature turn to you for help, you try to make your way, in a yet more desperate condition . . . You see humans and you call out to them, with no shame you alarm these humans in this atmosphere, which is continually being teased by the cardinal points . . . and you have buttoned up your jacket, and everything in you is tense, and your head is afraid of bumping into things . . . all those handbags and sticks, those hundreds of thousands of handbags and sticks . . . you think you have come down a very long way in the world, just as those others have come up, and in your disgust you don't know what to do . . . those crowds of people unleashed by precisely advancing clock hands . . . You seek refuge on a park bench, but it is already full of people cleverer than you are, they occupied all the benches from early morning on, and are reading enormous books, and eating extensive paper-bag lunches . . . the whole pathos of government employees hits you, the whole meanness of state pensions . . . and you wedge your head between your knees, and try not to sink . . . and you hear the world writhing in your own headaches, in grotesque cramps, in the terrible violence of the air . . . In your room you are menaced by shards of memory, they are birds, unbelievable black birds, endowed with incredible force . . . This incredible state of emergency, this synthesis of rejection by the world and alienation from the world, in which you suddenly find yourself, without any bearings, this condition that lands you in every conceivable human procedure . . . The police and the vegetable truck, they're all coming for you, as though to destroy you . . . the voice of the people . . . even as a child I could feel that devastating procedure in my brain . . . this people that darkens the passages of my ears . . . and accompanying all these impressions, you must know, each time I touch the ground with my stick, I knock a hole in my skull, everything is like being condemned to ceaseless torment by a metronome on Föhn days . . ." He often uses the word "suicide" now. In every sentence. With his great thumb that, when he stretches it, contains every ounce of his strength, he crushes himself, his surroundings, just as one might crush a beetle on a table or cabinet.

"I have no use for myself anymore," he says. "I'm just ordinary. As ordinary as the rest of the world. Gagging on ordinariness." On the rug under his feet, which "has always been pulled away. My awakening, like my going to sleep, ordinary. Even my dreams are ordinary. And I of all people, thought I had a claim to more-than-ordinary dreams. The nightmares I have are the nightmares of my childhood. Gruesome, when an old man has to dream them again. It's no pleasure. Advanced astonishment, nothing more, and always alone. On my left there is you, and in my right, my stick. The two things that keep me together. I trust you're not angry with me? My original concept, I don't know what it is anymore, maybe you know . . . And then the disqualification of the rest of the world . . . the impossibility of coping with talent . . . The whole person just black propaganda against himself. Is that right . . . ? I try to understand myself, you know, and I know that things are getting worse: it was always that way. Attrition of the muscles in the brain. And everything I see a reflection of myself, sometimes broken by a powerful stream of alien thought." I think it must be easier to stitch up a leaky intestine than to make these observations. I could read the whole thing back, but I would only give myself a fright. The way he says: "Everything is black." Everything as though determined for no one but himself, and as if he assumed the others were all wearing earplugs. Even the way he wipes his shoes with the rag he always carries in his pocket, the way he tries to prove everything with his Pascal, though he knows there's nothing to prove. "Nothing is jocund," he says. And then the smell of frying meat greets us in the public bar.

It was possible to drift on a raft with other people for years and years, pressed together, body against body, in a tiny space, without coming to know those people any better. "The darkness around one must be equal at moments to the darkness later on, that turns to stone inside us, at the end. Petrifies our blood, like the veins in marble." Quiet filled rooms with its curse, and day and night, at all times, there were hordes of "casualties of quiet." Strauch says he wouldn't be surprised to learn one day that he had really been someone else altogether. "To learn," he says, "that a faulty adjustment toward me on the part of nature kept me from ever gaining admission to myself. Possible, no?" He got on to a certain happy time of his youth, and then right away buried it again: "The little creeks that refresh us, are they not produced by storms?" Before going to sleep, humans stared at the foam-tipped waves, "futilely, mindlessly, not yet in dream.

"Youth is its own message. What happens afterward is without significance; a mode of fabrication, nothing more." But to complain about it was pathetic. And pathos constituted age. Age *was* pathetic. "At any rate, age isn't merit, much less triumph." You could find yourself waking in a setting that was made up of all your previous settings, "more and more settings."

Over recent weeks, he had called on many government offices, to see what information was kept on him there. "There were many things I wanted to have corrected," he said, "but they turned me away, even threw me out," he said. In such a way one was thrown out by thunderstorms, and wound up in the sea, pointless and purposeless.

I recalled how I had come by my internship in Schwarzach. Honsig had drawn my attention to it. In the dissecting room. How there was a hospital, not too small, not too large, with all kinds of possibilities. There was a registrar, and an intern, and other doctors, and nursing sisters. Situated at a major railway junction, and at the intersection of several highways. Many accident victims, widely famed for lung operations. A hospital that was continually bursting at the seams, summer and winter alike. The surrounding country offered sports facilities: skating, skiing. Good people, both from the medical and the personal point of view. Free board, and a quiet room.

The place was bland and claustrophobic like all mountain towns. It was near the source of a river that suddenly turned north, where it's a little less bleak.

I think of Schwarzach, and what there is there. Houses, almshouses, a church. And the hospital. A couple of barber's shops in competition with each other. A waterfall cuts the place in half. You see a lot of pregnant women, as you do in Weng. Not so many workers, because there is no industry. But just as many railwaymen. Postal workers. At any given moment, Railway Wrestling Competition, Railway Shooting Competition, Railway Ski-Jumping Competition, Railway Swimming Competition. St. Nicholas's Day: a bunch of apprentice lumberjacks, butcher's boys, and milkers put in an array of gruesome masks, with horns and braids, twisted ears and noses, gap teeth and split tongues, and set upon the bystanders, knocking over old people, beating up children, and, because it's a centennial festival, are not brought to court for it. Heavy thunderstorms and ensuing landslides continually alter the face of the town. The same bleakness in the houses as there is in houses everywhere. Men standing around, sitting around, in black jackets buttoned up to their Adam's apple, watching the waterfall, cursing their women-folk. In the small hours, the "wild" workmen. Deafening noises, that make you shut your windows . . . Visiting theater groups as well. The air is damp, and the children have rickets, they're all weak in the pleura and the bronchia. For no reason anyone understands, the water supply is the cause of a lot of illness in the place. The milk, though, is rich and fresh, because it comes straight down from the mountain farms up above.

Twenty-fifth Day

THE ANIMAL RUSTLING SCUM

". . . and so I made the most extraordinary discovery," said the painter, "one of those discoveries that hit you like a bolt from the blue. You must imagine, my exhaustion of today had already reached its apogee, I was continually threatening to keel over, I was hanging on in the knowledge that I would otherwise drown, I made a pitifully helpless impression, I even screamed, and tore up my sleeves. Look!" he said, and he showed me his sleeve, and I could see, yes, the sleeve was ripped, there was even a big piece of sleeve missing; he was walking quickly now, and he was saying he thought the land-lady would sew a patch of some other material over the miss-ing piece—"one of those crap materials they go around in here in the country," he said—and he suddenly grabbed hold of me, and knocked me into the ditch, which I hadn't even seen, the snow was deep, I was up to my knees in snow, it was a water drainage ditch, as I noticed right away, into which, with my superior strength and weight, I had also pulled the painter. "The icy water has established itself inside my boots," said the painter, once we had both pulled ourselves out of the "groin prison," and: "Imagine a man remains motionless in such a position, he'd freeze to death in seconds, from the feet up, there's a ruthlessness and thoroughness in this inimical cold that's terrifying and indescribable." But he didn't want to let himself be diverted from his extraordinary discovery by this minor incident, I for my part tried to distract him too (we had spoilt our walk by now, had to head back before, as the painter said, "the cold brought out a new illness in us," back to the inn, where they would surely have lit a fire by now, and the painter had said: "There are circumstances in which the landlady tries to dupe me, and she hasn't started heating yet, she dupes me by only lighting my stove just before my return, which is flagrantly in breach of the agreement I made with her, and is explicitly directed against me. By only lighting the fire at a time when she expects me back, my room doesn't get warm, my room doesn't ever get warm, it should be heated all the time, all the rooms in the inn are cold, cold, cold rooms, you understand, these appallingly inimical rooms"), but he pulled me close to him again. "I mentioned my extraordinary discovery," he said. "I suddenly saw, as I was emerging from the ravine, that the stream, you see, was red. I thought: a phenomenon, a natural phenomenon! But immediately I understood: blood! And I thought: That's blood, by God, that's blood! I couldn't trust my eyes, but the entire stream was full of blood! Now, I felt like running back upstream, I wanted to and I felt like it, I was even duty bound to run upstream, because what I saw was without question the product of a crime, as I very clearly saw, a human crime, 'a wonderfully hurried rhythm of blood' inscribed itself before my eyes, I wanted to run back upstream, but you know that's not possible, I found myself in a tormenting position: to know with perfect clarity, and to see, yes, also to see, that a crime was in progress, who could say how far upstream, perhaps no more than a hundred paces (it could be no great distance to this crime), the quantity of blood was quite extraordinary (it was a first-class spectacle), the blood-red stream running through the white snow blanket, and all scratched by the black branches, by these wild black branches . . . All this just a momentary impression, the work of seconds. I wanted to call out. I didn't call out. My attempt to make my way upstream was doomed to failure, I was up against such a huge impossibility that I was condemned to failure, I expect you're familiar with the sensation: you want to take a certain path, and you're unable to take a single step along the way, the brain gives its signal, the brain is like a whip against the body, but the body is an extraordinary instance of insubordination . . . But I did have one idea: I ran back into the ravine, and crawled, crawled, I say, crawled on my belly toward the stream, perhaps a hundred yards upstream of the place where I made the discovery, I looked back where I had crawled, and I saw: an animal! I saw: a monster! I saw a humiliation of fins! I was too crushed to be able to get up and make my way to the stream through the undergrowth. But, in order to encompass what I just related to you, I felt an extraordinary access of strength. The idea that there was a crime in progress here, or rather, further up, where that terrible garish blood sprang from, gave me such superhuman strength I no longer believed was possible. Well," said the painter, "all at once I heard a sound, a sound not from nature, a click as of a jackknife shutting, the sound of a blade, a rasp, a screech. I pressed myself down in the snow and tried to get some warmth into my shoulders by means of that particular turning of my head that I once described to you. All purely instinctively. Suddenly only my sense of hearing was functioning. I heard a scraping and the sound of gravel on railway ballast. The snapping-off of gigantic snakey leaves. Finally I heard the river being waded across three or four times. I immediately thought: men, men poaching fish, I thought, and crawled out of my hiding place. I was glad to be given the certainty that my discovery corresponded to fact, that my sense of color hadn't deceived me, that this mountain stream was not just a blood-red stream in my brain, not just some deranged precipitation within my thought processes, that what I saw in this section of stream was not caused by some mirage or unlucky human chance, but was in fact fact, like lightning suddenly trumped by thunder. What I now saw, having crawled as far as the bank of the stream, was so horribly ridiculous: the heads and tails and midsections of cows. The warmth and softness of freshly slaughtered meat was still in the air, the opposition between chilly void on the one hand and warm void on the other; the emetic of fear on the white canvas of snow, an unrepeatable scene: the chewed and shattered and sliced anatomy of dehumanization by Heaven and Hell. As I say, only a scene, and behind it, on the other bank as though out of range, the miscreants, fled and fleeing."—"The cow slaughterers," I said. "We are talking about common livestock thieves, men and women, presumably from one of the neighboring villages. In among the scraps of meat, the stains of blood, the bone and cartilage and bowel, were signs of footsteps made by men and women. There was a headscarf lying there, I pocketed it as evidence," said the painter. I was shivering and soaked to the hips as we walked in the direction of the inn, which we were neither of us able to see, because suddenly the fog had swathed everything, "down to the most rudimentary contours of the world." The painter said: "I want to call the scene 'slaughter,' in the moment I beheld it, everything seemed to soak into the picture. I could clearly see the butchers' fleeing footprints. One could see also the tracks of the livestock they had stolen. One could see the darkness of the planets, and the low proletarianism of murder. I saw the word 'innocent' on the ground, in the snow, this low code, you must know, and the word 'meanness' clearly in the sky. One thing was strange: even as the severed limbs and organs were still twitching, my interest instantly transferred itself to the process of rigor mortis, which here was being enacted in a million variations. I stooped and pressed my hand into the blood and mixed it with snow. I threw red snowballs! I threw red snowballs! Picture the scene. At first I prudently forbore to open any of the great eyes that were lying around, all of them strangely closed, I avoided the spectacle of those large, docile cow's eyes. I forbore till the moment when I was no longer equal to the temptation to give myself over to the sympathy that anything animal has with the human, and I opened one of the cow's eyes, one of those gigantic, stalled, chilled, bloodless orbs. The thieves," said the painter, "had proceeded by a scrupulous plan. Everything took place in a spot that hardly anyone but me has ever seen, one of the most inaccessible of spots, perhaps the most inaccessible spot there is. I still have not reported on what I took in. Of course I ought to go to the policeman and inform him. Probably word of the incident has already got out. Because, as I saw later, the ravine was full of blood too. The policeman walks through the ravine. The churchgoers walk through the ravine. They all must have seen the blood. At a certain place, the blood seemed to branch off, the traces of blood, in the direction of the scene of the crime. The thieves must have been equipped with all possible slaughterman's tools. I myself heard the sound of a knife snapping shut, there was the beating of a hammer, of a mallet, the scrape of a saw, which suddenly broke off. They had heard me, they must have. They packed up the meat. They plunged into the stream. They waded across, once on the other side, they were in the relative security of the woods. There wasn't the least thing I could have done about it. In my condition, a person in my condition is unable to do anything. Such a person can only flee, can only take flight, shrink back from the blood and the sounds of criminality. Baffling, the way the scene of the crime not only attracted me, attracted me with its natural horror, but was able to attract me. As I already said, I crawled up to it on all fours, like a beast. You understand: I was helpless against this setting, against this scene. The smell of slaughter, still warm, as under a bell jar," said the painter. "And then this silence in which, had I not rubbed my face with snow, I might quite easily have suffocated. It was a question of three or four cows, I thought, there had to be three or four cows at issue, I thought, and I found three tails, three tails. And yet there must have been four cows, I thought. It was inexplicable to me, and I continued to think in terms of four cows. A small calf's head lay in the bushes, already under water, bleeding dry. So there were three cows and a calf, three tails in other words."

At the inn, the painter showed me the headscarf he had found at the site of the crime. We had just come in the door. In the darkness that obtained there even at midday, he fished something bloodied out of his coat pocket and showed it to me. I held it up in the light that fell through the narrow glass panel in the front door, and saw the headscarf. "That's terrifying testimony, isn't it," said the painter; "it's all too easy to imagine the victims might have been human. And it wouldn't even be too grisly, because one wouldn't be able to laugh, not be able to burst out laughing. And when I saw the grisly chopped-up animals, I had to burst out laughing, I burst out into extraordinary laughter. Do you know what that means? It means horror demands laughter!" We went into the public bar, and from there to the kitchen, where we took off our jackets and coats, and above all our boots. And then we took off our trousers, and finally, called upon to do so by the landlady, and because the painter seemed to have no objection, our underpants as well. The landlady should sew a patch over the missing material in his sleeve, and make it good, said the painter. As we both stood facing the wall, while the landlady went up to our rooms, to find us some clean dry underpants and socks and pants, the warm air from the stove at our backs brought us back to life. "She (the landlady) is taking advantage of this incident to quickly light a fire in my room," said the painter, "because as I said to you before she won't have kept the room warm. We startled her by getting back so early. She just tricked me," he said. "How could I be so stupid as to follow her instructions to get undressed in the kitchen, and make an ass of myself in front of her. I do feel an ass standing face to the wall, half-naked. Don't you feel like an ass too, with your face to the wall like that, it's a moronic and undignified state to be in, a couple of grimacing individuals facing a firing squad. We are being executed here!" the painter called out. He now had his coat wrapped round his legs and belly, and said: "Please to keep the incident with the cows to yourself, just as I'll keep it to myself. To make such witness precipitately public, and in such an unpleasantly disagreeable case as this, can only lead to the nausea of a trial by public opinion. I prefer to avoid that. I would ask you not to waste a word on it. Not to anyone. Not the least suggestion of it." Then he said: "This is now the period of murder conspiracies, the farms are wiped out by the snow and cretinism. The gangs unscrew the padlocks on the barns, and gag the livestock. The air is slashed by the whistling of their sticks."

Once changed, he hunkered in the hallway and read to me from his Pascal. It was always "about the whole tragedy," he said, I didn't understand what he meant by that. Always about "a single coarse act." He said: "Factor in lethality." And: "Death renders everything infamous." He was continually leaving, only to get out at some city of thought, interrupting his journey; he had a destination "that would permit of no arrival, that discourages any arrival." I went up to my room and said to myself, but aloud, so that it bounced off the walls and its echo struck me: "I can't stand any more of this!" I lay down. I leafed through my Henry James, without giving the writer a thought. Got up. Walked to and fro. Lay down again. I detested the shamelessness of a sentence I had come across in the middle of my book somewhere. I threw the book to the floor. Everything stinks, I thought. Suddenly everything was just stench, even the merest notion, the merest, most distant notion was stench. Then I went downstairs, and sat down at the extra table. Everyone was eating with great appetite, even the painter showed such an appetite that I was disgusted by it. I could eat nothing at all, and even let my soup go cold. When the painter had gone up to his room, I stood in the kitchen and joined in the discussion that must have been in progress for some time between the landlady and the knacker. It was to do with rich people, and hunting parties. They came three or four times a year and chased with hounds, and there were a lot of wild shots into the bushes, and you often found natty buckles and belts and ear protectors and single gaiters in the woods and on the gravel. Sometimes the nobility (the painter said "the gentry") suddenly took over this "dirtiest corner of the world." What were the rich? they asked themselves. They didn't know either. It got to the point that they would automatically have to hate wealth, so as not to find themselves excluded by it. Then I remember a sentence the painter came up with yesterday: "Poverty can stare up at wealth, and that's as near as it gets." The knacker was often taken on by the hunting parties. Various venerable old families would assemble "in a spirit of megalomania, to shoot holes in nature." Last night, the painter described hunting as "divine sense with trivial human markings." I said to the knacker: "Have you been hunting in the Klamm valley at all?" The Klamm was a particularly sought-after hunting terrain, said the knacker, it still had a reputation for wolf barks from the olden days. I remembered happy hunting expeditions myself. As a child I had often gone along on hunts, high and low. "The hunt is the only institution between the world powers, man and beast, beast and man, man and man, beast and beast, not to involve sadism," my father had once said. To avoid the painter, I tried to slip into my room as quietly as possible. But he heard me, and summoned me to him in his room with his call: "Come along!" which was a strict command. I stood in utter darkness. "Feel these walls," said the painter, "having to freeze between walls like these is an act of catastrophic lunacy. Now sit down!" He pushed me down onto one of his chairs.

"Everything is actually without words," he says, "it is as wordless as it is loathsome, as conscientious as it is condemned by sense." He wanted to have my company. I could feel it. Everything he said was like forcing me into his coat, and buttoning me into it for all time. But in that state of torment he said: "Leave! Leave! I want you to leave!" And he forced me out the door. "It's a mistake to count on people. It's a grave mistake to count on anyone at all. I have always made this mistake. I have always made this most glaring of mistakes, I have always counted on people!" he said. I couldn't stand it anymore, and I ran downstairs and out of the house. Once I was out in the fresh air, I soon recovered myself. I had the feeling the painter, this man, Strauch, had me in his power again. "All right," I said, and I went to the cemetery. And: "All right," and I went back. All the way I saw nothing and thought nothing, except that the painter had me in his power. Forced me into his pictures, into the world of his fantasy. Me, his feeble observer. I felt imprisoned. But even that fantasy, I thought, is a fantasy of the painter's. I am no longer myself. No, no, I thought, I am no longer myself. It drove me wild, this violence was a sudden induration against which I kept banging my head. But isn't that metaphor, that sensation in my brain, isn't everything I think and see and speak and revile—isn't it all Strauch's? In the afternoon, I tried to sleep, and couldn't. I saw myself helpless and entrapped in sentences and perspectives of Strauch's, in his "morbidities" and "absurdisms." I continually heard myself blurt out the man's phrases. Not until dusk, when our walk was almost finished that we had gone on together, was I able to push myself off from him. As from some fatal shore. I don't know, is it all nonsense? Is what I'm writing now nonsense, because I'm writing far into the night, in the "boundless ignorance of darkness."

Of course they had all heard about the poachers and the slaughtering by now, and the knacker had to set off up to the stream, and stuff the remains of the cows into sacks, and carry them off. He had gone up there with the mayor's horse-drawn sleigh, I could have gone with him, but in the end I didn't want to go, I wouldn't have seen much because it had started snowing again. He had broken the horns off the skulls, and brought the tails along. He described everything differently than Strauch, but what he said was confirmation of what they both had said about the episode.

The people were pretty agitated, there had been quite a spate of cows being stolen, and slaughtered by some flowing water or other. "I should say there were three cows and a calf," said the painter down in the public bar. The knacker looked at him, and asked him how he knew. No one knew that, apart from him, the knacker. "It was a hunch," said the painter, "just a hunch." And he said to the knacker: "Well, didn't you find six horns, three tails, and four heads at the place?" "Yes," said the knacker, that was right, but he hadn't told anyone about it, or given out any figures. "You must have without realizing it," said the painter. The knacker was mystified.

There was talk about the cattle thieves until far into the night. The painter told me the whole story again, but now that I was hearing it for the second time, I found it repulsive, thoroughly repulsive. I just simply felt disgusted, I had the feeling the painter was reveling in the story, in this, to him, for whatever appalling and unfathomable reason, so extraordinarily congenial story. The landlady put the tails in the pot right away, and at lunchtime everyone was eating the soup from them without any show of disgust. I wasn't disgusted either, and I ate the soup. He had thrown the many fresh bones to the dogs, said the knacker. They laughed about the soup, "for which we have those thieves to thank!" they said. They almost couldn't eat for laughing. But they did, they ate it all up. All of them, they ate it all up. The painter ate in silence. He looked as though he were sitting on a big secret. And of course he knew more about the whole episode than any of the others. But he remained true to his resolve. He didn't tell anyone that he had heard the thieves, perhaps even seen them make their escape into the forest. "A black scurrying of bodies and a bestial lugging of sacks of meat across to the other side," he had said. He is not wholly sure whether his impression is the product of fact, and not imagination. "But it's not just imagination," he said. The talk was of other instances of poaching in recent times. No trace of the "poaching scum" had ever been found. Not the least trace. "We won't make any headway with this latest case, either," they said. "No," the painter had said. "The snow will cover over all footprints. The thieves are counting on the snow. The snow will cover their crime." The engineer, who had now also come to the table, said he had noticed something at lunchtime that might lead to the apprehension of the culprits. "Traces," he said. Then, two hours later, the traces had disappeared. Even at lunchtime, there had been "not the minutest lead."

Twenty-sixth Day

"I lay in my room all night, on the floor, if you must know. Another man might have called out, or knocked for help. If only the cold hadn't been so intense, coming through the floorboards," said the painter, "there was an intense cold coming through the floorboards. I freeze, because my head takes away all the heat from my body. It doesn't even have to be cold, I'm still freezing. I can pile on any number of blankets, I'll still freeze. And then my head started to swell up like a balloon: everything transpired in a sort of half-waking state: my huge head was breathing in and out, and almost crushing my chest. My thighs were so cold that when I touched them, I thought they must be dead; and my legs and feet, which I normally keep moving, to get some warmth into them, you know . . . I couldn't do it this time, and there was no way of getting myself warm . . . Can I hang on till morning? I wondered, and closed my eyes. But even closing my eyes was a painful intervention into my being. As for opening them again! I open my eyes more slowly than anyone I know, and I close them in the same way. My eyes, my mouth, my ears, are all terribly sensitive; because they are all so big, they cause me great pain. My collarbone and shins are covered by the merest layer of skin. The nerves have nothing to sustain or protect them. The hours pass more and more slowly, I find it increasingly difficult to get through a night. I can't read my Pascal anymore either. Not one word. Nothing. Before long, I won't be able to think of anything to make my nights bearable. There are no pressure points in my body, not to mention my head, that aren't extraordinarily sensitive to pain. It doesn't matter what I do, my constant headaches will be joined by the pains I suffer when I move my foot anywhere, when I put my hand on something somewhere: it makes no difference what I touch it with and how, it will hurt, and I will be in pain. And then there's the additional factor that incipient thoughts bat around the inside of my skull; each time, I think my head will break apart when I move from one subject to another. There is a continual imaginative assault, which is driving me half crazy. You must remember, no one has such self-restraint. Every object I see hurts me. Every color I am forced to take in. Every memory that surfaces, everything, everything. There isn't anything I can look at till the end, because I would either be wiped out or driven crazy, in the way that everything strikes me as being so crazy already, that I'm like a cursed animal, do you understand! I've already crossed the line . . ."

"I have the feeling," the painter said, "that my head is my body, and vice versa. Certain faint rowing motions with my legs, you understand, in the night . . . as if my head were filled with poison gas, as if I would feel the greatest relief if someone were to stab me in the head . . . then it would transpire that my head is made of some solid matter after all, it would split open . . . I am so afraid of encountering some hard object, some pointed object, it's ridiculous . . . as if I had a giant tumor over my left eye. The yawning holes of my nostrils are the muzzle of a prehistoric beast. I have the feeling: my nose is made up of an infinite number of little sucker nozzles. In every one of these nozzles I, my explorer character, is able to descend . . . the lungs, you know, no longer work by instinct, I am continually afraid they might tear. Whereas the lungs are the only organic part of me that doesn't hurt. Which in turn frightens me, you see: what if one wing no longer stands the pressure, then there's a chain reaction . . . such knowledge of the inner makeup of my body . . . I feel and empathize with every one of my internal organs . . . each organ is a firmly defined notion, a well-rounded pain . . . And the extraordinary . . . Liver, pancreas, kidney, those three torments, you understand . . . and then the torment of my head, which I have already described to you. Head torment and body torment, reciprocal, you understand, unyielding, you understand also: and then the whole subterranean empire of torments, the torments of the mind, and the free-floating torment of the soul . . . I could divide my head into millions of constituent parts and study its laws: that work of extermination! The brightly colored territory of my pains: no horizon, you know, no perception, no relief from unconsciousness . . ." He says: "I cling to people who have certain specific intentions, it's a mental torture."

And then: "The most promising plans, the most promising conditions, everything goes to rack and ruin, everything that contradicts absolute silence. And in you I seem to identify some admirable character traits . . . And you're able to listen as well. As far as I'm concerned, I am of unimaginable hardness. Not laughter and tears, as people might think. No. Admittedly, at your age the greatest danger is the ability to make anything of yourself, and then not to make anything . . . Because, like all humans, you aren't able to identify your moment. Nothing identifies its moment, that's it! . . . where there's a precipitate fall or climb, you don't know . . . where it goes down into the practice of letting live and vegetating along. Most humans lose themselves in the sexual at thirty or so. And thereafter they just eat. I sometimes detect a certain astounding cleverness in what you say, a radical clarity, a philosophical aptitude that sources everything in a higher plane. And that's the deadly thing."

"It might be the sound of falling snow or the smack of a bird on the cobblestones, the possibilities are endless . . . Often, it's just the smell of the millennia in my nostrils . . . I'm sure you sometimes come across some long-forgotten scene from decades past . . . You see a tree and you see a window, and in actual fact there's no tree and no window, but a city and a country and a river and a man who wakes up, who dies, who shakes hands with you or gives you a smack . . . Isn't that right? Those are the issues that have always preoccupied me. The sound of my stick on the road, the voice of the priest, or the groan of the knacker as he shoulders his rucksack . . . One might pursue one's investigations into these matters indefinitely, take them to inhuman lengths, indecent lengths, into religion, and into the opposite of religion . . . Religion, you see: my tree, my stick, my lungs, my heart, my taciturnity, my attentiveness, my crippledom . . . Progress with these things makes it all so much more megalomaniacal, the advance in my brain, wherever advance is possible, only where there is no advance, you understand . . . Perhaps that's what held me back from the ultimate! It's a leading character-

istic of mine to be modest and self-effacing. You might be sur
prised to hear it, but that's the way it is. Cause and effect are
almost indistinguishable to me. Science, you know, I have
nothing to do with, I resisted it all my life, it would be an
abuse against my nature . . . of course I'm at a disadvantage
in my sentimental preferences for the clear scenes of my past.
And another thing: vindictiveness! The way the past is put
together from vindictiveness is something that's worth considering. One has nothing to cling to, and feels pointless . . . Is
it that?" He says: "All at once my head had pushed everyone
in the public bar back against the wall, all of them, even the
ones at the extra table, the knacker, the policeman, the engineer, the landlady and her daughters, all of them. In my
dream, you know. My head was suddenly bigger than the
public bar, and it crushed them all. A firm lethal blow in all
directions, into the reaches of the furthest walls. A terrible
effect. But my head didn't have sufficient force to destroy the
inn. The juice of those humans that my head squashed,
annulled, was running down my face. Objects and persons
were pulped. And the feelings of the objects and persons,
likewise. Their feelings too! My eyes grew dark. My tears
mixed with the pulp, because of course I wasn't able to move.
In a corner of the public bar, between the bar and the window, my little body had found a refuge for itself, though it
was horribly cramped. I was unable to breathe. The sweetish
taste on my lips! I tried not to ingest the pulp, but I had no
alternative. My tongue was able to push it away, but not the
taste. I couldn't breathe. My ears were flattened against the
ceiling, you know, so I couldn't hear anything. Since everything had happened so suddenly, I wasn't able to warn anyone, not you, or the engineer, or the landlady, or the knacker.

I was terribly unhappy. I cried, because I had killed everyone. My head tried to break out of the inn, because it was afraid of suffocating. It was able to push the walls back slightly, but no air came in. There was no chink or crack, the walls gave like rubber. I went wild. With that, my head suddenly shrank back to its original dimensions, and the crushed persons and objects, the pulp, you remember, fell to the floor in large hard slabs . . . Then, these slabs were once more persons and things. They were sitting in their places, eating and drinking, and placing orders and paying, you know, and the landlady's daughters were jumping over the benches as if nothing were amiss. I woke up exhausted and saw that I had misplaced my woolen blanket. I stood up and lay down again and wrapped myself up as warmly as I could. Then, between waking and sleeping, I made my next highly interesting, albeit traumatic discovery: the landlady was standing in my room, and was shooing away a swarm of birds from a tree that stood in the middle of my room. She clapped her hands, and the birds took to the air, and everything went dark . . . Then I got up, and tried a cold footbath. The footbath afforded me some relief. At any rate, I didn't dream anymore. Maybe because I was sitting on my bed and browsing in my Pascal. Maybe."

VIEWS ON HEIGHT, DEPTH, AND CIRCUMSTANCE

"I must point out to you," said the painter, "that just one step further on the thinking is completely different, that just one step further on existence is completely different; the virtues

and the issues are the same, there are the same inattentive-
nesses, and the same impressions, and the same causes, but
the effects are terrifyingly different . . . It's difficult to make
myself clear to you, I could as easily be speaking to a tree,
and I am in fact speaking to a silhouette, yes, a silhouette, to a
concept flexible to the point of madness, but you are a person
whose being is always acute. I should like to point out to you
that, if you adduce the idea of a 'bloodless landscape,' merely
adduce it, and blow it up like a balloon, like an enormous balloon, with incomparable lung power, with the lung power of
an extraordinary universe, that it is then possible to move
about outside the shadow side of our imagination . . . I confront myself with the keenest frost, which to the thought is
true and acute, and pitifully ridiculous . . . I have been speaking in my cruel and hopelessly elaborate way, but listen now:
I am undergoing a 'chilling of my memory' which I should
like to call unjustified, or rather: I am distracting myself from
within, purely so that I leave myself alone! Or rather: my
brain is distracting from the relatedness of the world, distracting from myself, from the malice of inventions that have
enabled me to exterminate myself . . . In the darkest places,
only incomprehensibility carries any conviction, you understand, I should like to put you in the way of a fascinating
metaphor, as you might cast adrift a dog on an endless ocean,
as you set a bird deep underground, as you pitch a man in his
memory; it's not the height, it's not the depth, height and
depth are both laughable compared to the circumstance that
the catastrophic is laughable compared to the benign . . . but
for the sake of these notions of mine it is imperative that
I must soon disappear, I must soon burn: I have always
been attracted to the notion of burning, having to burn for
my own sake has always been my secret version of personal

fame . . . If I fail to die, I thought, if I fail to be confused . . . if I fail with my ideas . . . You understand! . . . I get ready for my journey, and deceive the world . . . I pack my bags and deceive the world . . . I board a thousand trains and deceive the world . . . I distract it from the point where I'll be arriving . . . Because the end is nothing more than the nausea that a decomposed human causes . . . Well, and even though the end is also a shipwreck, I will have to undergo that final stifling act of coition, that torment, that turns the calamity of my relinquished existence into a devilishly certain conspiracy. I'm not even thinking of dying," said the painter, "I'm not even thinking of fame . . . I'm not even thinking of indecency, of the indecency of dissolution."

THE RAVINE

"The way the brain reverts to being a sort of machine, the way it hammers out everything once more that it was hit and knocked with hours and days and weeks previously. The way a word can trigger a whole avalanche of logic, sending whole settlements of verbal constructions into the depth, without the least exemption. As if some runtish dictator, invisible, unapproachable, at least for humans, threw a vast machinery into action, with horrendous noise that one is helpless to oppose . . ." The painter continued: "You must imagine a rocky ravine in the prettiest colors of the universe, most especially watercolors, the colors of putrefying flesh, a ravine which a man enters, following orders. If you like, you can press a suitcase into his hand, set a hat on his head, give him tight clothes to wear, whatever your fancy might be, or your inner virtue, because such are the dreams, opposed to my version, that I now impose on you: a man with the fantastic on his back, with disappointment at his society, which, far from any social groupings, has done everything to set him on the road to ruin, a man with a monstrous memory, with an imagination that is majestic and unalterable, not capable of heightening, not capable of shrinking . . . This man, and me, his inventor, you now drive into the ravine, you yell at him, you smack him in the face, you simplify him, you imagine him as rustling leaves on trees, as crumbling of rocks, as teeth ground in fear, so that you can join him; you introduce yourself as terror, and slowly you take from him his fear by concentrating his mind on his last will . . . He senses his departure, but he no longer opposes it . . . he is lulled by the impossibility of actually feeling his pain, and by your stratagems . . . Well, now we have set someone en route to hell, created him and set him going, at a time one would have to call the seventh day of discreation, the seventh and last day of discreation . . . You must imagine that only the air still exists, everything else in this person is just a laughable extravagance, a feeling his brain—already dissolved into nothing—is limping in pursuit of . . . the man may still retain certain bearings in a fixed world, a sense of father and mother for example, of cities, of scientific experiments, notions of manual work, rudimentary anthropophagous impulses of an animal sub-brain, that we should imagine in the name of science . . . a designation occurs to me, a pitiful, a scandalous designation, a so-called cemetery name floating over his tomb, his cement tomb . . . can you guess the name? Can you guess the horror of horrors? I can see that my instruction, which makes up a fourth of my being (one fourth is the notion of instruction, one fourth is the notion of repugnance, one fourth is the

notion of futility, and one fourth the notion of no-longer-
and-not-yet), I have given you the pleasure of bewilderment,
which is completely what I had in mind, and completely what
my invented character would have had in mind as well,
whom we should think of as a teacher, to my mind teachers
are the best characters, the teacher is *the* made-up character
par excellence . . . well now, this teacher enters the ravine,
and gets to his destination, which is of course a schoolhouse.
But what is a schoolhouse? A house where things are taught
that someone doesn't yet know, can't yet know . . . I don't
want to go on, I say: the teacher understands that nothing can
be learned anymore, that everything is ignorant, that everything is finished, everything is beginning, and so on: he
unpacks, he unpacks his bags. Do you get the scene?" I say:
"Yes, I get the scene."—"Hold on to the picture: the teacher
unpacks his bags, he discovers that it's cold in the school. He
turns on the heating. He arranges his books. He finds the
classroom, he suddenly knows the names of the children he
will teach—you were thinking of children as well, I hope? He
says to himself: I wish I had my books in my head! Did you
think of that too? You see: the teacher is thinking of the past,
he can only think of the past because he can only think in the
past. There is nothing very remarkable about humans," said
the painter. "The brain believes in the progress it aims to
make, but the brain cannot make progress. The flesh is different there: it consists of the progress that is denied the
brain . . . What would you say to this: the teacher has been
ordered to the ravine to perish . . . in an obvious, a simplistic
way, nothing obscure, in a form of butting forward . . . Even
though he knows where his obedience has got him, namely
into the ravine, he is still thinking in terms of teaching and

the possibilities of teaching: because I am a teacher, he may be thinking to himself . . . Do you still see the teacher? As I've presented him to you in my art? In the perspectivelessness that I master, because I am so full of different perspectives? So, you see him: the polarity going from the animal to the animal . . . I don't ask myself what else shall I do with my teacher, not anymore . . . As it's winter, I have the pleasant conviction that I shall have snow fall, the holy snow of holy winter, I shall have the earth covered with snow, the ravine stuffed full of snow, the schoolhouse roofed with snow, I feel like proceeding with the delicacy of impotence, to make everything in this teacher impossible, to prevent his blood from circulating, to weld his brain to the freezing point, to the absolute freezing horizon . . . If you're still there, where the teacher is unpacking his bags . . . If you still picture him standing in front of the stove . . . on the way over to the hunting lodge, as it might be, yes, even before the onset of the great frost, I ventured to imagine a vicarage with all the ingredients of earthly felicity . . . Now, you see: the teacher, shut in his destructive fantasy, slowly he is forced back in on himself by his thinking, into the idea of 'never-ending snow' . . . One should be careful not to refer to such a procedure as 'story,'" said the painter. "You see: I am now involved in the falling snow, in the even falling of the snow . . . the world around, our idea of the world around, becomes softened to the degree that it is forced to assume demonic traits . . . a devilish silence makes concentration impossible, all the while it prompts him to raise his performance, suggests the unrepeatableness of all feelings . . . Now I know only too well," said the painter, "given my possibilities, you would have dealt very differently with the teacher, you would have integrated him in an idyllic peace, in a daily routine, in the vibrations of youthful sensitivity, into mutilated vices, into mutilated sorrows, into the mutilated notions of end and departure that typify youth, that youth makes possible, and not into the great vices, the great sorrows, not the great imaginings of end and departure that age allows ... You would have enclosed the teacher in your petty lie, you would, shall we say, have let him live! But I will not let my teacher live, I must not let him live, I cannot let him live, my teacher will not live, he has never lived, he must not live, the living teacher is anathema to me, it denies itself to me: I must kill him, I must let him die a fearful death, a second death, because as far as I'm concerned, the teacher has always been long since dead ... So, now I'm listening to the falling snow and the cracking of tree trunks ... the beginning of the ice age, the crumbling of human melancholy ... now I have a monstrous landscape of death crystals before me, for the teacher to walk into.—I see the occasionally moving way his being opposes extinction, how his head denies the summonses of death ... how his feet suddenly falter, how everything about this man fails as fail it must ... how this man, this teacher, is extinguished, is dead ... the teacher is dead ... Now, you see," said the painter, "I make my world anew: now I am once again on the first day of creation, on the second day of creation, I am busy imagining all the days of creation I need ... the teacher is dissolved in the air of my exemplary conditions, the teacher is dissolved in the lack of an answer, the lack of a face. The teacher has fallen prey to a wild transmogrification of intellectual dread, to a resurgent animal intellectualism ... Did you manage," said the painter, "to follow in every little detail the scenery I tried to lay before you?"

I didn't reply. "You see," said the painter, "the brain is capable of nourishing itself on the inventions, the great inventions of little and lesser and infinitesimal dread . . . it can make itself roar . . . make itself a world, an original world, an ice age, a vast stone age of organization . . . One proceeds from a very small and insignificant instance, from a little individual who falls into one's hands . . . From the principle of some desecration, the justness of such desecration, into the desecration itself . . . one leaves the victim lying there, one has snow fall on him, one has him decompose, dissolve, as an animal might dissolve that one once might have thought oneself to be . . . Do you understand? Life is the purest, clearest, darkest, most crystalline form of hopelessness . . . There is only one way to go, through the snow and ice into despair; past the adultery of reason."

In order to pre-empt any unclarities in this "horror," simply to rule them out, and to rule them out too in the mind of the reader once and for all, I would like to refer to the opening sentence of this attempt, I should say: let me begin again with the opening sentence of this report of an "unfortunate excursus," which it seems to me I have simply copied from the painter, with all the ruthlessness of his own brain, with the sentence, in short: "The way the brain reverts to being a sort of machine . . ." I am so exhausted I need to go and lie down right away, I am incapable of writing down one more word, not one more word today, even though I have reason enough today to continue, to continue without end, with words and with "notions" and with "omissions" . . . I am so exhausted, I am so utterly exhausted . . .

My Letters to Assistant Strauch

FIRST LETTER

Dear Assistant Strauch,
I have indeed succeeded in systematically inveigling myself into your brother's life, not without a certain measure of ruthlessness and dishonesty, alarming to myself: in the course of the first few days it was comparatively easy to find myself in your brother's society, truth to say, he forced it on me, if anything; which I might view as a stroke of especial good fortune, because you had the apprehension that your brother might have sealed himself off entirely, and that I might not be able to come anywhere near him. Great was my surprise, then, to find myself confronting a man, who, without the least reserve, speaks all about his condition. At this point I should say that everything I discovered here in Weng, in the person of your brother, and the conditions here, to which he is helplessly exposed, as exposed as they are to him, has exercised an extraordinary fascination on me, but one to which I am sure I will be equal. In my view it is possible, and in due course certain, that I will be able to adhere to the line of clarity and logic in my treatment of the prescribed subject (I feel naturally bound to the terms of our last conversation in Schwarzach). I want to emphasize at this point that I am sticking absolutely and in every respect to the agreed parameters, there can be no question of my

having pursued this assignment under false or misleading assumptions. From the very first moment, I have been at pains to exclude the purely medical aspects of the case, and confine myself rigidly and consciously to personal responses to the equally personal behavior of your brother. I think I may already have found the right scientific—not, *nota bene*, scientific in the medical sense!—approach, a way of connecting discoveries and angles of observation that should, I hope, in time, provide useful results. The only difficulty is this: your brother claims me entirely for himself, and the only remaining time to myself (and it is not nearly enough) is at night, for me to make notes, to record the inner and outer atmospheres, to compare him with my developing sense of him, from various, albeit inadequate angles, some more "acute," others possibly "obtuse," to do proximate justice to the always dual perspective of the case, to approach your brother, as it were, on a documentary footing—however fragile and occasionally even inadequate this strikes me as being. With this highly phenomenological and unassuming brand of failure, to try to order it and within its order to set it at variance to its order. So I write down at night what I take in during the day. It seems to me your brother is an instance of something it occurs to me to call a precipitous fantast. My thinking immediately arrows through such a notion toward its aim. The question is, how possible is it to advance into the *incommensurateness* of your brother. You probably will have no more from me than a suggestion of your brother's superficial nature, over a conscientiously recorded protocol of the phosphorescences of this surface, and of some of the latent (and presumably dark) currents and countercurrents (changes), a sort of secondary report taking account of the lapidary optical, and this will be what I will end up turning in to you, on the basis of my notes here. A secondary report of an extraordinary, delicate state of deficiencies, misguided, but I think no longer transferable. I take this assignment, given to me by you for whatever reasons, as a signal expression of confidence, as an, as I now already see, important episode of my increasingly medical life, indeed, of my entire development to date. As far as I can judge, this assignment is in many ways one of inestimable importance to me. However, it would certainly be a mistake if I were to present myself to you already as a grateful intern, before anything has yet been determined, before the first proper step in any direction has truly been taken . . . And this assignment has not yet entered the outer courts of reality. In view of which, and lastly, whatever I may have said in the past, I would urge you not to expect overly regular bulletins from Weng.

SECOND LETTER

Dear Assistant Strauch,
You taught me what shock therapy is, what it is to oppose madness with lunacy till the midpoint of the two is in uproar. I must say, what your brother is going through here is perhaps another and not inharmonious type of shock therapy, as you once briefly described it, which has nothing to do with technology, which is the countervailing suffering of a deranged nature, against which its exorbitant and misanthropic opponent mutinies. "He might be a person," you once said, "on the brink of millennia." If you hadn't said it yourself, I might have supposed your brother would have come up with it, he seems to say such things all the time.

The shock therapy in question is Weng, one of those
therapies you darkly and conscientiously described as
fiendish, that pursue absolute healing, not healing as
physical or mental process, what is described in Koltz as
"therapy of the inward detonation." Weng is a shock. For
your brother, of course, a totality involving a pitiless and
brain-corrosive recipe, which you once, in the course of one
of our evenings in your room, described as "flood damage in
the individual." I think the case in question is an extremely
unscrupulous—unscrupulous toward anything at all—
condition fed back (from some initial hereditary weakness)
that is incapable of registering anything but itself, its own
embodied idea of itself. Is it possible to speak of an
internalized inheritor disease? As I increasingly have come to
see, I occupy no point of view at all. All there is is "the
energy of different perspectives." Do you remember
something you said in the course of our only walk together
earlier this year: "The connections in the blood are suddenly
irreparable." This, I believe, is where your brother, from out
of some now forgotten place that it would be important to
learn, is currently placed. "My head could be somewhere
where I have no access to it," he said today. I must say, it's
the most I can do to reach a secondary precision where it is a
matter of presenting a sequence of events that have become
rigid and quasi-autonomous. This now is the time of
availability—where your brother is concerned. But all the
possibilities behind so many open doors exhaust me already,
and suddenly, it seems to me, I am no longer up to the
linearity of procedure that you called for, or to any cerebral
activity that insists on the lack of any fixed point of view. It
will make you suspicious: on occasion, I move in the same
mysticisms as your brother, in that "prescientific thought,

the unrevealing mysticism of one who is on the run from clarity." It is an extraordinarily compelling thing for me to observe how the only lately shamelessly dark world of your concepts is now suddenly opening. As though it were just a matter of stepping out and leaving behind whatever gets in the way of bold thinking; and I must tell you: of medical thinking too, because your thinking is a medical thinking, unlike that of your brother, which, as he says himself, is "an amoral interstitial thinking without any declared purpose." Basically, both the simple and the demonic sides of your brother's nature are headed in the same direction (his direction), everything "inhumanly bestially elevated"—as your brother says—in effect, toward death. But all that is a long way from diagnostics, from persuasiveness, from the linearity that, as you always say, must be in sole charge. Nothing so depresses your brother's spirits as the absence of contact with you. It would be too simple to talk of a *brother complex,* by analogy to the *father complex* that we would seem to have put behind us. But there is one piece of news that I must break to you today: it's as though your brother suffers from interjections, from "an army of hecklers," that "plunge a brain perhaps overly set on logical consequence into continual disorder." My thinking, yes, my *feeling,* based on my thinking, is that this constellation probably affects your brother's entire constitution, but it would be completely mistaken to think of any sort of conclusion to that effect, assumptions at this stage are rapidly overthrown, but what is tangibly there one might classify as a highly self-confident misanthropic degeneration. Everything turns microscopic. I am trying to be clear, but I am compelled to see that I understand very little about this type of thinking: rather, I seem here to be governed by my own intuitions.

And yet I think on the basis of my impressions I may be of
some use to you at the proper time. At worst I am an
attentive, if occasionally mendacious (at least on a banal
level: I claimed to be studying law) stenographer, characterized by submissiveness and obedience. It's like this:
everything here makes me ponder, in this case. Colors,
smells, temperatures—the ubiquitous and almost daily
advancing frost here strikes me as being of the very greatest
significance. I must simply forbid myself to lose myself in
particulars, and point out to you details of this climatologi-
cally (remember "flood damage in the individual") interesting, climatological and clinical whole. And I must not in
writing to you become involved in questions concerning my
observing function. I don't believe there is any chance of
altering your persuasion that your brother is lost. I don't
believe in normalization (healing), rather it is my constata-
tion that the case is deteriorating with each passing day.

THIRD LETTER

Dear Assistant Strauch,
Your brother is living in the delusion that he is several beings
at once, and in the delusion—to him, a terrible thing—that
he is oppressed by these various, simultaneous, unpre-
dictably fluctuating beings, whom he himself views as "the
unthinkable raw material of (his) episodes." He has spoken
of the "scourge of chromatic humiliation" and of the
"philosophy of the exacerbated bird's-eye view of impure
thought." This explains the compelling nature of his
constitution, his development, his unfruitfulness. It is this
unfruitfulness, understood as the adoption of inhuman

rights, that allows him to live—and of course condemns him
to death.

I have made the observation that your brother's existence is
fundamentally ("creating themselves in steady negation") on
two planes: the political, and what you call the "dream of a
relationship." These two lives course through the rigid
geometry of his pre-established positions, and also through
the commotion of his inner life, which you describe as "the
interconnected void." In the person of your brother, I think I
have found a notable instance of the political man as dream
and the simplifying dreamer as political, and the mutual
drama of the two. You yourself spoke once of an essay you
proposed to write, to be called "The Dreamer and the
Political Man." Your brother would furnish you with the
most outstanding manifestation of the subject; what you
wrote would be the reflection of a consciousness, of a
thought, that seems, or is, complete. I believe the relationship between dream and politics as exemplified in your
brother to be something utterly masculine. The dream of
such a person knows neither day nor night, knows nothing
political, just as the politics of such a person knows neither
day nor night, nor anything dubiously dreamlike. And all
that without boundaries, yes without even the thought of
boundaries. The way each thing, dream and politics, exists as
a separate whole in such a person, makes for complete
equilibrium. I would say that a person who is equally a
politician and a dreamer ought to be the one we classify as
nearest to perfection, if he didn't refuse any categorization:
he would be, yes, he is, the most self-evident human being!
But in such a "divine binary," which represents a summit of
human development (though without beginning and

without end), the sickness of separation is not just a tough adversary but a step comprising "all deaths at once" that continually requires to be taken. And your brother is just such an "object of all deaths at once."

To return briefly to the area where I saw the full human potential of someone like your brother, the political and the dreamlike, being united: while his political side may be as much invested in his day-to-day existence as in his dreamlike (or as his dream), I would still describe it as *the night of his life,* and the dreamlike as his day; the day and night of his self, but without boundaries, and hence his night without a day, and his day without a night. But what is a political person? What is a dreamer? Still, that is what happened to your brother, and in him, the deadly stasis of an entropic vehemence. Together we go on long walks, from one forest to another, into one ravine and out of another; the cold is such that it is impossible to remain motionless for long, to remain motionless out of doors, not even to stop and think, he and I if we stopped and thought, we would immediately freeze, we would die in midthought, as the animals die if terror prompts them to stop in this extraordinary frost. There is an "extraordinary seductiveness of frost" here. I am currently quoting your brother with the dispassion of someone assigned to report on him, to whom "the lines of the world memory" fit together. Today your brother said: "My brain has gone to be set." I find that an extraordinary pronouncement. Imagine if he had said: "My whole brain has been taken away to be retyped." He mentioned *you* only once; one of those dark places in his darkness appeared, in which from time to time "he mindlessly weeps down into." He has the oddest connection to your sister, who is now living in Mexico. He is one of those people who refuse to say anything at all, and yet who are continually driven to say everything. Who tie tourniquets round the arteries of their thought, but to no effect; who pour themselves out in suicidal word-spate, who hate themselves in truth because the world of their feeling, apprehended as enforced incest, daily smashes them to smithereens. I should like to say: attend to your brother.

FOURTH LETTER

Dear Assistant Strauch,

there is a perfectly ordinary dread, some way short of the greater dread that has your brother in its grip, pushing him into ever greater ruthlessness (ruthlessness principally toward himself). People avoid him. I avoid him myself, in my exhaustion, such exhaustion as I am incapable of describing, I avoid him, but then I am incapable of avoiding him. I am at his mercy. Forgive me! He thrusts his frailty at me and into me in the form of sentences, like slides into a projector, which then projects those terrors onto the blank and always available walls of my self (or his). Of course you want to hear more about your brother, and I will try to keep up my strength. Do you know about the Far Eastern languages he speaks? About his "Asiatic character"? About his time as a substitute teacher? These are all great and completely self-contained darknesses within his *perpetrated existence*. He was attacked as a child. By you. Do you know about that? Your brother is the opposite of you in every-thing, and then he became the opposite of that again, *you are* your brother, and then again *you aren't* . . . He lives in "world of conceptless concepts." His stick in his hand has great significance for him. Far from being systematic, I want to draw attention to the fact that even today he is frightened of doors that slammed shut in his childhood. He also suffers "for generations of insomniacs"! His intellectual world always took place in cemeteries, "hung around cemeteries a lot." Do you understand? Also of interest: his relationship to music, his horror of the state, the police, order. His outrageous pleasure in turning a question into a mutilated reply. Always the thought of the "hideous accidents on the street," of "lurking family disasters" in the distant past. A liking for circuses, for revues, for all sorts of oddities. He talks of his "kingdom of merriment." Did you never try to get close to your brother? By ruse? Because you are a doctor, and I think contact with him would have been important to you as well. Or did you, as I fear, never have any contact with your brother? He gets over his night by day, and vice versa. He always carries the *Pensées* in his pocket. I thought I would be spared your brother's aggression. But now I feel the contagion of his logically galloping illness. What illness is it? Your brother grows darker in the measure in which he thinks the world and everything in and around him is also darkening. "The world is a progressive dimming of light," he says. And, tonight: "Everything in me is dried out like the bed of a stream, like the bed of a stream of blood." As the notion of insanity is not clear to me, but merely familiar, I am unable to say whether I think your brother is insane or not. He is *not* insane! (Mad?) No, not mad either. "Echoes of death" go making noise in his head. Today I saw him sitting on his bed, stark naked, and preoccupied with his body.

· · ·

You will suppose I have been neglecting my duty, because I haven't written to you for so long. You may imagine I am using your money to buy myself a nice holiday! Whereas in fact my stay here is a terrible chastening, chastening in the double sense of the word. The fact is that I am steeped in your brother's thought. In his complaints against everything. I don't—yet—have his illness, but I am steeped in ridicule. He shows me "the malformations of the earth's surface, created by the malformations of the cosmos." At this moment, everything looks pretty dark to me as well. You must excuse me, this letter is dictated by a rambling for which I am not responsible. It's late. But I would still like you to think about the "childhood punishments" you imposed on your brother. About the "childhood lies" you spread about him, all the years of your growing-up and young manhood. I don't know whether my task can simply be abrogated at the end of thirteen or fourteen days.

Since you have failed to reply to any of my missives, I must assume that, even if you cannot be satisfied with me, you nevertheless do not desire any particular change to the current pattern, and do not insist that I immediately go back. Besides, such a move would be entirely pointless. Of course, I am thinking in terms of taking up my internship in Schwarzach in due course . . .

FIFTH LETTER

Dear Assistant Strauch,
medicine is dark, these are only dark paths I follow with "exposed brain" through the byways of our science, which I

should like to term the glorious one of the sciences, as the ruler of terror among all the sciences, which, unlike ours, are pseudosciences, even though ours is no better than a protoscience itself. I can't imagine its knowledge, it is only possible to feel it in all its presumed evolutions from our thinking. Medicine seems to me like a concatenated sequence of darknesses, intimately connected to superstition, bold incisions in the perhaps already lapsed geometry of the world. In the process, the substance, flesh, the nether possibilities of the organic, appears more and more insignificant against the only true natural, which is the illimitable dark. Our science is the one from which all others proceed and take their being. And, to quote your brother, with whom I feel an ever closer connection, founded on the stimulus of reversible ideas: "The study of sickness is the most poetic of the sciences."

I don't want to go without writing down a few of your brother's really remarkable sayings. Of course I won't proceed systematically. That's not possible for me. It's a stage, which I am going through as well. Among other things your brother today said: "The tragedy is connected to all the other tragedies." Also: "Worth is worthlessness, the calamity of worthlessness is the worthlessness of one's world and of the world *unconnected to one's own.*" He said that after coming round from a protracted period of unconsciousness, I found him lying in his room, you can imagine my consternation, my initial reaction was that he had suffered a minor heart attack. He said: "Everything is *nearly* black." He was going through the "nitrogen of the primal condition of the devil." In the evening he said: "The earth, the world, is bloodshot." This is unusual. He had always led an existence that "was both above and below any other existence, and had never approached his own *existential minimum.*"

Well, if one were able to establish overnight what our organs *are*. But perhaps you already have laid out in your mind in orderly fashion things that to me seem hopelessly entangled: perhaps an operation? Our science knows it, but doesn't act on it, in accordance with the "terrible principle" of *"here as there, illusion!"*

If only I could lay my hands on your brother's "scrapbooks"! Did you know of the existence of these "scrapbooks" in which for many years, decades even, he has written down everything that preoccupies him?

I am only able to note down a few headings, and even that strikes me as contemptible and mad.

We played a game together today: to see which of us can reduce the other to tears! (This game, as I now know, was one you often played with your brother.) Your brother lost.

SIXTH LETTER

Dear Assistant Strauch,
Suicide comes from the womb, as you once determined: its realization begins to occur at the moment of the suicide's birth. Everything your brother has lived through to date has been a "passion of suicide." A pursuit to the death of everything that was particular about this particular human being.

Against such a background of "deafening generality" he
now speaks incessantly of the "craft of suicide," the action
that will bring him to completion after a lifetime of suffering
and preparation. It's not possible to oppose the boldness of
the idea that each individual suicide is the maturation of
thousands of years of preparation. Your brother (who has
now almost entirely stopped sleeping!) refers to motherhood
as *suicidehood;* truly, the womb is the tomb. The breeding of
a human being (thinking most rigorously of himself) is
the decision of the father (first and foremost) and of the
mother (as well) to sponsor the suicide of their offspring,
the child, the sudden premonition "of having created a new
suicide."

Twenty-seventh Day

"A devilish fear, you know, has always kept me away from suicide. Then there were thoughts arising out of the dark, the
whole communing with self, very pronounced in my case.
The conviction of my nature, the monstrous condition of
spiritual development . . . Yes, I was always able to repel suicide, those innumerable cases of limitless disappointment,
excess, criminality, heredity, these inhuman difficulties . . .
You must know, like all humans, I have communed almost
exclusively with myself in this difficult world, where there

are practically no laws . . . no way of contemplating . . . I was
too little interested, you know, always a man of resolve, of
contradiction, of fear . . ."

The material about Strauch (in my memory) is monstrous.
What is written down is the best I can do. I am probably just
about able to draw up a report. But it's not possible to
describe the condition of a human being in the same way as
one can describe the state of an animal. My assignment
advances my education. I'm certain it won't benefit the
painter Strauch. Why? The assistant will question me. I will
be able to say things to him, and I can demonstrate the
painter's walk to him. I am now able to say what drew
Strauch to Weng. Why he left Vienna. Why he burned his
paintings. Why he hates so much. Why he runs into the
woods. Stopped sleeping. Why! I am able to say what he says
and how he says it and why it makes waves of insanity and
revulsion. I am able to say what he feels when he sees the
landlady, and when he sees the knacker with his rucksack.
Why he is indifferent to so much and what, I know what is
going on within him, who this painter Strauch is, this perse-
cuted, ostensibly useless person, who on paper may have a
brother and a sister and others besides, but in reality has
always been alone, much more miserably alone than one will
be able to imagine even after reading my report, alone in the
way that a fly is alone in an apartment in a city in winter,
being chased by the occupant and his cohorts, and finally is
splattered against a wall, if these people feel hounded and
maddened and under attack from this fly, so that they band
together in their dwelling, and silently decide to kill it off,

that vile, monstrous creature, as they call it in their aggression, that poisons their air and their evening—not knowing what a fly is, and what goes on in one, much less a fly in a city apartment in winter. I have observed the painter Strauch, I have lain in wait for him, I have lied to him, because that is what my assignment called upon me to do, I have driven him crazy with my questions, much crazier than he was before, and I struck him on the head with my silences, on his head that he fears so much. I bothered him with my youth. With my plans. With my fears. With my incapacity. With my moodiness. I talk about death without knowing what death is, what life is, what any of it is . . . everything I do I do in ignorance, and I compound his ruin with my own. Ruin? And finally today I even tried to list the various modes of death for his benefit, which completely cast a cloud over him. "Suicide is in my nature, you must know," he says. Swipes the air with his stick just as a monster that's no longer a monster might swipe at the air where there is no heaven, and not even any hell. The air he swipes at is just air and nothing else, and, as I see, it's not even one of the elements.

"One day you get home, and you know that from now on you have to pay for everything, and from that moment on you're old and dead. One day, everything is finished, though life itself might go on for a while. You're dead, and beauty and whatever happiness is and wealth, everything has withdrawn from you, forever." The painter is talking to himself, not to me. In the village square, which we've unexpectedly reached, because we walked in a circle, and were lost in thought, he said: "Ghastly, that dog barking! I have always hated it. Always been afraid of being bitten by a dog, and dying of rabies. Even on my way to school I ran the gauntlet of barking dogs! I felt cramps in my heart, you know. The dogs leap up at you, and knock you down with a violent swipe of the paw. The dog owners sic their beasts on people who have done nothing to them or their dogs. And then you have a terrible bite wound! The way that energized flesh jumps at you, it could easily kill you! Dogs . . ." said the painter, "butchers' dogs, wolfhounds! Barking and yapping wherever you go! How I hate dogs! My sister, you must know, had a bite taken out of her thigh by a dog in a pub once. The landlord never even apologized! If at least he'd been upset! . . . A beast takes a piece out of you, and all your efforts are in vain! They can rip the pockets off your coat! Attack deaf old men from behind, who, a matter of days later, die of a heart attack. When I arrive here, the dogs go for me, and I need to raise my stick at them once or twice to persuade them to leave me alone. Without my stick, I most probably wouldn't be alive!" After we had passed through the cemetery: "Peasant funerals are a ritual. The dead man is washed and wrapped in a shroud and laid out and unwrapped again and dressed in his Sunday best." At his feet, they recite prayers that have been in existence for hundreds of years. The brothers and sisters take turns praying, and then the parents, the grandparents, the children, the children's children. Or other relatives pray. They sing hymns with medieval words none of them understand. Or Latin. Pictures of the departed are hung throughout the house. His remaining possessions are put in order, and labeled with the name of the one who is to have them. They pray to him to intercede for them in heaven, as that is where they think he has gone. They ask him questions, and receive his replies. They sprinkle holy water over him, "and invoke his name, as if he were one of the saints."

It all went through my head: the showmen, the eccentric tramp, the movable theater, the dog's body, the burials, the behavior of the landlady, her husband away in prison, guarded like a dog, slaving away for tripe and gruel, never to get used to wooden clogs and burlap but who might yet find some relief in his straw sack and handcuffs. The cold went through my head, and drove me half crazy. It was a crazy morning, blown apart by brass-band music. Beer and salt pork and Sunday suits stunned me with their peculiar human reek. The previous night went through my head. I thought how far away everything is. It can't be really, but it is and that's how it is and it doesn't really matter. Today was the coldest day so far, and I wrote to the hospital for my winter coat, otherwise I would freeze. And the copy of Koltz, because I'm not thinking of leaving any time soon. I can't leave now. Always the same walks, they tighten round you like a noose, and discipline your thinking. There's a letter to my brother half written on the table, and the Henry James, which I've almost finished. It must be even colder outside. From one hour to the next it's dark as well as cold. When I hear the painter wheezing up the stairs to his room, I feel sick. I should think about him seriously. Because I have to write my report. I'm not sure how old he is. His walk, what does it mean? The way he stands up and sits down? What he says and the way he says it! And me? How do I feel about him now? First and foremost, I'm a liar. Yesterday he looked at me sharply: "Law is what you said, isn't it?" And I: "Yes, that's right. Law." And then silence. It was pitch-black in the valley, and the air could hardly be kept out. Then it started to snow. We could hear shooting from the forest, from the shadow side. But it couldn't have been a deer I heard as I made my way back to the inn alone. "The world is constricting in my heart," he said. Is it that? If I write down such coarse things, it's heartless of me. I have to. It's only because I have to that I can. Are they conversations that I have with the painter? Hardly. Clues? Something morbid about all of it, as his brother said, "and still a terrifying distance." Who's to blame? But now I know pretty much the major phases of his life. Doesn't help me. There's always a lot of snowfall between him and me. I was thinking about the way he sat on his bed, looking at himself. His dreams. His illness, which is also "in opposition" to him. It was horrible hearing him talk to the railwayman yesterday. How he kept conceding that the railwayman was right about everything, even though he didn't understand anything, not the first thing. How he always concedes now. Everything he says is concession. In fact, he's powerless all the time.

Every age was always miles from the world which it always abused. Occasionally he found himself under attack from conditions in the remote past, a smell that had to do with afternoon coffee at his grandmother's or the hens clucking on one of his grandfather's farms. Or again the smell of a bakery in the city, where ladies ate cake. "The moments of the three-year-old haunt the thirty-year-old." Now he sees them under conditions of a different terror. The trees of an avenue cool him down, they have to do with his homework in the second year of elementary school. Church visits, from a different period of childhood, along with having to get up and go to bed at fixed times and solving math problems. The magic of incense and Gloria and wooden Madonnas that the priest commissioned from the carpenter next door. The time of learning to walk, and learning to contradict. The time of devout evening prayers. "If someone in the pub says a certain word," said the painter, "it makes me what I was twenty years ago." And then: "You're not always the person you are." Retreats, fundamental experiences, forgotten and renewed where they broke off: a forest, a church, a schoolyard. City and countryside alternated according to the whims of his parents and grandparents, his walking and thinking remained subject to the whims of politics: all of it a checkered retrospect. "All of it softened," he says. "I could eat in such a way that was repulsive, even where repulsiveness was at home, and I could develop manners that would have impressed princesses." He had played the highest and the lowest parts. "I have always been a genius at transforming myself." He mastered, like no other, "the art of not drawing attention to oneself. A formal walk and formal meals, as much as eating off newspaper." And it had never been just a game either: "I was the person through and through who had to eat off newspaper, and also the one who eats formally, but mostly I was the one who has to eat off newspaper . . ." His childhood, spent in institutions: schools and hospitals. Career conversations that were the despair of parents and grandparents. Occasionally also of the guardians to whom he was given for foster care. Funds dried up at the precise moment when he needed money, "more urgently than ever!" Took a job, a succession of jobs. "I always did the dirtiest work." Attempts to slip in here or there, study, generally study. All failed. Lying in bed for weeks on end. Slinking along walls, too hungry to be able to make a decision. Brother and sister withdrawn to their "secret world." The deaths of grandparents, of parents. Retreat. The factory switches off all thought.

"I often get up in the middle of the night," said the painter. "As you know, I don't sleep. Picture my head to yourself. Once I've worked my way out of bed, I begin to palp my arms and legs, I slowly begin to move, which is very difficult, because I can't find my balance right away. With this head, you know, as soon as I get up, I experience difficulties with my balance: I have to be careful not to get up too quickly. I stand there stark naked. I listen, there seems to be nothing moving outside, nothing inside, as though everything had perished. There are probably birds sitting on the branches, the blackbirds of winter, but they're not moving. If you go over to the window and look out, if you have enough time, you can see the birds sitting there: fat bellies, incapable of singing. I don't know what sort of birds they are, but they're always the same kind. I try to walk up and down my room once or twice, without hurting my head too much with the strain of walking. Do you have any idea what it means to be someone who feels indescribable pain when walking and breathing at the same time? I sit down carefully at my table, and start making notes, notes about everything that preoccupies me. But I don't get very far, after every three or four words, I have to stop . . . of course, it's an alarming thing, trying to commit something to paper . . . but then there's this idea that's just come to you, and you feel convinced it's a good idea, and it goes. The nights are my martyrdom, you know, I abbreviate them by contemplating my body: I sit in front of the mirror, and look at myself. It's not always possible to choke back highly pertinent questions. And so I experience quite lengthy periods of mere looking. It's the only satisfaction I have; it lessens the pain; my head remains without uproar, without increase in heat and agitation. I get through the night, the terrible despair, you know, that appears in the walls when I scratch them with my fingers. You see," said the painter, "my nails are all broken off. The pain from my head is so inconceivable that I can't begin to describe it."

On my return to Schwarzach, I read in the *Demokratisches Volksblatt:* "The unemployed man G. Strauch from V. has not been seen in Weng or environs since last Thursday. In view of the heavy snowfalls currently being experienced there, the search for the missing person, in which members of the police also took part, has had to be called off."

That evening, I ended my internship, and traveled back to the capital, to resume my studies.

A NOTE ON THE TYPE

This book was set in Monotype Dante, a typeface designed by Giovanni Mardersteig (1892–1977). Conceived as a private type for the Officina Bodoni in Verona, Italy, Dante was originally cut only for hand composition by Charles Malin, the famous Parisian punch cutter, between 1946 and 1952. Its first use was in an edition of Boccaccio's *Trattatello in laude di Dante* that appeared in 1954. The Monotype Corporation's version of Dante followed in 1957. Although modeled on the Aldine type used for Pietro Cardinal Bembo's treatise *De Aetna* in 1495, Dante is a thoroughly modern interpretation of the venerable face.

Composed by Stratford Publishing Services,
Brattleboro, Vermont
Printed and bound by R. R. Donnelly and Sons,
Harrisonburg, Virginia
Designed by Virginia Tan